ACCLAIM FOR A
NEW VOICE IN FANTASY...

After living in New York, Cleveland and Chicago, Elizabeth A. Lynn is now settled in San Francisco, where, she says, she belonged all along. She is thirty-four. A DIFFERENT LIGHT, her first novel, was published by Berkley in 1978. THE NORTHERN GIRL completes her acclaimed new trilogy, THE CHRONICLES OF TORNOR, each volume of which is complete in itself.

THE CHRONICLES OF TORNOR

WATCHTOWER
THE DANCERS OF ARUN
THE NORTHERN GIRL

THE NORTHERN GIRL

ELIZABETH A. LYNN

BERKLEY BOOKS, NEW YORK

THE NORTHERN GIRL

A Berkley Book / published by arrangement with
the author

PRINTING HISTORY
Berkley-Putnam edition / December 1980
Berkley edition / April 1981

ISBN: 0-425-04725-3

A BERKLEY BOOK ® TM 757,375
Berkley Books are published by Berkley Publishing Corporation,
200 Madison Avenue, New York, New York 10016.
PRINTED IN THE UNITED STATES OF AMERICA

The author would like to thank the following people, without whose patient assistance this book would never have been finished: Jerry Jacks, Debbie Notkin, Charles N. Brown, Marta Randall, David Hartwell, Vonda N. McIntyre, and John Silbersack.

For Sonni

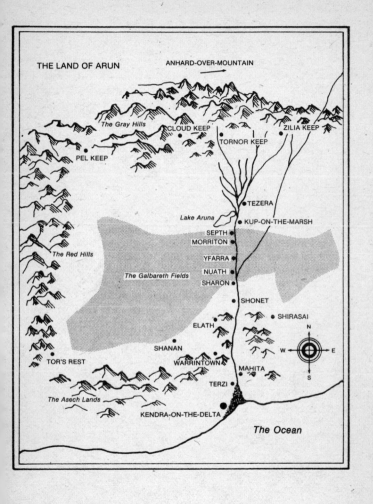

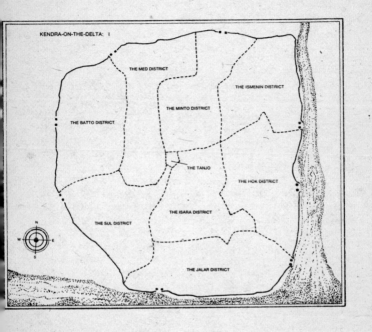

KENDRA-ON-THE-DELTA: I

THE MED DISTRICT

THE ISMENIN DISTRICT

THE MINTO DISTRICT

THE BATTO DISTRICT

THE TANJO

THE HOK DISTRICT

THE ISARA DISTRICT

THE SUL DISTRICT

THE JALAR DISTRICT

N
W E
S

THE NORTHERN GIRL

CHAPTER ONE

I hate you, Sorren thought at the ocean.

The summer air, heavy with salt, made her tired. The money bracelet which Arré had given her for shopping had left a red line on her arm. Behind her on the dock, the stink of fish steamed upward like smoke. Sails bobbed in the bay. An empty cart bounced by her, pulled by a weary gray mule. Flounder, she reminded herself. Flounder in four days.

She walked through the market, past vendors and shops and stalls, to the familiar slope of the hill. The ocean winked at her back, brassy as a plate. Shop banners hung limply in the windless morning. The cobbled streets were hot, but Sorren barely felt it through the tough calluses on her feet. By the time she reached the hilltop, she was plodding, and her cotton shirt stuck to her back and breasts.

She paused before the Med gate to gaze over the city. The red dome of the Tanjo shone at its heart. South, the ocean seethed and glittered, speckled with the fishing fleet's yellow sails. East and west of the city lay the cotton fields. She could not see the pickers with their great sacks over their shoulders, but she knew they were there. North were the vineyards, out of which she had come seven years back. She had only gone back twice to visit, the first time to show off her new clothes, the second time for her mother's burial. She arrived too late, and said her farewells by the grave, trying to recall clearly what her mother had looked like. That had been four years ago. Now when she tried to, she could not even remember the outline of her mother's face.

The big blue building to the east, beside the river bank, was the hall of the Blue Clan. Blue banners waved before it, and from shops and stalls and carts small blue flags declared their owners to be members of the Guild in good standing. The carts that carried wine barrels from the Med vineyards to the city had blue streamers on them. Beyond the vineyards lay the Galbareth Fields, where the grain grew; beyond the grain lay the steppe—and the mountains. Sorren closed her eyes a moment, and they loomed in her mind, hard and gray and incorruptible, the way they sometimes loomed in her dreams.

But there were no mountains near Kendra-on-the-Delta.

Sorren opened her eyes. The stone from which the Tanjo was built had come from the Red Hills, through Shanan and the Asech country, a long journey, days and days away.

She turned to the gate. The gate guard was watching her from his post near the shade of the kava fruit tree.

"Good day," she said.

He grunted. His dark red shirt was damp with sweat. He had laid his spear down on the stone. She wondered what Paxe would say if she came suddenly from the Yard, and saw her guard without his spear.

"Hot," she said.

"Yes," said the guard.

The green peel of a kava fruit lay in the gutter like a piece of green cloth. All the guards ate the kava fruit when they were on gate duty, but this guard—he was young, with a small sandy mustache—had not yet learned to kick the peel out of sight. He was not going to open the gate for her, either. She reached to do it herself. He changed his mind and reached, too, and their fingers touched. His were sticky.

She walked through the iron gate. "Thank you," she said.

He grunted again. The guards were never sure how to treat her. She was a bondservant, but half the time Arré treated her as if she were her daughter . . . and there was Paxe.

The gate closed. She strolled across the courtyard. Flowers grew along the sides of the path, drooping in the heat. As always, the pattern of the courtyard tile intrigued her. She paced along one edge of the figure. The blue triangle on the red field was uneven. She wondered if the artist who had designed the courtyard had made it so deliberately.

As she got to the front door, it opened, and a man strode out. They bounced off each other. More for balance than for courtesy, Sorren went down on one knee.

His perfume was familiar. She squinted. It was indeed Isak. It was harvest month; why was he not at the vineyards, overseeing the picking? "I'm sorry, my lord," she said.

He smiled at her. "Sorren." His soft voice always reminded her of a cat's purr. He wasn't angry, of course. Isak never grew angry. "Be more careful, child. You would not wish to topple one of our august Council members, would you?"

"No," she said.

"Of course not." Brushing his ringed hand over her head, he strolled across the courtyard to the gate. Sorren rose. Her left knee hurt, and she rubbed it. Isak spoke a moment with the gate guard; the sunlight glistened on his blue silk tunic. She wondered if he was telling the man to pick up his spear.

His muscles had felt hard as tile under the shirt. Now Arré would be in a bad mood; she was always cranky after she talked to Isak.

She went into the house. It took a moment for her eyes to grow used to the darkness. The long, cool hall smelled of lilies. A lacquered vase of them stood on a little table beneath the statue of the Guardian. This statue was new; it had been made by the sculptor Ramath, the same sculptor who had directed the making of the big image in the Tanjo. Sorren bowed toward the image. Stone lips smiled at her. Stone eyes gleamed.

She wondered what had happened to the old statue. Surely, she thought, you could not break it, as you might break an old unwanted pot. That would be disrespectful to the *chea*. She listened for the sound of Arré's voice from the workroom. This morning Arré had planned to meet with her surveyors, to discuss their blueprints for enlarging some streets. But she heard nothing. She peered into the large parlor. Elith was there, dusting, mumbling to herself as she passed the cloth over the wall screens.

Elith was old, fat as a feather mattress, and deaf, but she had been Arré Med's mother's personal maid, and Arré kept her on. Sorren raised her voice. "Elith! Do you know where *she* is?"

The old woman turned slowly. "Kitchen."

Sorren went to the kitchen. All the windows and doors were open, with nets across them to keep out flies, but the big room was hot, hotter than the market. Arré was there, talking to the cook. She turned as Sorren entered. "Well? What did the fishmonger say?"

Sweat jumped out on Sorren's upper lip; she rubbed it. "The fishmonger said that he could not get you perch, but he could get flounder."

"Flounder will do."

"That's what I told him."

"How do you want it fixed?" said the cook.

"I don't care. Not too spicy, that's all. Marti can't eat spiced meat."

Marti Hok was one of the Councillors. The flounder was for the Council meeting. The cook nodded and started calling to the apprentices. Sorren recalled her own time in the kitchen. She had hated it. Once she fainted, to everyone's disgust. The other scullions teased her for weeks for being afraid of blood, but it had not been the blood that had made her faint, but the heat. It was worse than the heat in the grapefields. Maybe it had been the heat and the smells combined. She was sensitive to smells, and there were always too many of them in the kitchen.-. . . No wonder cooks threw things.

Arré was wearing white. It made her skin look darker than it was. The heat furled her hair into small curls. Her hair was almost as short as Paxe's, but the texture was different, and her curls were striped with gray. She jerked her head at Sorren. "Come," she said, and marched out of the tiled kitchen. In the cooler corridor they both leaned on the wall.

Arré said, "I think it gets hotter every summer." She squared her shoulders. Her eyes glinted upward. "I'm glad it's you doing the shopping, and not me."

Sorren grinned at the thought of Arré Med, Councillor of Kendra-on-the-Delta, head of the Med family, buying flounder on the docks.

"What are you smiling at?" said Arré irritably.

"I was thinking how surprised the fishmonger would be."

"Wipe your face," said Arré. She started down the hall. "And don't laugh at me."

She *was* cranky. Sorren wiped her sleeve across her lip. Arré went into the small parlor. It was her workroom and sitting room. It faced south; by day its walls were bright, sun-drenched. Its inner walls, like those of the large parlor, were made of screens. The outside wooden wall was hung with a woolen tapestry, all reds and blues. The dyes for the wool came from the Asech country; no other dyes made such brilliant and durable colors. The floor was wooden and unmatted. Sun-light fell in bright streaks across it. The lines of the grain gleamed. Arré sat in her cushioned chair. Sorren stood by the door. The older woman glanced at her. "Sit down," she said, pointing to the footstool. "I need to talk." Obediently Sorren sat. A lacquer table stood at the right side of the chair, its red and black surface shining in the sun. Against the wall, a glass-faced case held a rack of scrolls: the Med accounts. Once a month a scribe came from the Black Clan—not a Scholar, they did not do such mundane work—and went over them for error, under Arré's watchful eyes. Arré had no steward; it seemed unnecessary in a household which consisted of herself and her servants. She did the bookkeeping.

"Did you see Isak?" she asked.

Sorren nodded. "We met at the gate." Arré's face was taut, as it always was when she talked about her brother. Silver bracelets, two on each arm, clinked as she folded her hands in her lap. The largest bracelet had a blue jewel in it. "What did he want?"

Arré grimaced. "Whatever he can get."

"But it's harvest. He should be at the fields."

"Nonsense. Myra manages the vineyards better than he ever could, or cares to." Myra was Isak's wife. "He asked to dance for the Councillors."

"Did you say yes?"

Arré's hands flew apart. They were big on her small frame, ungraceful, not pretty hands. Isak had pretty hands. "He's the finest dancer in the city—how could I refuse?"

Even Arré admitted that Isak could dance. It was his gift, his art, as administration was hers, and perhaps his passion, or one of them. He had been trained to it by Meredith of Shanan, who had been trained by Berenth of Shanan, who learned it from his mother Jenézia of Shanan, and she, every city child knew, had danced with Kel of Elath. It was his right to wear the *shariza*, the red scarf of the *cheari*, but, with greater delicacy than he usually showed, he chose not to. Sorren had asked him about it once. "The old chearis were trained in arms and in the warrior arts," he said. "I am not."

"Why not?" she asked.

"War is uncivilized; you know that," he had answered. "It's a crudity better left to soldiers. Besides, the wearing of blades is forbidden in Kendra-on-the-Delta."

But he danced the role of the warrior well enough. Sorren pattered her hands on her knees. "Does he want me to play for him?"

"Yes."

"We haven't had time to practice."

"It won't matter. Do something you both know. Anything."

Sorren had drummed for Isak for four years, the first year only at small parties, but the next year at the Festivals: Harvest Feast, Spring Feast, the Feast of the Founding of the City. "I guess. . . ."

"It won't matter. He won't care what he does, as long as he can get near the meeting."

Isak's political ambitions and Arré's contempt for them were no secret in her household. But, Sorren thought, that isn't fair. Isak does care about his dancing. She had watched him practice for hours, while sweat poured from him and his lungs heaved for breath, till anyone with less discipline would have stopped, rested, poured water on his head, something. His muscles were like Paxe's, smooth and stretched, and he moved with the same kind of economy, but with more grace.

"What are you thinking about?" Arré demanded.

Sorren blushed. She did not want to say, of Paxe; it seemed crass. "Being graceful," she said.

Arré Med laughed. "Never mind it," she said. She was a small woman, built like Isak. Though the stool Sorren sat on was lower than Arré's chair, when Sorren straightened their eyes met on the level. "You don't need to be graceful. People notice you anyway."

Sorren said, "That's because I'm tall, and pale." She frowned at her light skin. In the hottest sun, it refused to brown; instead, it turned an ugly and uncomfortable red. She touched her hair, which was long, and the color of wheat. "I would rather be dark, like Paxe."

"Dark is the fashion now," said Arré. "But never regret your height. We small folk find other ways to make people notice us. Like Isak."

People always noticed Isak. If they didn't, he made them. He could turn heads in a crowd faster than anyone. But people noticed Arré, too.

"Will you need something new to wear?" Arré said.

"What?"

"When you play for Isak, at the Council meeting." Arré tapped the chair arm. "Pay attention, child."

"I'm sorry," Sorren said. Reminded, she slipped the money bracelet from her arm and held it out. Arré took it, her fingers automatically counting the remaining shell pieces. "No, I have enough clothes."

"If you want something, just ask." Arré grinned like an urchin in a street fight. "Isak will pay for it."

A light tapping on the screen made her look around. Lalith stood in the doorway. She was thirteen, lithe and little and brown-skinned. Arré had picked her from the vineyards in the same way she had picked Sorren, and brought her to live and work in the house. "The cook sent me to bring you this," she said. She held out a bowl.

"Well," Arré said, "bring it here! What is it?" Lalith gave it to her. It was a dish of berries with sweet cream poured over them. Arré had a notorious sweet tooth. "Thank you, child."

"And this came." Lalith extended a letter. The wax seal had a crest on it.

Arré ripped it open. She scanned the writing and her dark eyes frowned. "When did this come?" she said.

"Just now. A servant brought it." Lalith shifted from one foot to the other.

"Bah." Arré put the letter down on the lacquered table top. "From Boras Sul," she said. "To inform me that he is ill and cannot come to the Council meeting, he regrets, thank you, my dear Arré." She waved at Lalith to leave, and picked up the bowl of fruit. "He will send his son, who is even more of an idiot than he is. Bah."

Sorren said, "Maybe he *is* ill?"

"Maybe he eats too much," Arré said contemptuously. Boras Sul was very fat.

Sorren ran a thumb along the smooth lacquer. "I can find out."

"The servants' mail?" said Arré. Sorren nodded. "Don't bother. Save it for something important. Tell the cook that Boras will not be at the Council dinner. Go on. I don't need you."

The letter had brought back her ill temper. Sorren left her alone to work it out. She went to the kitchen to tell the cook. He was playing the pebble game across the cutting board with Kaleb, the night watch captain, Paxe's second-in-command. She watched the design form on the grid.

She told him about Boras Sul, and he shrugged. "Thought it was bad news," he commented. "That's why I fixed the berries."

"I don't think it helped," Sorren said.

"Too bad," said the cook. Kaleb moved a pebble three spaces, and he scowled. "Don't lean on the board," he said to Sorren.

She had not been leaning on the board. She wondered if Paxe had seen Isak arrive. She glanced at Kaleb. Like her, he was from outside the city; he was Asech, brown and high-cheekboned, with stones set in his ears. "Is the Yardmaster in the Yard?" she asked.

Without lifting his eyes from the board, he nodded.

Outside the house, the heat fell on her again. She went swiftly through the rear courtyard. The tile here was a different pattern than in front of the house. The paths were lined with sour apple trees. She marched under the spreading, blossom-laden branches. There were petals scattered over the tiles. At the end of the row of trees, she balanced on one leg and picked the petals first off one, then off the other foot. Lalith swept the petaled tiles every morning, and three hours later they were pink again. She continued toward the Yard. The gate to it was on the other side, but she was not going in; she couldn't, not being a soldier. When she came to the high red wooden fence she pulled herself up and sat on the top.

From this vantage point she could see the whole Yard, from the gate to the weapons shed. There were perhaps twenty people in the Yard. They stood in a circle around a small moving human knot. The center of the knot was Paxe. Six guards ranged around her. They dived at her, and she dodged and waved and turned, throwing them easily, keeping two paces ahead of their steps, lunging at them to toss them when their tired steps slowed.

Paxe saw Sorren perched on the fence, and grinned, white teeth flashing, but she continued the demonstration without breaking stride. Finally she halted it with a shout. *"Yai!"* The watching guards drew close to listen. Her hands moved as she talked. She wore—they all wore—training clothes, the cotton shirt and drawstringed pants that reminded Sorren of Isak's practice uniform. She had said so once to him, and he explained that the old chearis had dressed like that, and the city guards continued the tradition without knowing where it came from.

"Are there any real chearis left?" she asked him.

A different man might have been insulted at the suggestion that he was not a *real* cheari. But Isak never got angry, and besides, he had said as much himself.

"Maybe," he answered. "In the north, somewhere. Legend says that a scion of the line of Van of Vanima still lives in the Red Hills."

Sorren tingled. She remembered that her mother had told her stories about the magical valley, called Vanima, where no one was every sick or cold or hungry, where it was always summer. "Is there such a place?" she asked Isak.

He had smiled that sardonic smile. "Legend says there is."

"But you don't believe it."

He shook his head. "No."

Sorren knew the story of the Red Clan. It had been told to her around the pickers' campfires. Once the city Yards had been public places, where children went to learn the arts of fighting. The strongest, surest, most graceful of these children went on to learn to dance. Those who could both fight and dance were called chearis, and the best of these bound themselves into companies, joined by love and respect and skill. Each company was called a *chearas*. They traveled from village to town to city, from steppe to sea, dancing, teaching the weapons' arts, and drawing the hearts of all who watched them, across the land of Arun, into harmony.

But as more people crowded into Kendra-on-the-Delta, the Council grew nervous; it banned the bearing of edged weapons and then the teaching of edged weapons within the city gates. Shanan Council of Houses followed suit. Finally even Tezera Council passed a Ban. The chearis, appalled at the abandonment of tradition, took their complaint to the Tanjo. The Council of Witches deliberated, and finally its chief, the *L'hel*, spoke. All things change, she had said. The chea manifests itself in peace. A ban on edged weapons will make the cities peaceful. Therefore, let the soldiers fight, and let the chearis dance. There is no more need for cityfolk, except those called to the guard, to learn fighting or weaponry.

Some chearis, like Meredith of Shanan, laid aside their knives, left the Yard, and taught the dance, as the witches commanded. Some joined the city guard, and taught the arts of spear and cudgel and empty-handed combat. These skills were permitted by the Councils to the guards, but to no others.

But most chearis, disbelieving, angry, and unwilling to change, left the cities.

"Where did they go?" Sorren asked first Isak, and then Paxe. The old history intrigued and enchanted her.

Isak said, "They went west, and north, looking, I suppose, for Vanima, where the Red Clan began."

Paxe said, "They went west."

"Then is there still a Red Clan?"

Paxe said, "Ask Isak Med. He could wear the shariza, if he wished."

And Isak said, "Ask Yardmaster Paxe."

But you could not push Paxe to talk when she would not. Sorren did not ask a second time. Instead, she assumed the answer: No. The Red Clan was no more. The thought made her sad. Though it was true, the city was peaceful. The guard troops kept order. Perhaps there were a few old chearis left, somewhere in Arun. But it seemed doubtful that they ever came within the city's borders.

Sorren gazed down into the Yard. Head cocked to one side, hands on her hips, Paxe was watching the practice. She was tall, as broad-shouldered as any of her guards, a stern and striking figure. She wore her tight-curled hair very short against her head. Sorren shifted on her perch. The Yardmaster looked at her, smiled, and jerked her head in the direction of the cottage. Sorren grinned. Swinging her legs around, she jumped from the fence. The cottage—Paxe's cottage, where she lived with her son, Ricard—was around the east side of the Yard.

The cottage door was open. Ricard was there. Officially he lived there, but in fact he rarely slept in the cottage, preferring the homes and haunts of his friends. He was curled in the sunlight on the mats. He opened his eyes as Sorren blocked the light. Slowly he sat up. "What are you doing here?" he said.

She wanted to laugh at him and tell him not to be a fool, but he was only fourteen, and hated being laughed at. She went around him. Where Paxe had muscles, he had fat. He was always morose; had she been such a sullen child three years ago, Arré would probably have sent her back to the grapefields in disgust. She went into the kitchen. Paxe's gray cat was sleeping on the tile top of the stove. It opened one eye—it only had the one, the other had been clawed blind in a fight a year back—and made a chirruping sound of inquiry and welcome.

She stroked its thick soft fur. It was sleek and as well-exercised as Paxe herself. It purred in soft growling chirps. There was a peach lying nearby on a flowered plate; she picked it up. The smell made her mouth water. She bit it, feeling fuzz on her tongue. It was perfect, ripe and sweet.

Ricard had followed her. "That wasn't for you," he said, grumpily but not seriously.

"Want some?" She held it out to him.

"Naw." He scratched his chin, which was beginning to sprout with beard. His skin was lighter than his mother's. "Listen, I want to tell you something."

"Tell." She stroked the cat, ate the peach, and listened. He told her a long, complicated story which seemed to be about a friend of his and a girl. She wondered if she was supposed to believe in the friend.

There was a sand-glass on the windowsill. She turned it over to watch the sand trickle from one compartment to the other. Ricard leaned over her. He was as tall as she, which meant he was almost as tall as Paxe. His voice stumbled. She glanced at him.

His lips were parted. He was looking down the open neck of her shirt.

They both lost the thread of his story at the same time. Ricard muttered something which Sorren couldn't catch.

Before she could swear at him, he backed away, whirled, and went into the front room. She heard Paxe's step.

"Where are you going?"

He mumbled. The cottage door banged.

"Sorren?"

Licking the tips of her fingers, Sorren laid the fringed peach pit back on the plate. "I'm in here."

Paxe walked into the kitchen. Her cream-colored shirt was patchy with sweat. "That Ricky," she said. "He's gone out to spend my money. I never see him except when he needs cash; it's all he ever asks of me."

"He's just a little boy," Sorren said. She opened her arms, and Paxe walked into them. Her body was hot and scented with dust. "Don't mind what he does." Gently, she reached to stroke the back of Paxe's neck.

They went upstairs, to Paxe's over-sized, feather-quilted bed. Smiling, Paxe took off her clothes. She lay down, waiting for Sorren to join her. They rolled together, half loving, half wrestling. Curling in the lovers' knot, they stroked and teased each other into shivering pleasure. Sorren's skin flushed with blood. She laid her head on Paxe's thigh. One hand cupped over Paxe's mound, she felt the pulse of pleasure leap, leap, and fade.

She ran her tongue over her lips, tasting Paxe.

Paxe's fingers reached for her. "Come here."

Sorren pulled herself up until she lay beside her lover on the pillow. She loved the way they fit together, like a thing and its shadow. Paxe turned on her side. Her right hand brushed Sorren's breast.

"I know why I love you," she said. "You're the only woman around this house near my size."

Outside the house, a woman's voice began to sing. "*In sunlight we must part, my love, in starlight we may smile; The moon is shining bright my love, O let me stay awhile....*"

Sorren joined it. "*Sing hey and a ho for lovers, sing hey for the setting sun. Sing hey for the girl who makes me smile when the harvest work is done!"*

Sighing, Paxe arched her long body upward, and twisted herself on top of Sorren. "You can't sing, you know." She bowed her head. Their lips met, and their tongues.

When they disengaged, Sorren said, "I know. That's why I play the drums." She wriggled. "Get off."

"Why?"

"I have to go back to the house."

Paxe made a face. "I suppose you must." She rolled over. Sitting, Sorren reached for her clothes.

As she drew on her pants, the mountain vision came upon her. *She was a bird (though without form or weight) soaring over the steppe. She smelled the northern air, thin and clean and dry as bone, tasted it, felt her lungs labor for it. The sun was hot. The hills rose below her, brown and green and white. The white was sheep. They grazed placidly on the grass, as girls with sticks watched them. A river, blue as a ribbon, threaded a path toward a valley. Behind the river, the mountains stood. Within the cleft of the mountains, a tower lifted a gray spike to the sky.*

She returned to present time to find Paxe sitting beside her, her brow wrinkled. She lifted her palm to her lover's dark cheek. "I'm back."

Paxe sighed. "Where did you go this time?"

"Where I always go," Sorren said. "The mountains."

She had been thirteen, riding a wagon back from the grape-fields, her mother's meager belongings scattered on her lap, when the visions first possessed her. She was too numb to be frightened. But when they continued, she asked questions in the city, and found that this power to go places with her mind had a name. Far-traveling, it was called, and those to whom it came were automatically named members of the White Clan, and whatever their stations, had to leave their lives to come within the Tanjo and serve the chea....

It was an honored task and an honored title, that of witch. But Sorren did not want it. The witches frightened her. Stubbornly silent, Sorren kept her gift to herself. The only person she trusted enough to tell about it was Paxe.

Paxe said, when Sorren told her of the gift, "You should go to the Tanjo."

"I don't want to," Sorren said. And Paxe accepted that. Arré, Sorren knew, never would; she cared too much for power to understand why someone might not want it.

"You might want to, someday," Paxe said. Sorren nodded, but she doubted it. The witchfolk lived in the Tanjo, and only talked to each other. For Sorren, used to the hustle of the markets, it seemed too straight, too confined a life.

Besides, they would not want her in the Tanjo. She only saw one place. She saw the mountains, only the mountains. She saw them in spring, when the blue river leaped down the sloping hills like a freed hare, and in summer; she saw them in fall, when rain turned the valleys to marsh, and in winter. Always she saw the same vista: the fields, the river, and the castle with its one tall tower. In winter, the tower glittered with ice. It was a real place; Sorren was sure of that. Sometimes she approached the tower at dusk, close enough to see a light through its amber panes of glass.

She had described it all to Paxe, but the Yardmaster did not know it.

Sorren thought, someday, when my time is all my own, I will discover where it is, and go to it.

But her mother had bound her to the Med house for the traditional eight years, and the time of her release was still one long year away.

"Isak was at the house today," she said.

"Oh?" Paxe reached for her clothes. "What did he want?"

"He wants to dance for the Council, when it meets."

Paxe twitched her shirt over her head. "Arré said yes, of course." Sorren nodded. "I wonder what he's up to."

Her tone was thoughtful. "Why should he be up to anything?" Sorren said. She stroked Paxe's thigh. There was a long runneled scar across it, and she wondered for the hundredth time what had made it. She did not think it was a spear cut.

"Because," said Paxe, "he hates her. I remember when Shana, Arré's mother, was alive, and Arré was learning to run the district from her. Isak hated her then, too."

From the Yard came the voice of Dis, the day watch second-in-command, calling orders to the guards. Paxe straightened. "I must go, *chelito*. I'll see you later." She laid her lips against Sorren's hair for a moment, and then rose, teeth gleaming in her dark, stern face.

She went downstairs. Sorren sat quietly, listening to her steps. Paxe's bedroom was like Paxe herself, bold, clean, and beautiful. The floor was unmatted; the walls red wood, bare of tapestries. Sorren started to braid her hair, and then remembered that she had nothing to tie it with. Letting it dangle, she went downstairs.

As she strolled around the corner of the Yard toward the house, she saw Ricard waiting for her. Internally, she grinned as he fell into step. She waited for him to say something, but he said nothing, only frowned. Finally Sorren grew bored.

"Did you want to finish telling me that story?" she said.

His glance was resentful. "No." Within the Yard, Paxe was instructing; her voice echoed through the fence planks. "What did you say to her?"

"To who?"

"To my mother."

She scratched her nose. "Nothing about you."

If anything, his face grew more sullen. But he managed a muttered "Thanks."

Sorren wondered why he stayed in the city if he so disliked it. "Ricard," she asked, "have you ever wanted to leave here? To travel?"

He looked at her as if she had started speaking in the Asech tongue. "What difference would it make?" he said.

Sorren couldn't tell if that meant yes or no. Ricard wandered off, kicking at the tiles of the courtyard. She had heard Arré and Paxe arguing about him; Arré thought Paxe should send him north, to the vineyards. "Myra will put him to work," said Arré. Sorren agreed. But Paxe did not want to.

Perhaps, Sorren thought, Ricard would be a nicer person if he had brothers or sisters. Paxe had had two children before him, but they had both died.

She went into the house through the kitchen door. Cook was gone. The apprentices crouched in a conspiratorial huddle. She smelled the sweet, distinct odor of heavenweed. They passed her the pipe as she angled by them, and she sucked on it slowly, breathing in the harsh narcotic smoke. She handed it to Lalith. It went around the circle and returned to her. She shook the pipe gently, to stir the flakes, and took one final puff.

Quietly she went upstairs. Her room was in the back of the house, near enough to Arré's so that she could hear the calling-bell when Arré rang it. She had to pass Arré's chamber to get to it. If Arré's door was shut, it meant she did not want to be disturbed. Sorren hoped it was closed.

The heavenweed was making her hyperaware of her body. She slid her feet on the patterned carpet of the upstairs hallway. Arré's door was open, but only a crack.

In her room, she took her drums from their basket. They were wooden, with deerskin heads. She had first started drumming in the grapefields, on the hollow logs which the pickers dragged out at Harvest Festival. She wedged the drums between her knees. There was a worn spot on the left-hand drumhead. If she caught Isak at the right time, he would pay for a new one, and that would please Arré. She tapped the skins softly. *Pah-pah-pah-dum-pah.* She wondered which dance Isak would do for the Councillors. It would be something slow and subtle, with lots of little changes, not the flashy fast dances he did at festivals for the crowds.

Pah-pah-pah-dum-dum. The heavenweed made it hard to concentrate. Her fingers felt tingly. She liked heavenweed. Especially she liked smoking heavenweed with Paxe (though Paxe herself rarely smoked it; she claimed it made her sleepy) and then making love.

Pah-dum-pah-pah. Her muscles moved under her skin. She felt the slight constriction of the bondservant's bracelet that she wore high on her left arm. It was brass, with a pattern of blue and scarlet enameled triangles. She did not mind wearing it; the life she was living as a bondservant was much easier than the one she had been destined for, that of a migrant picker.

The small room held little that was hers. The drums were hers; Isak had, in a moment of generosity, given them to her. The clothes she wore, by custom, were her own. The items in the cedar chest—brush, comb, bronze mirror, gold chain, sandals—were hers. The Cards were hers. They lay beneath her pillow, in a wooden box. They were very old—she did not know how old—and had been designed for telling fortunes, for seeing into the future. They had been her mother's. There were twenty-two of them, all different, and she had given them names from the images. They were numbered, too. Sorren had learned to read numbers in the grapefields. One of them, the Dancer, had no number; the rest did, and she kept them in order in the wooden box, wrapped in a scrap of red silk.

Her fingers tapped the drumheads. Telling fortunes was contrary to the chea, the Tanjo said so. But Sorren was not troubled by that prohibition; she did not know how to use the Cards. She could not remember if her mother had. She wished she could remember all the stories her mother told; they might have explained where the Cards had come from, and how they worked. They even might have explained Sorren's visions.

She had thought of showing Arré the Cards. But if she showed Arré the Cards, she might have to tell Arré about the gift, and Arré would tell the witchfolk, and then Sorren would be forced to leave the Med house and live in the Tanjo and serve the chea, and be shut away from all her friends, especially Paxe, and never go to the mountains.

That would be awful. Her fingers danced on the drumheads. *Pah-pah-pah, pah-pah-PAH*. She would hate it; she would run away.

CHAPTER TWO

Paxe's day began with the dawn. The birds woke her, and then the light, leaping through the eastern window. She lay in bed, not moving, sorting out the sensations of the morning. From the Med house she could hear the clatter and bustle as Toli, the kitchen apprentice, cleaned the ashes from the furnace beside the house and lit the new fire. The scents of pine and hemlock drifted on the wind. The breeze was moist and salty, blowing from the south. She stretched; her sinews creaked, and her joints popped softly. Lifting on her elbows, she cocked her head, listening for sounds from the lower room. But she heard nothing; Ricard had not slept in the cottage this night. She had not expected him to be there: on the rare occasions he deigned to use her house, he filled it full of heavenweed smoke, and she would have smelled it. Besides, she would have heard him stagger in.

She rose, and dressed. She was used to getting up early by now; she had been doing it all summer. The three Med commanders—Paxe, Kaleb, and Ivor—rotated from watch to watch four times a year, with the season's change. Day watch went from sunrise to midafternoon; late watch, Ivor's watch, went from afternoon to midnight, and night watch went from midnight to sunrise. The actual times of the watch were flexible, to allow for the variability of the seasons. Night watch was the most unpredictable and day watch the busiest of the three duties, and day watch was Paxe's current command.

Kaleb was waiting for her just within the Yard gate.

"Good morning," he said.

She smiled at him. "Good morning." They knew each other well. He had been her second-in-command for seven, and her friend for sixteen years. After the death of her daughters in the plague, Shana Med, Arré Med's mother, had given Paxe permission to leave her post in the vineyards and travel. She journeyed west, to Shanan, and then farther still, across the Asech territory to Tor's Rest, a small village at the southernmost tip of the Red Hills.

She had stayed there two years. On the journey back she met Kaleb and he followed her to the city and joined the Med guard at her recommendation. It was likely (though not certain) that he was Ricard's father.

"How went the night?" she asked.

Kaleb leaned on the Yard wall. "This district was quiet. There was trouble on the docks, but the Jalar guard broke it up."

Dock work was tedious and exhausting; sometimes the loaders and fisherfolk battled just for release. "Anyone injured?"

"Not really. There were a few cracked heads. The Jalar guards had to use their spearbutts."

That was usual. "Who started it?" Paxe asked.

"I don't know," said Kaleb. "But rumor says Col Ismenin was in it."

He would not report rumor to her if he did not think it had some truth. "This isn't the first time that's been said," she commented. The Ismenin brothers were known to be brawlers. She looked Kaleb up and down. His clothes were dusty. He was three years younger than she, and already there was gray in his hair, but he would never say he was tired. "Go to bed," she said.

"I'm going."

She watched him leave the Yard. Ricard did not look like him, not really. She wondered where her son had spent the night. He played around the city half the day, spending her money and smoking heavenweed. . . . He was fifteen. At fifteen, she had been pregnant. Perhaps it was time for her to admit that he was no longer a child.

She began her exercises. Standing in the center of the wide, quiet space, she stretched her body in a circle, north, south, east, and west. She tended her muscles the way her guards tended their weapons, honing them, oiling them. Her frame was still as hard and slim as it had been when she was Sorren's age, but now she had to work to keep it so.

"Good morning, Yardmaster!" A handful of her guards came through the Yard gate. She waved a greeting. "Heard about the fight last night?"

That was Seth; he liked fighting. "I heard," she said. "Were you in it?"

His chocolate face split in a smile. "Not me. I was home in bed."

"That's a wonder," said Paxe.

Seth mimed astonishment.

"Don't give me that innocent look. I know you." She had had to order him beaten twice, for fighting in the Yard. He threw his hands out, palms up, the picture of innocence, and she shrugged. The other guards jostled and teased him as they walked to the weapons shed. Paxe left them to train without her. This was the time of day when she normally made her rounds. She strolled to the Gate. The Med district was the most irregularly laid out of all the districts. It was shaped like a boot; the opening of the boot pointed south, and the toe east, and the heel of it came smack against the Northwest Gate. Paxe called it "the Med district," but deep inside she thought of it as hers: her territory, her realm, her piece of the city.

She stopped at the Travelers' Hall on Well Street to eat a morning meal. The cityfolk greeted her; travelers (who ate in the Hall for free) stared at her, obviously wondering who she was. She strolled through the Wine Market, picking her teeth free of sausage. In the Street of the Goldsmiths, she halted at a shop. The smith smiled and pulled out all his trays.

"Yardmaster Paxe, to what do we owe this pleasure? Is there something you would like? Just tell me."

Paxe looked at the lovely, expensive baubles. Once, years ago, she had purchased a bracelet at this shop for Arré. "I like it all, Tian, but I'm not going to buy it." She tapped the tray. "Put 'em back before the thieves get restless."

"With you standing here? Never." But he put the trays in the shop. She walked south, to the Tanjo guardpost. The Med guard, a woman named Orilys, saluted her with a palms-to-gether bow.

Four districts bordered the Tanjo precincts: Med, Minto, Isara, and Sul, and all four maintained a guard there. "How is it?" Paxe asked.

Orilys glanced at the Tanjo dome. Beyond the gate, the wide, white walkway shone in the sunlight. Near the entrance, an acolyte swept the already spotless pavement with a broom. A red bird skimmed over their heads, heading for its nest. A colony of them lived in the crannies of the building. "Quiet," she said. "It's always quiet here."

The traffic at the Northwest Gate was normal. Paxe stood to watch it. The guards fidgeted, and she grinned at them, guessing she was interrupting their dice game. They would return to it the moment she left. A green-clad courier arrived at the Gate, and the guards held back a cart to let her come in first. Paxe wondered where she'd been, and what her message was. It was not urgent; if it had been, the messenger would have been on horseback. That was one of the privileges of the Green Clan; they could ride horses within the city gates.

A gaggle of children swarmed around her as she left the Gate. "Yardmaster!" they shouted, and she patted them—all the ones she could reach—and gave the oldest a bronze piece with instruction to buy them all some pears. They ran off, dodging the incoming carts.

On the way back to the hill, Paxe walked through Oil Street. It was so named because it had once been lined with choba trees, which bore the long yellow pods from which choba oil was pressed. A mill for processing the oil still stood at the end of the avenue. But the trees had been pinched until they ceased to bear, and had been cut down some years back. The mill sat deserted. The houses here were ramshackle and old. Hard-eyed men and sullen women watched her pass, and the ragamuffin children squatting in the gutters did not call to her. A goat wandered untethered in the road.

Her steps seemed to echo on the cracked, dry street, and over everything hung the sweetish heavy scent of heavenweed. A few of the gardens sprouted corn, but most of them were dry, the plants withered and lifeless. It was not a good place for a stranger to walk. Paxe wondered what would have happened if the choba trees had continued to bear fruit. But there were few productive choba trees left in the city; most of them had been cut down to make room for more houses. Choba oil came from the orchards of Shirasai. Tattered banners, marking vacant buildings where once there had been flourishing shops, flapped over her head. Skinny cats prowled through piles of rubbish. The desolation made her sad, and she told herself that every district had an Oil Street. Hers was no worse than most.

She approached the Yard from the rear. As she walked around the high red fence, she smelled heavenweed. Some of the off-duty guards had been smoking, she guessed. She *hoped* it was the off-duty guards, and not the ones whose watch it was: she had strictly forbidden her soldiers to smoke or drink on watch. The Yard sounded empty; there were none of the shouts and grunts of people training.

Quietly she went around to the gate. The guard was not at his post. She frowned. But the Yard was not, after all, empty: a small knot of people stood in a corner where the fence posts joined. She couldn't see what they were doing; they seemed to be looking at something. Evrith, the gate guard, was one of them.

She felt her temper rising. If they were smoking heavenweed in the Yard, she thought, she'd have the hide off them in strips! She strode through the gate. Suddenly, one of them—it was Seth—stepped to one side and raised both hands in the air. Paxe saw what they were looking at and her muscles clenched in shock: they were looking at the summer sunlight, pouring like water off the hard edge of a naked sword.

At first, the guards did not see her walking toward them. When they did, they froze. She held out her right hand. "Give it here," she said. Silently Seth laid the hilt in her palm. She wrapped both hands around it. It was bronze, with a decorative raised pattern that made the worn metal easier to hold.

Automatically her body recalled stance and balance: she advanced her right foot, and swung the blade. She'd learned to use one in Tor's Rest, from Tyré, who had claimed to have trained with Doménia, last of the line of Van of Vanima. She swung the sword again, and it sang as it cut the air.

Her guards were looking at her as if they had never seen her before.

"You didn't know I've used these," she said. "Where did you get it?"

Evrith started to speak, and Seth elbowed him. "It's mine," he said. "I bought it from a smith's son."

"Where did he get it?"

"Made it," Seth said airily.

Paxe squinted at the single-edged blade. It was shorter than the one Tyré had taught her to use, but it looked just as old.

"Where's the sheath?" she asked.

Seth plucked it from the ground. She held out her hand for it, and he gave it to her. It was leather, old cracked leather. She scowled. The sword looked too used and too well-made to have been fashioned by some ambitious blacksmith's son.

Again Evrith started to speak. Fiercely, Seth said, "Shut your mouth!"

Paxe glanced sharply at him. He's lying, she thought. Insolently, he met the look, and her temper rose again. Sheating the sword, she bent to put it down and then sprang up, snapping upright as a plucked bowstring leaps to place. She fisted her left hand in Seth's shirtfront and shook him till his eyes rolled, and when she finished shaking him, she slapped him. "That's for lying. Where did you get it?" She waited till he was about to speak and then hit him again, very hard.

Tears came to his eyes, and a name jolted out of him, "Lyrith!"

"Who does he fight for?" Paxe said.

"Ismeninas," Seth muttered, swaying in her grasp.

Paxe let him go.

She picked up the sword again. "Would you care to have to account for your possession of an edged weapon in the Tanjo?" she said. Seth's face grayed. They all shook their heads. "Then I suggest you forget you ever saw or touched this." She lifted the sword.

Evrith said, "Yes, Yardmaster." They stepped out of her way as she turned to leave the Yard. As she passed around the outside of the fence, she smelled the heavenweed, still heavy in the air. The whole incident had taken almost no time at all.

She took the sword to her house and laid it upstairs, by the bed. The look of it disturbed her. What if Ricky came upstairs and saw the sword lying there? She went back down the stairs. Lifting the lid of her cedarwood chest, she nestled the blade in among the quilts and covered it until it was concealed by the folds. She would have to tell Arré about it, of course. Arré would want to know how it got into her hands, where it was from, who made it. She dug it out again and took it apart, as old Tyré had taught her.

On the tang she found scratched runes which were the maker's name. She puzzled over them, but the script was strange, and she gave up. Under the name was a little fish emblem; that told her enough. The sword had indeed come out of the north, from Tezera, and it was old. Rust streaked the steel. It had to have been made before the Ban.

She fitted it back together again. Even the discolored steel felt dangerous, both for what it was, and for what it meant. It was *ni'chea*. Edged weapons, so the witches said, shattered that harmony which drew people together in peace and made the land of Arun fruitful; it was forbidden to own them or use them in the city. The prohibition was not total, but the terms of the exceptions were clear and known to every child in the city streets—which only made the swords more fascinating, Paxe knew.

Her image of the Guardian sat in its niche in the wall. She rarely looked at it; it was part of her life, like her past. It was made of red stone, a rarity in Kendra-on-the-Delta: most of the statues in the city were made of clay, and were white. Kaleb had given it to her. The Asech were serious about symbols. Kaleb had not been back to the desert in ten years, but he still wore the token of the Rat Clan where it could not be seen, under his shirt.

Paxe gazed at the stylized face, wondering what to do. By law, she should bring the sword to the Tanjo, give it to the witches, and name Seth as its possessor. She wondered what they would do to Seth if she betrayed him to them. He could be banished from the city, whipped, fined, or worse. The last man to bring a sword into the city had had his right hand struck off.

Frowning, she returned the sword to the chest. Then she rose and left the house. Before she talked to anyone, Arré *or* the witches, she wanted to know exactly where the sword had come from.

She went down the hill to Spring Street, and there, turning east, she walked toward the river, toward the district which was named for and guarded by the Ismeninas.

The Ismenin house was made of stone. It sat on a bluff, with its broad back to the river. It was new. The original Ismenin mansion, like the other great houses of the city, had been built of red cypress, that beautiful wood which had the property of silvering as it aged. It was Rath Ismenin, Ron Ismenin's grandfather, who had caused the stone house to be built. In the Council Year Ninety-Three, he and others traveled to Tezera, to discuss the effects of the Ban on commerce. Visiting the high families of Tezera, Rath Ismenin walked through marble halls for the first time. When he returned south, he ordered the Ismenin mansion razed to the earth, and built himself a house of white granite, with architects and masons hired from Tezera, under the shocked gaze of his neighbors.

The street on which the house stood was called, with characteristic city humor, Rath's Alley. The Yard was next to the house. Like the Med Yard, it was a fenced, dirt-filled square. Paxe strode briskly toward it.

A guard stood outside the tall iron gate. "Good morning," Paxe said. "I want to see Yardmaster Dobrin." Dobrin had been Yardmaster of the Ismenin Yard for fifteen years. He was a small, dark man, older than Paxe. She knew him—not well, but all the Yardmasters of Kendra-on-the-Delta knew each other.

The gate guard said, "I'm sorry. The Yardmaster is teaching now."

Paxe stepped back to see him clearly. He was young, with a silly little mustache on his upper lip; it looked like a caterpillar. "My name is Paxe," she said. "I am Yardmaster of the Med Yard." Expecting him to move, she stepped forward. Courtesy demanded that he let her in.

Licking dry lips, he held his spear like a bar across the gate. Gray and gold tassels hung below its point. "I'm sorry, Yardmaster," he said. "No one is permitted to enter the Ismenin Yard who does not wear Ismenin colors."

Paxe had never heard of such an order. "Whose orders are those?" she said.

"Ron Ismenin's."

She looked him up and down, a measuring stare. He was sweating. They both knew how easy it would be for her to move him aside. She cocked her head, hearing the clash of wood striking wood and numbers being shouted ("*One*—and *two*—and *three*—and *four!*") through the gate. She said, "Tell Yardmaster Dobrin that I am here and wish to speak with him."

Gulls circled over her head, crying mockery. There were always gulls by the river. Hands on her hips, she stepped back to give the guard room to make up his mind what to do. If he refused to carry her message to Dobrin, she would go through him.

He swallowed. "Excuse me, Yardmaster," he said. He pushed the bolt back and slipped through the door. She heard him bolt it from the other side. She stared at the gate, holding her temper.

In a very short while, the guard was back. She heard him slip the bolt. He did not come out; instead, he held the door open for her. "Excuse me," he repeated.

She looked at him the way she would have looked at one of her own soldiers. "There are rust spots on your spearhead."

Within the Yard, the Ismenin soldiers were drawn up into two lines. The guards in the lines faced each other, making a row of pairs. They held wooden swords. Paxe watched quietly as they swung the swords up and down, halting at waist level

on the downstroke. The presence of the guard at the gate should
have forwarned her, she thought. A boy staggered by her,
carrying a bucket. Setting the bucket down, he flung water on
the blowing dust. The line of the swords arced upward. The
soldiers pretended not to see her. One man caught her eye: he
was tall, light-skinned, his hair was reddish brown, and he
wore silks, not cotton. He had a gold ring on his right middle
finger.

She wondered who he was. In the Med Yard no one, not
even she, wore rings. He saw her watching him, and smiling,
he lifted his weapon and brought it down in a clean, sharp cut.
At the lowest point, his body clenched. His hands did not
quiver.

"One—and two—and three—and four!" A woman's voice
counted cadence. Paxe watched the redhead, and decided that
he was probably one of the younger Ismenin brothers. She saw
no live blades, anywhere. She waited, and after a while Dobrin
appeared. He wore gray cottons, stained with sweat. There
was more white in his mustache than she remembered, but
apart from that, he looked as he always did.

"Welcome," he said.

"Thank you for admitting me to your Yard," Paxe said.

He scowled. His salt-and-pepper brows drew together. "You
should not have been kept waiting. The order was not meant
to apply to you."

The shadows of the wooden swords danced on the dust.

"I would like to speak with you alone, Dobrin."

"What of?" he said.

Paxe glanced at him. He was watching his soldiers, face
impassive. She admired his composure. "Of a guard in your
command," she said. "Named Lyrith."

Dobrin took her to his cottage. His home was even less
cluttered than hers. He had never married, Paxe recalled, and
perhaps that accounted for it; whatever children he might have
fathered remained within their mother's house. The front room
had no chairs, only cushions, and a low table on which rested
a spray of pink blossoms in a copper bowl. The walls and floor
were bare.

Paxe sat on a pillow. Dobrin went to the kitchen, and returned first with water and then with a dish of *fetuch* and a
small lacquered jar filled with salt. They sprinkled salt on the

crisp green stalks and ate them. The shared food had a pleasant sense of ritual. In a small niche on the eastern wall of the room sat a white clay image of the Guardian. Beneath it, on a shelf, sat a second spray of flowers. When they had eaten all the fetuch, Dobrin took the dish and salt jar back to the pantry. Returning, he seated himself on the pillow and folded his hands in his lap.

"It's been a long time," he said, "since we shared a meal."

Paxe's mouth twitched. Six stalks of fetuch! "So that's how you stay so thin," she said.

Dobrin smiled. "You wish to speak to me of Lyrith," he prompted.

"Yes," said Paxe. She could still hear the count from the Yard through Dobrin's window. She wished she were not facing the Guardian; the image seemed to watch her, seeing her thought before she spoke, as could the witches in the Tanjo, some of them.

"When I came back to my Yard from making rounds this morning," she said, "I found one of my men with a sword. A live blade. I took it from him. I asked him where it came from. He confessed to me that Lyrith, of this house, gave it or sold it to him, I don't know which."

Dobrin said evenly, "I see. Was it marked?" he said.

"It had the fish emblem on the tang."

Dobrin's hands clenched, and relaxed. Rising, he went to the door and jerked it open, and his voice cut like a knife across the cadence of the count. "Gavriénna!"

The woman ceased counting. In a moment she appeared at the cottage door. "Yardmaster?"

Dobrin said grimly, "Bring me Lyrith."

The woman bowed and vanished. Paxe heard her shouting. When she returned, she towed a young, dark-skinned man. Dobrin reseated himself and beckoned his soldiers inside. "Paxe-no-Tamaris, Yardmaster to Arré Med," he said, indicating Paxe. "She comes to this Yard with an accusation. Lyrith, do you know a Med guard named—" he glanced at Paxe.

"Seth," she said.

The man bit his lower lip. "Yes, Yardmaster."

"Did you sell or give to him a Tezeran sword?"

Lyrith looked at the ground. Gavriénna shook him. "Answer quickly!"

Lyrith said, "Yes, Yardmaster."

"Where did you get it?"

Lyrith gulped. "My cousin is a trader, Yardmaster. When we—when we began training with the wooden swords, I asked him to bring me one. He brought me two. Seth is bedmate to my sister; he saw them in the house and wanted one. I gave it to him."

"Even though, when we began training, you were warned that possession of live blades was and *is* forbidden."

"Yes, Yardmaster."

Dobrin leaned forward. "You have been forbidden to own a sword," he said. "You have been forbidden to even *talk* about the training here. If word were to reach the Tanjo that there is a sword in your house, do you realize what could happen to you? You could be banished, your hand could be struck off! Yet you ask some trader to bring you a sword, as if you had never heard me say, *You may not own a blade.* Do you know what the witchfolk could do to you for this?"

He had not raised his voice. But Lyrith was gray, and sweating where he stood. "Yes, Yardmaster."

"You are a fool."

"Yes, Yardmaster."

"I shall not bother to report this to Ron Ismenin. Tomorrow you shall bring me this blade you have. And today at noon you shall go to the post; Gavriénna, ten strokes, and I want every guard in the Yard to witness it." The watch commander nodded. "Get out of here."

"Come on, fool," said Gavriénna. She jerked Lyrith from the cottage. Paxe glimpsed the man's face for a moment; he was near to tears. She could not tell if they were tears of shame or of relief.

"Are you satisfied?" said Dobrin, folding his hands again.

Paxe was silent. The count resumed. ("One—and two—and three—and four!")

"No," she said finally. "No, I am not satisfied. Dobrin, why are you training with swords, when they are forbidden in the city?"

"Because I am Yardmaster," said Dobrin. "I obey the house I serve."

"Even though you break the Ban?"

Dobrin leaned forward. "I do not break the Ban."

"Because you have no live blades? Don't play with me, I am not a magistrate. You are knowingly breaking the Ban.

You know it, and Ron Ismenin knows it. Why else would you be telling your guards not to talk about their training, and why else would your lord have set a guard to keep strangers from your Yard gate?"

Dobrin said, "I am teaching the *komys*, Paxe, the short sword."

"Chea, what difference does it make, the word you use?"

"Do you know the exact words of the Ban?" Dobrin asked.

"No," said Paxe. "I have not read it. But I know what it says, and so do you."

Dobrin said, "It is written in the old tongue. I don't know it, but it has been translated for me. It lists the weapons which are forbidden in the city. There are two words for 'sword' in the old language; one betokens the long blade, one a short blade with a single edge. The Ban never mentions this second weapon."

The blade she had taken from Seth was short, with a single edge. "Do you tell me that short swords are not covered by the intent of the Ban?"

Dobrin shook his head. "I would not tell you that. But I do tell you that short swords are not covered by the language of the Ban."

Paxe's throat began to ache. "Dobrin, we are not Scholars, you and I. We are Yardmasters. Our oath binds us to uphold the law. If we break the spirit of the Ban, we break the law—and more. We break the chea."

"Ah," said Dobrin. "Do we?" He leaned forward, his face suddenly passionate. "I think not, Paxe. No, listen to me. We cityfolk are taught from childhood to reverence the witchfolk, to believe that, because of their powers, they are closer to knowledge than the rest of us. What we are taught to forget is that they are simply men and women, like you and me. Whatever their powers, they are only human, and I don't believe that they know any more than you or I, or anyone, about law, or truth, or the chea. More, Paxe. I am no longer sure that the chea asks that we do one thing within the city Gates, and another outside them. Outside the city, folk may wear and use edged weapons, inside not, and the witchfolk claim the chea wills it so. Yet the sign of the chea's presence is prosperity and concord among peoples, and look—outside the city walls there is no discord. It's been a hundred years since there was war! If the Ban is so necessary to keeping Arun peaceful, why, without it, has the country prospered?" He rapped on the table for emphasis. She had always thought of him as taciturn, and his volubility surprised her. This was the only speech she had ever heard him make.

For a moment Paxe's mind wheeled back to the Red Hills, to Tor's Rest, to Tyré. The old cheari had hated the Ban. "It makes no sense," he argued. "How can there be one chea for the cities and another for the Galbareth?" He was dead now; he had died in her arms, from a viper's bite so virulent that they had not had time to go for the Healer, three towns away. His death had broken Paxe's heart all over again.

"Then you believe the Ban—"

"Is human-made," finished Dobrin. "Made by the witches. I suppose they thought they had good reason to make it, when they did. But the world changes."

("One—and two—and three—and four!")

The face of the Guardian smiled serenely across the room. Paxe's mouth was dry. She said, "I will have to tell Arré Med that you are teaching the short sword, Dobrin."

"I know that," he said. "Think of what I have been saying to you, Paxe, about the chea."

Paxe rubbed the scar on her thigh. She could feel it through the coarse cloth of her pants. Tyré had given it to her, in training.

"Be assured," she answered, "I will."

CHAPTER THREE

The Council of Houses of Kendra-on-the-Delta met for the third time that year in the house of Arré Med, on the fifth night of the third week of the last month of summer, in the 146th year since the Council's founding.

Five families had seats on the Council. It had been three; it could be seven or nine. The odd number avoided deadlocks. The heads of the families, or their delegates, came to the meetings, which rotated each time from house to house in a set design.

Arré Med sat at the head of the table, facing the big double doors of the long parlor, as befitted her position as host. She was wearing new clothes in honor of the occasion; a skirt and tunic of blue and silver silk. She picked at her dessert, listening with half an ear to Boras Sul, who had changed his mind at the last minute and decided to come after all. He was describing a gold bowl which one of his pet traders had brought him from Tezera, and he was wearing red, which made him look even grosser than he was. Not for the first time, Arré decided that Boras was a tiresome, acquisitive fool.

They had started the meal early, and had been eating for— Arré glanced at the hour candle in its niche—almost two hours. The table was heaped with fishbones. Sorren stood by the door. She had directed the meal, the way the leader of a traveling show directs her acrobats and jugglers, and she had done it well. The Council officially began when the meal ended. Arré signaled Sorren to have the platters cleared from the table.

As the girl bent to take her dish, she said softly, "Is the scribe here?"

Sorren nodded. "She says, will you please not keep her standing in the hall, because her knees hurt."

Arré chuckled. The scribe was—had been, for fifteen years—an irascible old woman named Azulith-no-Alis. "Get her a chair."

"I have."

"Good." Arré relinquished her plate. "And my brother?"

"He arrived a few moments ago."

"Where did you put him?"

"In the little room off the hall."

"Fine. When we move to the chairs, bring glasses and two flasks of the northern wine." Sorren dipped her head in a half bow.

"Arré, my dear, you set a superb table," said Boras, settling back in his chair. It creaked. He waved one hand in the air, and then laid it delicately across his stomach. "I commend your cook."

Arré said, "I will be sure to tell him."

"I wonder—" Boras hesitated, in the manner of a man about to commit an indiscretion—"would you be willing to part with the recipe for the flounder?"

"I will have my cook copy it and send it to your kitchen," Arré promised, offering up a smile of thanks to the ghost of her mother, Shana, who had taught her that people were so much easier to handle when their bellies were full.

"The Med table has always been excellent," said Boras, pursuing his love with earnest single-mindedness.

"Thank you," said Arré. Her neck was starting to ache from being polite, and she was terribly aware of Isak waiting in the nearby room.

She was tired. The day before (and the day before that, and three days before *that*) she had spent with her surveyors, who wanted to dig holes all over the district, like children in a mudpile, and could not seem to understand when she insisted that they present her with a systematic plan for the street enlargements they wanted to make. Today she'd visited the district court, slipping into the rear unannounced to listen to her judges. She wanted very much to sleep. It was too much to hope that the meeting would end early, of course. She had no business to declare to the Council, but someone would.

She glanced down the table. Marti Hok sat at the foot of the table, as was her right; she was the oldest of the Councillors. She was also the one with whom Arré most often allied in the voting. Beside her, to Arré's right, sat Kim Batto. His head was bent, and the light gleamed on his bald spot. Kim was fussy and often obstructive, but his house had strong ties to the White Clan and for that reason Kim was both important and dangerous. Cha Minto sat next to Kim, closest to Arré. Boras sat across from the other two men.

Cha Minto looked up from contemplating the grain of the table. "Thank you for dinner, Arré," he said. He was the youngest of the Councillors, and normally he was laden with trivia, chatter, bits of gossip about this house or that. Arré wondered what was wrong, that he was so silent.

"You're welcome," she said. "You're very quiet tonight."

"I'm sorry."

Arré snorted. "No one said you had to talk."

"I could always talk about the food," he said, eyes on Boras.

She grinned at him. "Don't bother." She dropped her voice. "Boras does enough of that, for two."

It was meant to make him laugh. But he simply smiled perfunctorily, and looked at his hands. She gave up. Marti Hok was smiling, as if she sensed Arré's impatience. She looks, Arré thought, like a fat spider. It was no insult—it was the image she used when she thought of herself; a thin, dark, swiftly moving insect, ignorable, until it bit you.

The oldest Councillor tapped the floor with her cane. Its silver head was cast in the shape of a phoenix. "Shall we begin?" she called.

"Let's," said Kim.

Arré nodded. She gestured for Marti, as the eldest of the company, to rise first. At the other end of the parlor, a grouping of chairs sat beside the fireplace. The grate was empty, of course, though tongs and a tinderbox and a pile of seasoned birch logs sat nearby. The mantel of the fireplace had been freshly waxed, and the oak gleamed like silk. Two lamps with oilskin screens stood on the mantel, ready for lighting. A tall red lacquered vase filled with blue lilies rested in the arched hollow of the fireplace.

The Councillors made themselves comfortable. Sorren came in with a tray laden with glasses and the flasks of dry, amber wine. She handed each Councillor a wine glass. A scraping sound told Arré that the table they had just left was being moved against the wall to make room for Isak's dance. Azulith came in, and sat on the stool that had been placed for her at Arré's left. "Good evening," she said cheerily. Boras pretended deafness; Kim gazed into space. Marti smiled.

"Good evening, Azulith. How are your knees?"

"Terrible. It's the damp off the water, my lady, that makes them ache." Azulith settled her scroll case on her lap and took out her brush and ink stands.

"I know," said Marti. "So do mine."

"Shall we start?" snapped Kim.

"My goodness," said Marti, making her voice dulcet, "what

are you in such a hurry about?"

Kim pursed his lips. To forestall what he might say, Arré said, "Sorren, close the doors."

Sorren drew the big double doors closed. Arré lifted the wind glass to her lips. She liked the smell of good wine, although she rarely drank more than one glass. Drink made her sleepy, and too much made her sick. Sorren came round to the hearth and lit the two *chobata* on the mantel. They glowed softly through their painted porcelain skins. Arré set her glass down on the table which Sorren had placed, for that purpose, at her elbow. "Who has something to declare?" she said.

These words officially opened the Council meeting.

Kim Batto crossed his legs beneath his black and scarlet robe. "I do," he said.

Arré folded her hands in her lap. The Batto family and the Med family had a long history of enmity, going back two hundred years, to before the founding of the Council. Ewain Med, a captain of the city guard and the Med heir, had been killed by the eldest son of the Batto line, a man named Raven Batto. He had been outlawed, and with him, of her own desire and to her family's despair, had gone Maranth Med, next in line as heir to the Med house.

Tales of their travels to Anhard or to the Red Hills had persisted throughout Arun for years after their disappearance, but since they never returned to Kendra-on-the-Delta, no one had ever been certain where they had gone. The families had bickered and fought and blamed each other for the tragedy, until Lerril Hok brought them together again, some sixty years after the death of Ewain Med. The act had given the Hok house a reputation for peacemaking which they had never lost.

"The Council hears," said Arré.

The scribe lifted her brush. The Councillors, even Boras Sul, leaned forward a little in cushioned seats. Arré felt a flicker of excitement chase through her nerves.

"It concerns the trade in heavenweed. My guards tell me it has increased markedly lately, especially among the Asech youth."

The Batto family controlled trade with the Asech, whose merchants sold spices, beadwork, pottery, and dyes at all the city markets. For those goods, they received cloth, heavenweed, grain for their horses, and metal and leather goods. They still considered themselves desertfolk, but more and more of them were living in the city, or working in the cotton fields and vineyards. They had become a source of cheap labor, welcomed in times of prosperity, looked askance at in times of drought.

Arré said, "Are you making a complaint?"

"I am," said Kim.

"Don't you tax the trade?" asked Marti Hok.

"Of course we tax the trade," snapped Kim.

"Then the increased demand is making money for you. Don't complain."

Kim looked annoyed. "Marti, there are more important things than money. You miss the point. Have you noticed the effects of heavenweed on your servants, your dockworkers, even your guards? It makes them quarrelsome, *and* lazy. They stop wanting to work; they lie around all day and smoke, and at night they make trouble."

Marti said, "Heavenweed doesn't make people lazy, Kim. In case you hadn't noticed, people *are* lazy. And no, I can't say I've noticed any such effect among my guards, but then, my guards don't smoke on duty. Do yours?"

"Of course not!" Kim said.

Azulith said, "It's easy to say there are more important things than money when you have never lacked it."

"Azulith, be quiet," said Arré automatically. "Marti, be serious."

"I am being serious," said Marti. "Do you want to limit the trade, Kim?"

Kim frowned. "Well, I would not say that. It has occurred to me that more stringent controls might be in order. I might start by raising licensing fees. Fewer merchants would be able to afford it, and the trade might drop."

Marti said, "The Blue Clan would not like that. Also, raising fees will encourage people to buy from unlicensed merchants. You would not want to encourage that."

"No," said Kim. "No, I wouldn't." He sat back.

Arré said, "Cha, what do you think about the heavenweed trade?"

The young Councillor looked blankly at her. "I beg your pardon," he said automatically. "I was not listening. I am sure Kim will do the right thing."

Kim looked torn between pleasure at the praise and annoyance at Cha's inattention.

Arré said, "Is there more to be said on this matter?"

No one spoke. Boras Sul coughed portentously. "I have something to declare."

Marti Hok sighed.

"The Council hears," said Arré.

Boras wanted to talk about money. Since the thirty-fourth year of the founding of the Council, Kendra-on-the-Delta had used the polished shell pieces, the bontas, to buy and sell with, instead of gold and silver. Assayers sat at all eight city Gates, with weights and scales and measures. Merchants and travelers entering the city surrendered their metal coinage, and received bracelets of shells; when they left, they returned the remaining shell pieces and received back the equivalent in metal coinage, less the city's percentage, in exchange.

The Sul house licensed the assayers. They also oversaw the craftsfolk who cut and carved the pearly mussel shells out of which the bontas were made. The shells were cut in five sizes. The smallest counted least. Cityfolk called them "the bones." The little one was called by some the wishbone, by some the fingerling. The others were known as deuces, treys, tetras, and quints, also called largos. The careful measurements and weighing of the metal currencies was vital to the city; when every township up the river could stamp a crest on a piece of copper and call it a coin, the making of the bones in Kendra-on-the-Delta acted as a stabilizing force to Arun's economy.

But lately, Boras explained, the assaying tables had been glutted with coins made of bronze. "Like throwing pebbles in the scale! Might as well take a piece of clay, cut a mark in it, and call it money."

He has a face like a bronze coin, Arré decided. Round and flat and just that color. He was glaring at them all as if he suspected them of having engineered the glut. "Waste of the assayers' time!"

"Where do the coins come from?" asked Marti.

Boras scowled. "From Nuath."

Nuath was the largest of the towns on the river, after Mahita. Most of the grain for Kendra-on-the-Delta flowed first into Nuath, and then onto the great Blue Clan barges which carried it downstream. They must be doing well if they can afford a mint, she thought. Most of the towns on the river used coins from Shanan or Tezera.

"They have a face on them," said Boras. "I'm told it's the

face of the town barker. Calls himself a lord. Name's Tarn.
Calls himself Tarn i Nuath."

Kim Batto said, "I know of him. He's a Ryth." The Ryth
house was a prominent Blue Clan family, with a branch in
Kendra-on-the-Delta and another in Shanan. "He thinks he's
noble because he has money. He's ambitious."

Marti smiled. "Who is not?"

Kim looked pious.

"Dangerous?" asked Arré. Petty houses, especially those
which controlled or could control a key point of the grain trade,
could be dangerous.

"I think not," said Kim.

Marti said idly, "How do you know of this man, Kim?"

Kim smiled. "I sell him pots," he said.

Kim considered himself something of an expert on Asech
pottery. People had been known to consult him from as far
away as Shanan on the work of a particular tribe or potter.
"Does he have taste?" asked Marti curiously.

Kim flicked a speck of dust from his sleeve. "None at all,
my dear Marti," he said. "The man's a barbarian."

He sounded very smug. Arré found her fingers curling in
irritation around each other. "Boras," she said hastily—she
was not going to be rude to Kim, it only made the meetings
longer—"what do your assayers do about the bronze coins
now?"

"Ignore them, mostly," grumbled Boras. "Pass them through.
Some of the city merchants will take them, and some won't.
I don't like it, though. It undermines standards."

"You could set up separate tables for bronze coins," said
Arré.

"Too much trouble," said Boras. "Besides, it would only
encourage people to use them."

This was true, Arré thought. Occasionally even Boras
showed flashes of intelligence.

Marti Hok said, "Why not do nothing? It doesn't sound
serious yet. Tell the assayers to pass the bronze coins through
without weighing them, and tell the city merchants that bronze
coins cannot be used as payment for taxes or for any city
services."

"Um," said Boras.

"I like that," said Kim.

Cha Minto merely nodded. Arré wondered how much of

the talk he had heard. "I agree," she said.

Sorren, unasked, circled round to the window and slid back the screen. It was still light out, but it was cooling. A damp breeze made the lilies tremble. Azulith worked her fingers to uncramp them; she had been writing steadily. Arré tipped her head back in her chair. It still ached. Isak. What did Isak want? There was no reason she could think of for him to desire to attend the Council this evening. She watched Sorren move around the room. If she had had children, her daughter or son would be doing what Sorren was doing now, serving wine, lighting lamps, as she, Arré, had done for her mother. But she had never wanted to bear children.

She beckoned to Sorren. "Tell my brother we are ready. Fill the glasses before you leave." Sorren brought the decanter around once more. When she left the room, Arré knocked on the arm of her chair.

"Councillors," she said, "before our senses grow too dulled with wine to appreciate it, let me present you with a surprise."

The double doors opened. Sorren entered, drums in hand. She wore black silk with gold edging; a gold chain gleamed around her throat, and the black tunic had red butterflies embroidered on it. Arré guessed that Isak had chosen her clothes, and nodded approval; his taste, as ever, was exquisite. Boras Sul gazed at the girl with suddenly gluttonous eyes.

Sorren sat on the carpeted floor and put her drums between her knees. Skillfully she began to tape a soft entering drumroll. Arré's heart jumped as she waited for Isak to appear.

Isak came through the doors.

He wore red and gold. He carried two huge fans that spread out from his supple wrists like wings. His long hair was pinned to the top of his head by a red lacquer comb. In the wide red sash gleamed the ornate hilt of the ceremonial knife that all dancers wore, recalling the time when dance was a warrior's art.

He lifted the fans, veiling his face. This dance had a story—they all did. Arré rarely bothered to follow the story. This one she knew, however: it was the Tale of the Enchanted Eagle. The drumming and the soft sounds of the silk moving eased her senses. She leaned back into the cushion of her chair and let her eyelids droop.

The drum tempo changed, quickened. She opened her eyes.

Isak postured, arms extended like the eagle's wings. He turned his head from side to side, flick, flick, the way a bird would. He had darkened his skin with something. The tongue and straps of his sandals were beaded to give the illusion of taloned feet. He had even outlined his brows with black, and his eyes glowed like a bird's eyes, brilliant, impatient, and feral.

He shook his head, stamped, and turned. The comb fell from his hair. His hair washed down over his back. Now he was the Witch. He bent grotesquely. His face twisted into a mask of malice and mischief. The fans closed and became witch's wands.

The drum tempo grew martial. He straightened. The fans crossed and became a bow and arrow. Now he was the Hunter, young and eager, innocent as flame. The Hunter met the Witch, was tested, endured. At the end of the dance, the drumming lifted to a crescendo, and the dancer was an Eagle again.

Sorren rested her hands on her knees. Isak lowered the fans from his face and smiled. In the streets, Arré thought, they would be cheering and shouting. Even Azulith was still, tongue curbed, broad face rapt, ink and pages forgotten in the spell.

Rising, Sorren opened the doors. Isak swept through them, and she followed him. The Councillors sat for long minutes. Finally Cha Minto stirred in his seat. He said, "Arré, your brother has a gift."

Arré looked at him, surprised. Isak was a man for women, had his tastes changed? But no, Cha did not look like a man who had just watched a lover perform. Again she wondered what was wrong with him.

Marti Hok turned to Kim Batto. "Help me stand," she commanded. He rose and assisted her to her feet. "Old bones," she said. "If I sit in one spot too long, I have to be practically levered loose from it." She hobbled around the edge of the parlor. Sorren came back to the room. She had changed her clothes; she was wearing the soft blue tunic and pants that Arré liked her servants to wear. She sidled to the open window. The cool sea mist, blowing from the south, feathered her hair to one side.

Boras heaved from his chair. "I've been sitting too long," he said. "Excuse me." He wobbled out the door. Cha Minto turned his wine glass in his fingers. Sorren brought the flask to him and refilled his glass.

Marti stopped beside Azulith's stool. "You write beautifully, 'Zuli," she said. She leaned one swollen hand on the woman's shoulder.

"Thank you, lady," said the scribe. "The chea knows I've been doing it long enough. Twenty-eight years come the new moon."

"Who trained you?"

"Samia-no-Reo, lady."

"Ah," said Marti. Samia-no-Reo had been one of the great scribes of the Black Clan. "I knew her, when I was a little girl. She used to tell me stories. You must be almost as old as I am, 'Zuli."

"I'll be fifty-eight, harvesttime," said the scribe.

"Have you children?"

"Six of them," said the old woman.

Boras Sul came back. "Well," he said, "what's next, eh?" He sat. Marti made her way back to her chair, and Sorren helped her into it. Arré sat a little straighter. Her neck was aching.

"I have something to declare," said Cha Minto.

He had laid his glass aside, and sat with his fingertips together, a Scholar's gesture. It looked false on him. Arré thought of Isak, whose skill made all gestures look true. She wondered if he was still within the house, perhaps folding his clothes, those elegant dancer's robes, and waiting, impatient and feral, like the eagle.

For what was he waiting?

"The Council hears," she said tautly.

Cha Minto cleared his throat. "It has been," he began, "the custom of this Council to enlarge itself when families of the city grew strong enough and prosperous enough to deserve a place upon it. When the Council was first formed, its members were three, the Hok family, the Med family, and the Batto family. The Sul and Minto families were admitted to the Council in the Council Year Ninety-Six, that is, as you know, fifty years ago."

Boras Sul looked annoyed at the reminder that his family had not been one of the original Council members.

"Kendra-on-the-Delta has grown over those last fifty years. Truce and agreement was made with the Asech tribes, so that there has been peace between the people of Arun and the desert people."

That, Arré thought somewhat sourly, had more to do with

the influence of the witchfolk over the credulous Asech than with the machinations of the Council.

Cha continued. "The trade with Anhard has increased."

That was true.

"The members of this Council should, I think, be proud of what they and their parents have accomplished."

Get to it, Arré thought.

"But, without minimizing the actions of the families whose representatives sit here now, much of that growth has been created by the actions of the families Jalar and Ismenin. I therefore propose that we invite those families to join our Council, making seven members."

He paused. The only sound in the room was the noise of the wind on the screen and the whisper of the scribe's brush.

Oh, that's clever, Arré thought, as the names sank in. The Hok family, Marti's family, was the oldest in the city, and Marti Hok's second child, a son, was married to the daughter of Meredith Jalar. The Jalaras ran the docks and the fishing fleet. The Ismeninas owned the mines. For years, Kendra-on-the-Delta had been dependent upon trade with Tezera for metal, particularly copper and iron. But the Ismenin family had found copper deposits in the hills east of the river, and iron in the Red Hills, west of Shanan. Iron and silver, copper and coal, flowed first through the hands of the Ismeninas, and then to the merchants and the markets of the city. They were a rough-and-tumble crew, rich, boisterous, and powerful.

Ron Ismenin and Isak Med were good, close friends.

She lifted her glass to her face and observed Cha Minto through its wavy blue crystal, wondering what he was doing, and if he even knew.

Marti Hok said, "The family Jalar has long deserved a place on the Council." Boras Sul grunted agreement. Cha looked pleased. "However—" Cha's face grew wary—"I am not so sanguine about the Ismeninas."

Boras said, "They start brawls, that great bunch of boys, and they are all too young."

Cha Minto said, "Ron Ismenin is thirty-seven. And there are only four of them, Boras."

Boras purpled, until he looked like a turtle about to snap. Marti raised a hand. "There was a riot in the shipyards last week, Cha. The younger Ismenin brothers were right in the middle of it. They fight, they make trouble. That makes me uncomfortable. What if Ron Ismenin should drop dead? May the peace of the chea be with us all, I don't anticipate it—but I have no wish to be the eldest member of a Council of unruly children."

Kim Batto stroked his beard. "I think that is unfair, Marti," he murmured.

Oho, Arré thought. Does that mean the White Clan looks favorably upon the Ismeninas?

Cha echoed him. "That *is* unfair. What if any of us drops dead? What if you die, or Arré, here?"

Boras Sul coughed. "This is premature talk," he mumbled. "Even the witchfolk will not say when someone is about to die."

Marti Hok said, "Cha, that is very rude. Boras is quite right. If, may the chea spare me yet a few more years, *if* I should drop dead tomorrow, my eldest son Sironen is perfectly capable of taking my place on the Council, as he has in family business. If Arré dies, there is Isak. He is young, but he is an artist, and therefore civilized. The Ismeninas are not civilized." She beckoned to Sorren to refill her wine.

Cha Minto looked as if someone had just dropped a bucket of sand on his head. Arré grinned. Marti's tongue had grown no duller as she aged. Even Kim Batto had his hand to his mouth, half concealing a broad smile.

"I apologize," said Cha Minto. "I did not intend insult."

Kim dropped his hand. His voice was smooth. "I appreciate your arguments, Marti. I know Ron Ismenin somewhat. He is a reasonable man. The Jalaras are, of course, totally acceptable. I support Cha Minto in this matter, and am willing to attempt to deal with the Ismeninas."

"I'm not," said Boras Sul. Sorren filled his glass a final time, and he ran his hand in an avuncular manner over her bare arm.

She took a hasty step back, and nearly knocked over the table at Cha Minto's elbow.

Arré said, "Careful, child." She looked at Marti, remembering her own parents, unexpectedly dead in the plague that had gripped the city in Council Year 129. She had not wanted to be head of the household. But her mother had trained her well; she slipped into the vacancy with only a few mournful backward glances toward her lost freedom.

Marti said, "I agree that the Council should grow, as our

city has enlarged. I approve the nomination of the Jalar house
to membership. But until I see signs of sobriety from the
Ismenin brothers, I will oppose that house's presence in our
midst."

Azulith wrote furiously. Cha Minto said, "I think you are
mistaken." He was gripping the arms of his chair with such
force that the knuckles whitened.

Arré said, "Cha, is there another house you might propose
to make this an acceptable pairing?" There was one other house
of stature, the Isaras, who controlled the choba oil trade. Cha
shook his head. "Then I must say that I too find the Ismeninas—
unpredictable. I agree with Marti."

The screen rattled, as the wind blew against its panels. The
Councillors jumped at the sound, and Marti rubbed her hands
together.

"Sorren," said Arré, "close the window screen and lay a log
in the grate."

Sorren slid the screen across the window. The breeze died.
Moving the vase, she dragged the toothed grate into the center
of the fireplace. Carefully, she built a firebed out of tinder,
and twigs. She struck flint—the tinder flared, licking at the dry
logs' scaly underbellies.

Arré stretched. Her clothes felt harsh and sticky. Cha Minto
was looking at her, his mouth in a wry twist. Arré thought,
If my brother Isak is using you, I feel sorry for you, my friend.
"Cha," she said.

His lips closed tight, and he turned his head, refusing to
meet her eyes.

"Cha!"

He looked at her.

"Before you came here tonight, did you happen to mention
the intent of your discussion to anyone? To Meredith Jalar,
perhaps, or to Ron Ismenin?"

He said, "That would have been most improper."

Marti Hok said sharply, "I take it that answer means no."

"That is what it means," he agreed.

Pulling herself from her chair, Marti stumped to the fire.
"I get cold," she remarked. She leaned on her cane, and Arré
caught her breath. Marti looked feeble.

"Marti, are you well?" she said.

"Perfectly!" The old woman's eyes snapped. She glanced
at Sorren, who knelt on the tiles, tongs in hand. "I would not

be young again, I assure you, Arré. What's your name, girl?"

"Sorren, Lady."

Marti looked interested. "That's a northern name. Were you born in the north?"

"No, Lady," Sorren said. She held the tongs angled in her hand like a spear. The light gleamed on her hair and pale skin as if she wore armor, and Arré thought, she look barbaric, strange, like some warrior-woman drawn on an ancient pot. "I was born in the grapefields, I think."

"Your coloring's northern, too," said Marti. "Do you know the story of Sorren, the Lady of Tornor?"

"No," said the girl.

"It's a northern tale. I could tell it to you. It was Samia-no-Reo who first told it to me, when I was half your height. I did not grow much taller. Send her to me, Arré, and I will tell her the tale."

Arré felt a momentary twinge of jealousy. She did not want Marti Hok to be telling her bondservant stories. But then she shrugged. Marti had done her work on the Council for her. She deserved some thanks.

She turned her palms upward. The silver bracelets jingled on her wrists. "As long as you don't keep her from her work, Marti, you may tell her what you like."

CHAPTER FOUR

Pah-pah-pah-PAH.

Sorren hung the firetongs back on their hook. Arré and Marti talked above her. The knees of her pants grew hot with the flames; she barely felt it. Tornor. Where and what was Tornor? A trickle of sweat tickled the skin under her breasts, as the name rang like a note of music in her head.

She needed air, and space. Rising from the hearth, she sidled round the chairs to the doors. She slipped into the hall. Her cheeks were hot; she lifted her palms to them, to cool them. Through the crack in the doors she saw Boras Sul staring, and wondered if he was staring at her. She thought of several rude things she could never say to him.

Isak came from the room he had dressed in. His black hair was still pinned to his head with the red comb, but he carried his costumes—the Eagle's golden cloak, the Witch's rags, the Hunter's jeweled loincloth—carelessly over one arm, as if they were valueless. He stared at Sorren. "What's the matter with you?" he demanded.

Sorren dropped her hands. "I'm hot." She hesitated, thinking suddenly, He was schooled; he might have heard of Tornor. But he would want to know why it mattered to her and she did not trust herself not to say too much to him.

"Is that all?" He was no longer looking at her; he was gazing at the double doors as if he could see through wood. "Sorren."

"Yes, my lord."

"In three weeks, there will be a party at the Ismenin house. I shall dance. Can you be there to drum?"

"I think so. Will you be dancing something new?"

"Something old. The Courtship."

That was a betrothal dance. Sorren woundered which of the Ismenin sons was getting married, and to whom. "I shall have to ask permission."

"From my sister." He said the word "sister" as if it were coated with ash. He still looked at the doors. Sorren wondered what he thought was happening. She listened to the rise and fall of Arré's voice. Isak never questioned her about the meetings, although he knew she served at them. If he did, she would tell Arré, and probably he did not want Arré to know he cared enough to question servants.

He shifted the costumes from one arm to the other. "What are they doing in there?" he muttered.

"Being polite," said Sorren. He shot her an icy look.

The doors opened all the way, and Azulith came out, carrying her scroll and brush cases. She smiled at Sorren and turned to go to the kitchen.

"Scribe!" said Isak. His soft voice cracked like a whip.

Startled, Azulith spun back, nearly dropping her brush case. "My lord?" she said.

Isak said, still softly, "I think I am due somewhat more respect than that."

Sorren blinked in surprise. Azulith had bad knees, everyone knew that. But there was nothing she could say. Angry, she stood silently by as Azulith went down on one painful knee.

"Thank you," said Isak. "You may go." Azulith rose with a grimace. Eyes eloquent with contempt and fury, she marched toward the back of the house. Isak did not seem to care.

Cha Minto stepped through the doors.

Isak's expressive shoulders tensed. The youngest Councillor shook his head from side to side. Sorren thought, Paxe was right. Isak was up to something, and had been disappointed. A fold of her shirt was out of place; she put it back, and looked up to see Boras Sul regarding her as if she were something to eat. Hastily she went down the hall to the wardrobe where the cloaks were hung. Boras Sul's servant came from the kitchen, she heard the fat man fussing at him. She waited as long as she dared, pretending to be busy with the cloaks, until she heard them leave.

She walked back to the doors carrying Marti Hok's cloak. Arré and Marti were talking just inside the parlor. Sorren waited for them to finish. Toli, from the kitchen, was putting the empty flasks and soiled glasses on a tray. Kim Batto, the prissy one, had gone. Sorren stroked Marti's cloak. It was fur, a soft white fur, too hot, she thought, for summer. The old woman turned and saw her holding it.

She smiled. "Let me have it, child."

Sorren settled the cloak on Marti's shoulders. Marti's skin was light brown, almost yellow, and soft with a thousand wrinkles. Her hair was white, and she wore it coiled on the crown of her head in a thick braid. She was stout and small, like Elith, but Sorren thought she was older than Elith: she had sons and daughters and grandchildren and maybe great-grand-children.

The old woman looked up at her. "Child, you are too tall. Arré, how can you bear to have this young giant about you always?"

Arré said, "I like tall people, Marti."

"Yes. How old are you, child?"

"Seventeen, my lady," said Sorren.

"You will not forget that you have promised to come to my house."

"Of course she will not forget," said Arré. "Marti, it's nearly midnight, go away!"

Marti laughed. "I shall sit up half the night anyway, Arré. I sleep less and less each year. When I'm ninety I shall sit wakeful all night, like a featherless old owl in a tree, too weak to catch her own mice—and I shall be very, very wise."

Sorren grinned at this. Marti looked a little like an owl. She slid her hand in front of her face to hide her smile.

Arré said, "That may be. You are already too wise for your own good. But you're keeping me up, and I still sleep at night."

"Oh, very well, I shall leave you to your bed." Marti nodded at Sorren. "Call my litter, please."

Sorren went into the courtyard. Under the torchlight she saw the cloth-covered hump of a litter. The four bearers were sitting beside it. She saw a light pass from hand to shadowy hand, and the scent of heavenweed drifted to her on the night wind.

She crossed the courtyard. As she reached the bearers, she saw that the door guard had joined them. He was one of the oldest guards. His name was Borti. Paxe grumbled about his age and slowness but somehow she never got around to telling him to turn in his badges. Sorren liked him; when she had first come to the city he had taken her all around the house on his back. He called her "Beanstalk" and she did not mind it. "She's ready," she said to the bearers. They snuffed their smoke and uncoiled. One of them twitched the cloth from the litter and rolled it into a ball.

Sorren returned to the house to tell Marti Hok that her litter was ready. At that moment, Azulith came down the hall. There was grease about her plump mouth, and she carried, in addition to her scroll and brush cases, a small pouch. The smell of fish cake emanated from it. "Good night, Sorren," she called over her shoulder.

"Good night," said Sorren.

"Good night, Sorren," said a familiar, mocking voice.

Sorren whirled. Isak stood in the doorway, with Cha Minto at his back.

She was still annoyed at him. "My lord," she said. "I thought you'd gone."

"Not quite," he said. Behind him, Cha Minto was pale, and she wondered if that pallor was Isak's fault. "Come to my house in ten days. We need to practice the Courtship."

Ten days was just past the Asech Festival of the Ox. "I will if I can, my lord," she said.

He said, "Be sure you do." Before she could respond—and what could she say?—the two men strolled together into the darkness. Marti Hok came to the front door, leaning heavily on her cane. Sorren pressed against the house wall to let her pass. The bearers assisted her into the litter and trotted off, the brass bells around their ankles sounding into the distance.

Arré came to the door. She sighed; she looked tired. "Close the door," she ordered. "I want to go to bed."

Together, they went upstairs. Sorren trimmed and lit the bedroom lamp, while Arré undressed. (She did not like to be helped with that. When Sorren tried, she snapped, "I'm not decrepit!") Sorren poured a bowlful of water from the pitcher on the stand. It was scented with rose petals stripped from the garden. She brought the bowl to Arré, with a cloth. Arré wiped her face. She took off her bracelets, and Sorren laid them in their box. The box was wooden, carved with the triangle badge of the Med house. Arré had once told her it belonged to Arré's mother. It smelled musty. The little compartments were lined with amber velvet.

Arré sat on the bed, naked. "Did Boras bother you tonight?" she said suddenly.

Sorren went to the chest in which the quilts were kept. "A little."

"I'll tell him to stop," said Arré. "He grows more mannerless the older he gets, and he never had many to start with. What did you think of the Council?"

Sorren said, "I mostly don't listen. I thought Isak's dance was perfect."

Arré scowled. "Did he speak to you when he was dressing,

or after the dance?" She scratched her thigh, where an insect bite had raised a welt.

"Yes. He asked me to drum for him at a betrothal party at the Ismeninas."

Arré lifted an eyebrow. "Oh? Did he say whose?"

"No."

"When is it?"

"In three weeks."

"Rrmph." Arré made a grumpy noise. Sorren folded the quilt around her. Arré put an arm across her face. "Leave the light."

Sorren tugged the quilt even at the corners. When she looked up, Arré was leaning on both elbows, watching her. "What is it?" said the older woman.

The word filled her mouth; she almost could not say it. She took a deep breath. "What's T-T-Tornor?"

"Why are you stammering?" said Arré. "It's a Keep on the northern border."

"What's a Keep?"

"A castle."

"Does it have a tower?"

Arré lay flat. "I've never been there, how would I know? Leave me now, child, I want to sleep."

Sorren picked up the bowl of dirtied water from the stand. "Good night. Sleep well."

Outside Arré's door, she listened. The noise of shuffling feet and wheezing breath warned her that Elith was wakeful. The old woman rose early and slept late, and she often wandered about the darkened house. Softly, Sorren went downstairs. From the noises she guessed that Elith was in the long parlor, and she whisked herself past the double doors before the old woman could see her. The kitchen was quiet. She dumped the dirty water out the nearest window. It would help the herb garden.

In her room, the window screen was open partway. The garden scent filled her nostrils. Through the gap she saw the waxing moon, white and brilliant, riding its river of stars.

Tor-nor. Sorren drummed the syllables lightly on the wall. *Tor-nor Keep. Pah-pah-dum.* In her experience, north meant the vineyards. But she knew that the river traveled through the vineyards and kept on going to the sea, and since it did not start in the vineyards then it must have come from somewhere else, and rivers, she had heard, started in the mountains.

There were mountains in the west; Paxe had been to them, though she almost never spoke of it. But there were also mountains in the north, and she thought these northern mountains were the mountains she saw. She ran her fingers through her hair. What if the castle with the tower, the substance of her vision, was indeed a Keep? She sat on the bed, fingers tapping. Perhaps her mother had named her "Sorren" for a reason, to say, "You are different. You come from elsewhere." *Sor-ren of Tor-nor. Pah-pah-a-dum-pah.* In the fields picking grapes, she had dreamed of being something else, not a grapepicker, something wonderful, a princess, and she had gone with Arré happily, without a backward look, because secretly she believed that Arré would make her a princess. It seemed very silly now. But all children had such dreams.

It still might be true. She wanted it to be so. Even if she was not a princess, she wanted it to be so. She wondered what Paxe would say when told. If she went to the cottage now, right now—but Paxe might be asleep, and Ricard might be there. Sorren frowned out the window at the moon. She did not want to have to talk to Ricard.

There was a snarl, thick as glue, in one lock of her hair. She picked at it, trying to work it loose with her fingers. When it finally came free, she rummaged in the chest for the horn-backed brush that Arré had given her, and brushed her hair until it crackled.

As she laid the brush down, vision came upon her. Pictures rose behind her eyelids. *The room went away; she saw the castle, and the tower. The buildings changed: shrank, or enlarged, as her ranging mind brought her farther from or closer to them. The stars made a bridge across the world. Torches flared on the battlements; the air was clean and dry and chilly. She hovered suddenly at the open window of the tower. A man—or boy, for he looked young—sat within the many-sided chamber. He held a pen in one hand. The other was not there— at all, Sorren realized. His right arm was gone, cut off at the shoulder. His embroidered sleeve hung empty.*

The small face blurred. The vision faded. Sorren shivered. Cold bumps marched across her arms. Rising, she shut the open screen, and went downstairs to the kitchen. The moonlight silvered the pots, making them look like treasure. She went through the rear courtyard to Paxe's cottage. The door was unlocked; she pushed it open with a cautious hand. Ricard was not there. The cat, from its place on a cushion, lifted its narrow head to gaze at her.

Naked, she climbed into Paxe's bed. Strong arms reached to hold her. "Chelito," murmured Paxe sleepily.

Sorren put her cheek against Paxe's breast. The shared bed was warm and safe and pleasant as a cave. Content, she pressed herself against Paxe's smooth skin.

They woke early, while the stars were still vivid in the sky, and made love. In the dim room, Sorren's hair crackled around her head like sparks from a bonfire. She described her vision, and then told Paxe what Marti Hok had said. "What do you think of that?"

The cat came in and rolled on its back, demanding to be stroked. Paxe rubbed its soft white belly fur with her toe. "It's interesting," she said.

Sorren was disappointed. But there was a look in Paxe's face she had never seen before. The dawnlight, faint as a baby's breath, gleamed through the screens, giving the austere room the look of winter.

"Why are you looking at me like that?" she said.

Paxe said, "Because I love you."

Sorren grinned. Lifting Paxe's hand, she put her tongue into the warm hollow of her lover's fist. "Someday I should like to crawl into bed with you and stay there the whole day."

Paxe laughed. "You'd wear me out," she said, drawing her hand across Sorren's cheek.

The cat followed them down the stairs. Just inside the door, Paxe stooped to put on her sandals. She was wearing Yard clothes, coarse blue pants and a baggy white shirt. "Was Ricard here when you came in last night?" she asked.

"Nope," said Sorren.

They kissed at the Yard gate. Sorren saw Kaleb out of the corner of her eye, standing in the Yard. He was waiting for them to say farewell so that he could make his report. He had been waiting since sunrise; Sorren hoped the night had gone smoothly. If there had been any trouble, Paxe would be angry at herself for having made him wait.

She dawdled in the garden, savoring the morning air. When she got to the house, Lalith waved to her from the kitchen. The brown girl was wearing her hair in her favorite style, with lots of little braids. They looked like spikes. She glanced toward the hour-candle. "She's asked for you twice already."

"Damn." Sorren hurried. "Why didn't you come and get me?" she said over her shoulder to Lalith, who laughed. On her way up the stairs, Sorren grinned. If Lalith had come to the bedroom to tell Sorren that Arré wanted her, Paxe would probably have thrown the lamp at her head.

Arré was sitting on her rosewood stool. "Where have you been?" she snapped. She was wearing all her bracelets; they jangled as she moved. "When I need you, I want you here, not gallivanting around the city."

Sorren said, "I was at Paxe's cottage."

Arré glared at her. But after a moment her face softened. "Oh. Well. You're here now. Sit down, I hate it when you loom." Sorren sat cross-legged on the soft wool rug. "Your hair is tangled."

Sorren blushed.

Arré frowned. She reached beside her, to the small table on which stood the lamp, her jewel box, and a small brown stone statue which Sorren thought was a dog but which Arré said was a seal. She stroked the seal's back. "Last night, you told me Isak asked you to drum at the betrothal of one of the Ismeninas."

"Yes."

"You're going shopping today." This was not a question. Sorren went shopping every morning. "I want you to find out which one of the Ismenin boys is getting married, and to whom."

"I can do that," Sorren said. She rather liked it when Arré asked her to find out things.

"Be discreet," said Arré sharply. She held out a money bracelet. "Here."

Sorren took it and turned to leave.

"See if you can find some sweet berries," Arré called after her. "Cook says we've almost used them up."

As Soren went downstairs, she wondered why Arré asked *her* to find out about the Ismenin betrothal. Surely she had been invited. Maybe she simply wanted to know what they were saying in the market.

Lalith was waiting for her in the kitchen. "Well?" Sorren said.

The girl rolled her eyes. "Lamb and fish," she chanted,

"anise, cinnamon, and salt, carrots and onions, yellow apples, if there are any."

Choba oil, Sorren thought, and sweet berries. "Thank you," she said. Some people in the market carried written lists. But Sorren could not write or read, so it all went into her head.

She walked down the hill reciting it to herself. It was cold in the valley by the river. The fog was in; it blanketed the river and the ocean, and dripped from the horses' flanks and from the canvas market stalls. Some days it was so thick that it rolled over the whole city, even the hill, making old Elith's bones ache so that all she would do was sit around groaning with her feet in hot water, and *that* made Toli angry because it meant he had to feed the furnace twice a day.

Sorren didn't mind it; she walked through the damp mist smiling. She had six errands to run, not counting finding out about the Ismenin betrothal. She went first to the butcher's, liking it least. The stall was crowded, and she had to shout her order over the heads of smaller folk. She went next to the fishmonger's.

Thule hastened to her, rubbing his red chapped hands. "Did she like the fish?" he asked.

"She loved the fish."

He swelled with pride, as if he had caught them all himself. "Good, good. What can we do for the Med house this morning? More flounder? Hake? Sea bass?"

"Is Mirrim here?" asked Sorren. Mirrim was Thule's daughter, a thin, quiet woman who knew everything that happened or was about to happen in the city.

"Not today," said Thule. "Halibut?"

"Let me look," said Sorren. She could not tell one fish from another but she liked to look at them. Thule led her to the tubs, talking very fast, pointing out the fattest fish for her appraisal. The cart from the ice houses stood near the tubs, and the fish bounced and jumped as if they were still alive, though ice crystals clung to them. "Let's have some bass," Sorren said. Math, Thule's middle son, climbed into the tub of sea bass, and with a big net ladled the beautiful brown and gold fish into a basket, to be delivered later to the Med cook.

The vegetable stalls were busy, and the spice shop was jammed with people ordering salt. Sorren recited her list to the clerks, and left. She stopped at the oilseller's in the Isara district to leave the weekly order for choba oil. The woman there was

friendly and garrulous: she gossiped about the people whose
stall abutted hers, about the Council, and about her own relatives. She told a funny, scurrilous story about three witches.

"Are Arré Med and her brother still fighting?" she asked.

"They don't fight," said Sorren. "They just don't like each
other." The oilseller frowned, wanting something new.

She had not said anything about an Ismenin betrothal. Sorren
frowned as she walked from the shop.

She went toward the Asech corner of the market. At one
stall, an Asech woman was dancing with a snake, making it
twine and slither around her naked breasts. She was graceful
and demure as she coaxed the snake over her nipples. Two
people sat at her feet; one playing a flute, the other that peculiar
Asech instrument, the *sho*.

The fluteplayer caught Sorren's eye, and winked. She
leaned against the wall, waiting for him to finish. His name
was Simbaha, called Simmy, and the woman with the snake
was his sister. Sorren had drummed for them once, at Harvest
Festival.

When the performance ended, the spectators clapped. The
snake hissed at the noise. Simmy came through the crowd with
a basket. "Hey, Sorren."

"Isn't it cold for naked dancing?" Sorren said.

"I wouldn't know, I don't do it. Tani doesn't mind." A
woman tossed a bronze coin at the basket, and he swung it
deftly. "Thank you, lady, may the Guardian smile upon you."
He moved the basket in a seductive circle. His flute, which
he carried in a sling over his shoulder, was painted with flowers. "You going to play for Isak Med at the Festival this year?"

Sorren said, "I think so. Seen Jeshim lately?"

"That *chaba'ck*." The word meant something horrible in the
Asech tongue. "He's got a pitch in the Jalar district. Hey, I
heard you were spoken for! Why're you looking for Jeshim?"

"I *am* spoken for," Sorren said. "I just want to talk to him."

"Too bad," said Simmy. "I like tall women."

Sorren waved good-bye to Tani, who was trying to tease
the snake back into its pot. She walked south, toward the
ocean. This was Jalar territory. Yellow streamers, token of the
Jalar house, waved on poles; yellow-clad guards were everywhere. They looked tense, and Sorren wondered why. Carts
clattered over the boardwalks. The yellow sails of the fishing
fleet gleamed through the mist. Rings of seawrack on the pil-

ings showed the high-tide mark. The water was low, but not as low as it could get. On the ebb tide when the moon was full, it seemed as if the whole ocean pulled away from the land, leaving the entire delta steaming and stinking, naked to a merciless sun.

Sorren walked up to a guard. "I'm looking for Jeshim the juggler."

"Near the slipway," said the guard.

"Where's the slipway?"

"That way."

"That way" proved to be a maze of alleys. Finally Sorren circled around what seemed to be half a hundred warehouses, and came out facing the sea. Gulls swarmed overhead. In front of her there was a great scooped space in the mud, and, within the space, the ribs and planking of a ship. Men and women climbed over it, calling and making noises with their hammers. Smells smoked from it, the smells of tar and timber and heated metal. It was exciting. Sorren drew a deep breath.

She found Jeshim on the walkway. "Sorren!" He beamed. He was part Asech, and wore blue stones in his ears. "What a surprise. What brings you all the way from the hill?"

Sorren grinned. "I came to see you, of course."

The juggler sighed. "Ah, if only I could believe that." He snaked his hand up her arm. "You know how I feel about you. But Yardmaster Paxe—" he coughed—"would chop me into bits and feed me to the clams if I touched you."

"You're right, she would," Sorren said. She moved, and his hand dropped.

Jeshim shrugged. "Want some heavenweed?" He bent to his pack. From it he pulled a pipe with a bowl as big as her fist. He filled it, and brought out flints. His hands were scarred, as if from a hundred tiny bites, and she remembered that he threw knives, too.

Two guards at the tip of the boardwalk sniffed appreciatively as the heavensmoke blew toward them. "Can you smoke and juggle?" Sorren asked.

"Certainly," said Jeshim. "I'm a much better juggler after I smoke than before." He sucked at the pipe. "Ah." He passed it to her, and she took a little bit. The heady drug made her ears buzz.

A step sounded on the boardwalk. "Smoking again, juggler?" said a hoarse voice. "Get out of my way." A man in a gray cloak had come down the boardwalk and stood now facing Jeshim.

Jeshim laughed. "Drunk again, gimpy?" He brushed a speck from his sleeve. "What if I don't want to move?"

The man showed his teeth. "Showing off for your friend, aren't you. Move, or I'll move you."

"Not in front of the guards, you won't," said Jeshim. But he stepped aside, just enough so that the man could go past him toward the boardwalk's tip. As he moved, his foot went out. The man tripped, swore, and recovered.

"Sorry," Jeshim said. "An accident." The man in gray went on, and the juggler laughed.

"Who's that?" said Sorren.

"That's the gimp."

The man in gray stopped just before the end of the walkway, and sat.

"What does he do?"

"He drinks. And he sits. He comes here every day. He likes watching them build the ship." He sucked on the pipe again. "Forget him. I haven't seen you in a while, Sorren, what have you been doing?"

Sorren chose her words carefully. If she wanted information from Jeshim, she knew, she would first have to put him in her debt.

"The same old stuff," she said. "Drumming now and then. Last night I drummed for Isak Med at the Council meeting. In a few weeks, I'm drumming at the Ismenin betrothal feast."

"Nice," said Jeshim approvingly. "You'll eat well."

"I eat well now," she said. "I heard that you were juggling there."

"At the Ismenin betrothal?" Jeshim's teeth shone yellow through his red-brown beard. "I wish it were true. Who told you?"

She had made it up. "I don't remember. Isn't it so?"

"Naw." He held the pipe out to her, and she waved it away. He put it in his own mouth and sucked deeply. His chest swelled.

She said, "Maybe I can make it true. I can mention your name to Isak. That might help."

"If you would, I'd be very grateful. It might fill my flattened purse."

"Aren't you working Harvest Festival?"

"Of course," said the juggler. "The scribe of the Blue Clan came to see me herself, to ask me to juggle in the Blue Clan tent. But that's five weeks from now."

Sorren counted on her fingers. "So it is." She let her gaze wander. "Which of the Ismenin sons is getting married? I forget."

"Col," said Jeshim. "He's the oldest, next to Ron."

"Who's he marrying?"

"Some Blue Clan bitch."

His eyes were half-closed against the smoke from the pipe. He knew she was pumping him: he had to. Sorren untied the knot of the bracelet and slipped a wishbone off her wrist. She dropped it in Jeshim's pack. His eyes opened. "Her name is Nathis Ryth."

She didn't know who Nathis Ryth was, but Arré would. "Are you making any money down here?" she said.

Jeshim smiled. He glanced at the pack at his feet. "It's no better or worse than any other corner of the city." His voice had thickened and deepened; the heavenweed was starting to affect him. "Doesn't Isak Med know who is marrying who, up on the hill?"

The Ismeninas did not live on the hill, reflected Sorren. But she knew what the juggler meant. She said, "I don't ask Isak questions; he doesn't like it." That was a lie—Isak loved to be asked things—but it sounded good.

Jeshim nodded, and slid his arm around her shoulders. "Be friendly, Sorren," he said.

She peeled the fingers from her arm. "Jeshim, put your pipe away." He peered at her resentfully as she rose and strolled toward the end of the boardwalk.

The ocean seethed, writhing through the fog like a great supple snake. She listened to the crash of the waves.

"Beautiful, isn't it," said a voice. It was the man in gray.

"I guess," said Sorren doubtfully. She found it frightening. "Are you a fisherman?"

The man laughed. "Do I look like a fisherman?"

Sorren looked at him. He was dark, and his face was odd, with broad cheekbones and forehead and a tight, narrow chin, as if he had been put together from pieces that did not match, like a child's wooden doll.

He was also very drunk; his brown eyes were not quite focused, and his breath was strong with wine. "No," said Sorren. "You don't."

He wavered in place. "I know who you are," he said. "Arré Med's bondservant. The northern girl."

"My name's Sorren."

"Kadra. Kadra-no-Ilézia."

Sorren blinked. It was a woman's name.

She took a closer look at Kadra, noting the curve of hips, and another curve under the gray cloak that might be breasts. "Sorry," she said.

"It happens," said Kadra enigmatically. "Ah, I'm drunk. You know him?" She jerked a thumb at the juggler.

"Yes, We're friends."

"Friends." Kadra said the word as if she did not know what it meant. Yanking a silver flask from a pocket, she tipped it to her lips. A rivulet ran down her chin, and she wiped it away with the flat of one hand. "This isn't the Med hill. What are you doing here?"

Sorren bristled. "That's none of your concern."

Kadra gazed at her. "Maybe not. How kind of you to point it out."

Sorren flushed. "I didn't mean to be rude."

"How old are you?"

Sorren hated telling people how old she was. "Seventeen."

"A baby."

Sorren set her teeth to keep from answering. Kadra watched her, and then nodded, as if pleased. She lifted her flask toward her lips.

"Empty. Damn." She shook it.

Sorren said, "Do you work on the docks?"

Kadra laughed, not mirthfully. "No." She touched her cloak; it fell to one side, revealing a glint of metal beneath it. "I was a messenger."

Sorren looked hard at the cloak. Behind layers of grime, a hint of green gleamed through. The metal might have been a buckle or a button, but Sorren did not think it was.

Only messengers had the right to wear green out of doors. The color gave them passage through the streets before anyone else, even the rich in their litters. The folk of the Green Clan kept to themselves, but Sorren had met some of them on the hill. It was they who carried the Council's edicts or suggestions to the Councils of other cities, to the Asech tribes, and to Anhard.

"Were you sick?" she asked.

"I fell," said Kadra, "and broke my hip. I can't ride."

"Were you a messenger a long time?"

"Ten years," Kadra said. "Why?"

Sorren realized that she had been rude again. "I was just curious," she said.

"Asking questions can get you into trouble."

"I was trying to be friendly—" but she was speaking to Kadra's back. The woman had brushed past her and was walking along the boardwalk toward the street. She limped on her left side. The idea that had been in the back of Sorren's mind came wiggling to the front. A messenger, she thought, would know about the north.

As Kadra passed Jeshim, he heaved himself to his feet. He ambled to Sorren and started to put his arms around her. She elbowed him, not hard.

"Oof!" He rubbed his ribs theatrically.

"Don't do that." She watched Kadra limp between two buildings, and vanish. A messenger could tell her what roads to take north, and when it would be best to travel.

"Smoke some heavenweed with me."

"I can't, Jeshim. I have to go back to the house."

The juggler shrugged. Pulling three red balls from some pocket, he set them spinning in air. They seemed barely to touch his hands. "You had a lot to say to the gimp. Friend of *yours?*"

"No," said Sorren. "We just met. But why do you call her 'he'? She's a woman."

Jeshim grinned, behind the spinning balls. "Did the gimp say that?"

"Not exactly. She said—" She tried to remember Kadra's words.

"That's exactly right," said Jeshim. "Because Kadra isn't exactly a woman, nor exactly a man, either. He's both, or neither, if you like that. He's a *ghya.* He's got both male parts and female parts." He sounded pleased about it, or maybe it was just relief that he was whole.

"How do you know?" Sorren said.

"Everyone knows it. It's no secret." He made the red balls disappear, and then pretended to pluck one out of his hair and another out of his mouth. "Hold still, there it is!" he said, reaching toward her.

"Don't!" She struck at his hand. The ball, jarred loose, fell to the planks of the boardwalk. Jeshim made a grab for it, but it rolled over the edge and landed on the mud.

"Damn! Now I have to get it." He stared at her soulfully. "Come with me. You made it fall."

"It's your fault," Sorren said. "You shouldn't grab me. I told you not to."

He sighed. "Sorren, you are unkind."

Grinning at him, she reached into his pack and drew out the bone she had given him. "Am I?"

He snatched it from her. "No, no, you are a most generous and loving girl. Come back and visit me again."

"I will," she said. "I'm sorry about the ball, Jeshim."

"Oh, it's nothing." He blew her a kiss, and she pretended to take it from the air and drop it down her shirt. Before he could come and put his arms around her again, she waved and walked back along the boardwalk to the warehouses. It grew hotter as she left the water's edge. By the time she reached the streets, her clothes were sticking to her. She smelled wine, and hesitated for a moment, fingering the bontas on her string, knowing that Arré would not be looking for her yet. To her right there was a tavern with a swinging sign painted with a picture of a silver fish. But she did not truly like wine. She would stop at one of the public wells for water before climbing the hill. She turned from the tavern and went on, knowing as she did that it was not thirst that had drawn her toward the tavern's door, but the thought that Kadra the ghya might be there.

CHAPTER FIVE

It took Sorren a longer time to get back to the Med house than she expected it to.

On the border between the Med and Minto districts, a crowd was gathered. At first she thought it was an accident, the way people were bunched together. "Stay back," droned the guards.

"Is someone hurt?" she asked a woman next to her.

The woman turned huge brown eyes on her. "Oh, no," she said, somewhat breathless from being squeezed on all four sides. "It's a Healing."

The guards were trying to keep a lane clear, but between that and ordering the people back from the Healer's canopy, they were very busy. Over the heads of the folk around her, Sorren could just see the tent. The sick were lining up around her, waving and calling in febrile voices to get the attention of the acolytes who stalked around the perimeter of the crowd. It took two witches to Heal, Sorren knew: one, a Truthfinder, to question, and the Healer to effect the change. Some people they could not help; the very old, the very young, the crippled or blind or deaf. Some people they would not help: people who were already getting well, for instance, and who wanted the prestige and excitement of having gone to a Healer. Once Elith had gone to a Healer's tent, complaining of shortness of breath. The Healer told her not to eat so much and sent her away.

At last, she wormed through the press to a clear space. Stretching her long legs, she hastened home. Borti was talking to the gate guard under the shade of the kava fruit tree. "What happened to you?" he said, looking her up and down.

Sorren smoothed her clothing. "I got caught in a Healing."

Arré was in the garden. She liked flowers. She knew nothing about growing them, but when she walked through the garden, she would reach out to touch the blossoms with an odd, endearing tenderness. "Did you get sweet berries?" she said, as Sorren approached.

Sorren sighed. She had meant to. "I forgot." She took the bracelet from her arm. "But I did get the information you wanted."

"Go on."

"Col Ismenin is betrothed to Nathis Ryth, of the Blue Clan."

"Ryth," repeated Arré. Her voice sharpened. "Are you sure?"

There was no reason for Jeshim to lie to her. "That's what I was told."

Arré stared at the wall of the house, with the light frown on her face that meant that she was thinking. Sorren said, "What does it mean?"

Arré said, "It's interesting."

"Why?"

Arré flicked a bee away from her hair. "You know the custom," she said. "Folk may marry or not, but if a man and woman do not marry, the children are only hers, not his. He has no claim on them." Sorren nodded to show she understood. Her mother had not married; she did not even know her father's name. It didn't matter. "If they do marry, the children belong to both, but they still bear the mother's name. If—let us pretend—I had married Boras Sul, he would have come to live here. His brother, Emrith, would be head of the Sul house. But our children would carry the Med name."

Sorren tried to imagine Arré marrying Boras Sul and having children by him. She failed. "I'm glad you didn't."

Arré sniffled. "There was never any question of it. However—the Ismeninas have always had a problem following custom. To be wealthy, it follows, a house must be rich in daughters. The Ismenin sons almost always breed males. If their sons marry into other high families, the children take the mother's name, not the father's. Now, custom can be circumvented in two ways. The first is by adopting female cousins, when they have them, into the main branch of the Ismeninas, and marrying their sons to them. The second is by making alliance with the Blue Clan. Ron Ismenin married a daughter of the Blue Clan house Holleth, and Karya Holleth agreed to give up her right to name her children with her family name."

"I understand," said Sorren. She liked it when Arré thought aloud to her. "This is the same thing, isn't it?"

"I expect so," said Arré. She tilted her head to one side.

"What does the Ryth house trade in?" asked Sorren.

Arré frowned. "Grain."

Sorren worked it out until she was sure she understood. Then she said, "Why are there no daughters born to the Ismeninas?"

Arré spread her hands. "The will of the chea, I suppose." Her face glimmered with the sardonic look she always wore when speaking of the chea.

"There was a Healing happening on Apple Street when I passed there," Sorren said.

But Arré was not interested in the Healing. "I wonder whose idea this was," she said.

"The marriage?"

"Oh, that is clearly advantageous to both sides. The Ryth house gets a ruling-house connection and the Ismeninas strengthen their ties with the Blue Clan." She frowned. "Their ties with the Blue Clan may even be a little stronger than I like. No, I meant my ignorance of the betrothal. I think I do know."

Sorren guessed what she meant from the look on her face. "Isak."

"It's likely. He is friends with Ron Ismenin. Indeed, he makes friends wherever he goes, my charming brother. At the Council meeting, I noticed that he and Cha were like this." She crossed two fingers.

Sorren wriggled her toes in the cool grass. She remembered Cha Minto's face at Isak's shoulder. He had looked frightened, not charmed. She touched the bell of a lily; pollen came off on her fingers. "Isak's married," she said.

"Yes," said Arré, "so?"

"He lives in the Med house. His children bear the Med name."

Arré smiled. "That's easy to explain, child. Myra-no-Ivrénia is the daughter of Ivrénia Ishem of the Blue Clan. Isak married a merchant's daughter. The Ismeninas are not the only house in the city to bend custom."

That night, Sorren dreamed again about the castle. It was a quick dream. She saw the tower and then the castle wall. There was someone standing on it. She wanted to see who. She woke abruptly when she tried, within the dream, to make herself move closer to the wall.

The dream made her think of Kadra. In the morning, she went to the cottage at sunrise, hoping Paxe would be there, but the Yardmaster was gone. Only the one-eyed cat purred around her ankles. There was no sign of Ricard.

She returned to the kitchen. As she made ready to go shopping, reciting the list of what she needed in her head, she asked the cook, "Have you ever met a ghya?"

He blew at her through his beard. "Ha. Someone's been telling you tales. There's no such thing, girl. Where'd you hear it?"

She shrugged. "Never mind." She went from the kitchen before he could question her further.

The fog was in; vendors strolled the streets with bells on their carts. At the fruit stall, Sorren remembered to order a sack of sweet berries, and paid for them, and ordered that they be delivered at once. That would please Arré. Then she went looking for the slipway.

She got lost on the docks. The blank walls of the warehouses confused her. Finally, after wandering through narrow, muddy alleys that all looked alike, she saw a man writing in large letters on the wall, and went up to him. "I'm looking for the Jalar slipway."

He pointed down the street. His brown hands were white with chalk dust. "Follow that path and take the second right, you'll come to it."

"Thanks." She looked at the wall. "What does that say?"

"Niké the Steersman fucks goats," he said happily. "This is the fourth place I've put it." He grinned and flourished the chalk.

Sorren followed his directions, wondering who Niké the Steersman was. When she came to the slipway she hesitated before stepping into the open. Jalar guards, lounging at the tip of the boardwalk, were wearing cloaks over their yellow shirts. The noises from the ship seemed more raucous than they had the day before.

Kadra sat like a lump of coal on the walkway, wrapped in her dark, dirty cloak. Jeshim wasn't there. Sorren wondered where he was. She went to Kadra. She had mud in her dark cropped hair, and Sorren thought, She must sleep on the beach. Her clothing smelled of seawater and wine.

The ghya looked up. "You again. Your friend's not here."

Sorren sat without being asked. The boardwalk planks were warm. She swung her legs over the side. "I came to talk to you, not Jeshim."

"To me." Kadra scowled. "Did Norres send you?"

"No one sent me. I'm shopping—I mean, this is the time of day when I go shopping for the house. Nobody knows I'm here."

Kadra yawned. She rubbed the flat of one hand over her

face. "What do you mean, you want to talk to me."

Sorren swallowed. "You were a messenger."

"Yes."

"Have you ever been north, to the Keeps?"

Kadra drew her knees up and laid her head down on them. "Many times."

Sorren let out a breath. She had been holding it. She'd been afraid—it was silly—that the Keeps no longer existed, that they were all empty, ruined, vanished, and that her dreams were of nothing, an illusion, the past. "Will you tell me about them?" she said. "How to get there, who lives there, what they look like—things like that?"

"You don't want me," said Kadra. "You want a Scholar."

"No," Sorren said. "Scholars know history. I want to know—real things," she finished lamely.

"Why?" said the ghya.

Sorren had known she would ask. "Must I tell you?" she said.

"Yes," said Kadra.

Sorren rubbled her palm across the flat, splintery planking. "They call me the northern girl," she said. "My mother used to tell me stories—I want to go there, after I'm free."

A ripple of feeling, too swift to name, passed across Kadra's face. "When's that?" she said.

"In a year," said Sorren. It felt like forever.

A tern with a black head landed on a piling. It picked its feet up, inspecting them, one after the other. Ruffling its feathers, it began to pick at its toes with its beak.

Kadra said. "I'll talk to you." She rose. "Not here. If that pimp Jeshim comes back, he'll be offended if you don't talk to him."

"I don't want to talk to Jeshim," Sorren agreed. "Where can we go?"

"Somewhere," said the ghya, "where I can drink. You'll have to buy the wine."

They went to The Silver Fish. The tavern was dark and largely empty, and it smelled of the oil the street vendors fried their oysters in. They sat at a table in the back, near the kitchen entrance. The surface of the table was covered with nicks and scars. A woman in a leather apron brought Kadra wine in an amber-colored bottle. She raised her eyebrows at Sorren. "What'll you have?"

"I don't want anything," Sorren said, working the smallest bonta from her string. She handed it to the woman, who shrugged and went back into the kitchen. Kadra put the bottle to her lips like a greedy baby. Sorren watched her swallow, frowning. "If you get too drunk," she said, "you won't be able to talk."

Kadra set the bottle down. "That's my choice," she said flatly. "You want me to do you a favor, you keep a sweet tongue in your head."

"Sorry," Sorren said.

The ghya wiped her mouth. "You have any notion what a Keep is?"

"A castle."

"Yes." Kadra's voice softened. "There are four of them—Pel Keep, Cloud Keep, Tornor Keep, and Zilia Keep. They were built hundreds of years ago, when Arun was at war with Anhard-over-Mountain. They sit on the steppe, with the mountains at their backs. . . . I don't know which you want to go to."

The sudden evocation of her vision made the hairs at the back of Sorren's neck tingle. "I don't know either," she said. "What—" she hesitated, and then went on—"what do they look like?"

"They're stone," said Kadra. "The stone's dark now, though on Pel Keep's walls there are patches of white. They used to cover the stones with limewash to protect them. South of the castles the land is flat, and bare except for the pine trees and the huts of the villagers. They say life hasn't changed there in a hundred years. More. Behind the castles the mountains stand like—like a barrier, as if the land ended there, and beyond it was nothing, a void." She laughed. "It isn't, though."

"Yes," said Sorren. "Yes."

Kadra looked at her oddly. "Have you been there, then?"

"No," Sorren said. "Yes. In a dream." Her cheeks felt flushed. "Does one of them have a tower?"

"A tower? I think one did, but it fell. I don't remember which."

"Are there wolves in the mountains?"

Kadra laughed. "I never met one." Then her face grew serious. "But I've heard from travelers coming out of the north of strange sounds on the steppe. Perhaps there are wolves again."

"Are there eagles?" Sorren asked. "And archers?"

"Of course there are eagles, and people hunting them with bows and arrows. Why?"

Because of the Cards, Sorren thought. But she was not going to tell Kadra about the Cards. "No reason."

Kadra's eyes narrowed, and her hand curled around the bottle again. "Why aren't you drinking?"

"I don't want any, thank you."

"Manners." The word was almost a sneer. "Manners and questions. Who taught you such fine manners?"

"Arré Med," said Sorren.

"Huh," said Kadra. She drank. "You know what they call her, and those like her, down here on the docks."

Sorren did know. "A swank."

"What's she like?"

Sorren frowned. How could she say what Arré was like? "She's been very kind to me," she said.

The door opened, and two Jalar guards entered. They sat at a table in the front. With casual arrogance, they stared across the room. Sorren thought they looked overlong at her. There were no other bondservants that she could see in the tavern.

Her arms prickled, and she rubbed them. "I don't like it here," she said.

"I hate it," said Kadra. She drank again. "I hate cities. Soft places. Too many people and not enough room. Cramped little houses, cramped streets, cramped minds." Her voice got loud.

The guards looked at them, with that suspicious look guards got. "That wasn't what I meant," said Sorren. She tapped the table. "I don't like this place. Can we leave?" As she said it, she remembered that Kadra had been injured. Perhaps it hurt her to walk. But the ghya was already standing. Sorren followed her out. The woman in the leather apron watched them leave, framed like a statue in the open kitchen doorway.

Kadra angled toward the slipway. "Come with me," she said. "Come look at the ship." Sorren had little interest in the ship, but she went. They clambered down into the pit. The mud was cool, damp, and squishy.

As they reached it. Kadra began to cough, great hacking coughs that sounded as if they might split her chest. "Do you want to rest?" said Sorren. The ghya ignored her. Bales of wool lay scattered on the mud nearby. "What's the wool for?" Sorren said.

"Caulking," said Kadra. "They dip the wool in molten wax

and stuff lengths of it into the cracks between the planks."

The ship was much bigger than the fishing vessels; even Sorren, who knew nothing about boats, could see that. She stared at the great skeleton. "What's it for—the ship?"

"It's going south," said Kadra. She waved one arm at the sea. "Away from land, away from cities, to find new countries." She shaded her eyes. Shrouds of mist kept Sorren from seeing what the people on the ship were doing.

"Are *they* sailors?" she asked.

"No. They're carpenters, sailmakers, ropemakers. Most of them have never been out of sight of land in all their lives. They'll call for a crew when the ship is done."

"What if no one wants to go?"

Kadra smiled. "Someone will," she said. The look she gave the ship was one of a lover to a beloved.

"*You* want to go!"

Kadra lurched to one side in the treacherous mud. Her dark face twisted with pain, or longing. "Yes. O Guardian, yes."

Sorren tried to imagine what it would be like to trust oneself to a small wooden box, floating in the midst of all that water. She shivered. "When will it go?"

"When it's finished."

"Whose is it?"

"Jalaras and Isaras."

Sorren wondered if Arré knew about this ship. "You want to leave the city, too," she said to Kadra. "Is that why you said yes to me?"

Kadra sat in the mud. "That's right. I'll tell you the best route to take north, what clothes to wear, what villages to avoid. If I help you, maybe the Guardian will let me have a place on that ship."

Sorren said, "I didn't know you could bargain with the chea."

It was ill-spoken. Kadra said, "Are you a witch, that you know so much about the chea?"

"No. I'm sorry. I've angered you. I'll go." Living with Arré had at least taught her when to retreat. She turned to leave the slipway.

Kadra called to her. "Wait!"

Sorren looked back. The ghya was holding out a hand. She trudged back.

Kadra said, "I said I'd help you. I will." She thrust her

palm upward. "In earnest of our agreement. Take it." *It* was
a shell. Sorren picked it from Kadra's palm. It was shaped like
a teardrop. It was tiny, light as a bead, translucent pink, delicate
as a piece of foam.

Turning the shell in her fingers, Sorren climbed up the
muddy bank to the beach. She looked back once, to see Kadra
crouched on the muck beside the ship. Something about her
posture made Sorren shiver. She ought to go to a Healer, she
thought; she sounds sick. The bank steepened near the street,
and she had to use her hands to balance. Her feet slipped in
the litter of seaweed and broken shells.

As she trudged up the street, Ricard's dark face bobbed in
front of her. She stopped, surprised and annoyed to see him.
His eyes were bloodshot; his clothes dirty and reeking of heavenweed. He glared at her, chin thrust forward like a baby's
pout. She tried to go around him, and he spread his arms out
to hold her.

"What are you doing here?" she said. "You stink." She
made a face.

"I saw you," he said.

She clenched her fingers on the shell, wondering what he
meant. Saw her what? "Are you following me around?" She
tried to push past him. He would not get out of her way.

"I saw you," he said again.

She felt her temper beginning to climb. "Ricky, leave me
alone."

"Saw you talking to that man."

Sorren resisted the urge to shout at him that Kadra was not
a man. "Ricky, go away," she said.

"I saw you," he said, and fell on her.

At first, she thought he had simply overbalanced, and she
struggled to hold him upright. He dragged her onto the stones.
His hands plucked at her shirt. She shoved him. He was strong.
Someone whistled, a piercing sound. Ricky breathed hotly into
Sorren's face and she realized he was trying to kiss her. "You
idiot!" she yelled at him, and bucked him off. He scrambled
back to her, panting, and she swung a fist at his face. The
cobblestones hurt her shoulderblades as he threw himself on
her, bearing her back on the stone. "You stupid boy," she said.

"I'm not a boy," he grunted. He pinned her wrists and put
a knee between her legs.

She heard noises, a crowd. Someone laughed. She twisted and turned, trying to free her hands, while Ricky breathed heavenscent into her face.

Then he was pulled off her. She sat up. Her elbows were scraped and stinging. Two Jalar guards were holding Ricky between them. His shirt was torn. She grinned with fury and pleasure at the sight and climbed slowly to her feet.

"Names?" said one of the guards.

She dusted her palms together. "Sorren-no-Kité, bondservant to Arré Med," she said. She rubbed her side. It hurt. "This idiot is Ricard-no-Paxe, son of the Med Yardmaster."

The other guard, a big brawny man, shook Ricard by the collar. "What were you doing?" he inquired. Ricard scowled and would not answer. "Are you hurt?" the guard asked Sorren.

"No." Suddenly, she remembered the shell. She had been holding it. "Oh, damn!" She felt her clothes, hoping it had gotten stuck in a fold. It had not. Probably it was crushed to powder. Her temper rose again. "Oh, damn, damn."

"What is it?"

"He made me drop something."

"This?" said the first guard, holding out the bracelet of shells.

"That, too," said Sorren. She had not even felt it fall.

"You shouldn't play so rough," said the guard.

Sorren glared at her. "Play! He attacked me! You think I like dust and sores? We weren't playing."

"Aw," said Ricky, "don't listen to her. She's a cunt."

Sorren leaped at him. She wanted to scratch his face off; she wanted to break his head. She flailed at him. The two guards dropped Ricard's arms and reached for her. Ricky ran, slamming through the crowd which had gathered. The guards swore aloud, and the woman hit her. She had already stopped fighting. The woman wrenched her arm behind her back, making her helpless. Pain shot into her shoulder. Through clenched teeth, she said, "You don't have to do that."

They marched her all the way across the city and up the hill to the Med house. As they came to the gate, the woman dropped Sorren's arm. It was numb, and she shook it to make the feeling come back. The door guard stared. Elith answered the door. The fat old woman raised her eyebrows at Sorren, and then hurried to get Arré.

She came from the small parlor. "What happened?"

The woman guard started to speak. Sorren interrupted her. "It was Ricard. I was on the dock talking to a friend, and he saw me. He smelled of heavenweed. He jumped on me. I was fighting him off when they came. Ricky called me a cunt and I got mad and hit him and they grabbed me and he ran away." She was trembling. Her back and her arm hurt and she felt twelve again.

"Are you all right?" said Arré. "Did he hurt you?"

"No. He didn't hurt me."

"Well?" said Arré to the guards. They looked embarrassed.

"We didn't know who started it," said the woman defensively.

"Hè did," said Sorren. "He even knocked the bracelet off my arm." Reminded, the guard extended the bracelet to Arré. She took it and laid it down.

"Thank you for acting so promptly to break up a fight," she said to the guards. To Sorren she said, gently, "Why don't you clean up?"

Sorren went to the kitchen. She could hear Paxe in the Yard. The apprentices crowded around her, asking questions. She sank onto a stool. "I got jumped in the market," she said.

"Who was it?" said Toli. "What'd you do?"

"I fought back," She felt trembly, still.

The cook came round the chopping counter, holding his cleaver. "Did you get the orders in?"

"Yes." She leaned her head on her hand. He gave her a clean, damp rag, and she wiped her face and then her elbows. Lalith brought her some tea. She slumped on the stool, sipping it. Lalith fingered the torn shirt.

"I'll mend this for you," she offered.

Sorren shook her head. "I can do it." The tea had honey in it. The sweet taste was very soothing. The cook glared at the apprentices and they got back to work, kneading dough, cutting up vegetables. Every time she looked at them they smiled. She could no longer hear Paxe's voice. She leaned on the cutting board. the kitchen warmth was delicious, like a feather quilt.

The door to the kitchen opened. Arré entered, followed by Paxe. She was sweaty from the Yard. Sorren guessed that Arré had told her. "It was Ricard?" she said. Lalith gasped. Everybody was watching her. She lifted Sorren's face between her palms, and touched, with her lips, a bruise that Sorren had not even realized was there. "Did he do that?"

Arré had her hands on her hips. "I told you," she said.
"He's too old to be hanging around here, begging money off
you, working only when he feels like it. He needs to be responsible for something."

"He's still a boy," said Paxe.

Arré's silver bracelets jangled. "He's a spoiled brat."

"Do the guards have him?"

"No. He ran away from them. Send him to the grapefields,
Paxe."

"I'll talk to him about it," Paxe said. Her hands move
caressingly on Sorren's shoulder.

"Don't talk to him!" Arré struck the counter with the flat
of her hand. "Tell him, just tell him. You let him do what he
wants too much, and look what he does." She gestured at
Sorren.

Sorren pictured Ricky in the grapefields. He was too lazy
to be much use there. Thinking of him made her fists clench.
She never wanted to see him again.

"You don't know anything about it," said Paxe angrily to
Arré. "You have no children."

"I can see what's in front of my eyes," said Arré. "Some
people can't."

The scullions, even the cook, had stopped work, and were
listening avidly. "I don't give you advice on the Council,"
retorted Paxe. "Don't give me advice on my son."

The quarrel proceeded over Sorren's head. The noise made
her head ache. The heat of the kitchen had turned stifling. She
felt suffocated. Her back hurt, her elbow hurt. She had lost
the shell Kadra had given her; she had used Arré's money to
buy wine for a drunk. . . . She shifted on the stool. Her throat
hurt. Her eyes stung.

Like a baby, she burst into tears.

The quarrel stopped. Paxe put both arms around her. They
went upstairs, to Sorren's bedroom, and Sorren curled on the
bed and cried. Paxe sat beside her, stroking her, her fingers
gentle. After a while, Sorren stopped crying. Her body felt
heavy and stiff, as it did on the days of the month when she
bled. "I feel silly," she said. "I'm sleepy."

Paxe kissed her mouth. "You're not silly." She stroked
Sorren's hair back from her face. "Rest. You'll feel better
later." She rose. Sorren started to call out to her, to tell her

that she had torn Ricard's shirt, but the Yardmaster was already through the door. Sighing, Sorren pillowed her head on the arm that did not ache.

Arré's door was open; Paxe knocked on it anyway.

Arré knew the knock. "Come in," she called.

Paxe walked in.

"Is she all right?" Arré asked.

"She's sleeping." The Yardmaster's tone of voice said, *Don't talk about it.*

Arré said gently, "She'll heal. Children heal fast, and she's still a child in some ways. She's not that much older than Ricard."

Paxe said, "She's a lot older than Ricard," and Arré could hear her frustration and anger in the way she said her errant son's name.

Holding her hand out, she said, "Please don't fight with me, Paxe. I'm sorry I pushed you. Do whatever you think best with Ricky."

Paxe nodded. "I shall." She sat on the rosewood stool. Her size made the furnishings of the room look small. Picking up the stone figurine on the table, she ran her fingers over it. "What's this supposed to be?" she said.

"A seal."

"It looks like a bear." She set it down. "Arré, I didn't come to talk about Ricky, or Sorren." Her face was stern, her back straight as a board. Arré leaned back on her bed pillows, fingering the tassels of the cover, as Paxe talked about walking into the Yard one morning after her rounds, and finding her guards looking at a sword.

Her hands sliced the air as she described the swordplay: forgetting that Arré had never used the weapon in her life, she told about taking the blade apart and what it told her. She was slim and tough as she had been thirteen years back, only her eyes and her hands had aged, and Arré stayed very still in her nest of cushions, feeling the old pull rise in her blood. If only, she thought, if only, if we could have stayed together—but it was too late for regrets. She listened intently as Paxe described her visit to the Ismenin Yard, and what she found there.

When Paxe mentioned the lines of soldiers with wooden swords, Arré felt a shiver down her back. *No* Yard taught the sword art. It was forbidden. "How has Ron Ismenin persuaded

his soldiers to break the Ban?" she said. "I should think they
would be terrified to touch even wooden weapons."

Paxe explained what Dobrin had said to her about the Ban
and about the witches. Her voice was strained; it was evident
that Dobrin's conversation had upset her. Arré nodded. It made
sense to *her*; but then, she had never believed in the chea. She
knew where the Ban had come from. It had been devised by
the Council with the connivance of the White Clan to break
the power of the Red Clan, which had grown much too strong
for the Council's taste; and also, to end the drain on the city
treasury which the metal trade was making. The demand for
weaponry meant that a third of the city's funds were siphoned
off to pay for metal and finished steel, and all that money went
north, out of the hands of the city's rulers and merchants, to
Tezera. The White Clan had supported it because it served
their interests to dam the Red Clan's power.

Arré's grandmother, Tabitha Med, had helped create the
Ban. By the time her granddaughter was born, there were no
more chearis in the city. And now we have Isak, Arré thought,
my dear, manipulative brother. I wonder how he managed to
ensnare Cha Minto. . . .

Paxe's voice broke sharply into her ruminations. "Arré, are
you even hearing me?"

"I heard every word," Arré said firmly.

"Was Dobrin telling me the truth?"

"About what?"

"About the short sword not being included in the Ban."

"I'm sure of it," said Arré. "I have a copy of the Ban in
my study, we could look at it, but I doubt it's necessary. A
lie would be too easy to disprove."

Excited, she slid from the bed and walked to the window.
The Ismenin family owned mines. It would be to their advan-
tage if the Ban were to be lifted, or if they could arrange a
way around it. When is a sword not a sword? she thought, and
answered, when it's a short sword. Kendra-on-the-Delta was
the largest concentrated market in the land of Arun, and what
better things would there be to make with metal?

A thought struck her. She said, "When did this happen,
Paxe?"

"Four days ago," said Paxe.

"*Four* days ago? Before the Council meeting?" Paxe nodded. "Why did you wait so long to tell me?"

Paxe looked at her hands. "I needed to think about it."

"You should have told me! It's my job to think, not yours. If I had known this at the Council meeting—" What difference would it have made? she thought. No real difference. "Is it common knowledge in the city that the Ismeninas are teaching the short sword?"

Paxe shook her head. "No. They have a guard at the Yard gate, keeping everyone not wearing Ismenin colors out. Dobrin told the guards not to talk about it."

"You saw no real weapons."

"None, and Dobrin was very clear about that: the possession of live blades is forbidden to his soldiers."

"Lyrith had one."

"Lyrith got a whipping."

"But why train with wooden blades if you do not eventually plan to use real ones?" said Arré.

I wonder if the White Clan knows about this, she thought. They must not. Someone would have to tell them, and she did not think they would be pleased. She tried to imagine what the Ismeninas were doing. They might be hoping to stimulate a black-market trade. But that would be easy to stop; the first few people found with swords would lose their right hands, and the rest would get frightened. "What do you think the Ismeninas are doing?" she said to Paxe.

Paxe said, "I don't know. I know it's dangerous." She stroked the sculpture, holding it between her big palms as if it were alive.

Arré snorted. "Of course it's dangerous!"

"What will you do?" said Paxe.

"Me? There's nothing I can do. For one thing—" she walked back to the bed and sat—"there's nothing in the Ban or in the Council ordinances to forbid the possession of wooden short swords."

Paxe frowned. "You can kill with a wooden sword, if you know how," she said.

"Can you?" said Arré. "I didn't know that."

Could the Ismeninas be training a private army? Stranger things had happened. But there had been no armies in Arun for eighty years, and anyway she could not imagine what Ron Ismenin would get with a private army that he could not get by spending a little money. She sighed. "I must talk to the Council," she said, meaning Marti Hok. Suddenly, she felt weary; hunger for something sweet gnawed her belly. She leaned on her cushions. Lines, a pattern of alliance, splayed through her thought. The Council ruled the city, but power existed beyond the formality of Council laws. She felt as if she, the Council, were being manipulated—by whom? Cha Minto? Bah, Isak? The Ismeninas?

"What should I do?" said Paxe.

She had almost forgotten Paxe was there.

She wanted to do something which would bother the Ismeninas. "Can *you* teach the sword?"

"Yes," said Paxe. "I could. I can have a carpenter make wooden swords, *sejis*, and bring them to the Yard."

"Do so."

"Why?" Paxe sounded troubled.

Arré smiled at her. "Because the Ismeninas will not expect that. Do it, Paxe. There will be no trouble, unless and until the Council bans the short sword."

"Very well," Paxe rose fluidly. She put the stone animal down on the lacquered table, and quietly walked out.

Arré reached from the bed. Picking up the stone thing— perhaps it was a bear, after all—she petted it, fingers finding the crevices and hollows that Paxe's warm hands had touched. She had bought the thing from an Asech peddler, years ago. She turned the figure in her palms, trying to remember the day. She had lived in this city, in this house, in this room, for eighteen years. She sniffed the house smell, a mixture of flower scents, food scents, human scents. She put the figure on the table. Sighing, she slipped to her knees and laid her cheek on the rosewood stool, trying to smell Paxe's scent through the scent of the wood. Foolish. She stood up. Her knees creaked. She was too old, to be feeling what she felt.

Was she jealous of Paxe and Sorren? A little, she thought. Pacing to the window, she unlatched the silk and paper screen and slid it back. Houses, streets, shops spread out before her like a tapestry. She watched a hawk wing north along the river, recalling afternoons when she had strolled along the river bank watching the barges pole downstream, with Paxe's arm around her shoulders.

Those had been happy years. She had been learning her trade, rulership; Paxe had been second-in-command of the guard. And Isak—Isak had been in Shanan, studying the dance. *Did* Isak know about the swords? she thought. He was Ron

Ismenin's friend; he had to know. Of course, he would not tell her. She was his sister, whom he hated, and wanted to supplant or, at least, to equal. An image filled her gaze for a moment, of a boy, dark and thin and graceful as a cat, with brilliant dark eyes, crowing with delight as she tossed him in the air, his long hair swirling in the breeze. "Ré," he had called her. "Ré, wait. Ré, can I come with you? Ré, I want to sit with you—" She had adored him, as had her mother and everyone who met him. When had his delight changed to jealousy? She could not remember, save that it must have happened early. At seven and eight, he had been sullen in her presence and lavish with attention to his mother, as if he thought loving would somehow change the fact that he was the younger of them, and not the heir. He had wept for Shana Med. Arré closed the window. But then he had gone to study with Meredith, and when he came back from Shanan he was brittle, hard as the surface of a chobata, and inaccessible, to Arré at least, as if he lived in the depths of a cave.

It was well into the dinner hour when Sorren came from her room.

The lamplighters were calling their high-pitched signals to each other down the winding streets. On nights she had no guests—which was most nights—it was Arré's custom to eat her evening meal in her bedroom. She was lingering over dessert when Sorren came in. The scrape on the girl's forehead was puffy and red. "Sit down," said Arré, ringing her bell for Lalith. "Did you put comfry on that bruise?"

"Yes." Sorren sat on the stool. Lalith entered, and Arré ordered her to bring a second plate of food. "I'm not hungry."

"Nonsense," said Arré. "You ought to be, after sleeping all day and fighting all morning."

Sorren touched the edges of the bruise with her fingers. Arré told herself that it looked worse than it really was. She herself bruised easily; the tiniest cuts took forever to heal. Sorren's skin was white, and all marks showed up strongly on it. She did look like a northerner; it was her coloring that had first drawn Arré's eyes to her, years ago in the vineyards: her hair the color of sunshine, and her eyes, as blue as the trumpet-flowers which grew up the grapevines. When I was a little girl, Arré thought, I wanted to look like that.

Sorren said, "I didn't mean to sleep so long."

Arré smiled at her. "I'm not scolding you, child."

"I'm not a child." The tall girl's back went as stiff as Paxe's could get.

"I know, I know," said Arré gently. But she looked younger than seventeen, with her hair tousled from the pillow and her white eyelids heavy. "How do you feel?"

"I'm all right."

Lalith brought the food in. Sorren took the plate on her knees. She picked up a piece of ham. "I guess I am hungry," she admitted. She glanced up shyly through her lashes. "Maybe it's the sea air. I was down by the docks when Ricard—saw me."

"Oh?"

"I was watching the ship; the one Isaras and Jalaras are building to go south."

Arré nodded. Edith Isara had told her about the ship, half mocking her own investment. "It will probably sink and never be heard from again," she had said. "But who knows; it might come back with interesting news of other lands, strange places where gold and silver pour out of the very soil and jewels grow on trees."

"But I thought you wanted to go north," Arré said.

She meant it teasingly, but Sorren blushed. "I do," she said. "A—a friend was showing me the ship."

Arré licked her spoon. She said, "I don't blame you, for fighting with Ricard."

"I didn't want to!" Sorren said. "He made me!"

"I expect he did."

"What will happen when he comes home?"

"That's up to Paxe," said Arré, thinking, I hope she has the sense to send the young lout to the vineyards. Looking at Sorren now, she saw a tall, golden-skinned girl who, she thought angrily, was worth two of Ricard.

Softly she asked, "Are you too bruised to drum?"

Sorren looked shocked. "Of course not!"

Good, thought Arré. She hesitated, considering her words. "When are you going to Isak's to practice?"

Thickly, through a second piece of ham, Sorren said, "In a week. If I may."

"You may," Arré said. "I want you to do something for me when you go to Isak's." She did not like using Sorren, but there was no other method she could use to find out what she needed to know. Isak talked to Sorren—not freely perhaps, but with less calculation than he talked with anyone else. "Tell Isak, if you can, that you have seen Paxe with a new thing in the Yard—a short sword. Ask him about it, and see what he says."

Sorren ate another strip of ham. The light from the chobata gleamed steadily on the fine smooth grain of her skin. She's lovely, Arré thought, with a pang, lovely as I never was, even when young.

"Does she really have a sword?" said Sorren. "I thought it was forbidden."

"It may be. We will see," said Arré. She wondered how much Isak would read in Sorren's manner. She was not, by nature, deceptive.

"What if he asks me where she got it?"

"Tell him the truth; you don't know."

"What if he asks me why I am asking him?"

Arré smiled. "You know Isak, child. Tell him, because he knows *everything* that happens in the city."

CHAPTER SIX

When Paxe woke in the morning, her bed was stained with blood.

Swearing, she leaped from the mattress and stripped it of its covering. It was not her time to bleed. She dumped covering and quilts in a heap on the floor and went to the basin to wipe her thighs and legs clean. Opening the chest at the foot of the bed, she took out her sponge, and, crouching, inserted it. Her back twinged. Scowling, she dressed, and stamped downstairs with the soiled linen in her arms. Against the waistband of her pants, she felt her belly's bloat.

It was cool out. Eastward, the sun touched the river, and the clouds caught the reflection so that they gleamed with the light. Paxe dumped the linens in the laundry. Her time had come early because she was worried, about Sorren, about Arré, about the city, and, most of all, about her son.

She wondered where he was. He had not come home; she hadn't expected him to; he was probably working up his courage to face her. Arré was right, she thought, I have been too soft with him. But after losing two, she had hugged the third to her, too tightly. She left the laundry. A boy wearing a Hok bond bracelet was coming up the walk. Paxe watched the gate guard speak to him, nod, and then open the gate.

She did her morning exercises with extra vigor. By the time the sun cleared the city's lower roofs, she was sweating. Guards wandered into the Yard, greeting her quietly. Kaleb was late. Wondering where he was, Paxe watched her soldiers pair for practice. Seth came in. "Good morning, Yardmaster," he said. His voice was sullen. As punishment for having brought the sword into the Yard, Paxe had set him to cleaning all the weapons in the weapons shed, and the hair on his hands and forearms was matted with grease.

The guards squared off for pike drill. She watched them thrust and turn. Kaleb came in, moving so silently that only his shadow slanting on the hard dirt told her he was there.

"Good morning," he said.

"Good morning. How went the night?"

"More fighting on the docks."

She shook her head. "How bad was it?"

"Bad." Rough-voiced with fatigue, he recited the tally: seven guards hurt, one stabbed in the stomach with a fisherman's dirk, two with scalp wounds from blows from a ship's spike. "They're in the Tanjo. The Healers say the stabbed one will recover, but one of the men with head wounds may not see again. Correo-no-Samantha is furious."

Correo was the Jalar Yardmaster. "I should think so," Paxe said. She shuddered. If those had been her soldiers. . . . "Were the Ismenin brothers in it this time, too?"

Kaleb shrugged with his hands. "I don't know. The people caught by the Jalar guards were reluctant to say."

"I'll bet they were," Paxe said. "You think they were paid?"

"It would need a Truthfinder to say that."

"It may come to that," Paxe said. She cocked her head to one side, surveying Kaleb's dark, seamed face. "You look worn out, my friend."

"I am," said Kaleb bluntly. The admission was unlike him, and it surprised her.

"Are you going home?" she asked.

"Yes." Kaleb lived west of the hill, in a cottage near the Northwest Gate.

"I'll walk you home. I have something to tell you."

They strolled from the hill. Already the streets near the Gate were crammed with carts. The scent of trumpet-vines floated in the morning breeze, overlaid with the harsher smells of spice and fish and human labor. In the vineyards, Paxe remembered, trumpet-vines grew up the grapevines, so that at the harvest it looked as if the grapes themselves bloomed with bright blue flowers.

She told Kaleb about Seth, the sword, her visit with Dobrin, and Arré's orders. He listened, one ear cocked toward her, walking with the peculiar gliding gait of one trained to walk on sand. "What do you think?" she asked him.

He made a soft sucking sound through his teeth. "What can I say? The Asech elders have never forbidden us weapons. But we respect the knowledge of the White Clan, and within the city, all desertfolk honor the Ban."

"Then you think I should not teach the sword?"

He shook his head—a learned gesture. The Asech did not do it. "Arré Med is a Councillor. She must have good reason for her order."

"Ye-e-e-s," said Paxe. They had reached the cottage. "The news from the docks will not please her."

"There should be no more such news," said Kaleb. "Correo is doubling the guard."

"Very wise," said Paxe. She raised a hand. "I shall leave you here, my friend. Sleep well."

Kaleb caught her hands. "I heard about Ricard," he said gently.

Paxe did not ask him how. He had his own sources of information.

"Have you seen him?" she said.

He shook his head. "No. But don't worry about him, Paxe. He comes of good stock. There's no malice in him."

To her astonishment, Paxe felt her eyes fill with tears. "Yes," she said. "Well, if you see him, tell him to come home."

Perrit the carpenter worked in the Hok district, across the city from the Med district, nearly an hour's walk. The sun, bowling swiftly up over the horizon, was beginning to heat the cobblestones. Paxe decided to break her routine and walk east. Her stomach rumbled, and she remembered she had not eaten. A boy strolled near, carrying a basket of cherries, and she hailed him. "What's your price?"

"I'm not selling, Yardmaster," he said, eyes flicking nervously from side to side. "I'm taking them to my gran; I bought them at Seri's stall, it's that way, two blocks down—"

Paxe lifted a hand to halt his chatter. "All right, all right. Go on." She turned down the Street of the Carders and crossed the line into the Minto district. At a stall near the Tanjo, she bought fish cakes; she talked a while with the vendor, and managed to wheedle him out of a glass of wine.

He told her all about the fight on the docks. "Forty people hurt!" he said, with relish and horror.

"Seven," she said. "Only seven."

He seemed disappointed. She listened, as she walked, to the conversations of the passersby. They talked about the fights, and about the approaching Harvest Festival. Three times in the Minto district Paxe saw old men bending over straw patterns cast in the street. The patterns were thought to be able to tell the future. Fortunetelling was ni'chea; the White Clan had declared it so years back, but whenever events grew uncertain in the city, the strawcasters appeared.

The market seemed more crowded than usual, and dirtier, as if the street-sweepers had not been working. The heaven-weed smell was thick. Once at a busy street corner, Paxe thought she glimpsed her son. But when she reached the spot she thought he'd been, there was no one there who even looked like him.

A beggar brushed against her, whining, and she snarled at him. He backed away. Paxe tried to remember when the beggars had come. Most of them were fakes, and all were pick-pockets. She strolled past the Hok Yard with her head cocked, half listening for a count ("One—two—three—four!") but heard only the usual grunts, thumps, and shuffling. The district guards, wearing the blue and white Hok badges, bowed to her.

When she entered the shop in Carpenters' Row, Perrit was busy, bending over a piece of wood locked in a vise. She knew better than to disturb him. She leaned against the wall, just within the doorway, till one of his apprentices saw her and scurried to find a stool for her. She watched Perrit's hands work a gouge. The room smelled of cut wood and turpentine. Planks, all shapes, all kinds, all colors, were stacked every-where.

Perrit put the gouge down and drew the wood from the vise. "Good day," Paxe said.

Perrit nodded. He was dark-skinned as she, white-haired, old, but his shoulders were like the oak he worked with. "Yar'master Paxe," he said, slurring over the sounds he could not say. His front three upper teeth were rotted from his jaw. "What we 'o 'or you?"

Because the city guards occasionally had to cope with drun-ken sailors or drunken countryfolk carrying smuggled weapons, Paxe taught her guards knife counters. For this training she used carved white oak blades, called *nijis*. Perrit's workshop supplied them to her and to two other Yards.

Paxe leaned forward, resting elbows on knees. "I need some training equipment."

Surprise danced over his dark face. "You shou'na."

Paxe chose her approach with care. "Perrit, does your mem-ory go back before the Ban?"

Two boys marched by, with lengths of red cedar balanced on their shoulders. Grains of sawdust clung to their hair and clothes. Perrit said, "It 'oes. I was boy o' t'irteen when it was make. Why?"

"You're almost the only woodcarver I can think of in the city who might remember how to carve sejis."

The old man rubbed his beardless chin. "T'ere be ot'ers," he said. "You nee' some?"

He sounded neither shocked nor surprised. Paxe wanted to ask him which of his compatriots had made Dobrin's sejis, but she knew he would not tell her. "I need some. Say, twenty."

He nodded. "I make."

"Do it yourself," she said. "Deliver them yourself, too."

He grunted. "I 'on't nee' you to tell me t'at. When you want?"

"How long will it take you?"

He calculated, staring into space. "T'ree week."

"That's time enough," Paxe said. "You'll find the Med response will be—generous."

As she left the shop, her back twinged. She walked through the Isara district with her lower spine pulsing at every step. At the Tanjo gate, she stopped. Orilys bowed. "Yardmaster."

"How is it?"

"Quiet as ever."

Nothing stirred on the immaculate pavement. The acolytes kept the stones well-swept. On impulse, Paxe gestured. "Let me through." Smiling, Orilys pulled the iron gate back.

It was dark in the red stone building. Slowly, Paxe's eyes adjusted to the dimness. When she could see, she put her palms together and bowed. The floor was tiled with blue and silver squares. The walls were bare of ornament. Light came from slits in the dome, and from the silver-filigreed lamps which hung overhead, affixed to the sloping wall by long chains and hooks. A soft warbling bespoke the presence of birds. Paxe stepped forward, and slipped off her sandals. The tiles were cold. She folded her arms across her breasts, and lifted her face upward, staring at the white pillar in the center of the room.

The stone was polished, toward the base, by the sweat and oil of fingers. The image of the Guardian, everyone knew, was only that, an image of a thing which did not exist—for the Guardian was not a real being, but itself a symbol of that mightier reality which scholars named the chea. But in the charged, heavy stillness, it was easy to forget that the Guardian was a symbol and its statue was only a piece of graven stone. *O Guardian*, said the people of the city; *May the Guardian smile upon you*, they called to one another. They kept statues of it in their homes, to which they bowed. Once, Paxe recalled, she too had come here, weeping for her children. She looked at the changeless, ageless alabaster. It was easy to see it as real, a being, stronger than she, wiser than she, not woman, not man, birthless and deathless, without the strains and scars that mark the passage of even the most fortunate of human lives.

Closing her eyes, Paxe said a brief, silent prayer into the secretive darkness, that no harm would come, through her, to the folk of the city she loved.

As she reached the border of her district, Paxe began to feel uneasy. She knew better than to look openly around; instead, she slowed, turned into a few alleys, and then doubled back. Softly she slid into a shadowed doorway to wait. In a moment, her sharp ears caught the patter of bare feet over stone. A small figure with a basket was coming through the alley she had just left.

She grabbed him. "Taking them to your gran? You little liar!" She cuffed him, hard enough to sting. The basket slipped from his hands and fell unheeded to the street. He twisted in her grip. Paxe closed her hand over his thin arm. "Stand still!" She shook him. "You were following me."

Ragged and dark-skinned, like a hundred other denizens of the street, he glared at her.

"What's your name?" she demanded. "Where do you live?"

He shook his head, as if daring her to question him more hurtfully.

Paxe scowled. Then, struck by a sudden idea, she seized him by an arm and a leg and swung him upside down. He yelled; two coins, one dull and heavy, one bright, fell from his pockets. The bronze piece skipped twice and fell in the gutter. Paxe put her foot quickly over the bright carved bone.

"That's mine!" said the boy. She set him down, and he scrambled for the bronze piece.

"Tell me who gave it to you and you may have the bone," Paxe said. The child's lower lip began to tremble. "Crying won't help."

The threatened tears receded. "I don't know his name," said the boy.

"I don't believe you," Paxe said.

"I don't!" His eyes watched her shrewdly. "He has red hair, though."

"There are a lot of redheads in this city."

"He has three brothers, and they all have red hair, too."

Grinning, Paxe took her foot off the bone. "Unless you want a beating," she said, "don't tell him I caught you." She stepped back. Swift as a striking snake, the boy plucked the trey from the road and raced for the alley.

Forgoing rounds, Paxe went directly to the Med house. She went in the kitchen entrance. Toli was kneading dough on a bread board, singing a popular song. Lalith was shelling shrimps, and the translucent pink shells were scattered over the kitchen steps.

"Is Arré in her study?" Paxe asked.

Lalith put the shrimp bowl down, and wiped her hands on her apron. "Yes, Yardmaster, do you want me to announce you?"

Paxe smiled at the girl. "No, don't bother." She hurried through the long kitchen. The oven was lit, and the heat made her cheeks prickle with sweat.

In the study, Arré was seated in her chair. A piece of paper lay in her lap; it was cream-colored, thick as calfskin, and sealed with a dollop of red wax. The seal was imprinted with the Med house's triangular seal. "Good morning," Paxe said.

"Good morning," said Arré.

Paxe sat on the stool. She could not help looking at the letter; it made an imposing packet on Arré's knees. She could not quite see the superscription. "What's that?"

Arré flicked the paper with one finger. "A letter to the Tanjo. From me," she added.

Paxe was surprised. Arré, she knew, had little use for the White Clan. "About the swords?" she said.

"About the swords," Arré confirmed. "The witchfolk need to know what the Ismeninas are doing. Whatever action the Council chooses to take about the swords will need the White Clan's approval."

"To whom will you send it?" Paxe said.

"To Jerrin-no-Dovria i Elath," Arré said, rolling the name on her tongue.

Jerrin-no-Dovria i Elath was L'hel—chief—of Kendra-on-the-Delta's Council of Witches. Paxe remembered him from Festival ceremonies: a stocky man, with powerful shoulders

and cornsilk hair. Three years ago, he had presided over Spring
Festival. That year Ricky turned twelve, and Paxe brought him
to the Tanjo for the Ceremony of Recognition. Paxe, like most
who grew up outside the city, had never seen the ceremony;
the witchfolk had created it to replace the tradition which had
once been the mark of passage toward adulthood, the giving
of the knife. In the ceremony, the twelve-year-olds were each
presented to the L'hel, who brought them solemnly before the
Guardian. Her impression of him then had been favorable; he
had seemed both confident and gentle. Good, Paxe thought.
He should know what to say to the Ismeninas.

She recalled Dobrin's impassioned speech about the witchfolk. "... Whatever their powers, they are only human...."

"You aren't pleased?" Arré said. "You're scowling. I
thought you'd be pleased." The sardonic note that crept out
whenever she spoke of the witchfolk infused her voice.

"I'm pleased," Paxe said.

Arré frowned. "I hope I won't have to go to the Tanjo."

Paxe decided to change the subject. "There was trouble on
the docks last night. Seven hurt. It may have been instigated
by the Ismeninas."

Arré said, "Ron had better do something about those brothers of his!" Then she stretched, and her voice turned wry. "I'm
a fine one to talk."

"Isak doesn't fight," said Paxe.

"I'd be happier if he did, at least I'd know what he's doing.
He lives in his house, he dances, he visits, he does no work—
what does he do with his mind?" Her voice rose in exasperation.

Paxe thought, She sounds like me, worrying about Ricard.
She was sick of worrying about her son. "I went to Carpenters'
Row, and ordered twenty sejis, as you said to."

"Excellent."

"Arré—" Paxe hunted for words. "If swords are returned
to the city, more people could be hurt than seven. A sword is
deadlier than a stick or a knife."

Arré spread her hands. "Have I said I want swords returned
to the city? I have not."

"Then why order sejis?"

"Because it makes political sense," Arré said. "The Ismeninas have them."

Paxe shook her head. She tugged her clothes into some
pretense of order. "Wait here." Politics were not her concern.

"I was followed to the carpenter's," she said.

"By whom?"

"A child. I trapped him in an alley, and he admitted the Ismeninas had set him at my heels."

Arré snorted. "Idiots! Did they think you would not notice a follower?" She scratched her chin. "That's interesting, though, that they feel they must know where you go and who you see."

"Do you want me to chase him away?"

Arré pursed her lips. "No. Let him hang about. Let the Ismeninas think we are both stupid." She lifted the sealed letter from her lap. There was a second letter beneath it, smaller, open. "Is Sorren back yet?"

"She's not in the kitchen," Paxe said.

Arré tapped the second letter. "Marti sent an invitation to Sorren to visit her. She was quite taken with her."

"Sorren told me."

"Marti wants to tell her stories, all about the Keeps in the north. The other evening, Sorren asked me what a Keep was."

"Did you tell her?" Paxe said.

"I told her."

Paxe wondered if Sorren had told Arré about her visions. "She has dreams about the north," she said. "She wants to go there when her time of service ends."

Arré said, "Children have all kinds of strange ambitions. She'll get over it."

Paxe shook her head. "I don't think so."

There was a small silence. Arré broke it. "Has Ricard come home yet?"

Paxe looked at her hands. "No." A brittle buzz filled the room, as a fly swooped from the window and circled their heads.

Arré said gently, "I'm sorry if I talked out of turn."

Paxe knew she was referring to their arguments about Ricard. "You didn't," she said wearily. "What you said was correct; I have spoiled him." The ugly word seemed ominous.

Arré said firmly, "Paxe, don't trouble yourself so. He'll come back."

"I hope so," Paxe said.

Sorren was troubled.

She had found her way back to the slipway, this time without

assistance. It had taken her a while; the fog was in. It swallowed
the fishing boats, leaving them blind, and the docks resounded
to the bellows of the conches, and each boat sounded a separate
tone to warn away its sisters.

Jeshim was gone from the docks; gone, she guessed, to seek
a warmer place. But—though she hunted everywhere, even
going down to the mud for a look beneath the boardwalk—
there was no sign of the ghya.

She went up on the boardwalk again. The Jalar guards were
standing on the end. She walked toward them.

The wind blew scraps of their conversation toward her.
"Stabbed," said one. "Stuck in the gut like a pig." They broke
off when they saw her coming toward them, and one of them
reached for his spear.

The other one caught his arm. "Looking for your friend?"
he said.

"I'm looking for Kadra," Sorren said, standing well away
from them. She was not feeling particularly friendly to Jalar
soldiers.

"Did you look under the walk?"

"Yes. She's not there."

"You might ask at The Fish."

It was a good idea. "Thank you," Sorren said.

The tavern doors were closed against the chill, but when
Sorren pushed them, they opened. The woman in the leather
apron came from the kitchen. Her hands were soapy. "What
is it?" she said.

"I'm looking for Kadra," said Sorren.

"Huh," said the woman. "That one. Try the street." She
went back to the rear of the inn.

Sorren scowled after her. That's no help, she thought. She
went outside again. Then, because she had been taught to take
commands literally when they did not make sense any other
way, she walked around the inn.

The rear door was open; from it she could hear the banging
of pots and a woman's voice, swearing. On the east wall of
the half-timbered building, a bundle of rags caught her attention. They looked familiar. She approached them. They moved.
She knelt. "Hey," she said. She poked the cloth. The long
bundle groaned, and an eye glared at her from the flapping
fold of a hood.

"G'way," said a voice.

It was Kadra.

Sorren turned back the cloak. The ghya's face was bruised on one side. Her left lower jaw looked swollen. Her clothes seemed surprisingly clean, but the space around her stank of stale wine and vomit.

"Can I help you?" Sorren asked.

"Get away from me," mumbled the ghya. She moved her mouth as if it hurt her. With a shaking hand, she tried to pull the hood of the cloak back over her head.

"You don't want to do that," said Sorren. "Do you need to be sick?" She pushed the cloak from Kadra's head.

"No!" Kadra said. She pushed upright. "I need to wash." Her voice had gotten strong. "Since you won't go away, help me stand." Sorren stood and held out a hand. Kadra grabbed it and hauled herself up, using the wall as well. "Guardian, my head." She tugged her clothes into some pretense of order. "Wait here," she said. She went toward the rear door of the inn, weaving a little. "Norres!"

A shriek answered her. It seemed to mean something. She staggered through the doorway. Sorren glanced around at the ghya's resting place. It was bare of all comfort; the only good thing about it was that it was protected by the surrounding buildings from the wind.

After a while, Kadra emerged from the inn. Her hair was dripping wet. With more steadiness, she walked to Sorren. "You're persistent," she said. "How did you know where to find me?"

"That woman told me," Sorren said, pointing at the inn's back door.

"She would. What do you want?"

Sorren said, "You said you'd teach me how to go north."

"Chea, so I did. Does that make you my keeper?" She hunkered down with her back to the brick and timber wall.

Her left lower jaw was definitely swollen. "Were you in a fight?" Sorren asked.

"There was some nonsense on the docks last night," said the ghya. "I got trapped in someone else's quarrel."

A cart rumbled along a street on its way from a warehouse to the docks. Sorren said, "If you don't want me to come here, I won't. But I need to know where to meet you, and when. I can come in the mornings, after I finish shopping, but I can't come every day or someone will notice."

More carts followed the first one. Absently Kadra said, "They must be unloading a ship." She rubbed her eyes. "You're serious about this, aren't you? You've got it all worked out. Where did you get that scrape?"

For a moment, Sorren had no idea what the ghya meant. Then she remembered the bruise on her forehead. "It's nothing," she said. "A scuffle."

"Did you win?"

"I didn't lose."

"Do you know anything about fighting?"

Sorren shook her head. Servants did not learn such things. "I'm strong," she said.

"Strength isn't enough," said the ghya. "Can you hunt? Can you use a spear or a knife?"

Sorren shook her head.

"You'll need hunting skills when you go north," said Kadra, "and a way to protect yourself. The folk of Galbareth will leave you alone, but after Lake Aruna, the roads get wild. It's not the kindest country for a solitary traveler."

"I just want to know how to get there," Sorren said, trying not to sound impatient. It was growing near to noon, and she did not want Arré to need her and notice her absence.

"It would help if you had a map," said Kadra.

Sorren had never seen a map. She knew what it would show her: the land, Arun, made small enough to fit upon a piece of parchment. She wondered if it would be possible for her to get one.

"You know where Plum Street is?" said Kadra.

"I can find it," Sorren said.

"It's in the Batto district. An aunt of mine has a house there; I stay there sometimes. I'll meet you there next week, three hours after sunrise."

"What day?"

"Fourth day. She goes to the baths the fourth day of every week, in the morning, and stays there for two hours."

"How will I know the house?"

Kadra said, "Just ask for me. Ask anyone."

She was hurrying up the hill when a voice hissed at her from a doorway. "Sorren." She looked around, annoyed at being stopped. Was it Jeshim, chasing her? A shadow stretched across the street. "Sorren!"

It was Ricard. He was standing under a kava fruit tree. He looked exhausted, and worried, and young.

"Please," he said.

She walked to where he would not have to shout at her. "What?"

"Sorren, I'm sorry," he said. His voice was like a little boy's, wavering and high. She wondered if he were doing it on purpose. His clothes were filthy, and his shirt was still torn. "I am, I was so high I went a little crazy. I'm not high now. I haven't had a taste of heavenweed since I ran away from the guards."

It could be true. "What do you want?" Sorren said.

"Is my mother angry at me?"

"Probably," Sorren said. "We didn't talk about it."

"Are you all right?" He looked anxiously at the bruise on her forehead.

"You couldn't hurt me," she said. "Ricky, I'm going to the house now. If you want to talk to me, come along."

"I'm scared to go back," he said.

It was as honest an answer as she had ever heard from him. "You'll have to, sooner or later," she said. With some surprise, she realized that she was no longer angry at him. "I think you should go back."

He shuffled his feet. "Can I go with you?" he said.

"I said you could." She wondered where he had last slept. He came out from under the tree. Carefully, he fell into step with her. It was odd to be walking with him like this. "Where have you been?" she asked.

He hunched his shoulders. "Running around. Running away." He sighed. "At the docks."

"I'm surprised the Jalar guards didn't find you," she said.

"I was upriver. Hok district. I saw her—my mother. I was hiding around the Hok Yard."

Sorren said, "It's not fair of you to trouble her. She has work to do."

He kicked a stone. "I don't mean to be a trouble. It just happens. I'm so stupid."

She could not help saying, "Just what I was thinking myself." He glanced at her, and then away, and she felt ashamed for teasing him. Their strides matched as they climbed the hill. "What are you going to say?"

"What can I say?" he asked.

She shrugged.

As they neared the Med Yard, Sorren said, "She'll be busy now. She likes to teach, this time of day."

"I know," he said. His shoulders hunched again. "I suppose I'd better wait for her in the house."

"Yes," she said. She touched his sleeve. "Good luck."

He ducked his head. "Thanks." She wondered what Paxe would say to him. He was too big to beat. She watched him go toward the cottage. Like a child, he dragged his feet, making shallow furrows over the dusty ground.

Lalith was waiting for her in the rear courtyard. She had pink petals all over her spiky hair. Her black eyes snapped with curiosity. "Wasn't that *Ricard?*"

Sorren nodded.

"How could you talk to him after what he did?"

Sorren sighed. "It was easy. I just opened my mouth." Lalith giggled. "Where's Arré?"

"In the parlor." They went into the house. Lalith went to the kitchen. Sorren went toward the parlor, wondering if Arré had missed her. She hoped not. The door was open, and she went in without bothering to knock, holding out her string of bontas.

Paxe was there.

Sorren immediately felt shy. She hated interrupting conversations, and she was never sure how to act toward Paxe and Arré together. The last time she had seen them, they had fought. She took a step back, thinking she could leave and return when their business was finished. Paxe turned and smiled at her.

"Come in," said Arré, "don't hover. Where have you been?"

From the slant of the sunlight across the wooden floor, Sorren knew it was late. "Shopping," she said.

"Shopping keeps you later each morning," said Arré, holding out her hand for the string of bontas. Sorren dropped it into her palm.

"I met Ricky," she said.

Paxe turned on the stool. "Where?"

"On the way. He came back with me. He's at the cottage."

Paxe rose. "I'd like to talk with him," she said.

"Of course," said Arré. "Go on." Her bracelets jangled as she pointed at Sorren. "You go clean up. Put on a fresh shirt. I want you to take a message for me."

"Where?" Sorren asked.

"To the Tanjo."

Sorren froze. Arré went on. "And tomorrow you can go and hear stories about the north. An invitation arrived today for you from Marti Hok." She stopped, and then said, "Well? Aren't you pleased?"

Sorren swallowed. She said, "I don't want to go to the Tanjo."

The room grew very quiet. In the stillness, the shouts of the guards in the Yard came clearly through the open windows. Sweat slicked Sorren's back. A hand brushed her from behind, and she jumped.

It was Paxe, still there.

Arré said, "What do you mean, you don't want to go to the Tanjo?"

Sorren said, "I—I'm afraid of them."

"Nonsense," said Arré. "Go clean up."

Paxe said, "Arré, why don't you let me send a guard with the letter. It's more formal."

Arré scowled at her. "I thought you were going to talk to your son."

"I am." Paxe didn't move. The older women looked at each other.

Arré sighed. "All right. Send a guard." Paxe's hand withdrew from Sorren's hip, and she left the chamber. Sorren bit her lip and waited for Arré to ask her why she feared the witchfolk.

But Arré simply said, "What are you standing here for? Have you no work to do?" She flapped a hand in dismissal. Sorren left the room as if her feet had wings. Later, when she was sure that Arré was not annoyed at her, she would ask about the invitation from Marti Hok. She wondered what she should wear.

As she ran through the kitchen, Toli said, "What are you so happy for?"

"Tell you later," she called over her shoulder. She ran to the cottage, to thank Paxe for her intervention.

But the cottage door was emphatically closed.

The weather changed that evening. The wind, whipping out of the south, brought the fog streaming up the city streets in long feathery strings. At sunset, the trees were tossing as they did during the autumn rainstorms. Cold weather put the cook in high spirits; he sang as he worked. Lalith, for reasons of her own, set a place at the table in the big parlor. Sorren lit the chobatas and went to tell Arré that dinner was ready. The cook had outdone himself; he had made turtle eggs and baked shrimp and yellow apples in honey.

Arré stared at the display of dishes. "What's this for?" she said.

"He likes it when it isn't hot," explained Sorren.

She had gone twice more to the cottage, but the door had been closed each time. She watched Arré eat, thinking of Marti Hok. When she brought the final dish from the kitchen, Ricard was standing in the hallway. He had cleaned up; his hair was damp, and he wore clean clothes. Sorren guessed that he had been at the baths. "What do you want?" she said.

"I want to speak to *her*."

"I'll ask." Sorren brought the dessert, a frothy delicacy of cream and sherbet, to Arré's place, and took the cover off.

Arré smiled. "It looks wonderful."

"Ricard is in the hall. He wants to talk to you," Sorren said.

Arré picked up her spoon. "Have him come in," she said.

Sorren beckoned Ricky in. He sidled past her as if he were afraid or ashamed to touch her, and she wondered what Paxe had said to him. He looked chastened. Standing at the foot of the table, he cleared his throat and said, "Thank you for permitting me to disturb you, Lady." It was the first formal speech Sorren had ever heard him make.

Arré ate some sherbet. "You have something to say to me?" she said. "Go on."

He wet his lips. "I have been living in a house on your land, and eating in your kitchens, and living off the money that you pay my mother for her work. The other day I did something very stupid." He glanced at Sorren, and then away. "If I worked for you, and I did—what I did—then you could have me fined, or beaten, or whatever. If I were a child, then I could be punished like a child, by my mother. I can—my mother says I can be a child or I can be a man."

"Which do you want to be?" said Arré.

"Whichever keeps me out of trouble," Ricky said.

"You should have thought of that before," said Arré.

"I know. I didn't think."

"Well? Think now. Which will you be?"

"Is there a choice?" said Ricky. "I want to be a man."

Arré nodded. "Your mother asked you this."

"Yes."

"What did you tell her?"

"What I just told you."

"What did she say?"

Ricky wet his lips again. "She said I should come here, and tell you, and then do whatever you told me to do."

"Very well," said Arré. She brandished her spoon. "I want you to go to the grapefields. You can leave tomorrow. I will write a letter for you to take with you. You will bring it to Myra-no-Ivrénia Med, and you will do as she directs, even if it means working the fields." She paused. Ricard nodded. "Since it's harvest, it probably will. You'll earn a wage, like everyone else, and in six months, if you wish, you will be permitted to leave the fields and return here, and we will see what happens then. Between now and then, I want six months' uncomplaining work from you. Do you understand?"

"Yes, Lady."

"Good. Go say good-bye to your mother." She dipped her spoon into the sherbet. Ricard bowed, and left. The chobata flickered in the draft as the door opened and shut.

"What do you think of that?" said Arré.

Sorren returned to her place by the hearth. "I think it will be good for him to have to work."

Arré scowled. "No doubt." She tapped her spoon on the plate. "But that's not what I meant. Will Paxe be angry at me for sending him away?"

Sorren considered it. It hadn't occurred to her that Paxe might want Ricky to go and still be angry. "I don't think so," she said. "*She* couldn't do it. That's why she sent him to you."

CHAPTER SEVEN

The following morning was chill and fair. Sorren rose early. Before anything else, she reached under her pillow for the piece of paper from Marti Hok. Arré had given it to her the night before, admonishing her not to lose it. Her fingers touched the thick paper and she grinned. It was still there.

She dressed in the clothes nearest to hand, and went to take Arré her hot water. The jug was waiting for her. She filled it from the pipe, and then lugged it up the stairs. Moving as quietly as possible, she brought it into the bedroom, filled Arré's basin, and set the depleted jug beside the table. Arré kicked under her quilt and murmured something, but did not wake.

In the kitchen, Sorren found Lalith chopping fish cakes. "You have to do the shopping today," Sorren said.

"What?" Lalith's braids quivered. "Why?"

"I'm going to Marti Hok's."

"Lady Fancy," jeered Toli. "There's soot on your shirt, are you going like that?"

Sorren made the moon sign at him. "No. Lalli, it's easy. You know the shops; I've showed you. Tell the clerks, and they'll have everything delivered."

"Do I need a money string?" said Lalith.

"No. They can send the bill."

Toli said, "I'll go with you if you're scared to go alone."

Spine stiffening, the thirteen-year-old drew herself up. "I'm not scared. I can go."

Sorren went to the cottage. But it was empty, except for the cat. Thinking that Paxe might be in the Yard, she went to peer through the gate bars. Dis was showing a new guard how to counter a pike thrust. Borti, thumbs in his belt, was rocking on his heels just within the gate.

He came out to talk to her. "Hey, Beanstalk." He winked. "Want a ride?"

Sorren pretended to be insulted. "I'm looking for the Yard-master, and that's not my name, old man."

"Who're you calling an old man?"

"Your mustaches are gray," she said, "and look at you. You're getting fat."

He slapped his paunch. "That's all muscle, girl!"

"Huh." She tried to see around him into the Yard.

"She isn't in there."

"You know where she is?"

"She made rounds early. I think—" he tugged on his mustache—"I think she went to the Gate to say farewell to her son."

So Ricard was really going. "Thank you," Sorren said. She leaned forward and kissed Borti's cheek. "You're a nice man, you know?"

She left him staring after her as if she had turned into a fish. She went through the kitchen, past the parlor. Elith caught her at the foot of the stairs. Her breath stank of garlic. The big parlor had a torn window screen, she said, and the lamps needed more oil.

"I ordered choba oil three days ago," said Sorren. The old woman's mumblings made her impatient. "Tell Toli to fetch it for you from the storeroom."

She dressed in fresh clothes and knocked on Arré's door. "Come in," Arré said. Sorren slipped in. Arré sat on the edge of her bed, putting on her bracelets. "Aha, let me see. Turn round. You look very nice, child."

"Thank you," said Sorren. She glanced about the chamber. "Is there something I can do for you?"

Arré chuckled. "I won't detain you. Have you seen Paxe this morning?"

"She went to the Gate to say good-bye to Ricky."

"Ah. Very well, child, go on." She waved both hands in a shooing motion. Habit made Sorren tug the corners of the coverlet as she passed it. She wanted to say something—do something—she didn't know what. Her feelings were all askew.

She went out the front door just as a boy in an acolyte's robe came through the gate. He looked very self-important. "I have a letter for the Lady Arré Med," he announced, to her and to the courtyard, "from Jerrin-no-Dovria i Elath." Sorren's pulse raced as it always did at the mention of the White Clan.

"Inside," she said, and stepped off the path to let him enter. He strode by her without thanks, as if deference were his due.

This, she thought, was the answer to the letter she had refused to deliver.

The Hok guards appeared to be expecting her.

She had brought the paper with her name on it to show them, but they didn't need it; they waved her up the path as soon as she said her name. She had put on sandals; they clicked on the tiles as she walked to the front door. The Hok house was huge, much larger than the Med house. It was built of silver cedar, and shaped like a U, with a large garden in the open courtyard. Trumpet-vines climbed up trellises and dangled from the peaked roof.

The Hok family lived all together. A girl in a white dress took Sorren to a blue tiled washroom so that she could rinse the dust from her hands and face, and then brought her to the alcove where she could leave her sandals. It was piled with at least a dozen pairs of sandals and shoes.

Marti Hok's chamber was wide and light, with windows all around it to let in the sunshine. Marti sat in the center of it, in a great wooden chair. The arms of the chair were carved like the heads of snakes.

"Come in, child," said the old woman. "Let me look at you." Sorren obeyed. She was glad she had put on clean clothes. "You look charming. Sit." Sorren folded her legs beneath her and sat on the floor. The mats were woven of bright gold straw, and they were very soft and sweet-smelling. A child ran in, and then another. "These are my grandchildren," said Marti proudly. Voices rang through the hallway; a third child ambled in. Sorren wondered how many grandchildren Marti Hok had—six, ten, dozens?

They tramped in and out of the chamber to show their grandmother live frogs, dead newts, sore knees, disagreements, uncertainties, treasures beyond price. The children—adults— looked in, asked an occasional question, said, "Don't annoy your grandmother."

Each time one of the Hok children entered, Sorren, mindful of propriety, went to one knee. A servant came in with bowls of sherbet for Marti and the visitor. Sorren stood, to take both bowls. "Sit!" said Marti Hok. "And stop getting up and down every time one of my daughters walks by. You are my guest, you are just Sorren, and I am just Marti. Get off the floor; sit on a pillow. I am pleased you could come."

Sorren grinned. "I like floors," she said. She let the servant hand her the bowl.

"Then you should sit there. Would you like tea or wine or water?"

"I would like some wine," Sorren said. "Thank you, La— Marti."

Marti told the servant to bring a glass of wine. Sorren spooned sherbet into her mouth. It tasted of raspberries; the flavor broke against her tongue like a bubble bursting. "This is good," she said.

"It is good," said Marti. "What do you think of this house?"

Sorren glanced around. The room smelled lovely; there were flowers in tall vases in every corner. The pillows were silk, stuffed with goosedown. In a wicker cage, hanging from a tall wooden pole, a lucky cricket sat singing. "I like it." Cautiously, remembering her length of leg, she stretched out in the sunlight.

A girl-child with long black hair scooted into the room. "*Abu*, look!" She held out her cupped hands. Marti bent over them.

"Remarkable," she said with conviction. "Where didst thou find it?"

"In the garden."

"Good. Take it outside and let it go. It needs light and air."

"But I want to keep it!" She opened the hands enough for Sorren to see a huge feathery orange butterfly, clinging to her palm.

"Thou cannot, it will die. Let it go, chelito."

The girl pouted. Marti fanned the butterfly's wings. "See chelito. It is growing. It wishes to be free." The orange wings were fluttering, trying to extend. "Let it go. It cannot live like the cricket, in a cage."

The girl sighed. "I want to keep it."

"There are some creatures thou cannot keep."

The girl went from the room, eyes fixed on the drying butterfly. In the next room, someone began to sing. "*Hush-a-bye, sleep my child, nothing fearful, nothing wild, shall disturb thee, take thy rest, here against thy mother's breast. Hush-a-bye, go to sleep. . . .*" The song broke off.

Marti smiled. "That's my youngest daughter, Alanna. She's pregnant."

Sorren said, "How many do you have?"

"Grandchildren? Children? Three sons, four daughters.

Only the Guardian knows how many granddaughters and grandsons; I surely don't keep track. Arré's house is not like this, is it?"

"Oh, no," Sorren said. She spooned up the last of the sherbet, which was melting into a creamy red puddle in the dish. "It's much quieter."

"Too quiet," said Marti Hok. "Arré burns too low. She's like a piece of coal, solitary on a grate. She needs people around her. She needs a lover."

"Arré?" said Sorren. She put the dish beside her. She could not imagine Arré with a lover.

"You think she's too old?" said Marti, amused. Her face crinkled into laughter. "Wait until you're forty, you'll know better."

"No," Sorren protested, "I know—" After all, Paxe was nearly forty. But Paxe was Paxe.

"She should have had children, too," said Marti. "But then, she has you." She stretched out her hand for her cane, and rose. Sorren jumped up. "Come. We will go to the library."

The library of the Hok house reminded Sorren of Arré's study, except that, instead of only one scroll case against the wall, this room was filled with glass-faced cases lined with scrolls. There was a big wooden chair, twin to the one in Marti's chamber, behind an equally massive desk. Marti lowered herself into the chair. She said, waving her hand at the cases, "Have you ever seen so many pieces of paper in one place?"

Sorren shook her head. She eyed the cases, wondering what it would be like to dust them all.

"My grandfather, Mordith, was a Scholar. He collected all these scrolls. He would pay people to bring him old records and histories, the older the better. He used to read to me from them. Samia-no-Reo was his friend. She would come to visit, and they would sit poring over the records, tracing the course of this lord and that lord, happy as children. He never let the servants in here, he cared for everything himself."

"Is he dead?" said Sorren.

Marti laughed. "Quite dead. Were he alive, child, he would be very, very old."

Sorren felt foolish. Bending, she peered through the streaked glass into the case. "Is the story of Sorren in here?"

"Not in that one. Move two more cases down and bring me

the leather binding with the papers in it." Sorren opened the door to the case. Dust flew out. She sneezed.

The leather binding was rusty red, cracked, peeling, old. She carried it to the desk and laid it in front of Marti. The old woman touched the leather with careful hands. "I think this is the right one," she said. She looked up. "Tornor. You know where it is?"

"In the north, in the mountains. It's a Keep."

"You know what a Keep is?"

"A castle."

"You know what a Keep is for?" said the old woman.

Sorren remembered what Kadra had said. *They were built . . . when Arun was at war with Anhard-over-Mountain.* "For war," she said.

"What do you know of war?" said Marti Hok.

"Nothing," said Sorren, but she remembered stories she had heard around the campfires. "A little. My mother told me some, about a time when we fought the Asech folk. They came from the desert, burning and killing. . . ." She shivered, remembering the firelight flickering off the faces of the old women in the fields, and their hard knobby hands moving in time to their words.

"I was told the same stories," said Marti Hok softly. "My grandfather remembered it. He used to tell me tales of villages and fields aflame, and riders galloping out of the desert. . . . I had nightmares about my room burning, and me burning up with it, and I wept into my pillow, until my grandmother found me and made him stop the stories, and told me that the witches in the Tanjo had made peace with the Asech for all time, and that they would never let the city burn."

For a moment, Sorren saw in Marti Hok's face the little girl she had been, sixty years before. "Did you live in this house?" she said.

"This very house. Well. That time is gone, and will never come again, Guardian willing. I pray that war will ever be something you have no knowledge of. There is a time in our history that is called 'the war years.' At least, my grandfather taught me, that is how they name them in the north. The Keeps were built a long time ago, to protect the folk who lived on the steppe from the plundering of the Anhard raiders. We used to fight with Anhard the way we fought the Asech. But that war was over two hundred and fifty years ago."

"We trade with Anhard now," Sorren said. She touched her arm. "In the fields, they used to tease my mother, saying that I might have Anhard blood."

"You might. They are fair, sometimes. But their skin is yellower than yours."

"My mother always said no, it wasn't so."

"Then it must not have been. Well—these records are from Tornor. Even two hundred and fifty years ago the Black Clan existed, and northern scholars kept records of the battles. My grandfather collected some of them."

She opened the leather binder. Sorren leaned over the table. For some reason, she had thought the records would have pictures in them, of women with swords, horsemen, castles, strange beasts, like the painted pictures on her Cards. She was disappointed: the yellow, brittle pages held no pictures, just long lines of writing going up and down the page. The ink was faded to gray.

"Can you read them?" she asked.

"Not those," said Marti. She laid those pages aside. "But these I can." Here the ink was clearer and the characters went from right to left across the page, the way they were supposed to. Reaching out, Sorren traced a piece of curling script with her finger, very lightly. Dust filmed her fingertip, and a tiny scrap of paper cracked beneath her touch and fell, like a petal, to the floor.

"This is the story of Sorren," said Marti. She pointed to a block of writing. "This is the name: Sorren." Sorren stared at her own name. "Here it appears again. Sorren. Sorren."

"Tell me the story."

Marti bent over the page. "I'll read it," she said.

"*This is a tale of courage and high adventure, having been copied by Elin, scribe to Berent, 22nd Lord of Tornor Keep, in the Council Year 89, in the third month of winter, the seventh year of the Lord Berent's reign.*" She stopped. "That year, the year 89, is the year the Tanjo upheld the Ban in Kendra-on-the-Delta."

"Oh," said Sorren.

"*This is being copied from a copy made in the year 32 by Josen, scribe to Morven, 19th Lord of Tornor Keep.* She goes on to explain that the older record, which appears to have been copies from the original, had been damaged by fire. *And it came to pass*—she likes that kind of language—*that in the twenty-fourth year of the reign of the Lord Athor, a warlord rose out of the southern villages, out of the village of Iste near the city of Tezera, and his name was Col, known as Col Istor. Out of his pride and without thought for the peoples of the land, this evil man gathered to him an army of malcontents and evildoers, and set out to make himself and his followers wealthy and great.* I am not going to read it, it will take all day. It seems that Col Istor gathered an army from around Lake Aruna, and led them north to make war on the Keeps."

"Was this during the war years?" Sorren asked.

"No, that time was past. Arun and Anhard were at peace."

"Then why did Col I-I—"

"Istor."

"—Col Istor want to fight?"

"It doesn't say," said Marti. "He was trained to war, he had fought the Asech in the south. Probably he was bored. He captured three of the four Keeps. In Tornor Keep, Athor had a daughter, Sorren, and a son, Errel. These two were made prisoner by Col Istor. They escaped—in winter. The story makes much of that, that it was winter. *The snow drifts that season were of the height of a tall man, and the steel so cold that it froze the fingers to it, so that a man might grasp a sword hilt and come away without his skin.* Ugh. They went south and west, and the story goes on to say that they came to the land of always summer, the magical valley, Vanima."

Sorren started. "It says that?"

"Yes." Marti read. "*It came to pass that as they drew near to Vanima, the mountains slid aside to permit them entrance, and closed behind them. Thus was the magical valley defended.*"

It did not sound real. Probably it wasn't real. "What else does it say?"

"It says that Errel and Sorren approached Van, its ruler, and asked for help. He told them he would help them against Col Istor, but that they would then have to pay a price."

"What was it?"

"He wouldn't tell them."

Sorren said, "That isn't fair!"

"No," said Marti, "but it's very likely. Shall I continue?"

"Yes, please."

"They agreed, so he gathered his chearis and they traveled north to Tornor Keep. They stormed the castle and killed Col

Istor and all his men. Then Van asked for payment." Marti
paused to turn a page. "His price for his help was that one of
Athor's children had to come and live in the land of always
summer, and never leave it. So the two children of Athor
fought, to see which one of them would stay and which one
would return to Vanima with Van and his chearis. Errel lost.
Sorren became the Lady of Tornor Keep, and her daughter
ruled Tornor after her, and hers after her. *And so it came to
pass that the line of Tornor Keep has continued even to this
day."*

*...Even to this day....Sorren sighed with pleasure. Kité
had never told her that story. Probably she had not known it.
She wondered what it would have been like, to fight a brother.
Surely they would not have wanted to hurt each other.*

"Did they look alike?" she asked.

"Sorren and Errel? It doesn't say," said Marti. "Of Sorren
it says,*Her hair was pale as northern grass, and her eyes were
blue as the sky in winter*. Errel it doesn't describe at all. Oh,
it also says that Sorren was tall." The old woman smiled. "If
you like, you may imagine that she looked like you."

Sorren nodded. "You said I had a northern look."

"You do," said Marti. "Many of the northern folk are pale
and light-eyed. Did you enjoy the story?"

"Yes, thank you." Sorren wondered if her mother had heard
the story sometime, perhaps when *she* was a child, and, remembering, chose to name her daughter after the northern
warrior woman. "Could I hear more?"

Marti said, "Chea, girl, there are a half a hundred of them!"
She shuffled the pages back into their original order. "Besides,
child, the past is a trap, and you are too young to be caught
by it. Wait until you are old and ugly and it is all you have
left."

Sorren did not know what Marti meant. "I don't think you're
ugly," she said.

The old woman laughed. "I thank you." She closed the red
binder. "Put this back."

Sorren lifted the flaking leather case in her arms. A piece
of paper slipped from the pages and fluttered to the floor.

"Wait," said Marti. She nudged the scrap with her cane.
"What's that?" Laying the binder back on the desk, Sorren
picked up the paper. It had pictures on it. They were cramped
ink drawings with borders around them, and writing underneath.

them. The pictures looked familiar, like something she had seen before.

"What is it?" Marti said, leaning forward.

"It fell out of the pages." Sorren turned it over. There were more pictures on the back.

"Let me see," commanded Marti. She took the paper delicately from Sorren's hand. *"The Dreamer,"* she read. *"A woman sleeping. A window overlooks her couch: through it we see two bright red stars. The Weaver is a woman in a green dress, seated at a loom. The Lady is a golden-haired woman, standing outdoors. She is smiling.* What is this?"

Sorren said, "It's the Cards."

"What are you talking about?"

Sorren took the paper back. "The Lady. The Dreamer. This one is the Dancer."

"Let me see—" They bent over the page together. "Yes. You cannot read, child, how do you know the name?"

"My mother gave them to me. There are twenty-two of them. This big." She made a rectangle with her hands to show the size. "They have pictures like this, only with colors, and more in the pictures. The Lady has a dog beside her."

Marti counted. "There are eight Cards pictured here. This is what you called them, Cards? Where are the rest?" She pulled the binder across the desk. "They must be here."

She opened the binder, and began to lift the pages from one pile to another. Sorren pounced on a second piece of paper. "This has eight more," she said. Marti continued to lift the pages, and a third paper appeared. "This has the rest." She recognized the pictures, crabbed and strange though they seemed. "The Tower, the Wheel, the Demon, Old Boney, Moon Lady, the Village."

"Let me see." Marti peered at the pictures. "They have names, child. This one that you call Old Boney is Death. The one you call Moon Lady is the Moon, and the one you call the Village is the Sun."

Sorren said, "My mother never told me what to call them."

Marti leaned back in the chair. Her soft brown cheeks had darkened. "Do you know what you must have?" she said. "According to this paper," she said, tapping, "someone who is trained to it can tell the future with your Cards. You say your mother left them to you?"

"Yes."

"I wonder—" Marti laughed. "It must be so."

"What must be so?"

Marti touched the paper. "Once, those Cards were in the keeping of the ruling house of Tornor."

Sorren swallowed. She gazed at the pictures again. "They can't have been," she said. "My Cards are newer than those drawings."

"Hmm." Marti frowned. "Do your Cards have a pattern on the back?"

"No."

"Ah. It says here, the pattern on the back of the Cards was a red star on a white field. The badge of Tornor is a red, eight-pointed star on a white field. You must have a copy of the original deck." Her face creased with amusement. "I wonder how your family got them. Could your mother use them?"

"I don't know," Sorren said. "She died."

"Perhaps," Marti said, "perhaps she could. Perhaps you have a right to your name. Perhaps, scores of years back, your family, your mother's line, was part of the ruling house of Tornor."

Sorren blinked. She did not know whether to laugh or weep. "My family?"

"Yes. Certainly. Such things are not given away." Marti laughed. "Shall I tell you something else? The ruling house of Tornor was originally started by a rebellious scion of the Med house. You could be a distant, very, very, distant relative of Arré!"

Sorren wanted to pinch herself to make sure she was not asleep. She was really a northerner, born in the south but with the blood of the north running in her veins. She was even— no. She caught herself. She was no princess. She was a bond-servant whose great-great-great-many times-great-grandmother might have been the younger sister of a noble house. "I wish I knew," she said.

Marti Hok's face grew somber. "Don't let me confuse you," she said gently. "It's only a fantasy, child."

From the corridor a voice called, "Mother?" A woman poked her head into the room. She was young, and very pregnant. "What on earth are you doing *here*?" she asked.

"What concern is that of yours?" said Marti. "I'm busy. Is it important? If not, go away and leave us alone."

"Whoops!" said the woman, and vanished. Marti laughed. Sorren held the pictures. She had told herself it was only a story, about a dead princess. But now she felt as if the Lady of Tornor had reached out a dead hand and touched her, over centuries and centuries. . . . Perhaps she had had the Cards, once, touched them, dealt them, used them to see into the future. Did she see me? she thought. "Does Tornor have a tower?"

"A tower?" said Marti Hok, but she did not ask why. She drew the binder to her once again. "A tower. Tornor *had* a tower. Elin the scribe speaks of it, giving the date it was built. *It looks north*, she says, *and has looked ever northward since its building, so that the many rulers of Tornor might have a place to stand to direct the battle against the Anhard raiders*— one cannot direct a battle from a tower, but how would she know that? Silly woman."

"Do the other Keeps have towers?"

"No."

It *was* Tornor she had seen, Tornor she had traveled to in her far-seeing. Blood beat in her head, and the tower of the Keep, far away, rose again in her gaze.

Marti Hok said, "Sorren?"

Sorren swallowed. The image vanished. "Yes. I'm sorry, La-Marti. I was dreaming."

"Have I given you pleasure with my stories?"

"Oh, yes."

"That is well. You might do something for me, then, in exchange."

"Of course," said Sorren.

Marti took the pieces of paper out of her hands. "I should like to see those Cards."

Sorren was silent. She could go to the house, get them, bring them back—but if she returned to the house on the hill, she would turn from Sorren the guest into Sorren the bond-servant. Arré would find her an errand, Cook would find her an errand, there would be dinner to serve, laundry to wash, tasks to do.

Marti said softly, "Never mind, child."

Sorren said, looking at the old woman, "But I want to."

"When you can, you will. No, leave those—" as Sorren started to return the papers to the binder. "Someone else will do it. It seems I was right in naming you a northerner. Tell me, have you thought of going north when your time of service is over?"

Sorren thought of Kadra, and her visions. "Yes."

"You would go now, if you could," said Marti. "I see it in your eyes; don't trouble to deny it." She groped for her cane, and Sorren put it in her hand. "It's just as well you cannot leave now. You have a lover, I think? Yes, I remember, the Yardmaster. She cares for you. So does Arré, and you for her, a little, and that is important; she needs people about her who love her. You know her brother?"

The abrupt question confused Sorren. "Yes," she said. "I drum for him."

"He is an evil man," said Marti Hok. "I am old enough to know evil when I see it."

Sorren did not think that Isak was evil. Malicious, perhaps, even cruel, but not evil.

"You don't believe me?" said Marti. "Well, we shall see." She set her cane firmly on the floor, and stood. "Meanwhile, you may practice patience by being cordial to an old lady for a while longer. Do you like flowers? Good. Come and walk with me in my garden."

CHAPTER EIGHT

"*Ha-ha-ha-ha-tay-ha-ha-ha* . . ." Strings of song echoed through the alleys. Paxe strolled through sunlight on her way to the Northwest Gate. It was the Festival of the Ox, an Asech feast. It went on for three days, while interesting smells floated from the Asech houses, and the women chanted in tones that went higher and higher before slurring into laughter. Men played music on reed flutes, and children ran about with clappers carved in the shape of oxen. It was the most important Asech feast, next to the Festival of the Horse, which was celebrated in the spring, after the sowing. Paxe found herself pacing in time to the strange music. A clear voice rose in song from a house and she saw a girl's frame silhouetted against a screen. "*Ya-ha-ha-ha-tay* . . ." It made her think of Sorren.

She had not seen Sorren—except for the casual greetings she could not avoid—for four days. She wasn't angry with the girl, nor did she blame her for what her own fool son had done—but she just did not want to see her, for a while. The last four afternoons Sorren had come to sit patiently on the Yard fence, and Paxe had stayed with her soldiers, pretending not to notice the lithe golden figure perched on the wood.

Arré had noticed, and had said bluntly, yesterday morning, "Sorren's unhappy. I suppose you know that."

"I know."

"Are you going to do something about it?" Arré said.

"When I'm ready." It sounded cruel. Arré shrugged.

"I think you're being foolish," she said, and that was the end of it. Paxe hadn't meant to be cruel, but whenever she looked at Sorren, something held her back from stretching out her hand. She hoped that no one, besides Arré, had noticed.

Traffic at the Gate was slow; there was a line of carts waiting to come in. Paxe wondered what was holding up traffic. She looked around for the captain on duty. His name was Sereth; he was city-born.

"Where's Sereth?" she called to one of the other guards.

"Round the guardhouse!" called the guard.

"Yardmaster!" Paxe turned, to find Sereth waving at her from the side of the tall guardhouse wall. She waved back and worked her way across the cobblestoned street to him.

His thick, sandy hair was standing straight out from his head. "I have something to show you." She followed him around the guardhouse to the small weapons shed in which the Gate guards kept their pikes and slings. He knelt beside a box and threw the lid open. "Look!"

Paxe knelt. The stamp on the outside of the box said it contained wool. She looked inside. There was a bolt of orange wool within the box, and something bright sticking out between the wool's soft folds. She reached in, feeling carefully along the fabric. Sereth grew impatient. Leaning over her shoulder, he pulled the wool back. The orange cloth concealed one—no, two, no, more than two—sheathed weapons. Swords.

Sereth hunkered down beside her. "There are seven knives and ten swords in that box. Vanesi the merchant brought them. She swears she had no idea they were there. She's in the guardhouse; we held her, thinking you might want to talk to her."

He was slightly breathless—with excitement, Paxe guessed. She wondered if he had ever seen a sword before. "Did you find other weapons amid her goods?"

"None. We took the caravan apart."

"Have you found any other weapons at all?"

"Not yet. We're double-checking all weapons, especially the ones from the north."

Paxe turned the first sword in her hands. It was bright and shiny, without stains or nicks or rust. "When was the last time someone tried to smuggle edged weapons into the city?" she said.

"Three years ago," said Sereth promptly. "Ben-no-Shana brought two swords in through the West Gate. He had his right hand cut off."

Paxe rose, letting the sword fall back in the box. "I had forgotten his name," she said. "You have a good memory, Sereth." Sereth flushed with pleasure. "Bring me Vanesi."

The captain hurried off. He brought Vanesi from the guardhouse himself. The merchant strode from the building. Her red hair was curled in Tezeran fashion. She was wearing yellow silks and high-topped boots of brown leather. She saw Paxe and hastened toward her, outstripping Sereth. "Yardmaster Paxe!" She thrust her hands forward. "I assure you, I know nothing about weapons hidden in my wool."

"When did you first learn of it?" Paxe said.

"When your guards opened the box and found them. I am appalled by this, of course."

Paxe looked the merchant up and down. "Who could put weapons into your goods without you knowing, Vanesi?"

The woman sighed, and put both hands on her ample hips. "Anybody with a purse. Few of my folk are unbribable. There's petty pilfering on every journey, but this is the first time I have had someone put things into the boxes instead of taking them out. Yardmaster, you know me, I have been coming through this Gate for six years. I am a trader; why would I bring weapons into the city, risking fine, or banishment, or worse?"

Paxe scratched her chin. Someone outside the Gate was wrangling with a guard about the length of time entrance was taking, and Sereth hurried off to keep order.

"Vanesi, I do know you," she said. "I'd like to believe you. Who's your caravan master?"

"Leth-no-Chayatha. He stays on Amber Street in the Minto district."

"I will see that he is questioned. The wool and the box it came in is yours, I suppose."

Vanesi scowled. "Unfortunately, I cannot deny it. My stamp is on the outside of the box."

"You know the law," Paxe said. "I must report this."

"I know," said Vanesi. "I expect to be summoned by my Clan. But may I go now? I live on Third Fountain Street, you know where it is."

Third Fountain Street was also in the Minto district. "If you're needed—"

"I will be reachable," the merchant promised.

"You may go, then," Paxe said. "I am sorry you were detained."

The fat merchant shrugged. "I've had worse treatment." She marched away. Sereth came from the Gate; Paxe saw him gaze after Vanesi's retreating bulk.

"I don't think we need to hold her," she said. "Send someone to Amber Street to question Leth-no-Chayatha, the caravan master. In fact—you do it."

"Gladly." Sereth jerked his thumb at the Gate. "Do you want us to keep searching the caravans?"

"Yes, of course."

"It slows the line."

"Let it."

Sereth bowed, palms together. "Yardmaster." He went off to inform his guards. Paxe felt momentarily sorry for the people at the end of the line who might have to camp outside the walls when the Gates closed at sunset, but there was nothing else she could do. The shouts from the caravans had lessened; already the news was filtering beyond the city wall.

She cut short her rounds to return to the house; Arré would want to know this. As she reached the top of the hill, a voice hailed her. "Yardmaster!" She turned. It was Ivor, commander of the late watch. He was as dark as she, with a natty little beard and mustache of which he was quite proud. "Vain as a peacock," his guards said; but they liked him, especially because he could beat them all at dice. He was a very good watch commander.

She waited for him to come to her, debating whether she should tell him about the smuggled swords, or wait until she had told Arré. She decided to wait. Ivor came up to her, dark face lined with anger and worry. "Yardmaster, I've lost a man."

"What do you mean? Who?"

"Seth," said Ivor. "He's deserted."

Paxe scowled. "Are you sure?"

"He's definitely gone. No one's seen him since yesterday, and he didn't report for muster."

Seth had been in Ivor's command for two seasons. "Where do you think he's gone?" she said.

Ivor said, "He's a country boy. He might have gotten tired of shining pikes, and gone back to his village."

"Yes," said Paxe, doubtfully. "Do you think he did?"

Ivor put his hands on his hips. "Actually, I doubt it. I never heard him speak of the country with anything but contempt. He likes the city too much to leave it. I'd bet he's still inside."

Paxe rubbed her nose. A fly buzzed at her, and she batted it absently. She couldn't remember the last time she'd had a deserter. "Did he say anything to anyone?"

Ivor said, "He's been mouthing off since you set him on cleaning duty. But no, he said nothing to anyone about leaving."

Once out of her district it would be easy for him to evade capture, but it would not be so easy for him to find work. He'd end up in a laborer's job. "Send a notice to all the Yards and to the magistrates, Seth-no—"

"Lenia," supplied Ivor.

"Seth-no-Lenia, deserted from his duty and his post, please notify the Yardmaster of the Med house if seen, reward will be paid for information leading to capture, blah, blah. Damn the man, why did he run? I would have released him. I've never kept a guard who didn't want to stay."

"There's more," said Ivor grimly. "As far as I can tell, he walked off with the extra key to the weapons shed."

"Oh, damn," said Paxe. "How the hell did he get it?"

Ivor looked wretched. "I gave it to him. He didn't return it."

It was clear she did not need to point out to him the foolishness of that act. After a moment, she said, "We'll have to get the lock changed. Find a locksmith, and put a guard at the shed—all we need is someone coming in and stealing half our equipment. Tell Kaleb to do the same."

She went into the house. "Arré," she called, not troubling to be ceremonial.

Elith stuck her head through the doors of the large parlor and glared at her. "The Lady Arré is in her study," she said.

Arré was sitting in her cushioned chair. "What brings you into the house with such a noise?" she said.

Paxe sat on the stool. "Listen," she said, and proceeded to tell Arré about the smuggled swords.

Arré clasped her hands in her lap and bent her head, concentrating. When Paxe finished her recital, she said, "What order did you give your Gate captain?"

"I told him to search all the caravans as they arrive, without exception."

"That's good. Do you trust Vanesi? Do you think she told you the truth?"

Paxe rubbed her nose. "I think so," she said. "But if you want to be sure, you can always call a Truthfinder."

Arré's hands unclasped. "I will tell the Tanjo about this myself," she said. "But I don't want to bring in a Truthfinder if I can help it. Paxe, pass the word to the other Yardmasters that swords are being smuggled into the city through the Gates. Ask them to take the same precautions you are taking."

Paxe nodded. "Who do you think is bringing in the swords?" she said.

Arré said, "Were they new swords or old swords?"

"New," said Paxe, wondering what difference it made.

"Ah," said Arré. "Then I can guess who's bringing them in. The Ismeninas."

"How do you know?"

Arré held up one finger. "One. The Ismenin Yard is teaching sword techniques. Two. The Ismeninas own land to the west in which there are great iron deposits. Three. The Ismeninas own foundries and smithies in which new swords could be made. Four." Four fingers waved in the air. "The sword your soldier had came from an Ismenin soldier."

Paxe frowned. "Why did you ask if they were new or old swords? What did it tell you?"

Arré said, "Because if they had been old swords, it's conceivable that someone else could be bringing them in. But only the Ismeninas would be bringing in new ones."

"The first sword was an old one."

"The Ismeninas must have brought some old swords from the north, to use as pattern for their smiths."

It sounded reasonable. Paxe could only think of one objection. "Dobrin said that possession of live blades was forbidden to his soldiers."

Arré said, gently, "He would say that anyway, Paxe. He must have been terrified that you would go straight to the Tanjo."

"No," said Paxe. "He wasn't terrified. And he wouldn't lie to me. He is not that sort of man."

"Wouldn't he?" said Arré. "I don't know; I don't know him."

The cadence count ("One—and two—and three—and four!") echoed for a moment in Paxe's mind. She said, "The swords must be coming in through all the Gates, not just one."

"I will write letters to the heads of all the houses, and to the Blue Clan as well, informing them of this," said Arré. "If I am right—and I think I am—the Ismeninas will be bringing the swords in on the river, on the barges and ore boats. They own the ore boats, after all."

"The Hok guards are supposed to keep an eye on the boats."

"And do they?" said Arré.

"They tend to let the Ismenin guards do most of the work."

"The Hok guards can do their share of work, for a change. And even Dobrin—ai, I'm sorry, Paxe, forget I said that— even the Ismeninas will have to order their river guards to search the barges. Is there any talk in the city about the training in the Ismenin Yard?"

"I've heard none," said Paxe. "Dobrin told all his guards to say nothing." She leaned forward. "Arré, why do the Ismeninas want swords in the city? What are they going to *do*?"

Arré said, "If I knew, I would tell you. I don't know. Shall I go to Ron Ismenin and ask him? He won't tell me." She leaned her head against the chair back; the skin at the hollow of her throat flashed, startlingly white.

The sound of a flute came faintly into the room from outside. Over its notes, Paxe said, "Why did you tell me to order sejis, and teach the sword?"

"Because," said Arré, "it gives the Ismeninas tremendous power in the city if their guards are the only ones in the city trained in sword technique."

The flute sound changed, as the flute player found a song she could play. Paxe cocked her head to one side to listen. *I am a stranger in an outland country; I am an exile wherever I go. . . .*

She said, "In the west, they say that song was sung by the chearis as they left the cities."

Arré rubbed her eyes. "It's older than that." She looked very tired.

Paxe said, "When are you going to the Tanjo?"

"In four days."

"That's the last day of summer."

"So it is." She half smiled. "I hate the summer heat, but I always miss the season when it ends. Isn't that silly?"

"No," said Paxe, "it's not silly." She rested her hand on Arré's for a moment. It seemed strange to her, sometimes, that they had both grown into people with so many responsibilities, so much to concern and trouble them. She smiled, recalling other summers when they had worried less. They had walked in the gardens of the country house—the trees and hedges had been smaller then—and there had been no children to fight about (Ricard was a baby), no Isak to disturb Arré's sleep (he was in Shanan, earning the shariza), no swords, no smugglers—and no Sorren.

Sorren was going to Kadra's.

The smells of *kadashi* and *pitof*, the spicy Asech breads, permeated the streets. Sorren squinted into the sunlight. She liked the Asech festivals; she liked the way they alternated with the city feasts: Winter Feast, the Spring Festival, the Feast of the Horse, the Feast of the Founding of the City, Midsummer

Festival, the Festival of the Ox, Harvest Feast, and so on. "*Ya-ha-ta-ha-tay*," sang a woman, and Sorren tapped her fingers on her thighs, drumming in and under and around the beat.

The only thing troubling her now was Paxe. Since Ricky's leaving, Paxe had grown silent and withdrawn from her. It hurt. She hoped it would be over soon. She had even asked the Yardmaster if Paxe was angry with her, and Paxe had said no. But she had not seemed to notice Sorren for the last four days when Sorren perched in her usual place on the Yard fence.

Plum Street was in the Batto district, in the northwest corner of the city, where the roads led inward from the Asech country. It was not a prosperous street: tiles dangled from the roofs, and the cottages were old, narrow, and unkempt. Sorren wondered how she would find Kadra's house. This was an Asech enclave, the smells alone told her, and many of the lintels sported the ox-sign in token of the festival.

A little girl wandered into the road. She was carrying two blocks of wood. Singing tunelessly, she banged them together. Sorren called to her. "Chelito," she said, "dost thou know where lives Kadra the messenger?"

The child cocked her head at the tall stranger; gold hoops bobbed in her small brown earlobes as she nodded.

"Wilt thou show me?"

Again the rings bobbed.

The cottages at the far end of the alley were set back from the road, and between the houses and the streets sat patchy gardens. Some of them had heavenweed plants mixed in with the other herbs. The Asech child stopped in front of a house. "*Bé*," she said, meaning "There." There was no ox-sign on the lintel, and no music coming from inside.

"Kadra lives here?" said Sorren.

"*Dosh*." That meant yes. Sorren squared her shoulders. She walked up to the cottage door. The Asech girl watched her. She knocked. No one came to the door. She knocked again.

"Bé!" called the girl. Sorren glanced back at her; she was pointing to a dirt path that went around the west side of the house, between it and the wall of the next cottage. Puzzled but willing, Sorren started around the side of the house. Halfway there, she remembered the girl and turned back to thank her, but the roadway was empty, and the child had disappeared.

Behind the house, there was bare ground, and a wooden hutch with a peaked roof. It smelled of goat, and something else. If there had been a goat in it, Sorren decided, it had long since eaten its way into someone else's garden. The something else—she went closer to the hutch. There was a leather bottle on the ground beside the hutch. "Kadra?" she said.

"Ya," said Kadra's voice. Sorren went to the hutch. The ghya was sitting inside it, holding another bottle. She looked drunk.

The smells of goat and wine made Sorren's stomach lurch. "You're drunk," she said.

"Ya."

"You were going to help me. You said so. How can you help me when you're drunk?" Disappointment and anger made Sorren's voice sharp. She turned to leave.

"Damn it, girl, come back here," said the ghya. She rose from the hutch and stood swaying. She knuckled her eyes. "I thought you wouldn't come."

"I keep *my* promises," Sorren said.

"Snippy, aren't you?" said Kadra. She folded back onto the ground. "Come here. I have something for you."

Reluctantly, Sorren went to her. The ghya picked a scroll from the filthy ground and handed it to her. She unrolled it gingerly. It showed a collection of lines with little marks beside them. "What is it?" she said.

"Guardian, girl, it's a map!" said the ghya. "I made it." Sorren caught her breath. Kadra leaned close to her. "That's Kendra-on-the-Delta." She pointed to a circle on the bottom portion of the map. "I put the 'K' rune on it, that's the symbol on the bones, look at the ones on your string, you'll see." Her finger moved up the scroll. "This line is the river. This is Lake Aruna. Tezera is here, with the fish symbol next to it." She pointed to each place as she named it. The flat squiggles looked like a child's drawing.

At the top of the map were little humps. Sorren pointed to them. "What are those?"

"Mountains," said Kadra. "The Gray Hills, where the Keeps are."

Mountains, thought Sorren. Her fingers crooked as she leaned over the map. She imagined herself a bird, flying over Arun, the way she flew over the steppe in her dreams. This map could teach her every road, every bend, every curve of the river. She traced the line flowing north. "How do I go there?" she said.

The ghya plucked a straw from the hutch. Gently she

touched it to the paper. "Here is the city, where we are. The road follows the river, so. To get to the Keeps one must ride to Tezera and then go northeast, to Zilia Keep, or northwest, to the others. Have you decided which Keep you're traveling to?"

"Tornor," Sorren said.

"That's here." Kadra brushed the straw to the page. "The road goes north beside this river, the Rurian. When will you go? I'll mark the route for you with the villages' names."

"Next summer," Sorren said.

"Fall would be better," said the ghya. "It's hard to cross Galbareth in summer. The heat drains life. In fall the air is cooler, and the roads are not so dusty. The only problem then is to get to the north before it rains."

"What happens then?" asked Sorren.

"The steppe, the roads, everything turns to mud. The horses hate it."

Sorren had not thought about horses. "I can't ride."

"Then you'll walk," said Kadra, "and it will take you even longer. If you have a little money, the traders might agree to let you ride in a wagon as far as Tezera."

Sorren swallowed. Kadra's words were building unpleasant pictures, of heat, and muddy roads, and strangers who might not be friendly. "How long will it take?"

"On foot the whole way? Two months, at least. If you ride with the caravans to Tezera, less. Say, two weeks to Tezera and another ten days from Tezera to Tornor. That's how long it would take *you*. A messenger, even on foot, could do it in less."

It was a long time. Sorren bit her lip.

"Having second thoughts?" said Kadra.

Sorren wanted to say, No, of course not. But it was silly to pretend to be stronger than she was. "Yes."

"Good," said the ghya. "You should be." Deftly she rolled and tied the map.

"I still want to go," said Sorren.

"Do you." Kadra's voice got that curiously flat tone. "Then you ought to think about having one of these." She reached under her cloak, and with a motion that sent Sorren jumping back, drew her knife.

Knives could not be wholly banned from within the city gates; they were too useful. So the Council had enacted statutes spelling out exactly how long and wide the knives could be, and who could carry them, and where. Messengers were permitted to carry knives in the city, but they had to be within the legal limits. Kadra's knife was small and very thin. "It's single-edged," said the ghya. She showed Sorren the hilt, which was metal inlaid with bone. The blade curved backward, and there was a mark scratched on it near the point which looked a little like a stylized horse's head.

Sorren said, "It looks sharp."

"It is," said the ghya. "It's for stabbing, not slicing. I can get you one like it."

"No," Sorren said at once. "No. I don't want it." The rules against bondservants carrying even legal weapons were severe. "No."

"You'll need something," Kadra said.

"No." The whole talk of weapons made her tense. "I don't want anything."

"We'll see," said Kadra. She tapped the map. "You want me to keep this? I'll mark it for you."

"Would you?"

"Isn't that what you want? Come back next week. I warn you, I'll be drunk as a pig and you'll have to rouse me again."

"Why?" said Sorren.

The ghya said bleakly, "As you once said to me—none of your concern."

She rose. She was not quite steady. She stank, she was dirty, her face was mottled yellow where the bruises from the fight she'd been in were taking a long time to heal—Sorren stood. "Will they take you on the ship if you're drunk?" she said.

Kadra hit her.

The blow knocked her sideways, almost throwing her on top of the map. She caught her balance with both hands on the ground and scrambled out of reach. Kadra stood in the center of the path, staring at Sorren, her eyes stony, lips pulled back in rage from her teeth.

After a moment, her knotted hands relaxed. "I told you," she said, "to watch your tongue."

Face burning, from shame and from the blow, Sorren said, "I'm sorry."

Kadra stepped from the path. "Get out."

Numbly Sorren went by her to the street. She hadn't expected Kadra to hit her; she hadn't known the ghya could move that fast. She didn't know why she had said what she had. Stupid, she told herself. You are stupid. Every time you speak to Kadra you end up saying something wrong!

Furious with herself, close to tears, she hastened toward the Med district. Part way there, she stopped to wash her face at the public well. The old men who sat about the well gossiping moved aside politely so that she could work the pump. The cool water felt delicious against her hot skin.

"So, my lord," said a wonderful voice at her elbow, "how went your courier's meeting at Nuath?"

It was the name—Nuath—that made Sorren turn. Water dripped from her eyelashes as she glanced to see who was speaking. White flashed in her eyes; she caught her breath, and realized that a witch was gazing directly at her.

"The man's as stubborn as a mule!" said a male voice, answering. Sorren knew that voice well; she had heard it not so long ago in the Med parlor. The witch woman's companion was Kim Batto.

She bowed, palm to palm. She had never been this close to a witch before. "What lovely hair you have, child," said the witch. She had a remarkable voice, low and musical and as enticing as honey. "You've been crying, have you not? Are you troubled? May I help?"

She was beautiful. Her dark hair fell around her gown like a black river through a field of daisies. Sorren tried to speak calmly. "I'm fine, *damisen*. I had a quarrel with a friend."

Kim Batto coughed. "I know this girl, *lehi*. She's the northern girl, bound to the Med house. Don't concern yourself; it's probably nothing."

"Pain is never nothing, my lord."

"She's not hurt! You can look at her and see that. What's the matter, Sorren?" he said in a loud voice, as if he were addressing a dog or a cow.

Sorren touched a knee to the earth, and stood. "My lord, I'm going home. I was shopping."

"There," said Kim Batto triumphantly.

The Healer ignored him. "She is afraid," she said. "I believe she is afraid of me." She stretched out one hand. "Child, you needn't fear me. I am vowed to the chea, to harmony." Her voice was seductive.

"Lehi, it's trivial!" said Kim Batto. He laid his hand on the witch's shoulder.

She whirled from beneath his grip. "My lord, I did not give you permission to touch me," she said, clearly enough so that the old men around the well heard, and tittered. Kim Batto went scarlet. "Nor did I ask for your help." She turned to Sorren again. "You called me 'damisen'; that is a word of the old tongue. Where did you learn it, child?"

Sorren said hesitantly, "I was a picker, lehi. I learned it in the fields."

"You were a picker? Then why do I feel—" the witch broke off. Suddenly, Sorren felt—sensed—knew a touch, a presence, soft as spider web, strong as sunlight, inescapable as her own heartbeat. Her senses seemed to dim, and then flame more brightly. The wind struck her face; she smelled the scents of leather, sandalwood, linen, water. Unable to move, she endured the witch's entrance into the sanctuary of her skull.

The contact lasted for an instant, and then vanished. Released, Sorren cried out. Awkward as an infant, she bounced into Kim Batto, who swore. Catching her balance, she fled like a criminal from the scene of a crime, ducking through the mélange of shoppers, merchants, children, oxen and goats. At last, sobbing for breath, she reached the Med house. The gate guard stared at her in astonishment. "What's after you?"

She did not have the words to tell him.

"Go to hell!" She slammed through the gate before he could touch it. Paxe was in the Yard, she could hear her talking, giving instructions. It sounded as if she were teaching pike drill. Sorren started toward the cottage, and then halted. Paxe had not looked at her for four days. If she went to the cottage, Paxe might be angry. She could not bear that. If she went to the house, Arré might see her and want to know what was wrong, and then what would she say? Panting for breath, she stumbled into the garden and sat on the lawn.

Borti found her. As if she weighed nothing, he picked her up and took her around the back of the house, near the laundry. "Here." He put a piece of fruit into her hands. "Eat." She bit into it. The sweet juice made her gasp, it tasted so fine.

"How—"

"Ruath told me." Ruath was the gate guard. "Said you looked as if a demon was chasing you."

"Oh."

"I told him I doubted that. But I thought I'd come and find you." His deep voice grumbled on, like a lullaby. "You know you don't have to tell me anything, we're friends, right? But if you were running, you'd be hungry, so I brought some food, and thirsty." He put a leather flask in her lap. "So I brought this as well."

Sorren took the cork from the flask—her fingers shook, but only a little—and tipped it to her lips. The wine was tart and powerful. She choked, recovered, and drank again. "Thanks."

"Nothing. You'd do the same for me, wouldn't you?"

"Yes," she said. She smiled tremulously into his mustached face. There was white in them, but they were still long and luxuriously thick. "Except I don't think I could carry you."

He pursed his lips. "You'd do whatever you had to." The certainty in his voice made her straighten. He clapped her hard on the back. "You're all right?"

"I'm all right."

Rescuing the flask from her lap, he corked it and stuffed it beneath his belt. "Then there's no more to be said. Better get in the house."

CHAPTER NINE

Isak was being Stallion.

Bare-chested, with a huge reed prick fastened to his waist, he pranced and played. Sorren made her fingers gallop. This was the third time they had gone over this particular section of the dance. She saw his hand move as he counted. His black hair tossed. It was loose, like a horse's mane.

The dance began with Peacock, strutting and posing, the male posturing for the female, and went on to Bear, trying to dance, lumbering about the circle of the stage. They had done that part. In the final part of the dance he became Swan, cold, graceful, regal. The Bear part was most difficult because it had two kinds of rhythm in it. *Pah-pah-dum*. Sorren watched Isak's shoulders sway in time to her drumbeats. Stallion exited. Isak turned his back to her; that meant he was offstage.

She kept drumming. Sweat slicked her breasts beneath her shirt. The rhythm softened, smoothed. . . . Isak nodded at her. He was ready. She began to play Swan's entrance. For this part of the dance, he wore a feather cloak, but he was not bothering with it now. His arms lifted, making wings.

He came on stage again, gliding now, his head thrown back, his neck somehow lengthened, at least it looked longer. It was the dancer's magic, to draw the viewer into illusion. This part went better when there was a fluteplayer. *Pah. Pah*. The Swan furled his wing around the lady Swan who, invisible, was the object of his attention, as was the Mare the Stallion's, the she-Bear the Bear's, the Peahen the Peacock's. Isak sank to the floor, holding his arms up so that the cloak would drape his face and body. Sorren tapped the final beats of the dance, and rested her hands.

"How does it look?" he said, working his shoulders and lowering his arms.

"It looks good," said Sorren.

"Let's end, then," he said. Striding to the door, the dancer thrust his head into the corridor. "Bring water!" He came back into the room and sat on the mats. "Sorren, I'm getting old."

He reached for a towel to rub his face and eyes. His muscles slid smoothly beneath his amber skin. Sorren grinned. He did not look old.

"You laugh," he said. "How old are you now?"

"Seventeen."

"Guardian, you're an infant! I'm thirty-three, nearly twice your age."

"It doesn't show," Sorren said.

Isak laughed. After a good practice, he laughed a lot. "Teneth!" he called. The door slid aside and a plump girl sidled in, carrying a tray with a pitcher of water and two goblets.

"Thank you," said Sorren. She took the tray from the girl's hands. "I can pour."

"Let her," said Isak. "She needs the exercise." Sorren put the tray down. Teneth, blushing, poured water for Isak and then for Sorren.

"That's all," said Isak dismissing the servant-girl with a gesture. He lifted the goblet to his lips and drank without stopping. He sprinkled the last few drops from the goblet onto his upturned face. "Aah."

Sorren loosened her drumskins. It had been a good practice. She sipped the water. The girl had flavored it with lemon. The last time she had come to this house a boy named Koré had served them. "What happened to Koré?" she said.

"He isn't here anymore."

Isak grew tired of people quickly; Koré was probably back in the grapefields. Sorren picked up the towel Isak had used and rubbed her hands and face. She wondered what he was like to keep house for.

He stretched his legs out flat on the mats and began to touch his head to his knees. Sorren had seen Paxe do that after a session in the Yard. It stretched the muscles; if she neglected it, she got cramps. "So," he said, from his bent position, "how is my dear sister?"

"Arré Med is well."

His mouth turned up at the corners. He knew she hated to talk with him about Arré. Before he could say anything, she said, "How is your wife?"

"Quite well. She will be coming to the city for the Festival."

During the Festival, Myra and her children lived with Isak in this house. "And the children?"

"Well, I suppose. Myra would let me know if they had died."

He was like a mirror; you could never get anything from him but glitter and your own questions. Sorren rose. Her knees hurt from staying in the one position for so long. "When is the betrothal party, my lord?"

"In fourteen days."

"Do we need another practice session?"

"I don't know." He lay on his back. "What do you think?"

"Whatever you like."

He laughed. "I don't think so. Today went well. The party begins an hour before noon, but you had better get there a bit early."

"All right." Betrothal parties lasted until sunset, and often beyond. "Do you think the Ismeninas would like a juggler?" she asked, remembering Jeshim.

"They might," said Isak. "Why, do you know one?"

"His name is Jeshim. He's part Asech. He juggles balls and plates, and he throws knives, too. He's very good."

"If you see him between now and then, tell him to come by and show me what he can do. Ron left the entertainment up to me."

"I'll tell him," said Sorren. "Is there anything special you want me to wear?"

"Wear something good."

"I could wear the silk with the butterflies that I wore for the Council."

"Yes, do." He flicked her knee with a finger. "You looked very nice that evening."

Sorren blushed. "Thank you."

She walked to the window. It overlooked a small garden: sunlight sparkled on the flowers, red and yellow tulips marching in sedate rows. Isak kept the garden and courtyard beautiful, but Sorren did not think he cared a whit for flowers; he simply liked to have beauty around him. Even in this room, which was only the practice chamber, the wall hangings were expensive silk, the cushions were stuffed with goosedown, and the chobatas were of the finest painted porcelain.

She took a deep breath and let it slowly out. She was nervous. Over morning meal Arré had said, "Don't forget to tell my brother about the sword!" A week ago, it had seemed easy to say yes to the telling of a little lie; now it did not look as simple. Isak was clever.

On the other hand, the lie was much more likely than it had been a week ago. Someone *was* smuggling swords into the city. The guards at all the Gates were searching the caravans for weapons, and everyone in the markets knew that they had so far uncovered more than thirty blades, in bales of cotton and bolts of wool, on timber barges and ore carts, in a grain sack, and even in a bundle from Tezera which contained children's toys.

Tomorrow Arré was going to the Tanjo to speak to the L'hel about the Ban. That, too, was common knowledge in the street. Sorren wondered if the Ban would be lifted. She doubted it, but if the Ban were lifted, the Red Clan might return to Kendra-on-the-Delta. She knew how unlikely that was but it was exciting to think so.

Isak was rubbing his hair with the towel. To the back of his neck, Sorren said, "My lord, can I ask you something?"

"Of course."

"This morning I saw Paxe training in the Yard with a sword."

He dropped the towel and turned to face her. His voice grew soft, like a cat's purr. "Really? How interesting."

"It worried me. I thought—I know someone has been bringing swords into the city, everyone knows that—I thought it was forbidden to have one."

"You should ask Paxe about that," said Isak.

"I don't talk to her about such things," said Sorren. It was true. She let her gaze wander to the wall hangings. They were in the Med colors, red and blue.

Isak pulled his hair behind his neck with one hand, feeling with the other for a clip. "Don't true lovers share everything?" He found the clip. "Why are you asking me?"

Sorren's heart beat faster. Because your sister told me to, she thought. "Because I thought you would know," she answered.

Isak rubbed a hand along his shaven jaw. "It *is* illegal to have a long sword, a war sword. But there's never been a Council ruling on the short sword, the komys. Was this a short sword?"

"I don't know. I've never seen a long one."

He measured length and width with his hands. "About so by so."

"I couldn't tell. I was far away. I'm only a bondservant, so I'm not permitted inside the Yard."

Isak rose. "Have you and Paxe quarreled?" he said.

She looked down at him, astonished. "Why would you think that?"

"That scrape on your forehead."

Isak had sharp eyes. Sorren felt the bruise with her fingers. She had almost forgotten it was there. "That was Ricky," she said.

"Who is Ricky?"

"A fool kid," she said, "who knocked me down in the market a week ago."

"An admirer!" He cocked his head to one side, waiting to see how she would respond to his teasing. She wondered what he would say if he knew that Ricky was Paxe's son. He would make a joke of it. "I'm glad," he said. "I would be desolate to hear that you and Paxe had quarreled."

He liked to say these sorts of things to her. Sorren reached to the tray. Pulling it toward her, she poured them both another glass of lemonwater. "Who's getting married?" she said, being casual.

"Col Ismenin is marrying Nathis Ryth, of the Blue Clan."

So Jeshim's information had been correct. Sorren drank. "So she will be an Ismenin daughter?" she said.

Isak's eyes narrowed. "As a matter of fact," he said slowly, "no. The agreement is that he will be a Ryth. Why did you ask?"

"I was curious," Sorren said, meeting his eyes. After a moment, he smiled.

"It is, after all, traditional," he said. "The Ryth house is very pleased with their new son."

Sorren set her glass down. "I should go, my lord."

"I suppose you must. I will see you at the Ismenin house. Do give my regards to my dear sister."

"Yes, my lord."

"I presume she's still sleeping alone." Sorren didn't answer. Isak went languidly on. "She needs a bedmate, I think, to keep her from getting old and ugly and bitter. I would recommend one for her, but I suspect our tastes don't coincide."

Sorren hated it when he talked in that tone about Arré. She looked over his shoulder at the wall hangings.

"*You* might look around for her," Isak said, "since your taste in lovers appears to be the same as hers. You know that she and Paxe were bedmates?"

Sorren stared at him, shocked and stupid. "No," she said.

"Thirteen years ago, when they were both young and ardent and beautiful." He raised his voice. "Teneth! Bring me a clean shirt." The plump girl hurried in with a blue shirt over her arm. It had the Med crest on it, in red and darker blue. He pulled the shirt over his head. Sorren moved away from the window, rubbing her arms. Her skin felt cold.

She went to the door, carrying her drums. Isak's face emerged from the shirt. He was smiling. "Good-bye, Sorren. I'll see you at the betrothal."

She walked along the street with the drums hugged to her chest like a baby in arms. She pictured Paxe and Arré in the sunlight, walking through the garden under the sour apple trees, Arré's arm around Paxe's slim waist, Paxe's long arm around Arré's shoulders. It was easy for her to see Paxe young.

Thirteen years ago, she thought, I was a little girl of four.

"Hoy! Girl!" She turned. A girl with the browned face and straw hat of a grapepicker stood below her on the slope of the hill, holding a piece of paper in one dark and dirty hand.

"Yes?" she said.

"You serve the Med house?"

"Yes."

"You know the Yardmaster?"

Even more warily, Sorren said, "Yes."

The girl showed white teeth in a grin. "I was supposed to leave this at the Gate for her, but it took us so long to get inside that by the time we got through, the Gate Captain said she had gone." She held out the paper. "Here, take it! It's a letter for her from her son."

Sorren took the paper from her fingers. "Thank you," she said. "I'll give it to her." The girl waved her hat and ran like a goat down the hill.

Sorren went to the Yard. Paxe was not there.

Holding the letter in front of her like a flag of truce, she went to the cottage and knocked on the door.

"Come in," called Paxe. Sorren went in. Paxe sat cross-legged on the mat in front of her table. She had writing implements spread all over the table and all over the floor.

"What is it?" she said.

"It's a letter from Ricard," Sorren said.

Paxe's face lit. "Give it to me," she said. Sorren brought it to her and she tore it open. She read it, and her whole body seemed to smile. She put it on her lap and held out her hand. Sorren went to her, and Paxe took her hand, turned it palm up, lifted it to her lips, and put her tongue into the hollow.

"You've been very patient with me," she said. She touched the letter with her other hand. "Where did you get this?"

"A girl off a caravan gave it to me." Sorren wanted to throw herself into Paxe's arms. She was still thinking of Isak. "What does it say?"

Paxe held it up. *"To Paxe-no-Tamaris, Yardmaster to Arré Med, from her son Ricard, greeting.* I can tell a scribe wrote this," she added. *"I am working in the fields. I am well. Celénia-no-Tazia is my field boss. The work is hard. I have learned to take grapes from the vine without bruising them. I am being paid four treys a week. Please send me a pair of soft boots or money for same. I miss you. I wish I were home. Your loving son, Ricard."*

Sorren sniffled. "I could have told him the work is hard," she said.

Paxe stroked her hair back from her face. "But you know he would never ask you."

So that was all right. Sorren sat on the mat, drums beside her. "What are you doing?" she asked, looking at the curling sheets of paper and the inkpot.

Paxe put the letter on the table and picked up a brush. "Day after tomorrow is the first day of autumn. I'm making a new watch schedule."

"Which watch will you take?"

"Night watch," said Paxe.

Sorren sighed. "I never see you when you take night watch command."

"I know," Paxe said. "I'm sorry, chelito. I have to."

"What else will change?"

"Kaleb will take late watch, and Ivor day watch. He's never commanded day watch before, so I'm making Borti his second-in-command."

Sorren grinned. "He'll like that."

"I know. I hope Ivor has the sense to listen to him. He may be old and lazy but he knows more about this city than any two other people." Paxe stretched; her muscles showed beneath her shirt. "Where've you been today?"

"I practiced with Isak this morning," Sorren said. She edged closer to Paxe along the mats.

"Was it a good practice?"

"Yes," Sorren said. "But I *hate* Isak."

Paxe said, "Why do you hate Isak, chelito?" Her arm came

around Sorren's shoulder, and Sorren leaned against it happily.

"He's a chaba'ck. He likes to hurt people."

Paxe's whole body went stiff. "Did he hurt you?" she said.

"He said something."

Paxe looked grim. "What did he say?"

"He told me—" Sorren gazed at the mats. Suddenly, it was not so easy to say. "He told me that you and Arré were lovers, a long time ago."

"Ah," said the Yardmaster, and her fingers stroked Sorren's neck. "He was in Shanan, studying with Meredith." She wound both arms around Sorren and pulled her close. Sorren smelled the ink on her hands. "You want me to tell you about it?"

"Yes, please," Sorren said.

Paxe's breath moved in Sorren's hair. "I was second-in-command of the Med guard. Kemmeth-no-Vira was Yardmaster; he's dead now. I was twenty-four, Ricard was a baby, and Arré was thirty. It was three years after her mother's death, and she was learning how to be head of a house, and a Council member. She was much the way she is now—small and arrogant and willful as a hurricane—and I—" Paxe hesitated— "I was a lot like you, in many ways. She needed someone to talk to; I liked to listen—"

"Was she beautiful?" Sorren said.

Paxe chuckled. "I would not say that. Enchanting. Infuriating. Not beautiful."

Sorren twined her fingers in her lover's hands. "You must have been beautiful."

"I doubt it," Paxe said.

"What happened?"

"We were lovers for two years. Then we just grew apart."

Sorren frowned. "That doesn't tell me very much."

"It's been a long time," Paxe said gently. "You know the silver bracelet with the blue stone that Arré wears?"

"Of course," Sorren said, "It's her favorite."

"That was my gift."

"Oh." Sorren contemplated that for a moment. "Are you sorry it's over?" she said, unable to keep the bite of jealousy from her voice.

Paxe's arms cinched her tight. "I have a lover," she said.

They made love right there on the mats, and the woven pattern of the straw pressed itself into Paxe's bare shoulders.

After lovemaking, Sorren sat naked in the downstairs room

and told Paxe about her visit to Marti Hok, about the story of
Sorren of Tornor, and about the finding of the Cards. "It's
true," she said. "Marti Hok said so. I truly am a northern girl."

Paxe said, "Did you tell Marti Hok that you want to go
north?"

Sorren gathered her hair into her hands to braid it. "She
knew," she said, and blushed, remembering that Marti Hok
had known about Paxe as well. "She knows a lot." She halted
her braidmaking, recalling Marti's words. "She said that Isak
is evil."

Paxe leaned back against a cushion. "Evil is a strong word."

"*You* said he was up to something," Sorren pointed out.

"And so he is. You need a ribbon, chelito." Rising, Paxe
went upstairs. Sorren heard her in the bedroom. When she
came back down, she held a strand of indigo ribbon.

She snaked it over the top of Sorren's head and down across
her breasts. Sorren grabbed for it with one hand. "Don't. It
tickles." She tied the ribbon around the tip of the braid and
pulled the knot tight. "What is he up to?"

"*I* don't know," Paxe said. "Why was he so ready to make
you unhappy, today? I thought he liked you."

"I think," Sorren said, "it was because I asked him about
the swords."

Paxe froze in the act of sitting. Slowly she lowered herself
to the mat. "What about swords?" she said.

"Arré told me to tell him that I saw you in the Yard with
a sword."

Paxe frowned. "What did he say?"

Sorren said, "He asked me if it was a short sword or a long
sword. I said I didn't know, and he said that long swords are
illegal but that the Council never ruled on the short sword.
Was he telling the truth?"

Paxe was looking grim again. Sorren wondered for a moment if she should not have told her about Isak. But then she
answered. "He was."

Sorren shook her head to test the braid. It switched like a
horsetail. As she gazed at Paxe's frowning face, a suspicion
struck her. "Paxe, *do* you have a sword?"

"Yes," said Paxe. "It isn't mine; it came from one of my
soldiers." Her frown deepened. But Sorren wanted to shout.
If swords returned to the city, maybe the Red Clan would, too!

"Can I see it?" she said.

Paxe looked up. "Why do you want to see it?"

Sorren remembered the faces of the storytellers around the pickers' fires, and the way their eyes gleamed when they spoke of the chearis. "I—I've never seen a sword."

"Neither have most of the folk in this city," said Paxe. "Have you ever seen a knife? I don't mean a kitchen knife, I mean a weapon."

Sorren thought of Jeshim's knives, and then of Kadra. Her face reddened. What would Paxe say if she knew about Kadra? "Yes."

"It looks like that," said Paxe, "only longer."

Clearly, Paxe did not want to show her the weapon. Sorren tried not to look disappointed. "Is it one of those swords the smugglers are bringing in?" she asked.

Sharply, Paxe said, "How did you hear about those?"

"Is it secret? All the folk in the market are talking about it."

Paxe reached for her shirt. "Yes," she said. "It's one of those."

Sorren wondered what Arré would say when she told her about Isak. Tomorrow Arré was going to the Tanjo. . . . "Do you think the witches will lift the Ban?" she said.

Paxe's face came through the shirt neck. "It hadn't occurred to me," she said. She felt behind her on the mats for her pants. "I don't know."

Sorren wondered if she should tell Paxe about the lehi. But the memory made her stomach tense. "If the witches lift the Ban," she said, "the Red Clan might return. I'd like that."

Paxe's hands clenched in her lap. Emotion flickered over her face like a flame. "Would you?" she said. "Why?"

Sorren said, "It would be exciting! The Yards would be open to everyone, the way it used to be, and the chearis would dance. . . . Nothing ever happens in the city now. Don't you think it would be exciting to have the chearis back again, dancing and teaching?"

Paxe said, "I knew a cheari once."

"What?" Sorren blinked. "You never told me—"

"He's dead now," Paxe said. "I put him in the grave myself. He looked so small there. . . . I wrapped him in my own blanket. It was all I had to give him. He was so old, and so dried out from the fever—lifting him into the earth was like lifting a child."

Sorren swallowed. "You never told me," she said, shaken by the upwelling grief in Paxe's face.

"No."

"What was his name?"

"Tyré."

At dusk, the Yard gate shut. Paxe, drawing her cloak about her, glanced through the bars of the gate as she passed it, and the emptiness made her shiver, without reason. It was that in-between time of night; light lay in the western sky, but eastward stars were glittering. The moon had not yet risen; tonight it would not rise till after midnight. Along the avenues the lamplighters were calling: "Aahoo! Aahoo!"

Paxe passed a guardpost. Her silhouette was distinctive— "Damn it!" someone whispered, over the rattle of falling dice. She did not turn. Tonight she was not Paxe, the Med Yardmaster, but Donita, a farmer from outside the city. Kemmeth had taught her this trick. "Go sit in a tavern and listen," he said; "and you'll learn more from the gossip than you'll ever hear on rounds."

The smells of onion and anise told Paxe she was passing an herb garden. Kneeling, she kneaded dirt between her palms until it ground into her pores and under her nails. A dog barked in the nearby cottage, and Donita the farmer scrambled up, hands realistically dirty, a stalk of anise between her teeth.

It was Sorren's talk of swords that made Paxe decide upon this action; that, and her memories of Tyré which would not let her rest. Tonight she needed noise and laughter and the speech of strangers. She passed The Cup, the biggest tavern in the district. Its doors were open, and through them drifted inviting sounds; laughter and the clink of glasses. Someone inside was playing a sho. But The Cup was well lighted and popular; someone in it would be sure to recognize the Med Yardmaster. It would not do for tonight. She turned north, knowing that Donita the farmer would stay near the Northwest Gate. Travelers tended to keep to the particular sections of the city in which their business got done. Sailors went to the dockside bars in the Jalar district; merchants and caravaners frequented the inns near the Blue Clan Hall.

Just west of Oil Street lay an alley called The Mouth. Few people lived there; it was lined with warehouses and some dirty shops. At the foot of the alley sat a bar called The Tongue.

It was a squat building, half wood and half red brick. The door was open, and through it Paxe saw the mobile shadows of people walking. Choba dishes, too shallow to be called lamps, hung from the ceiling on tarnished chains, and the scent of heavenweed coiled from the doorway and hung like smoke along the grimy walls.

Three people were playing the pebble game on the steps. Paxe strolled up to them. Without looking up, one of them made a gesture. "Go 'round."

"I can't," said Paxe. "No room."

They looked up. "Then go over, if you must," said one, moving a leg a handsbreadth. Paxe turned sideways and stepped over the game. Deliberately she struck the edge of the board with her heel, knocking down pieces—"Clumsy," muttered the player. Within the hood's shade, Paxe grinned. She knew two of the players, they both worked in a Med warehouse, and neither of them had recognized her.

It was hot in the tavern's common room. The smell of broiled fish came from the kitchen, mixed with the scent of wine. Unfastening her cloak, Paxe signaled a server to bring her a tankard. "Hot in here," she remarked to the man nearest her.

He glanced at her and then away, uninterested. "Uh-huh."

A cluster of Asech in the corner were playing dice and smoking heavenweed. Smoke hung over their heads in a blue cloud. A noisier dice game was going on at a table near the kitchen. Paxe pushed her way to the table and joined the row of spectators. People talked over dice games. A big woman with tricolored hair was tossing the dice. She had more bontas in front of her than anyone else at the table. "Come baby, come sweetheart, come lovey," she crooned into her cupped hands. "Eeyah!" She let them go. They bounced across the varnished top and stuck in a groove between planks. "Seven! Pay me!" She snapped her fingers at the other players. She had a scar running up one bare arm, and her brown eyes were shrewd and hard as glass. The other players grumbled, and one of them threw down three fingerlings and left the table. Another man immediately took his empty place.

"Heard about old Scivith?" said someone.

"What about him?" said the woman with the scar, shaking the dice.

"He ran off with a girl from Shanan. Took all the bones in the house. Beria's mad as a hornet."

"She's better off without him. Come baby, come lovey—" The dice rolled again. "Four." She passed them on. "Your turn, Toby."

Toby lost. The dice went around the table. Someone else left, and Paxe took her place. The big woman smiled heartily at her. "A newcomer. Welcome to the table, friend. You know the rules? Evens lose, odds win, seven, nine, and eleven double the stake. The bet is three fingerlings."

"Thank you," said Paxe, lengthening her syllables into a farmer's drawl. She reached into her pocket for her money string and laid three small bontas on the table.

The other players exchanged surreptitious smiles. "Where you from?" asked the big woman.

"The valley," Paxe said vaguely.

The woman on Paxe's right thumped the table. "Quit yammering and play."

The dice went round. Paxe won a little; so did the big woman. No one else won anything. "My name's Annali," said the big woman.

"Donita-no-Elli." Elli was a common name.

"Been in town long?"

"I came in today." Paxe watched the dice fall. They looked all right. But Annali did not. Paxe recognized the swindler's manner without ever having seen this particular swindler. She wondered if Annali worked alone or with a partner, and how long she had been milking this district. "Almost didn't make the closing. It took an hour to get through the Gate. They searched my wagon down to the axles. What were they looking for?"

Four or five voices told her. "Swords. Weapons."

"In my wagon?" Paxe looked shocked.

"In all the wagons," said Toby. He leaned back in his chair. The server brought Paxe her tankard.

"A round for the table," ordered the man standing behind Paxe. She maneuvered a look at him. He was small and thin, wearing baggy gray clothes. He did not look the sort of man with money to waste in a dice game, but he was watching the table avidly, fingers tapping his hips, thumbs tucked casually into his sturdy leather belt.

So he was the partner. Paxe wondered how much money she was going to have to lose to get the information she wanted. The scam had not been going on very long, she guessed, no more than a few weeks, or the guards would have tumbled to it. The game was honest until a stranger joined it, and then Annali switched the dice. If the stranger stayed sober, she simply lost. If she got drunk, sometimes she lost and sometimes she won, and then got robbed on the way home.

Paxe wondered if the other players pretended to themselves not to know what Annali was. Some of them might even be honest, or stupid. Annali threw the dice and lost. The big woman's hands were in constant motion. She gestured, she clapped, she rubbed them together.

One of the players was staring fixedly at Paxe. "You sure you know how to play this game?" he said. "I know some farmers who lost all their money playing dice."

Annali frowned at him. "Chano, how rude. You can see Donita knows how to play. Besides, we don't play like that. This is a friendly game." Her smile at the man showed all her teeth. "Donita, what did you have in your wagon?"

"Corn, melons, cherries, and peaches."

"How are the melons this harvest?"

"Fat as a baby's bottom." The dice came to Paxe. She tossed them and caught them again. She thought the weight was different but could not be sure. "I thought edged weapons were forbidden in the city," she said.

"They are," said the woman on her right. She yawned, gap-toothed. "But someone's bringin' them in."

"Who?" said Paxe.

The woman shrugged. "No one knows."

"You gonna play?" said Toby to Paxe.

Paxe threw. "Nine! Pay up." She gathered her bontas into stacks as the other players groaned.

Chano was down to one deuce. The dice came to him; he threw, and lost. Cursing softly, he stood, swaying like a sapling in the wind. "That's done me. Good night, all. Good night, farmer. Watch who you spend your time with." He hiccoughed. A spectator slid into his seat as he staggered away.

"I seen a sword," said the woman on Paxe's right.

Everyone looked up.

"My man brought it home from the river. Said someone there sold it to him. Said the metal wasn't very good. Hid it in the woodshed."

Paxe said, "The guards at the Gate told me to stay away from the river. They said people have been getting hurt there."

Toby grinned. "That's the Ismenin boys; they just like to play. Jalaras got no sense of humor." Everybody guffawed.

Toby threw and lost. "Damn, looks like luck's just not running my way."

The talk turned to the harvest. Paxe listened, pretending to drink. She wondered how many of the people in the tavern had seen a sword. Weapons were not real to cityfolk, she decided. The dice went round again. The pile of bones in front of Annali was bigger than ever. Paxe finished her wine and pretened to nearly knock the empty tankard down. "Whoo. I must be drunker than I thought I was." She rubbed her temples with her fingers but made no move to leave.

"Another round for the table," said the man she'd marked as Annali's accomplice.

"You get fights in this district, too?" Paxe asked. The man who had taken Chano's seat threw and lost.

"Here?" Toby laughed. "Not here. The captains would skin anyone who tried it. This is a quiet part of town. This game's the most exciting thing in it." He slapped the table, and the bontas jumped. "This is the Med district, and Arré Med wants it that way. Quiet."

"Where are those swords going, then?" said Paxe.

"Guardian knows! Over to the river district, maybe, so that the Ismeninas can play with them."

The woman on Paxe's right said, "I heard the White Clan might say something about the swords."

"Maybe they will," said Annali. "No one knows what the witchfolk will do. Toby, play."

Toby played and lost. "Fuck it." He passed the dice to the woman on Paxe's right and glared at Annali. "Don't know what we got a Council for. Council could stop the sword trade if it wanted to. Witchfolk run this city now, and the Council's just for show. Babe at breast can see that." The woman on Paxe's right threw the dice and won. "Fuck. Everyone wins but me."

"Patience is a virtue," Annali said softly. She scooped the dice from the table and passed them to Paxe. Paxe fumbled and dropped them.

"My head hurts," she complained.

"Looks like our farmer's gonna leave us," said the man who had taken Chano's place.

Annali smiled. "Play one more round," she said. Her voice was butter-smooth. "Last time lucky."

Paxe played one more round, and won. She slapped the table. "That's it. I'm getting out." She shoveled her winnings into her pockets. Someone moved to take her chair. "Thank you all."

"Come back anytime," said Toby, his good humor restored. The man she'd picked out as Annali's partner had vanished. Paxe weaved to the door, still pretending drunkenness, and noticed that the Asech dice game, too, had broken up.

The gamesters had left the tavern steps. Paxe stood in the road, breathing softly, and listening. She heard nothing except the tavern noise. She began to walk, taking big, unsteady strides. After a while, she heard the telltale tap of bootheels at her back.

She grinned into the darkness. Tyré's training had honed her skills to a sharpness that only the desert-born Asech could match. She led her shadower on for two more blocks and then melted into the night. Annali's accomplice wandered forward, and then began to search the gutters and doorways for his quarry, as Paxe sat on the roof of a shed, listening to him puff and grunt and swear. She slid from the roof and staggered beneath a lamp. He immediately saw her, and she led him into a cul-de-sac, her own mouth stretching with laughter as he tried to be secretive behind her back. Finally she stopped, swayed, and pretended to be sick. Abandoning caution, he loped forward, and Paxe bent backward, balancing on one hand and one leg, and swung her other leg like a scythe.

He went sprawling down. She jumped him and locked his elbows behind his back. He tried to break her hold by falling backward, and she tightened the grip and closed thumb and forefinger over his nose. "I'll snap it," she said, twisting, and he whined and went limp. She put him belly down in the dirt and put her knee in the small of his back. "I could give you to the guard," she said.

He breathed painfully.

"Who was the man who left the table early?"

"Chano. He's a pimp."

Paxe closed her hand around his windpipe. "Who is he?" she said, squeezing.

"Ah—don't!" he gasped. "He—he lives on Eel Street. He's a weaver."

"Why did he try to warn me?"

"Guardian, I don't know. I wish he hadn't."

"Don't blame him," Paxe said. "I knew what was happening before I sat down."

She contemplated handing him to the guards, and decided

not to. She was sure they would not stay in the district, not now. Besides—she smiled to herself—the little scuffle had made her feel good, and she could afford to be magnanimous. She let the thief rise to his knees. "Next time don't be so quick to follow a stranger," she said. "Get out of here. Don't look behind you." Shakily, he stood and then stepped away from her, carefully not turning. Silent as a ghost, Paxe followed him to the alley's exit, resisting with difficulty her impulse to at the last minute yell, "Boo!"

She was halfway home when she realized that she was again being followed.

It was not the thief, she was sure of that. Who was it? She doubled back to look, but the street was bare as a plucked field. She stood in a doorway, listening, but heard nothing. She walked from the doorstep and before she'd gone three blocks, heard the barest rhythmic whisper of cloth on the dirt. She froze in a pool of shadow. The sounds stopped.

Furious, she let herself in a gate, traversed a garden, and climbed a fence. The light had grown. She looked west. The moon, not quite full but nearly as bright as the harvest moon itself, was rising like a beacon over the line of the horizon. It gleamed on some white shells in the garden. Paxe picked up a shell and threw it into a nearby yard, starting a noise of chickens. A dog barked. A door banged. "Who's there!" Under the concealing shouts, Paxe drew her hood over her face and returned to the street.

In two more blocks, she heard her shadower. She did not stop to think. There was a grape trellis at hand; in four strides she was up it, and from it onto the slippery, slimy tiles of a roof. She lay flat, squinting over the edge, waiting for her shadower to come to find her. He did not. Grinning, she wriggled along the ridgepole to the other side of the house. The top of a rainbarrel made a convenient stepping-stone to the ground. Taking her boots off, she hung them, around her neck. She walked through a stand of kava trees, and emerged with her bare feet sticky from the fallen kavas. The only way her pursuer would catch her now was if he had the nose of a wolf.

On the Street of the Smiths, she heard the sound of footsteps.

She ran, silent as a deer on the desert, stretching her legs, feeling the wind beat at her face. He was good, very good, but now she was five blocks from home. She went into the public baths and out again. She ran through an alley, into the back door of a pipe den, and out the front door, while the drowsy patrons gaped at her. She climbed one fence and slid across a potter's clay pit, and climbed a second and came down into a rose bush. Thorns pricked her ankles. She went into a stable and shinnied out the window, as the mules and horses turned puzzled eyes in her direction, looking much like the people in the pipe den had. She went twice into the same alley and came out each time a different way, and then she stopped, and listened.

She heard footsteps.

Grinning, she went to meet them, plucking rose petals from her hair. A shadow detached itself from the night and met her. They embraced, breathing hard. "When did you know?" Kaleb said.

Paxe laughed, and lied, tucking her arm around his shoulders. His came around her waist. "I always knew."

They strolled up the street. Paxe's breathing evened. "I saw you in the tavern," Kaleb said.

"I didn't see you. Were you playing dice, there in the corner?"

"Yes. What brought you there?"

"I wanted to hear the gossip."

"That's a good place to do it. What did you think of Annali?"

Paxe chuckled. "She's very good. How long has she been working this district?"

"Three weeks. You spoiled my plan. I was looking forward to cleaning them out."

"Ivor didn't spot them."

"No. He's young; he'll learn."

"Why did you let Annali and her friend go on for three weeks?" Paxe said.

Kaleb said, "I didn't know about them till three days ago. They're smart; they halt the game at change of watch."

"They know your reputation." Paxe hugged him. "Guardian, that was fun."

"It was, wasn't it." His tone was wistful.

"Kaleb, are you homesick?" They were two streets from the Med house. They walked beneath a lamp, and the lamplight shone on Kaleb's face, giving it a bronze glow. The red stones in his earlobes gleamed like drops of blood. Paxe halted, and turned Kaleb to face her. "Are you?"

"Sometimes," he said. "When the wind blows off the sea, I get restless. This is a chilly town for a desert rider, and it's

difficult to feel at home in a city without horses or a place to
let them run."

Paxe had never been much of a rider. She put both hands
on Kaleb's shoulders. "Do you want to leave?"

"No," he said. "My home is here. I like my work. Besides,
I would miss you."

She swallowed. She had feared suddenly that he would say
yes. They walked a little further. "I wonder where Ivor is?"
she said, and put her hand up to her face to hide a yawn.

"In the Yard," said Kaleb. Suddenly, he stopped. "Paxe—
when this is over, when the smuggling has ceased, after Festival—let's leave the city. We could go west, into my country,
and ride, and hunt. My people would make us welcome."

The breeze blew through the kavas. Paxe sighed, remembering the brilliance of the stars in the desert, away from the
fog and the city's dust. "For how long?" she said, tempted.

"For as long as Arré Med could spare us."

Paxe grimaced. "Arré would not want us to go at all." But
it could be managed, she thought, Sereth was competent, she
could take him from the Gate and name him second, Ivor would
play Yardmaster. . . . "We can't. Kaleb. Not now. Maybe in
a year."

"I suppose." He kissed her cheek. "Good night, my friend."
As he turned to go, the scent of heavenweed tickled her nostrils.

She went to her cottage. It felt very empty. The cushions
were all over the place, and she straightened them. The lower
room smelled of sex. Moonlight shone through the window
screen, making a line of light on the wall. The house was cold.
Her bed was cold; she sat on it, yawning. She played the chase
that evening over in her head, wondering what Arré would say
if she knew her commanders had gone capering over rooftops
and in and out of bathhouses like children.

She pulled her clothes off, and hugged her pillow to her.
It had been fun. So had her scuffle with Annali's little friend
been fun. For a moment that night, though, Kaleb had frightened her. She did not want him to leave the city. She loved
him; she needed him. Paxe's eyes stung. Tyré was dead, Ricard
was gone, Arré was preoccupied and growing more inaccessible as she aged. . . . Paxe turned in bed, determined not to
weep, not to pity herself, and not to think—how could she not
think!—of Sorren.

CHAPTER TEN

Smoothing her clothing with one hand, Arré scowled at the litter. It sat in the front courtyard. Paxe stood at the front gate, waiting to see her off. She had ordered the Med flag tied to the litterpoles, so that everyone it passed would know who was inside it.... Arré wished she had not decided to take a litter. She detested them; they made every journey public. She was in good health, and it was ostentatious to ride. The only people who used litters, besides the old and sick, were wealthy city merchants who liked to display their lack of taste, or strangers who might otherwise get lost.

She was nervous, and it made her ill-tempered. She glanced at Sorren, who stood behind her, inside the hall. Something had happened to the child; it had put a hard edge to her voice and a fierceness in her laugh. She had reconciled with Paxe, or Paxe with her. That was good. The reconciliation had occurred soon after Sorren's return from Isak's house, and Arré wondered how much Sorren's new humor had to do with Isak.

Isak. All her thoughts returned to him. Her mind went around the patterns. Isak was allied to Ron Ismenin. Ron Ismenin was bringing swords into the city. Cha Minto was allied to Isak; *he* wanted the Ismeninas to have a Council seat. Kim Batto wanted the Ismeninas on the Council, and he was allied to the White Clan. The Ismeninas were stirring up fights in the Jalar district. One of the Ismenin brothers was planning to marry into the Ryth clan, and, for reasons Arré did not know, to become a member of that house. His inheritance portion went with him. Arré wondered why the Ismeninas would so easily agree to give up money. She was reasonably sure that it had nothing to do with tradition.

The letters she had sent to the heads of the great houses telling them about the swords had done their work; the city was humming like a wasps' nest, as the innocent acted to stem the smuggling of blades and the guilty sought to conceal it. Paxe had reported that morning that the number of weapons found at the Gates had dropped. But that might mean the smugglers had found another way of bringing them in. Even if no new weapons were entering the city, the ones that had gotten past the guards were still inside—hidden by the Ismen-

inas, Arré guessed. Unless the Council ordered the Ismeninas
to submit to a search of their property, all their property, Arré
doubted that the weapons would be found.

And that, she was sure, the Council would not agree to do.

The Council, if it chose to, could announce that the Ban,
despite its flawed construction, applied to short swords as well
as long ones. But the Council's declaration would mean little
without the support of the Tanjo. Arré frowned. Kim Batto
had voted to put the Ismeninas on the Council, he was the
voice of the White Clan. Did that mean the White Clan was
somehow allied to the Ismeninas? What if the White Clan
wanted weapons returned to Kendra-on-the-Delta?

There was only one way to find out, and she was doing it.
Her stomach ached, with the plaintive pain it reserved for
telling her it wanted something sweet, but Arré ignored it.
Sweets made her complacent, and for a meeting with the L'hel
she wanted all her wits about her.

How had the White Clan—and the L'hel, its chief—come
to have so much power in Arun? She wasn't sure. The Clan
itself was only a hundred years old. They seemed like upstarts
compared to the Med house, which could count its generations
back five hundred years, to before the founding of the city.
It was true that the country had enjoyed great prosperity and
peace in those years. But why give the witchfolk credit for
that? Arré thought. It's we, the wealthy families of the city,
who have had to find ways to deal with increased trade and
rising population. The witchfolk received the praise, but it was
the ruling families whose shoulders bore the responsibility.

She looked at the angle of the sun on the courtyard tiles:
it was time for her to be going. She nodded to Paxe, who
signaled to the litterbearers. They took their places at the litter
poles. A line of polished spearheads marched to the Gate and
stopped; it was her escort. Pushing the silk hangings aside,
Arré entered the litter. No matter how they aired them out, the
damned things seemed to stink. She tapped on the wall of the
silk-paper box. The litter lurched, throwing her forward and
then back, and she set her teeth, loathing the motion, the
confinement, her helplessness. . . .

"Yai!" said Paxe, her voice a muffled shout.

"Ho—and ho—and ho—and ho—" The litter bounced in
time to rhythm as the bearers chanted softly. Arré clutched the
cushion. Through the gap in the swaying curtain she saw her

own gate, the kava tree, the escort moving backward—no, she was moving forward. The two lines of soldiers had split to let the litter fit between them. The litter tilted again, and Arré seized the cushions and swore under her breath. "Ho—" chanted the bearers, and flanked by guards, Arré rode away from her house, down the Med hill.

The journey was mercifully brief.

The litter-bearers were careful, and when at last they set her down within the Tanjo precinct, Arré was so grateful to be stationary that she smiled at them and told the captain of the guard to give them a little more money. She was amazed to be on the ground all in one piece and without a bruise. With the guard behind her looking very formidable, she walked toward the Tanjo entrance. The great red building was imposing. She told herself not to be too impressed.

At the Tanjo door she hesitated, and as she waited a man came from it. She recognized him, and was jolted, not to see him, but to see him here, now. It was Kim Batto.

"Arré!" He smiled. "You are expected. Go right in." He stepped out of her path and strolled away. Thoughtfully she watched him. He hadn't brought a guard, and he had taken pains to let her know he knew what she was doing there. . . . It was a good way to make himself look important. She caught one of her guards making the moon horns at Kim's retreating form, and suppressed a smile.

"Thank you, Captain," she said. "I expect to see you in an hour."

The wide white pavement was very clean. Arré watched the guard march away. Then, turning, she went through the Tanjo door. It was dim inside. Stolidly the Guardian stared down at her, at the other people in the red room, at the city, at the world. . . . It was only a statue. She stared at it grimly, refusing to succumb to the lure of awe and worship. It was only a statue. She had one like it in her front hall, made by the same sculptor. It was only a statue.

Someone whispered her name; she had been recognized. Two women kneeling near the statue's base were staring at her. They blushed as she looked at them, but continued to whisper to each other. She put her hands together in the posture of supplication and bowed, hating the political necessity which made her do so.

"Arré Med." This was not a whisper. An acolyte approached her.

"Yes?"

"Please come this way." He beckoned, and she followed him.

He took her around the statue to a door dimly remembered from the last time she had met with Jerrin-no-Dovria i Elath. The blue tiles which formed an archway over it matched the blue tiles on the floor. The door was a screen, easily opened. The acolyte gestured for her to precede him. She stepped through into a similarly tiled hallway.

"You are Arré Med," said the woman standing there. She had an extraordinary voice, deep and husky. Her face was smooth and sensuous beneath a heavy drape of long black hair. The hem of her white gown brushed the patterned tiles. "You are welcome to the Tanjo. I am Senta-no-Jorith."

She said her name as if she expected Arré to know her. Her poise and graceful bearing made the older woman feel awkward. It was a feeling Arré was used to and she waited for it to pass.

"Please come with me," Senta said. The hallway was short and it ended at an archway which opened directly onto a sunny courtyard.

In the middle of the courtyard was a grassy garden filled with flowers, a pool with red fish swimming in it, and a bench. Jerrin-no-Dovria i Elath was sitting on the bench. He stood when Arré appeared. He was much as she remembered him: dark-skinned (though not as dark as she) light-haired, with dark blue eyes, and scars across both cheeks. He wore white silks. A gold ring with a white stone ornamented the middle finger of his left hand. He was stocky, with a wrestler's broad shoulders, and he was only a little taller than she was.

"It's a pleasure to see you again, Arré Med," he said. His voice was pleasant. "Please sit." He pointed to one end of the stone bench.

Arré sat. "Thank you, L'hel," she said. With a swirl of his robes, Jerrin sat opposite her. The black-haired woman, graceful as an acrobat, sat at his feet, hands folded in her lap. Her robes were dazzlingly white against the green.

"I told my guards to return for me in one hour," Arré said.

"I am sure we will have our business done within that time," said Jerrin. "May I offer you refreshment? Wine? Water? Tea?"

"Wine," she said. She expected him to call for a servant. Instead, he simply glanced toward the red stone building. Arré heard the sound of a screen sliding on its runner. A blue crystal ewer and three blue cups floated from the building and, as if invisible hands held them up, sailed across the sun-filled court-yard and deposited themselves at the L'hel's feet. Senta picked up the ewer and poured wine into the cups. She handed one to the L'hel and one to Arré.

Arré took in firmly in both hands. "I didn't know you could do that," she said.

"My gift is lifting," Jerrin said. "And since I thought it best that we speak in private, I arranged to have wine set out beforehand."

"Can you lift anything?" Arré asked. The cup was light.

"Heavy objects are more difficult," he said. "I could not lift this bench. I might be able to lift you from it."

Arré managed not to reach out and clutch the edge of the bench. "You needn't demonstrate," she said.

He laughed. "I won't. Within these walls, everyone has seen such tricks; it's refreshing to talk to someone to whom they are still impressive." His voice grew self-deprecating. "I was showing off, I'm afraid."

Arré smiled, and sipped her wine. It was very tasty. She said so.

"From the Med vineyards," Jerrin said.

She nodded her appreciation. She recognized the wine; it was not cheap. Nor were the goblets and pitcher, nor the silks the witches wore, nor the gold on Jerrin's finger, nor the blue and silver tiles that made such lovely patterns on the Tanjo floors. The White Clan paid for part of this with money given it by the city, apportioned from city taxes. The rest of its money came from other sources; from the Blue Clan, from the crafts-guilds, and of course, from the grateful populace of Arun.

She smoothed her silks. The fine feel of the fabric gave her pleasure and reassurance. She had left off her bracelets when dressing this morning, thinking that the L'hel might find them frivolous, and she missed them. She wondered who Senta-no-Jorith was, and why she was present at this discussion. She decided to begin it, obliquely.

"The harvest is excellent this year, my managers tell me, L'hel. It would be a shame if Harvest Festival were to be spoiled by the presence of edged weapons."

"Please," he said, "call me Jerrin. Titles are formal, and

we are not strangers, therefore we do not have to be formal.
You are right, it would be a terrible shame. We must hope it
does not happen. The Guardian has blessed us this year; the
harvest is indeed abundant, and the Festival will no doubt be
crowded. I plan to be there myself, to open it with the Invocation. I know the Blue Clan and the Guilds have arranged the
usual entertainment for the people. I understand your brother
is to dance—?"

Arré tensed. "My brother dances every year."

"He is very good," said the L'hel.

Even Arré did not like hearing her brother patronized by
Jerrin-no-Dovria i Elath. "He is more than very good," she
said tartly. "He has the right to wear the shariza, which no
other dancer in this city has."

"Indeed," said Jerrin. "You praise him, yet I believe you
do not get along."

"That is correct," said Arré. Witches knew everything, some
people said. Arré doubted this, but she was sure that Kim Batto
had told the L'hel everything he knew, thought, or suspected
about the Med family, including that sister and brother detested
each other, and that Isak had never adjusted to the fact that
Arré, not he, had stepped into their dead mother's shoes.

"It is a matter of some concern to me," said Jerrin gravely,
"that families, particularly noble families, should not be at
odds with one another."

"Oh?" said Arré.

"For instance," Jerrin went on, "I understand that you object
to the seating of the Jalar house and the Ismenin house on the
Council. May I know why?"

"It is not customary for Council business to be discussed
outside the Council," said Arré.

Jerrin smiled. "But you can tell me," he said, his voice
smooth as cream. "Unless you prefer that I hear it from Kim
Batto—?"

Arré folded her hands. Her buttocks ached, and she found
herself wishing for a cushion, and shade. "I have no objections
to the membership of the Jalaras on the Council," she said.
"I object to the Ismeninas, because they are young and ambitious and cannot be trusted."

The L'hel pursed his lips. "It might be easier to control
them on the Council."

"I have no guarantee of that," Arré pointed out, "and it
gives them access to power they do not now possess. I think

they and the city are better off without it."

The woman at Jerrin's feet said softly, "Why do you think the Ismeninas are not to be trusted, Arré Med?"

Arré turned the faceted cup between her palms. "Because I believe they are responsible for the presence of swords in the city."

"Have you proof?" said Senta.

"No," said Arré. "But consider. One. The Ismeninas own the iron deposits which were found west of Shanan. Two. The Ismenin Yard is teaching sword techniques. Three. The Ismenin brothers like to fight. This is well known in the city. They are not a peaceful family."

"I know all this," said Jerrin. "I also know that the Ismeninas are not the only family to teach the sword. At least one other noble house has plans to do so." He smiled.

"I admit it," said Arré. "However, I am sure you can see why. I would be pleased to cancel my order to my Yardmaster if Ron Ismenin were to interrupt his Yard's training."

"I doubt he will," said Jerrin.

"But," Arré said, "I did not come here to accuse the Ismeninas of anything, though it must sound like it. I came to ask the Tanjo and the White Clan what the White Clan plans to do about the swords in the city."

"What the White Clan will do?" said Senta. "Or what the White Clan would like to see the Council do?"

"The Council would not presume to dictate to the White Clan," said Arré. "Will the White Clan dictate to the Council?"

"No," said Senta. "But if the White Clan had a position on the Council, the two could act as one."

Arré had not expected the conversation to turn to this, but the arguments against it were burned into her mind. "There are two good reasons why the Council refuses to give the White Clan a place on it. The first is the matter of function. The White Clan heals, makes weather, and speaks the truth: those are its functions, which the Council cannot duplicate. The Council rules. That is its function, which the White Clan cannot duplicate. Second; if the Council admits the White Clan to membership, it would have to admit the Black Clan and the Blue Clan, and I suppose the Green Clan as well."

"What about the Red Clan?" said Jerrin.

"There is no Red Clan."

Jerrin lifted his cup. "Your second argument is more valid than your first," he said.

"What do you mean?" Arré said.

"You are correct to say that if the Council admitted the White Clan to membership, it might also be expected to admit the other Clans, which would make ruling that much more difficult. However, no individual member of the Council rules the city. The Council as a whole does so. Thus, to admit the White Clan to membership would give the White Clan no more power to rule the city than has any individual house."

"Ruling is a charge upon the noble houses of the city," Arré said. "We are trained to it. We have experience."

"I am also trained to it," Jerrin said. "I rule the Tanjo."

"If you were a member of the Council, who would rule the Tanjo?" Arré said.

"But I would not want to be a member of the Council," said Jerrin. "As you might say, that is not the L'hel's function."

Arré waited, until it grew clear that he was not going to go on without coaxing. "Who, then, would the White Clan propose to be its member on the Council?"

"A Truthfinder," said Jerrin.

Diplomacy, Arré thought grimly, is not a matter for truth. "No. When it becomes necessary for the Council to have proof of the Ismeninas' actions, proof will be found. This is an internal matter."

"Then why did you write to tell me about it?" he said.

"Because bringing weapons into the city is not only against city law, but, by the terms of the Ban, it is ni'chea," said Arré. "Also—I thought you would want to know."

Jerrin smiled. The silence deepened. Arré's stomach rumbled; it was begging for a sweet. She drank a little wine to calm it. She wondered if Ron Ismenin ever sat here. "Have you considered," she said, "that you have a moral authority the Council lacks? You might, if you chose, approach the Ismeninas directly and suggest to them that bringing swords into the city is an unwise move."

"I might," said Jerrin, "if the Ismeninas had ever asked for my opinion. But Ron Ismenin has never spoken to me."

How convenient, Arré thought. But Kim Batto talks to you, and Kim Batto supports the Ismeninas. . . . Jerrin's indigo eyes were fixed on her face, and she had the uneasy feeling that he knew her thought.

"Are you a Truthfinder?" she asked.

He looked startled, and his eyes slid from hers. "Me? No, I am a mindlifter. Witches usually only have one talent. I have no access to your mind, and if I did, I would not use it. That would be discourteous."

"And you are not discourteous." She wondered if she could believe him. "How old are you, may I ask?"

He touched his fine silky hair. "Forty-seven. I was named L'hel at thirty-nine."

"Is it a lifetime office?"

"It can be. There are three *L'helis*; one here, one in Tezera, and one in Shanan. The other two are much older than I am." He turned his cup in hand, and the ring on his finger caught and reflected the light. "In my case, I think it will not be. I grow tired."

She did not believe him. He was winding her about with charm, like a spider winding silk around a victim. Openness could be a deceit; she had used it so, and knew the tactic. "Where did the scars on your face come from?" she said. "They look regular, as if they were put there deliberately."

"They were." Jerrin brushed his left cheek with his hand. "The Asech made them; they mark their witchfolk that way. The scars were once marks of shame but now are badges of honor."

"You are not Asech, why do you have them?"

"I lived with the Asech witches for two years."

"What do Asech witches do?"

"Heal," he said, "make weather, and tell the truth. They also serve to keep the tribes in touch with one another. Sending a courier across the desert is slow, and not always safe. Sending a thought is faster."

Arré drained her cup. Talk made her thirsty. She lifted it. "May I trouble you for more wine?"

He floated the cup from her hands and refilled it without touching it. Watching the pitcher lift and pour all by itself gave her an eerie feeling, as if the objects in the garden, the flowers, the bench, the stones, the gliding fish, were sentient and could listen and maybe talk.

"Thank you," she said. "May we talk further about swords?" Jerrin inclined his head, agreeing. "They say witches know everything that happens in the city. Were you aware that the Ismeninas have been smuggling swords through the Gates, and that they have been teaching swordplay to their soldiers?"

Senta answered. "We knew this."

"And you let it continue?"

"What would you like us to do?" said Jerrin.

"Declare the Ismeninas ni'chea," suggested Arré.

Jerrin chuckled. "That would tear the city apart."

"Declare swords ni'chea."

"We have. The Ban exists."

"Short swords are not covered by the Ban, and the Ismeninas are bringing in short swords!"

"Let the Council state that short swords are covered by the Ban, and they will be," said Jerrin.

"Will the White Clan support the Council?"

Jerrin's voice was silken. "The Council rules. The White Clan heals, makes weather, and speaks truth. Does the Council depend on the White Clan's support?"

Arré gripped the crystal cup so tightly that she feared it would shatter. "In this matter, yes."

There was silence: an angry silence on Arré's part. She had been pushed to an admission she had not wanted to make. The quiet was broken by a bird's loud singing. A red bird swooped from the sky, to land at Senta's feet. She smiled at it and held out an elegant hand. Ruffling its feathers, it flew from the grass to her wrist and perched there as she stroked it gently with one finger. "This is Leeka," she said. "For two seasons now, she and her mate have built their nest in the Tanjo dome." Her voice was warm. Arré glanced toward the L'hel, and froze. He was staring at the two, woman and bird, with rage in his face. He saw Arré looking at him, and smoothed it away at once, but not fast enough. She wondered what he could possibly object to in Senta's affection for the dove. She had seen that look before, on her brother's face; it betokened injured pride, and bitter jealousy. She rubbed her arms, which felt suddenly chilled, despite the hot sun.

Senta flicked her fingers upward. "Go, Leeka," she said. The bird soared into the air.

"Arré Med," said Jerrin, "have you ever heard of foreseeing?"

Now what? Arré thought. "I know it is a witch-gift."

"Do you know how it works?" Arré shook her head. "Witches who can see things before they happen are called foreseers. It is an uncertain gift; we do not understand it yet, and so, when we see things, we don't know if the things we see *are* going to happen, or *may* be going to happen."

"How can you—" Arré scowled. The future was the time that had not happened yet, how could it exist to be "seen"? It made no sense to her. "Why do you tell me this?" she said.

"Our foreseers have seen a time when people in Kendra-on-the-Delta battle in the streets, with swords." Arré caught her breath and he lifted a hand to keep her silent. "We see another time when short swords are banned in the city by order of the Council. We see *another* time when the city is filled with strangers who come from ships like our fishing boats but bigger, much bigger, sailing out of the south, strange men and women who wear odd clothes and cannot speak our language, and we see *another* when ships come from the south bearing warriors who enter the city and pull down the walls, and burn the houses of the people."

Arré shivered. Automatically her hand made the "avert" sign. "Are any of these futures going to happen?"

"We do not know," said Jerrin. "Perhaps none of them will. I tell you this not so that it may frighten you but that it may teach you a lesson that we in the Tanjo have learned. It is not an easy one but it is simple. *Do nothing.*"

Arré gazed into the depths of her cup, thinking: Is this the advice you give to Kim Batto?

"And," continued Jerrin, "when next the White Clan requests membership on the Council, do not refuse it."

"I am only one vote on the Council, L'hel; *I* do not make that decision."

"But you are its strongest voice," said Senta. "Boras Sul is not worth mentioning, Cha Minto is—biddable, shall we say, and Marti Hok is old."

"You don't mention Kim."

"Kim Batto will do as I—as we—tell him," said the woman. Her eyes lifted to Arré's; they were as black as the bird's and opaque as stone.

Steps rustled in the grass. A dark boy in a short white gown approached the bench. "Excuse me, L'hel, Lehi, but the Lady Arré's escort is within the Gate, and they wish to know where she is."

"As you can see, Niko, she is here," said Senta. She reached to take one of Arré's hands in both of hers. "Tell them she is sitting in the garden, enjoying the sun, and that she will come presently."

The acolyte bowed and scurried away. Arré took her hand back. Steadily she eyed the white-gowned woman. "You are a Healer," she said.

Senta nodded. "I have that gift. I am also a Truthfinder."

Jerrin said, "Senta. See the Lady Arré to the Gate."

Senta rose. "L'hel," she murmured, and bowed. Arré stood. Her knees crackled, and her back hurt. Senta led the way through the pillared, tiled hallway to the domed building. Within the dome, she turned to face the statue of the Guardian and bowed, long hair dipping to the tile, her body strong and graceful as a willow. The statue smiled enigmatically upon them both.

The guard troop was drawn up in two lines before the Gate. Arré started toward it; Senta put a hand on her arm. "Arré Med," she said, "I have a favor to ask you. You have a bond-servant in your employ, a girl of northern birth. Her hair is gold. You know the girl I mean?"

"Yes."

"I should like to speak to her. I mean her no harm, I assure you. Will you send her to me?"

Arré's thoughts jumbled. What could a Truthfinder want with Sorren? "She will not want to come," she said. "She fears the Tanjo."

"I know," said Senta. She bent her head close to Arré's ear. "She is right to fear some of us. And wrong to fear others."

She's not talking about Sorren, Arré thought. "Who is it right to fear?" she murmured.

"Power is dangerous," said Senta. "Fear who needs it most." She smiled, as if she had just said something trivial. "The L'hel is your enemy, Arré Med." In the depths of those remarkable eyes, something glittered—truth? Arré thought. "Farewell." Turning, she nodded at the soldiers, and walked with long, graceful strides back toward the Tanjo dome.

CHAPTER ELEVEN

Arré's stomach churned.

Is that so, she thought. But the warning shook her. What had *she* done to incur the enmity of the L'hel? And why should she trust Senta-no-Jorith, who appeared to be no more than the L'hel's mouthpiece? She squinted toward the dome, but the Truthfinder had vanished.

A man's voice said, from above her head: "Lady?"

She looked up. The guard captain loomed above her. She scowled. "What do *you* want?"

He took a step back. "We are ready to escort you home," he said.

"Thank you," Arré said. She contemplated walking. But it would take too long, and Paxe would be rightfully furious if she did it. "Call me a litter." He bowed and whistled between his teeth.

"Be sure it's clean," she snapped at him, and he bowed again. The litter appeared, blue flags flying, on the other side of the Gate. Arré climbed into it, ignoring the captain's outstretched arm. She wondered what her mother would have said to the L'hel. It helped her to think of her mother. Shana Med had never been afraid of anything, including the ugly plague that killed her.

The litter heeled suddenly, tossing her against its wall, and then stopped. The captain came to the side of it and extended his arm to help her out. Arré climbed down without using it. "Thank you, Captain." she said. "Please tell the Yardmaster that I want to see her." She went into the house; Elith was mumbling to herself in the hall, and Arré thought impatiently, She's getting senile. I should send her to the grapefields; she could sit in the sunlight, and talk to herself, and die in peace.

"Bring me some food," she snapped at the old woman. Elith blinked. "Go tell Cook I want some berries and cream." She went into her study. The sun glistened on the silvery cedar floor, on the bright tapestries, on the glass of the record case. Arré sat on her chair and kicked off her shoes. Leaning back luxuriously into the cushions, she thought, I am a spider, and this is my web.

It was childish, but the impudent image made her feel better.
Her stomach sizzled with hunger, and she patted it. "Patience," she said.

"Patience is a virtue," said Paxe from the doorway.

Arré grinned at her. "Who said that?"

"A woman I met last night." The Yardmaster's broad mouth
turned up at the corners. "She was a thief. Firth said you
wanted to see me."

"I did. Sit down." Arré pointed at the stool, and Paxe sat.
"How long ago did you order those sejis?"

"A week ago," said Paxe.

"How long before we get them?"

"Perrit said three weeks. He often delivers early, but I don't
know that he will this time. Say, twelve days."

"I want them now," Arré said. "Offer him double pay to
get them done. I want the Med Yard training in the use of the
short sword, and I want Med soldiers to be proficient in their
use by Festival."

Paxe's brow furrowed. "Proficient?" she repeated. "It can't
be done. It's less than four weeks to Festival."

"I know when Festival is! I want as many of my guards to
know swordplay as possible by that time. Get them good
enough so that they can hold swords and look convincing and
not cut each others' silly heads off. Can you do that?"

The door opened, and Lalith came in, carrying a blue bowl
with cherries in it. Arré took it from her. "Is Sorren back from
shopping yet?" she asked.

The pigtailed girl shook her head. "No, Lady,"

"When she comes in, tell her I want to see her."

"Yes, Lady," said Lalith. She shot a curious glance at Paxe,
and left. Arré ate a spoonful of berries. The sweet strong flavor
made her sigh with pleasure.

She looked sidelong at Paxe. The Yardmaster was frowning,
thinking, no doubt, about the swords. Should I tell her what
happened at the Tanjo? thought Arré. She trusts the White
Clan. The L'hel's venality will break her heart.

"Where are those swords that came through the Gate?" she
said.

"The ones we found are in the Gate guardhouse, locked
up."

"Bring them here," said Arré. "Bring them to the Yard."

Paxe nodded.

"Does Ron Ismenin still have that child following you around the city?"

Paxe smiled. "When I let him."

"Can you find me someone—not a child—whom you trust, to follow Kim Batto?"

Paxe scratched her chin. "Yes," she said. "I think so. Double pay?"

"Whatever you think is fair," Arré said, "but I want him followed everywhere, even at night."

"Why?" asked Paxe.

Arré drew a breath. "Let's just say," she said carefully, "that I don't believe our Kim is as pious as he appears to be."

Paxe stiffened. "You think he is involved with the Ismeninas?"

"He may be."

"The Tanjo thinks very highly of him, it's said."

"I know that," said Arré. "I just want to make sure. When you arrange matters with your spy, tell her to report directly to me."

"As you wish," said Paxe. "Anything else?"

"No." As Paxe rose, Arré said, "Have you heard from your son?"

Paxe smiled. "Yesterday," she said. "A letter came with one of the caravans. He's fine. He wants me to send him boots."

"That's good," said Arré. "I'm glad he's well." Paxe left. Arré put her feet up on the stool, wondering about Kim Batto, and about Sorren, and why Senta-no-Jorith could possibly want to see her.

Sorren was at a wedding celebration.

Tani, the snake-dancer, was getting married. The actual ceremony hadn't happened yet, and would not happen until Tani returned to her tribe. The man she was marrying was still in the desert. Tani was happy because she liked the man. Simmy was happy because Tani was not going back to the desert to live; part of the wedding agreement was that the husband-to-be agreed to move to Kendra-on-the-Delta after the wedding. Tani's snakes were happy because they had been fed to the point of somnolence.

The celebration had started in the Isara market, but after a while it grew raucous, and Simmy suggested that they move to his cottage before the Isara guards came around to break them up. It was a tiny place; it smelled of goatskin and heavenweed and the strong, hot spices the Asech used in cooking. Sorren sat on a cushion, drumming. Simmy played the flute. Sothri and Tani were dancing, twining scarves around their breasts and bellies in slow erotic motion, while Nerim, their young partner, stood in the doorway, mouth against the boxlike shape of a sho.

Asech drums were flatter than the drums Sorren was used to, and they were usually played with sticks. But Sorren had discarded the sticks. Their sound was more tinny than her drums, less resonant, more of a rattle. It didn't matter. The music of the sho was wild and strange and it tingled in her blood like wine; she thumped the drum with both hands, while Simmy's flute went up and down the scale. Everyone in the crowded room was smoking heavenweed and swaying from side to side. Tani and Sothri chanted; it sounded like the Festival chants, but faster. Soon the chant had words in it, and the men joined in, shouting and laughing. Tani's face began to redden. From the few words Sorren could catch she knew it was a very bawdy song.

"You know what it says?" said an insinuating voice. An arm came around Sorren's shoulders. It was Jeshim, breathing heavenweed. "It says, *As the stallion, rearing, calls for the mare; So do I, rearing, call for my love.*"

"Huh," said Sorren.

"And how are you, my sweet drummer?"

"I'm not your drummer, Jeshim, and I'm fine." She wriggled her shoulders to make him drop his arm. He didn't seem to want to. His fingers cupped her breast. "Jeshim, if you hold me, I can't play." She stopped drumming. Simmy took the flute from his mouth and scowled at Jeshim. Jeshim shrugged and took his hand away.

"Where's the food?" yelled someone. Tani and Sothri went into Simmy's tiny pantry and returned with platters piled with Asech delicacies: seed-cakes and little balls of lamb meat dipped in batter and other things that Sorren didn't know. Tani put the tray in front of her. She took a seed-cake.

Jeshim took a long thin strip of meat and popped it into his mouth with evident relish. "What is that?" Sorren asked.

He grinned. "Lizard." She pulled her hand back quickly from the tray. "Guardian, girl, I'm only fooling."

She didn't believe him. It probably *was* lizard. She took another seed-cake. "I have a message for you from Isak Med," she said. Maybe if she gave him good news, he would leave her alone.

"What?"

"If you want to juggle at the Ismenin betrothal, go see him."

"Wa' hai!" Jeshim bounced to his feet. Then he leaned down to kiss Sorren exuberantly on the cheek. "O most lovely one, I am in your debt." He wormed his way into the kitchen and came back with a wineskin. "Here, want some?" He held it out to her; Sorren shook her head.

It was nice to be able to spend a little time at a party. Arré was at the Tanjo, and had not expected to leave it before noon. *Ta*-ta-ta-*ta*-ta-ta . . . She hit the drum. Her own shoulders were swaying. Nerim was watching her; Sorren smiled at him, and he blushed all over his face, and turned his head away. He looked like Ricard, only more pleasant. His shyness was attractive. She pounded the drum until her fingers stung.

When she left, Simmy followed her out to the street to bid her farewell and thank her for playing.

"Thank you for asking me. I would have brought a gift if I had known." The Asech at the party had brought gifts—pots and leather goods and pieces of jewelry.

"Don't worry about it. Your presence was gift enough." He glanced at the sky. "You won't get into trouble, will you?"

"No, its all right, I have time this morning."

"I'm sorry about Jeshim." His voice was grim. "I *didn't* invite him, but he's hard to keep out."

Sorren walked home with the Asech songs pounding in her head. When she entered the kitchen, Lalith said, "Arré wants you." She wrinkled her nose. "You smell funny. Where have you been?"

"At an Asech wedding feast," Sorren said. "I ate lizard."

Lalith's eyes got huge. Grinning, Sorren went to the parlor. "Where have you been?" said Arré, in much the same tone as Lalith.

Sorren sat on the stool. "A party. I drummed. An Asech party."

Arré made a rude noise. "I never get to go to parties in the middle of the day."

Her voice was sharp—was she in a good mood or a bad mood?

"Whose party was it?"

"A snake-dancer's," said Sorren. She wondered how the meeting with the L'hel had gone. She had been afraid for days that Arré would command her to go to the Tanjo with her, and that morning she had deliberately left the house early and stayed away late so that she would be out of the way.

Arré's right hand reached to touch the bracelets which normally reposed on her left wrist. They were not there. She looked at her hands. "Now, why did I—oh." She smiled. "I was wondering why I left the bracelets off this morning. It was because I didn't want to seem frivolous. Frivolous! Bah." She snorted. "Go get them for me, child."

Sorren went upstairs to the bedroom. Picking the bracelets from their box, she brought them to Arré, who fitted them over her hands. Her fingers lingered on the one with the jewel, the one that Paxe had given her.

"Sit down, child," she said. Sorren sat, wondering if something was wrong. Arré tilted her head to one side. "Tell me," she said, "why would a Truthfinder want to see you?"

Sorren grew cold. "I—I don't know," she said.

"Have you ever met one?"

"Once. In the market."

"What did she look like?"

"She—she had black hair, and a beautiful voice. She was walking with Kim Batto."

"Senta," said Arré. "What did she say to you?"

"She—I was upset, and she asked me why I was crying. She frightened me. I ran away."

"Have you always feared the witchfolk?" said Arré. "I remember you would not go to the Tanjo with my letter to the L'hel—Sorren, stop shaking!"

"I can't," Sorren said.

Arré reached forward and took her hands. "You can," she said firmly. "Sorren, the witchfolk may be strange but they have never done hurt that I know of. Why should you fear them? Is there something you have or do that they have forbidden?"

Sorren swallowed. This was worse than she had thought it would be. She did not dare tell Arré about her visions; Arré would surely want her to go to the Tanjo.

But she did have something she could show Arré: the Cards. She said, "I—I'll show you. I have to go upstairs."

"Go," said Arré, releasing her.

She carried the box downstairs and laid it in Arré's lap. "That's why," she said.

Arré opened the box and took out the Cards. Gently she

unwrapped the red silk and, lifting the first Card, turned it over to the picture. Her eyebrows lifted. "Huh." She turned over the second Card, the Weaver. "What are they?"

"My mother left them to me," Sorren said. "They're from the north. They're fortunetelling Cards."

Arré turned over the third Card, of the woman sleeping. "What do you mean, they're from the north?"

Sorren explained about finding the images of the Cards in Marti Hok's grandfather's records. "They're from Tornor Keep," she said. Tornor. The word still felt strange in her mouth.

Arré stroked the painted pictures lightly, the way she touched the flowers in her garden. "They are beautiful," she said. "Why did you never show them to me before?"

Sorren bowed her head. "I thought you might take them away. It's against the chea to have them."

"Because they are fortunetelling Cards? But they're yours, child, they're an inheritance." She laid them back in the box and folded the red silk over them. "Can you use them?"

"No. I left the grapefields—and then, my mother died. She never showed me how."

Arré sighed. "That was my fault," she said. "I took you away." She held the box in both hands. "I think you should learn to use them."

"How?" said Sorren.

"I don't know," Arré put the lid back on the box and handed them to Sorren. "Put them away, child."

Sorren took the Cards upstairs.

When she returned to the parlor, Arré had taken out her writing materials and was writing a letter. Sorren watched the pen flow across the page. Arré finished the letter, which was very short, and sprinkled it with sand. "I told the Truthfinder I would send you to her," she said. "However, you know how forgetful I am." Arré never forgot anything. "I must have forgotten to tell you."

Sorren said, "Won't she be angry?"

"Possibly. I don't care, nor should you. You are my bond-servant, and under my protection. But you had better avoid both Healings and the Tanjo for a while."

"I do anyway," Sorren said.

"Did you finish your shopping?" said Arré.

"Yes."

"Is the house clean? The laundry done?" Sorren nodded.

"Good." Arré folded the letter and sealed it with the Med stamp on red wax. "Then you may take this to Marti Hok."

But Marti Hok was not home. The Hok guards remembered Sorren, and passed her through to the front door without even asking to see the Med seal on the letter. The door was opened by the girl in the white dress. "I have a letter from the Lady Arré Med to the Lady Marti," Sorren said. "Is she at home?"

The girl made an apologetic face. "She's at the docks with her son. Is it urgent? I can have the letter taken to her by a guard."

"I don't think so," said Sorren. Arré had not said it was urgent.

"Yona, what is it?" called a woman's voice. A door in the interior of the house shut, and a woman came into the hallway. She wore a soft silver gown that belled out over her obviously pregnant body. The girl and Sorren both bowed.

"She has a—"

"I have a—"

They both stopped at once. Alanna Hok laughed. "One at a time," she said, taking the letter from Sorren's hand. "What's this? Oh, I see. I'll put it on Mother's desk." She had a round pleasant face, and her hair fell in soft brown curls around it. Her back was swayed slightly forward as she tried to balance the weight of the baby inside her. "I remember you—the northern girl. Tell Arré Med that Mother will get the letter this evening. It must be important if she sent you." She flicked the stiff paper back and forth like a fan. "Do you know what's in it?"

"No, Lady," said Sorren. She thought she did, but Arré would not thank her to talk about it, even to a member of the Hok family. Alanna fanned herself idly, and Sorren smelled in the light breeze the sandalwood scent she used on her hair. She bowed again. "I will give Arré Med your message."

That night she could not get to sleep. Restless, she lay in her bed twitching like a fish on a hook, trying to think of nothing. At last she sat up. Feeling by the bed for her tinderbox, she made a flame and touched it to the wick of her candle. Her shadow blossomed on the wall. She took the Cards from beneath her pillow and held them in her hands.

She picked up the first Card, the Dancer, and laid it on her lap. Beautiful and joyful, he smiled from the painted scene as if he were alive. She wondered if he was supposed to be a chearl. She poured them all onto her lap and picked up a second

at random: the Sun. It showed a farmland scene, a barn, a
field, and people dancing. She picked another: the Rider. The
Rider's cloak was green. Was she supposed to be Kadra? Sorren
looked closely at the painted figure to see if it bore a face she
knew, but the face was too small to see. She picked another
Card: the Lady. In the picture, she had golden hair. Sorren
wondered if, in the fortune she could not read, the Lady was
supposed to be her mother. The Wolf glared at her from the
pack. The malice in its red eyes was terrible. The Juggler made
her think of Jeshim, and then of Isak. She picked up the Phoenix. This, she thought, was the most beautiful of the Cards;
the bird's wings, through the fire, gleamed with rainbow
colors.

This was silly. She had no idea what the Cards meant, and
all her staring at them would not help. She piled them up again,
ignoring their usual order, and returned them to the box.
Throwing back her quilt, she went to the window. The waning
moon looked as if it were diving toward the sea.

She found herself aching for a vision. But perversely, nothing happened. The world stayed stable and secure about her.
Sighing, she returned to her bed, wishing that she knew where
Toli kept his heavenweed pouch. Smoking alone was no fun,
but at least the drug would help her to get to sleep.

On the morning of the watch change, Paxe had a headache.

She rubbed her temple. The ache had started in the night,
and though it had diminished, it was still there, wriggling and
probing, like a worm in her head. She told herself it would go
away as soon as she stopped being idle. She went outside.
Ivor, standing in the Yard, hands on his hips, flashed her a
joyful grin. She beckoned to him, and he strode happily to her
side.

"Yardmaster, thank you for naming me to this watch. I'll
do my best, I promise you."

"I know you will," she said. "Don't let Borti bully you;
he'll try to."

"I won't."

"But don't try to do everything yourself, either. Day watch
is hard, because there's a lot to keep track of, but I wouldn't
have put you here if I didn't trust your good sense and your
ability."

Ivor's eyes shone at her words. "Thank you," he said.

"Have you made rounds yet?"

"I was just about to."

"When you go to the Gate, tell Sereth to load those swords we took on a wagon and deliver them here. Arré Med wants them stored in the weapons shed."

"I will."

"Has the lock been changed yet?"

"The locksmith's coming this afternoon."

"Good." Her temple throbbed, and she resisted the urge to rub it. "I'll see you later."

He bowed, and with a jaunty step, went back through the Yard gate.

She went the shortest route possible to the Hok district. As she passed the Tanjo, she realized that her muscles were cramping with tension. She shook her arms, hard, to make them relax. The guards at the precinct border bowed to her. The Hok district was busy; people and carts crammed the streets shouting at each other, all in a hurry. They looked at Paxe and got swiftly and quietly out of her way. She went to Perrit's workshop. The old man was in the back of the shop, showing a new apprentice how to use a hammer. "See t'ose mark?" he said, pointing at a plank laid across two sawhorses. "We call t'em owl eyes. T'ey happen when you hold t'hammer too loose or too tight." He picked up the hammer and struck the nail cleanly. "T'hammer bounce when you hit because you hold it too har'. When I hit, I hit only nail. No bounce." He gave the girl the hammer. "You try."

Paxe interrupted the lesson. "Perrit," she said, "I need to talk to you."

He frowned. "A moment, Yar' master."

"Now."

"You try," said Perrit to the girl. "I be back." Frowning, he walked to Paxe's side. "What is it?"

"I need those sejis."

He shook his head. "I can't 'o it."

"Double pay?"

He tilted his head to look at her. She saw the question coming. "Don't ask," she said. "You don't want to know. How soon can I have them?"

"Ten more 'ay. No sooner."

"Do it. Ivor-no-Akia is day watch commander; he will show you where to put them if I am not available." Behind them, the apprentice swung gingerly at the mauled piece of wood.

She went back to the Med district the same route, her feet finding the path automatically. A block from the Tanjo she noticed a small, familiar face behind her. She doubled back, and caught the ragged boy as he was coming through the alley, looking for her in doorways. She picked him up and shook him till he quivered, terrified. "You tell Ron Ismenin," she said through her teeth, "that if I see you again behind me I'm going to throw you in the river, and that goes for anyone else he tries to get to follow me!" He trembled in her grip, and she scowled at him, her rage only half pretense. Her head throbbed. She left him on the road like a discarded shoe; when she looked back to check on him, she saw no trace of him. She continued on toward the hill, a little ashamed of her ferocity.

Jenith-no-Terézia was a small brown woman. Paxe had known her for years. She had been a worker on the estate at the grapefields during the years when Paxe was a guard there, and had come to the city about the same time Paxe did. She was now a head worker in one of the Med warehouses. Paxe found her inspecting a leaking wine barrel and swearing murder at the cooper who'd made it. "Look at that!" she said, pointing to the puddle of red beneath the cask. "Some son of a mongrel donkey used green wood in this thing, and it shrank before we got the wine it! Damn it. May the winter demons carry him off, the man who made it." She grinned at Paxe. "Yardmaster. What brings you here—thirst?"

"No. Have you got anyone who can watch over things while you come out for a while?"

"Sure." She went and found her second, and gave him some brief orders. "Let's go. I'm curious as a virgin in an orgy."

Paxe laughed, and took her to The Cup. The folk in the kitchen recognized them both. They brought Paxe wine and would not take her money. Jenith ordered water.

"Don't you drink?" said Paxe.

"Chea, I don't have to! The fumes in that place send me reeling home at the day's end. Tell me how you are! I don't see you often enough, you busy woman. Tell me, does Kaleb still work for the Med Yard? A lovely man." She smiled. "How is your son?"

"In the grapefields," said Paxe. She sipped the wine. "Working."

"Good. My daughters are there, too. I told them they could

come to the city when they had enough money not to need mine for a year."

Jenith's daughters had been born about the same time as Paxe's. Paxe remembered the four children playing together in the courtyard of the estate house. "Are they well?"

"Well enough," said Jenith. "What can I do for you, Paxe?"

"Not for me," said Paxe. "For Arré Med. Jen, can you still vanish in the city?"

Jennith grinned. "I haven't tried in a while. But I suppose I could." She was Asech, and had been brought up for her first twelve years in the desert. "Why?"

"Arré Med needs that talent. She will pay you double whatever you're making now to follow someone around the city and tell her where he goes."

"For double pay I'd strip and dance naked in a nest of snakes," said Jenith. "Who do I follow?"

"Kim Batto."

Jenith pursed her lips. But she did not ask why. She drank her water, hiding her face behind the cup. Putting the thick clay mug down, she said, "All right. Shem can handle the warehouse for a while. How long is this going to go on, and can I get someone to help me if I need to?"

"You can get someone to help you, but you pay her," said Paxe. "As for how long—" She frowned. Arré hadn't said. She'd have to guess. "It ought to be over by Festival."

"When do I start?"

"As soon as you can. Report to Arré Med every three days, unless she tells you differently."

Jenith nodded. She leaned closer, her voice dropping. "Paxe—what did the L'hel say to Arré Med yesterday, about the smuggled swords?"

"I don't know," said Paxe. "She didn't tell me."

Jenith drew a little circle on the table with one finger. "They're saying in the streets that the Tanjo is going to lift the Ban, and that the Red Clan will come back."

Paxe lifted her cup. "I haven't heard that," she said, lying a little. Sorren had said it too. What if it were right? she thought. A spark of anger burned in her as she thought of Tyré, exiled from his city, unwilling to teach a truncated art, hating the witchfolk, hating the Ban.

"And another thing," said Jenith. She dropped her voice even lower. "They say the Ismenin Yard is teaching swordplay to its soldiers! I asked an Ismenin guard and he said it was a lie, but they have a guard on their gate now so that no one can look in. Do you think it could be true?"

Paxe was tempted to say, yes, it's true. But something—loyalty to Dobrin, perhaps—held her back. She wondered how long it would take for the rumor to sweep the city. Why, she thought, had Jerrin-no-Dovria i Elath not banned short swords at once? Maybe he would; maybe the White Clan was waiting for the Council to act. She wished Arré had told her something. Jenith was watching her, eyes anxious. Paxe shook her head and said, "I don't know anything about that, Jen."

She decided to go back to the cottage, to sleep. Perhaps sleep would ease the headache that rode her forehead like a burning coal. As she passed the Yard gate, she glanced in to see who was there. A stranger knelt beside the door of the weapons shed—the locksmith, she thought, but remembering Seth, she crossed the Yard to make sure. He was a little man, with tufts of black hair on his head that stuck out every which way; they made him look as if he had the mange. He scrambled respectfully to his feet as she peered over his shoulder.

He had the old lock on the ground. "Go on with what you're doing," she said. "If the watch commander hasn't come back when you're done, give the key to the gate guard." He bowed. She walked across the Yard, aware that her guards were slowing their training pace to stare at her. She wondered what she looked like.

A noise from the street made her turn; it was the sound of bells, mingling with the chant of litter-bearers. She got to the corner in time to see an empty litter vanish down the slope of the hill. She went to the gate guard. "Who was in the litter?" she asked.

"The Lady Marti Hok, Yardmaster," he said.

Paxe nodded. Of course, she thought, Arré would call upon Marti for counsel. She went to her house, feeling her muscles ache. The cat cried at her ankles: she scooped it up, rubbing it under the chin until it purred and stretched in her hands like wax, paws in the air. Its body vibrated with pleasure. "Come on, kit," she said to it, and dropped it on the floor. It blinked its one eye at her, and yawned. "Let's sleep." It licked one paw, and then, tail waving like a flag, padded up the stairs behind her as she went to her bed.

CHAPTER TWELVE

"Do nothing," said Marti Hok. "What *interesting* advice!"

She sat with Arré in the bright, fragrant study. All the window screens were open, and the flower scents were drifting upward into the little room. Arré's letter had said, "Come as soon as you can," and Marti had taken it literally, canceling two other appointments to come to the Med house. She and Arré had eaten morning meal together in the parlor, while Arré told her the details of her conversation at the Tanjo. She sat now in a cushioned chair, sipping rose tea from a green-glazed cup.

"So Jerrin-no-Dovria i Elath thinks I am too old to matter?" she said.

"And Boras is too stupid," said Arré.

Marti scowled. "Well, I *am* old, and Boras *is* stupid, but he is not so stupid nor I so old that we cannot discern a threat when we encounter one." She made a sour face. "Faugh. 'Do nothing.' The White Clan would love that." Her dark eyes under their yellow lids were as hard as Senta-no-Jorith's had been, and her voice rasped with anger and scorn. "What fools they must think us, Arré!"

Arré grinned. Marti was as bracing as a dip in the cold pool after a sojourn in the hot room of the baths. "Thank you for coming so quickly," she said.

"Your letter said 'Important,'" said Marti. She glanced around the study. "Have I ever told you how much I like this room?" she said. "Your mother used it as her study, too. She had a yellow rug on the floor."

"Yes," said Arré, "it's in my bedroom."

"Do you remember her?"

"Yes," Arré said.

Marti smiled. "I *intend* my children to remember me. The old lady—I can hear them say it—the old lady wouldn't have done that. They say it now when they think I'm not listening: 'The old lady wouldn't do that, and she won't let *you* do it either!'" She leaned back in her chair.

The teacups had red and blue fish painted within their bowls. The fish reminded Arré of the Tanjo. She had told Marti every-

thing, except the Truthfinder's parting words. They had frightened her; they still frightened her. But they had nothing to do
with swords, or the Ismeninas, and besides, she did not even
know if they were true. Truthfinders did not lie, it was said.
But it was also believed that the L'hel was an honest man. If
he thinks to terrify me with his tame Truthfinder, Arré thought,
he will be disappointed.

"Well," Marti said, "what are we going to do about this
nonsense, Arré? Do nothing, and give the city into the White
Clan's rule?"

"No," Arré said firmly, "we are not."

Sorren had filled a tall vase with lilacs and put it on the
lacquer table that morning before she went shopping; the bright
blue spears were reflected from the black lacquer, as was the
red vase. Med colors, thought Arré. She touched the petals of
one flower. This is the way it was before the Council, she
thought, when first one House and then another ruled the city.
"Should we call Boras Sul into this discussion?" she said. He
was their ally, after all.

Marti raised her eyebrows. "Do you really want Boras
here?" she said. "He will fidget and mumble and fall asleep,
and be shocked at all he hears without offering one useful
idea—besides, I don't think he has any, any more, or if he
does they are all about food. No, Arré, I think we should not
call Boras."

Arré grinned. "We might call Meredith Jalar and Edith
Isara."

"They are not on the Council."

"Yet," said Arré. "It is true that the Batto House is as old
as the Med House and almost as old as the Hok, but right now
I would rather have Meredith Jalar on the Council than Kim
Batto."

"Oh, I agree," said Marti. "Kim is going to be very sorry
when this is over, I think. I agree with you; he must be the
link between the Tanjo and the Ismeninas. Pompous man that
he is, he is going to be lucky to come out of this situation with
a whole skin. But he is only a little, little problem." She held
her hands in the air. "We have two big ones. Ron Ismenin and
the swords are one. The White Clan's ambitions are the other.
Each believes it is using the other to get what it wants. Imagine
a skein of wool. It has two ends but only one piece. If you
pull either end, the skein unravels. What we must do here is
decide which end we want to pull."

"I wish you had been with me at the Tanjo," said Arré.

Marti sipped her tea. "I am sure I would have handled it no better. Arré, don't underestimate your strengths, or overestimate theirs. They must be vulnerable—we all are. I, for example, am subject to colds."

Arré began to laugh. "Marti, you are irrepressible," she said.

"So I should hope," said the old woman. "Now that I have made you laugh, shall we get on with this Council of two? You have had time to think about it all, while I have not. Tell me what you have considered."

"Well," Arré said, "I have considered giving the L'hel what he wants."

"A vote on the Council."

"Yes. But we would stipulate that the White Clan member could *not* be a Truthfinder."

"And how would you know the witch's gift?"

"Ask for a demonstration," said Arré. "Witches have only one gift."

"Who told you?"

"The L'hel—but I think it's true."

"It doesn't matter," said Marti. "We cannot give in to the White Clan. If we give them the vote because they force us to it, our power is negligible; we are an impotent and useless body, and sooner or later someone will come and sweep us away." She made a sweeping gesture with one hand.

"That time may be upon us," Arré said.

"I think not. But that is surely the basis of the L'hel's threat, that through silence he will permit Ron Ismenin to do what he likes, whatever the Council desires or decides. Shall we approach the problem from the other end? It may prove easier. How many swords are there now in the city?"

"We stopped thirty-five of them at the Gates, and those are locked up in the guardhouses," Arré said. "As for the rest— I think we can assume we caught most of them after we started looking, but we have no idea how many got through before we started looking."

"And Ron Ismenin has them," said Marti. "Might they be enough to equip a guard troop?"

"They might be. I thought of that."

The old woman shot her a shrewd look. "Is that why you instructed your Yardmaster to order sejis, last week?"

Arré smiled. "What do you know about that?"

"Nothing stays secret in this city," said Marti. She scowled into her teacup. "What good is it going to do Ron Ismenin to build an army? This city has too many people in it to rule by martial law."

"Do you want more tea?" said Arré. She reached to ring the bell for Lalith.

"No," said Marti. "Why are the fish in this cup blue and red?"

"Because the Med colors are blue and red," said Arré. "I have six like that one."

"But I've never seen a blue fish," said the old woman.

"Nor I have. Maybe the maker of the cup has."

"Humph." Marti considered that. "I think the painter was just being inventive. I am glad you ordered your Yardmaster to find someone to follow Kim, by the way. That was inventive."

"It was not my idea," Arré said. "Ron Ismenin thought of it first. He sent some poor child to follow my Yardmaster."

Marti said slowly, "I don't think it was Ron Ismenin's idea, Arré."

"Oh?"

"I think it was your brother's," said Marti. Her voice was gentle, and very firm. "He is friends with Ron Ismenin. I have watched your brother over the years. Your brother is a predator. Cha Minto is a polite and decent man—what was the word you said the L'hel used; ah, yes biddable—Cha is biddable, and your brother has trapped him into something. I saw them together at the Council meeting. Did you think Cha was happy? He was not; he was angry and frightened and he did not know what to do to free himself from the trap. I feel very sorry for Cha."

Your brother is a predator.... The words made Arré shiver. "So do I," she said. She remembered Isak as the Enchanted Eagle, eyes burning with the eagle's passion. What, she thought sadly, happened to my baby brother?

She said, "I can do nothing with Isak."

Marti said, "He is your heir, is he not?"

"Yes," Arré said, "and after him, his children. He has three; the oldest is Riat, he is eight."

"Which does he resemble, father or mother?"

"He looks like his father," Arré said, "but he has his mother's sense and her sweetness."

"His mother is an Ishem, is she not?" said Marti. "A good choice." She looked into her cup again. "I will have more tea now, Arré."

Arré rang her bell, and Lalith came in. Bowing, she took Marti's cup and returned it to her, refilled. "Bring me wine," Arré said, and when the wine was brought, she took a large, reckless swig.

"What do you think of the Ismenin betrothal?" said Marti.

"I was about to ask you that." The wine warmed her belly. She drank again.

"You know, of course," Marti said, "that Col Ismenin is giving up his name and that Nathis Ryth is the daughter of the head of the Council of Nuath, the man whose face is on the bronze coins."

This was news. "I did not know that," said Arré.

"I have spoken to my caravan masters of him," said Marti. "They say he keeps a private army. They also say that his coins are accepted along most of the river towns."

"What does he do with this army?" said Arré.

"Nothing. It's very small. But swindlers and thieves stay well clear of Nuath, preferring to go hungry rather than be caught by the Ryth soldiers. It is said they are very efficient."

"So are our city guards efficient." Arré turned her bracelets on her wrists. "And Kendra-on-the-Delta has no need for a private army, no matter what is done upriver. If Ron Ismenin thinks it does he is mistaken. Perhaps *he* ought to live in Nuath, and be a Ryth." A thought struck her. "Is this Blue Clan barbarian coming to the betrothal?"

"I imagine so," said Marti. "Do you wish to speak with him about his relative-to-be's conduct? I will stand beside you, and look forbidding."

Arré smiled. "I cannot go," she said. "I was not invited."

Marti grasped the head of her cane in both hands. "What? That's ridiculous. Isak is dancing—"

"Oh, I know that," said Arré. "Sorren is drumming for him. My servants are more in demand than I am; I have said it before." The wine glowed in her belly. The outrage in Marti's face made her want to laugh.

Marti thumped the tip of her cane on the floor. "You *will* go."

"Will I?"

"Naturally you will! Can't you see how foolish Ron Ismenin

will look? He can hardly turn you away at the door."

Arré tried to imagine Ron Ismenin telling her to go home. "No." She began to grin. "Marti, you are a demon." What would Isak do when she walked into the party? "I will go."

Marti looked smug. "So Sorren is drumming at the party. They will do The Courtship, of course. She is a lovely child, Arré; well-mannered, charming, everything one could wish for."

"I know," Arré said. "I could not be prouder of her if she were my own daughter." The words seemed to hang in the air for a moment, like smoke.

Marti sighed. "Swords, Arré." Her voice was somber. "Swords, and the Ismeninas' ambitions. . . . What are we going to do about them? Do you have a plan? For though you called me here for advice, I will tell you truthfully, I have none."

Arré said, "I think I do." She wondered what Marti would think if she told her about the times the Tanjo's foreseers had "seen," in which all the things that happened contradicted one another, and still existed, somehow, to be "seen." Which is true? she thought. The one in which people of this city battle each other in the streets with swords? The one in which the Council bans the kyomos? The one in which the city burns? Yet another? To which future will my acts contribute?

It did not matter.

She touched the flower with her fingertips. A petal detached itself, and fluttered to her lap. "My plan," she said, "is one which will, I hope, precipitate whatever action Ron Ismenin is planning to take with his hidden swords. It could be dangerous. But if it works, it will insure two things. One: that his plans will be rushed, and hence ill-made, and two: that by his actions he will condemn himself in such a way that the L'hel *cannot* support him."

Marti folded her hands in her lap. "Tell me," she said.

When Sorren returned that afternoon from shopping, she found Elith screaming, Lalith in tears, and Arré, sleepy, and drunk.

"What's wrong?" she said to the old woman in the hallway. But Elith, redfaced, was busy scolding Lalith. Sorren caught Arré's name in the tirade, and went gingerly to the study. There were two empty carafes on the lacquered table. Sorren sniffed them, and wrinkled her nose at the smell.

Arré sat in her chair, scowling. Her hair was wild.

"What happened?" Sorren said. She had never known Arré to drink enough to be more than tipsy.

"Nothing," said Arré.

Elith appeared at the door. "No more!" she said, shaking her finger at Arré. She reminded Sorren of a hen with its feathers ruffled in anger.

"I'll drink if I want to drink!" Arré shouted back, and hiccoughed.

"Why do you want to?" Sorren said. But Arré simply stuck out her chin and glowered, looking very much like a stubborn child.

Elith said, "I leave the house for a few hours, only a few hours, and this is what I get when I come back!"

Sorren went to her. The old woman smelled of jasmine soap; she had been to visit her friend the soapmaker. "Why are you so angry?" she said.

Elith sniffed. "No one listens to me." Her voice grew into its familiar whine.

Arré said, "I don't want to hear it." She hiccoughed again and licked her lips. Her voice was slow, almost stuporous. "I'm thirsty."

"You can't have any more," said Elith.

Arré raised one hand and flung the glass. It bounced off the wall, leaving a tear in the screen, and shattered on the floor.

Sorren went to the kitchen. She found a mug and a pitcher; filling the pitcher with water, she put both on a tray. Lalith was sitting on the steps, snuffling into a rag. Her cheeks were streaked with stains. Sorren said, "Lalli, why did you bring her all that wine?"

Lalith said, "She asked for it! What else could I do?"

"Nothing," said Sorren. She wondered if Arré had drunk enough to be sick. She hoped not. "She broke a glass," she said. "Better come clean it up."

Picking up the tray with both hands, she brought it to the study. Elith was still in the doorway; Sorren had to squeeze past her. She put the tray on the table, poured water, and handed Arré the glass. Arré drank from it eagerly. Her face was flushed. "Good," she whispered. She slumped deeper into the chair, and her eyes closed.

Sorren sat on the stool. Lalith crept in with a broom and a damp cloth.

"Wouldn't you like to go to bed?" said Sorren softly. There

was no answer. "Lalli, get the cook," she said.

"I knew this would happen," proclaimed Elith from the doorway.

Sorren felt her temper rising. "Instead of saying I told you so, you could get her bed ready."

But Elith muttered something and refused to budge. The cook looked in the room. "What's this?" he said, and made a face. "Oh." He approached Arré and with a gentle, deft motion, lifted her closed eyelid. She opened her mouth, breathing heavily, but did not move. "You take her feet," he said to Sorren. Stooping, he put his long arms under Arré's shoulders. Between them, they carried her out of the study and up the stairs.

Sorren filled a basin with cool water and brought it to the bedside. She wondered what had happened to make Arré drink so much. She sponged Arré's face, which was scaly and dry. Arré was breathing loudly now, and her breath was sweet as new milk. Suddenly, Sorren shivered, and the cloth dropped from her hand. Arré was often tired but she was never sick. What if she had some illness, a fever, the lung fever, even? What if she was sick enough to die?

She put the basin on the floor and leaped for the door. Arré muttered, and extended one hand into the air. Sorren went back to the bed. "Arré?" she said.

"Uh," said Arré. She opened one eye. "Sorren. Don' go."

Sorren sat down again. "How do you feel?" she said.

"Thirsty."

That evening, Paxe came to the house. It was just sunset. Lalith brought her upstairs. She was wearing her boots with the wooden heels, which made her even taller than she was. Sorren was very glad to see her. Arré was awake; she had been waking and sleeping at intervals all afternoon. She was sitting up, propped against cushions. She opened her eyes as Paxe sat down.

"Ah. You." She struggled to sit up. "Did—did you get the sejis?"

Paxe said, "I could not get them sooner than ten days from now. Will it do?"

"It will have to," said Arré. "And the spy?"

Sorren thought, What spy? She took a step nearer the bed.

"Her name is Jenith. She used to work in the grapefields."

Arré licked her lips. "Thirsty," she whispered.

The water pitcher and glass were at Paxe's feet. Bending, she poured water and held the glass to Arré's mouth. Arré gulped feverishly, and then let her head fall back on the pillow. She looked at Sorren. "Cloth."

Kneeling, Sorren dipped the cloth in the basin. She laid it gently across Arré's forehead. Water ran down her neck.

"What are they saying in the city about the swords?"

"Not much, yet," said Paxe.

"And about Ron Ismenin?"

"There are rumors that the Ismenin Yard is teaching the sword. But the Yard denies it."

Arré nodded. The cloth slid from her forehead, and Paxe caught it. She dipped it in the basin herself, and laid it gently back on Arré's forehead. "Of course," said Arré. "They have to say that. Ron Ismenin is being very careful. He does not want to alarm people, or make them think he is doing anything ni'chea. Well, next time someone asks you, tell them what you know. Don' say you know it, say you have heard it. Say you've heard that the Ismeninas are training with the short sword, the kyomos."

Sorren said, "Are they?" She had not heard this before. Paxe had said nothing to her about it.

"Yes," said Arré, "they are."

"Does Isak know?"

Arré smiled. "Isak knows all about it. He is friend to Ron Ismenin." Her eyes suddenly filled with a drunk's easy tears. "My little brother. Ré, he used to call me. Ré. You can say, too, that the Tanjo does not approve of this, but is waiting for the Council meeting in two months, because at that meeting the Council intends to ex-ex-extend the Ban to short swords. You can say how lucky you think Ron Ismenin is that training with the short sword has not been declared ni'chea." She waved her hands in the air. "Tell everybody. Let the whole city know."

Paxe caught her hands and held them, gently. "Arré, is it true?" she said.

Arré said, "Does it matter? People will believe it, anyway."

Paxe said, "I want to know."

Arré said, "A part of it is. That's enough, isn't it, Paxe—part truths? Ron Ismenin will think he knows wh-wh-which part is true and which not, but it will make him very unhappy, it will burn and pickle and fester in his soul until he no longer knows who or what to believe—" She hiccoughed. "The bed is going around."

Paxe said suddenly, "Arré, what did the L'hel say he would do about the swords?"

Arré shook her head. The cloth fell onto the quilt. "Oh, no," she muttered, "you don't trap me like that." She closed her eyes, sighed, and seemed to sleep.

Paxe stood. Her eyes were troubled. "Has she been like this all day?"

"Since I came back from shopping. I found Elith yelling at Lalli, and her drunk in the study. She drank two carafes of wine."

Paxe scowled. "She shouldn't drink. She knows that." She laid her hand against Arré's cheek. Arré did not stir. Despite herself, Sorren reached for her lover's hand.

"How sick is she?" she said. The words made her throat hurt.

Paxe said, "Not sick enough to die." She put her arm around Sorren, and hugged her gently. "Don't worry, chelito."

Heavy steps and harsh breathing in the hallway warned them, and they moved apart as Elith came to the door. "How is she?" said the old woman.

"Asleep," said Paxe.

Elith said, "Her mother went like this."

The words chilled Sorren to the bone. But Paxe said, "Shana Med died of the plague!"

"Ai, yes," said Elith, "but it was this that killed her, as it took her mother before her." The old woman's voice took on a keening sound. "I have nursed three generations of the Med house, and I know the weakness of the line. The Healer told me. It is a sickness; it makes the muscles limp and the mouth dry and the breath sweet. She has it, as her mother had it, as her children would have had it." She caught her breath. "I have seen it; I know."

"Enough," said Paxe. She took two strides to the door, seized the old woman by the shoulders, and pushed her into the hall. Then she came back to the bed. Again she stooped and felt Arré's forehead. "Elith is an old crow," she said. "She's not that sick. But she needs to be watched."

Sorren swallowed. "I'll stay with her."

"If you need help, leave a message with the gate guard. He knows how to find me."

Sorren said, "I will."

When Paxe left, Sorren went to her room. She dragged her quilt and pillows into Arré's chamber. The candle flickered over the small sleeping form. She did not want Arré to die. She sat beside the bed, listening to Arré's steady, stertorous breathing, and wild thoughts swirled in her head. Maybe Arré's illness was meant as a sign for her, maybe it would cease if she went to the Tanjo, told them what she was, gave up her dreams and became a witch. . . . But she knew better. You could not bargain with the chea. She had said so to Kadra herself.

Arré slept for two days.

Sorren stayed by the bed as much as she could. Lalith did the shopping; Toli, the cleaning. The guards were simply told that Arré was not well, and that she did not want callers. Paxe came upstairs every few hours. But she said only that if Arré's breathing did not change and she was neither too cold nor too hot, then they should let her alone, and let her wake by herself. What if she doesn't? Sorren thought; but she did not say it. Saying it made it too real.

The second day, Jenith was among the callers.

Sorren did not know her, but she recognized the woman's name. She went to the gate herself. "I'm sorry," she said, "but Arré Med can't see you now. Can you come back?"

"I'll come back," said the dark woman. She smelled of wine and heavenweed. "Make sure you tell her that I came."

The third morning, Arré woke.

She was very weak; Sorren had to help her to the chamber pot. She did not believe it when Sorren told her how long she had slept. "Two days and nights? That's not possible." But the sweat-soaked bedclothes helped to convince her. "I want a bath, and breakfast," she said. She sniffed. "Guardian, open the window!"

Sorren pushed the screens to one side. "I was afraid you'd catch cold," she said.

Arré was looking at the nest of blankets on the floor. "Who's been staying here? You?" Sorren nodded. Arré touched her arm. "Thank you, child," she said. "I frightened you, didn't I. I frightened myself." She ran her hands through her hair. "Faugh. I'm hollow as an empty jug, and I stink worse than any goat."

After bathing in hot water, she insisted on being helped

downstairs to her study. "I have work to do. Who came while I was asleep?"

"Jenith was here," said Sorren.

"Jenith—ah, the spy. When will she come back?" Sorren shrugged. "Why don't you know?"

As if to make up for two days of silence, she was irritable as a trapped bee.

Finally Sorren said to Cook, "I'm going to do the shopping. Tell Lalith to answer the bell, if it rings." It was the fourth day of the week, and she wanted to go to Kadra's. She sped through the shopping, praying that the ghya would still be at the house.... She would go to the dock to find her, if she had to. But Kadra was there, sitting in the goat hutch, map on her lap.

"You're late," she said.

"Arré needed me."

"Huh." The ghya coughed. "Here." She put the map into Sorren's hand. "I marked your route. The circles are villages. The blue crosses are where the merchants stop. You may be able to find some friendly trader who'll let you ride a wagon. The big red mark is over Elath, the witch town. The fastest route takes you to the east bank of Lake Aruna, right under the Tezeran city wall. A few traders go from Tezera to the Keeps, and you may be able to coax a ride to Tornor from one of them. Otherwise, you'll have to walk or buy a mule. The country's marshy there, where the rivers meet."

She named the villages. "Terzi, Mahita, Warrintown, Elath, Shonet, Sharon, now you're in the Galbareth, Nuath—"

"Stop," Sorren said. Her head was spinning from the litany. "Go slower." Kadra repeated the names more slowly, and Sorren said them after her, pointing to each circle on the map.

"You'll know Mahita because it's bigger than the others and it sits on both sides of the river, with a bridge crossing from side to side. In Shonet, there are great heavenweed fields, you can smell them half a day from town." Her wine-scented breath was warm on Sorren's cheek. "People don't ride through Shonet, they float." She broke off speaking to cough. Her face reddened, and she put both forearms over her stomach.

"Do you want some water?" said Sorren, half rising. There was a water barrel beside the house.

"No. Sit there," rasped the ghya. She struggled, and the spasms subsided. "Near the Tezera road, there are plenty of inns. You'll have no trouble finding food. After Nuath—" she pointed to the map—"comes Yfarra. The riverfolk live there. Then Morriton, Septh, and Kup-on-the-Marsh. Then Tezera."

Sorren repeated the names.

"Your memory's good," said Kadra.

"Thank you," Sorren said.

Leaning over the map, she said the names to herself, trying to make them stick in her mind. Terzi, Mahita, Warrintown, the witch-town to which she would *not* go, Sharon, Shonet—no, that was wrong, it was Shonet, *then* Sharon. The strong aminal smell in the debris of the pen was making her dizzy. But there was no shade in the space behind the house except in the goat hutch.

Kadra coughed again. When the fit was over, she said in a hoarse voice, "What do you know about the Ismenin Yard teaching forbidden weapons?"

Sorren said, "Why should I know anything?"

The ghya said, "Because Arré Med talks to you, girl, that's why. Don't play stupid. Is it true?"

Terzi, Mahita, Warrintown, the witch-town, Shonet, Sharon, Nuath. Yfarra. She drummed it on her knee. "I don't *know*," she answered, remembering Arré's instructions, to talk. "But I've heard it in the market."

"Well, don't say if you don't want to," said Kadra.

"What do you think about it?" Sorren asked.

"What do I care?" said the ghya. "I'm leaving—one way or another."

Drawing her knife from the sheath in her belt, she began to pare her nails with it. The nail of her little finger on her right hand was long, like a scribe's. She trimmed the others short. "You ought to have a knife," she said again. "Something."

"No." Sorren frowned. Terzi, Mahita, Warrintown, the witch-town, Shonet—

"A bow then, to hunt with. Guardian, girl, you're planning to go on foot into a countryside you don't know—what if you get lost? What will you eat? Berries and nuts, like the chipmunks? What if you get hurt, or you drink bad water and fall ill?"

"I'll make traps."

"Traps don't always catch anything. Can you throw stones and hit what you aim at?"

"Not very well."

"You need a bow and arrows. I can get one for you, and

I know a place you can practice. You're a northerner—the skill's in your blood. You ought to learn it."

The skill's in your blood—Sorren's imagination stirred. She remembered the Card, the woman drawing a bow silhouetted against the crescent moon. The Archer had gold hair, like her hair. "Bondservants can't have weapons."

"I'll keep it for you."

"It's ni'chea. What if someone saw me practicing?"

"They won't," said Kadra. "I know a perfect place. But even if they do, you're wrong. Bows and arrows are ni'chea only if the arrows have iron points. I'll make you arrows with blunt points. They're better for small game, anyway."

"Can you make arrows?" Sorren said. "I didn't know that."

Kadra grinned, not nicely. "Spare me the list of things that you don't know." She coughed again, bending double, and spat in the dirt. "Cursed city air," she muttered.

It's not the air that makes you cough, Sorren thought, it's the drink—but she did not say it. Warrintown, the witch-town, Shonet, Sharon, Nuath, Yfarra, Morriton, Septh, and Something-on-the-Marsh. Kup. Paxe had a sword, which was ni'chea, why should she not have a bow?

She crooked her arms, trying to remember from the Card of the Archer how one held it. Kadra chuckled. "Want to try it?"

Sorren glanced sideways at her. "I suppose I do."

"Good," said the ghya. "Meet me here next week and I'll have it for you. Stand up; let me see how tall you are." Obediently, Sorren scrambled up. She was taller than anything in the scrubby yard except the house itself, and it made her feel large and clumsy, as usual. Kadra rose. "Hold still," she directed, and proceeded to measure Sorren from feet to armpit with her hands, as if Sorren were a horse. "All right." She sat. Sorren reseated herself on the ground.

"Why did you do that?" she asked.

"The bowyer needs to know your height to make the bow."

"How long will it be?"

"When you stand with the lower tip on the ground, the upper should touch your armpit. I'll tell her to make yours shorter; a short bow's best for hunting, because it doesn't snag on the brush."

Timidly, Sorren said, "I can't pay for it until Festival. Arré usually gives me a money string then."

Kadra scowled, as if mention of money made her angry. "Never mind. The bowyer owes me a favor. It won't cost me; why should it cost you?"

Sorren had the uneasy feeling that she was lying. But she was not about to say so. She ran the string of names out in her head—Warrintown, Elath, Shonet, Sharon— "What should I wear to travel in?"

"Sturdy stuff," said the ghya. "Boots, and a cloak, and warm clothes for cold weather."

"But I'm going in the summer," objected Sorren.

"It gets cold in the north at night, even in summertime."

Sharon, Nuath, Yfarra, Morriton, Kup-on-the-Marsh. "How much money will I need?"

Kadra shrugged. "How much will you have?"

"I don't know," Sorren said. Part of the bondservant's agreement stated that there was money set aside for her, which would be given her when her time of service ended. Arré would know. She wondered if Arré would be feeling better when she got back to the house. "What's happening with the ship?" she asked. "Is it finished yet?"

The look of longing came over Kadra's face. "The hull and keel are finished. The lower decks are done, and they're working on the upper deck. When it's laid, the carpenters will come aboard to make cabins. Ten days ago, they brought the masts downriver. It may even be ready to sail by Festival."

"What's it called?" asked Sorren. Even ships, she thought, must have names.

"A name in the old tongue," Kadra said. "It means 'starfinder.' Starfinder—*Ilnalamarê*."

CHAPTER THIRTEEN

The sejis arrived at the Med Yard on the sixth day of the first week of autumn, four days earlier than Perrit said they would.

Paxe was sleeping when a hand on her naked shoulder brought her striking up from the pillow. She had been dreaming about the Red Hills. She recognized Kaleb even as her hand sliced for his throat, and grimaced apology as he jumped swiftly out of range.

"Sorry."

"You wanted to be told when the sejis arrived," he said.

She rubbed her eyes. "They're here so soon? Perrit's a marvel." The sky gleamed hot blue through the window. "How has the day gone?" she asked.

"Quiet, so far," said Kaleb.

Rising, Paxe walked to the wash basin and rinsed her face. "Did Perrit bring the swords himself?"

Kaleb nodded. "He's downstairs in the weapons shed, putting them away."

They went to the weapons shed. Perrit had bullied one of the late watch guards, Sekki, into helping him. He grumbled at Paxe as she ducked under the shed's low lintel, "I knew you wou'na have racks."

She glanced quickly to the back, to be sure that the live blade which had been brought from the Gate guardhouse were stowed out of sight. But they were securely covered by silk and canvas. She gazed at the shed walls. Perrit had made racks for the sejis to lie on. She took a wooden blade from the rack and ran her thumb along the wood. "White oak," she said.

"O' course."

The finish was like satin. She held the blade on her palm, feeling the balance. "They're beautiful, Perrit. Thank you. No one in the city could have done this work but you."

"Wait till Arré Med see t' bill." He grew suddenly shy. "My wagon's here." He left the shed and walked quickly across the Yard, a small, squat man with immense shoulders. Kaleb closed the shed door and locked it. The metallic sound was harsh in the silence.

Sekki bowed. "Excuse me, Captain, Yardmaster." She walked toward the gate.

Kaleb said, "The news of the Ismenin Yard teaching the short sword is everywhere around the city."

"I will tell Arré Med."

Kaleb said, "Paxe, does Ivor know that you intend to teach the short sword?"

Paxe said, "I haven't told him."

"Then he doesn't know." Kaleb rubbed his chin. "He may have trouble accepting it. He's city-born and -bred. To him, a sword in the city is ni'chea, whatever its length."

That night, Paxe made her rounds in the darkness as she had been wont to do in the daylight, from post to post, past the Travelers' Hall, through Wine Street, along the Street of the Goldsmiths. At the Tanjo guardpost, she halted. The dome sat outlined by stars in the clear night. A light shone from the entrance, and a second light gleamed from the apartments behind the great red structure. "Who lives there?" she asked, and guessed the answer before it came.

"Those are the rooms of the L'hel."

At sunrise, she went to the Yard to give Ivor the report. As always, he looked fresh and dapper as a dancer, his hair in a topknot, his clothes washed and scented with lavender. "Come to the cottage," she said.

He followed her to the cottage. "Sit," she said, gesturing to the mats. He seated himself cross-legged on the mat beside the table. Paxe sat opposite him.

"Is something wrong?" he said.

She folded her hands on her lap, wondering how best to say it. Better to be blunt, she thought. "Ivor," she said, "have you ever used a sword?"

His face changed subtly. "No, Yardmaster."

"Why do you look at me like that?"

He touched his face with the fingertips of one hand. "I don't know what my face looks like."

"You have heard the rumors that have been filling the city?"

"About the Ismenin soldiers learning the short sword? Of course."

"They are true," said Paxe.

Ivor bowed his head. She wondered if it was so that she

could not see his face. He glanced up again. "The swords that were smuggled into the city—the ones we found, at any rate, were short swords."

"Have you ever seen a sword other than those?" Paxe said. He shook his head. "Then how do you know that?"

He fidgeted with his mustache. "Borti told me. He said it might be important."

"It is important. Short swords are not covered by the Ban. That's why the Ismeninas are not afraid to teach them. Days ago Arré Med went to the Tanjo, to talk with the L'hel about the swords in the city. I don't know what they said to one another; she didn't tell me. But short swords are still not covered by the Ban. And we, too, are going to teach it to *our* soldiers."

"How?" said the captain.

"With sejis. Wooden swords. They've been made already; they're in the weapons shed." Paxe took the key to the shed from her pocket and laid it on the table. Ivor picked it up. "Arré Med desires the guard to have a decent familiarity with the weapons by Harvest Festival."

Ivor swallowed. "Yardmaster," he began, and stopped.

"Say it," Paxe said.

"All my life I have been told that swords within the city walls is ni'chea."

Paxe looked at her hands and found that her fists were clenched. She opened them. "If they were ni'chea, don't you think the White Clan would have spoken by now?"

"I suppose so," he said. "But—Yardmaster, have you ever walked across ground that looked and seemed solid, only to have it quiver and shake under your weight like the sand beneath the tides? You tell me short swords are not ni'chea, and my stomach feels the ground give under my feet."

"I know," Paxe said. "I feel it too. But I am the Med Yardmaster, and those are my instructions from Arré Med, to teach the sword. All I need to know—all you need to know, Captain—is that it is not illegal."

He bowed from his seated position, palms together, and then rose fluidly. He started toward the door.

"Wait!"

He turned. "Yardmaster." His face was stone.

"You have not heard my report," she said.

"Yardmaster."

"It was quiet." Too damn quiet, she thought. He was still

watching her with eyes like agate, and she wanted to smack his head, hard, or else put her arms about him, whatever might thaw that frozen expression. "The guards at the baths found two men sleeping near the furnace and sent them to one of the travelers' shelters. Two drunks had a fight on the Batto district border and the Batto guards broke it up. A woman was found ill on Oil Street and one of the guards delivered her to the Tanjo—" She made him listen to the recitation, watching his eyes slowly change, and see her. When she finished, her right temple was throbbing as if someone had struck her. But Ivor no longer looked as if his blood had changed to ice.

He bowed. "Is there more, Yardmaster?"

She wondered if she should tell him about the shadower Arré had had her find for Kim Batto. But no, that was none of his business, and it would only upset him further to know. Whatever balance he had found was precarious, and till it was strengthened she did not want to impair it. "Nothing, Captain. Dismissed."

Two hours before sunset, the Yard was full. When Paxe came from the cottage, she counted forty people inside the fence. Most of the day watch was there, and the tension of suppressed excitement was stifling, like the pressure of air before a rainstorm. She wondered how the word had gone around so quickly.

Some of the soldiers had formed fighting circles. But when Paxe stepped into the Yard, the circles broke apart. The guards all turned to watch her. The door to the weapons shed was, of course, locked. She caught Kaleb's eye; he crossed to her side. "There are not enough sejis for all of them," she said. "Who ordered this?"

"Not I." He fished the shed key from his pocket. She opened the shed; the sejis lay on their racks. Paxe lifted one, then a second from its place. She gave one to Kaleb.

"Remember?" she said. "It's been a long time since the desert."

His teeth flashed in the shadowy hut. "I remember."

As they stepped into the sunlight, the waiting guards drew a collective breath. Paxe pointed at random. "You. Stand outside the Yard gate. No one not wearing Med colors is to enter."

Disappointment surged across the face of the soldier she had picked, but he bowed without speaking and went to the gate.

Paxe pivoted to face Kaleb. "Let's show them something," she said. "Slowly."

He dipped the point of the wooden blade in salute and fell into stance. She struck at him, and he countered. She struck a second time, and he countered again and then struck at her, making her leap out of range. The strokes of defense and attack made a pattern which they both knew: This was a *naïga*, a prescribed series of thrusts and parries, which she had learned from Tyré and taught to Kaleb in the desert. This particular naïga had twenty-five steps.

Slice, slice, thrust, parry, backstep, cut at the legs. As she moved, her chest tightened; she was breathing wrong. She forced the air out with her strokes. Huff. Huff. At the fourteenth step in the dance, Kaleb faltered, and she leaped inside his guard and bore his sword hand to the side and away and threw him, with a motion that left her in possession of his sword. He rolled and came up standing just out of her reach.

Kneeling, Paxe slid his sword toward him, hilt first. He scooped it up, careful not to touch the edge with his fingers.

Paxe said, to a silence so thick she could almost smell it: "The first rule of sword practice is to treat the wooden sword as if it were not wooden, but steel. Never touch the point or the edge of the blade with your hand. Never play with it, nor permit others to play with it around you."

The soldiers drew closer. A few nodded. She went on. "This sword is a komys, a short sword. It is not covered by the Ban and is therefore legal to use. *However*—" she paused, gathering their attention to focus—"at present, use of the short sword, like use of a spear, is reserved for properly trained guards, and must be confined to the Yard. Any soldier of mine who takes a blade—" she tapped the seji so that they would be sure to understand she meant even a wooden one—"beyond these walls will be punished *and* that transgression will be reported to the Tanjo."

More nods. She grinned, and dropped the formal manner. "You got that? Good. No talk about them either, you donkeys; to your mothers or your bedmates or even to each other outside the fence. What we do in here is our concern. If you're asked, look innocent. The asker won't believe you but it doesn't matter. Now—" She picked four soldiers from the circle and told them to take the sejis from the weapons shed and hand them out. "There won't be enough for you all. Don't worry about it. No!" This to Kepi, who had wrapped her fingers around the blade above the hilt. "You just lost four fingers from your left hand. Drop the blade." Scarlet, Kepi dropped the seji on the dirt. "Now go and stand against the wall. Kinith, you pick it up." Kneeling, Kinith grasped the seji as he had seen her do, fingers around the hilt.

"Have any of you ever used a blade?" she said.

Four voices murmured assent. "Fine. You're instructors. Don't get puffy about it. All right, those with the sejis stand in two facing lines. Hold the sword out, so." They copied her stance. "Right foot forward. Right hand first on the hilt, like holding the spear but close together. Get those shoulders down. Hands level with your waist. Your grip should be firm but light." Laying her sword down, she checked the four "instructors" to make sure they did, indeed, know what they were doing. The guards without swords watched jealously. "Yes. All right, you four give up your blades. Go and check stances. No, that's not how you pick it up! One knee down and back straight so that you can look around you, idiot." She imitated the man who had bent from the waist to pick up the sword. "Best way I can think of to get stabbed in the rump. Go stand next to Kepi."

She taught them the first stroke, the downward slice forward. In a little while, the Yard rang with a count. ("One—and two—and three—and four!") A light breeze from the south cooled the space, but even with it, soon she and Kaleb and all the guards were sweating. "Tighten your butt muscles at the end of your swing, but keep your hands and shoulders limber. The stroke should be firm. Don't let the point dip. If the blade wiggles as you strike, your grip is wrong, probably too tight. And one—and two—and three—and four. And one—and two—and three—and four. First line, lay your swords down, *kneeling*, assholes, yes, that's right. Back up. You ten, step forward and take them. Why are you holding the blade above the hilt? Idiot. Against the fence. You, pick it up. And one—and two—and three—and four."

By the end of two hours, all the guards, including the man at the gate and the ones who spent most of the time by the fence, had a chance to learn the naïga's first three steps. Paxe called them all together and repeated her warnings to them before she let them go. Kaleb supervised the return of the sejis to the shed.

He came to stand beside her. "What do you think?" she asked him.

He nodded. "They'll do."

"As long as they don't talk about it." She stretched, feeling her joints pop. Her muscles were sore and tense. She touched Kaleb's arm. "Train with me for a bit. Empty-hand."

He grinned, and shifted his weight. "Yai!" She reached for him and he spun around her. They struck and countered and threw each other to the ground, and Paxe's muscles loosened. At last she signaled halt. Her hair and clothing were caked with dust.

"Ah, that's better," she said. "I feel more like a human being."

Kaleb said cheerfully, "You smell like a donkey."

"Wretch. Is that how you speak to your commander?" She grinned. "Guardian, I do, don't I. I'd better bathe. Give me the shed key."

He handed her the heavy key. "When do you plan to hold a second session with the swords," he said, "one that the late watch can attend?"

"Tomorrow afternoon," Paxe said, "before watch change."

Two days later, Paxe walked into the Yard at midnight to receive Kaleb's report, and found two men waiting for her: Kaleb, and Sereth, the day Gate Captain.

The Yard was empty, except for those two. She nodded greeting to them, wondering what Sereth was doing there. Since watch reassignment, she had not seen him at all. He had not come to the sword training, but she assumed it was not because he was shirking but because he was exhausted after a day on the Gate. Kaleb, too, looked weary. But he also looked annoyed.

"How was the day?" she said.

"I've had better," Kaleb answered. He gave her a brief report, and then pointed his chin at Sereth. "Your Gate Captain, here, desires to have speech with you. He refuses to talk to me, or to Ivor."

Sereth shifted from one foot to the other. "Yardmaster," he said, "I know it's unusual but I do have reason."

"You'd better," Paxe said. All complaints or suggestions from the captains were supposed to go first to their watch commanders or to Kaleb. Sereth's thick sandy hair was sticking out from his head, as it did when he was alarmed. "Well," she said, "let's go to the cottage."

The house was dark. Paxe reached for tinder and flint and lit a lamp. As the room brightened, Sereth said, "Yardmaster, please forgive me for coming to you in this fashion."

Paxe said, "It's not I who should forgive you, but Ivor and Kaleb. You insult them when you disregard their authority in this way."

"I mean no insult, truly," said Sereth. "Only, this is important!"

Kaleb's brows drew together.

Paxe said coldly, "You are impertinent and tactless, Captain. Sit down. What's this about?"

Sereth seated himself. Kaleb loomed ominously at his shoulder. "It's about Leth-no-Chayatha," he said.

"Vanesi's caravan master."

"Yes. You told me to question him, about the swords."

"And you did."

"And I did, and he knew nothing, he swore it, by the Guardian, on his mother's grave, by all the demons of winter, he knew nothing." Sereth frowned. "I didn't believe him. Something in his manner—but the Blue Clan would not let a Truthfinder be called, and I didn't think I was going to get anywhere by asking him the same questions over and over again. He kept repeating his answers. So I stopped."

"When did you stop questioning him?" asked Kaleb.

"The last day of the Feast of the Ox," said Sereth. "I stopped but I kept an eye on him." He paused, then stuck his jaw out stubbornly and continued. "I asked my second to cover for me a few times so that I could leave my post, and I asked some friends on the late and night watches to help me."

"Go on," said Paxe grimly.

"The night of the half moon–three days ago—he left his house and went to a place he'd never gone before. The other days he spent doing mostly the same things: going to taverns and over to Seller's Alley."

"Did you follow him *there*, too?" said Kaleb, his voice dripping sarcasm.

"Yes. But I stayed in the shadows, and I don't think he saw me. He's got a fine body—" Sereth's teeth flashed—"and I guess he likes making money with it. Anyway, he went to this house, and when he came out he had a *lot* of money. He spent it on clothes and jewelry and gambling in the taverns and he's been eating in places a caravan master can't usually afford."

"He got paid for something," said Paxe. "All right, Sereth, what house did he visit?"

"Isak Med's," said Sereth.

Paxe blinked. Isak. Arré had suspected Isak of having something to do with the swords. "What do you think happened at that house?" she said.

"I'm sure he got paid for something," said Sereth, obviously trying not to sound surprised at the question. "I thought—well, it seemed likely that it has something to do with the swords."

"Why?" said Kaleb. But the concentration in his dark face showed that he was taking Sereth's story seriously at last.

Sereth said, "Because the Ismenin Yard is teaching the short sword; has been, since before we found the swords in Vanesi's wagon. And Isak Med and Ron Ismenin are friends."

Paxe said, leaning forward, "How do *you* know when the Ismenin Yard started teaching?"

Sereth said, "My sister's son's father has a brother who is a guard there. He got drunk three nights ago, and told me."

So Dobrin's rules for secrecy were breaking down at last. With rumors flying about the city like bats, the Ismenin soldiers must be feeling that it doesn't matter who they talk to, Paxe thought. She nodded at Sereth. "You are right," she said, "and you were correct to come to me about it. I take back my harsh words."

"Unfortunately," Kaleb put in, hunkering down beside Sereth, "nothing you've said is evidence of a crime. So a man has money. So what? Would you like to go in front of a Med district magistrate and bring a charge against Isak Med?"

Sereth ran his fingers through his hair. "Of course not. But I thought, if Leth were to be talked to—" He glanced at Paxe, hopeful and uncertain. "You're more forceful than I am, Yardmaster. He might tell you what he wouldn't tell me."

At his side, Kaleb gave a low chuckle. "Paxe, he wants you to beat it out of the man."

"It wouldn't have to be that," Sereth said hastily. "Only— he's *very* vain."

Kaleb's teeth gleamed. "Threaten to cut his nose off."

"Wait a minute," said Paxe. "Just wait. I am not going to go chasing Vanesi's caravan master around Kendra-on-the-Delta with a carving knife."

Sereth bounced a little on the mat. "You don't have to. I know where he is. He went to the public baths this afternoon.

Right now, he's in a pipe den in the Batto district. It's called the House of Pleasant Dreams and it's in the Street of the Whispers. He's planning to be there until two hours after midnight, and then he's going to Sellers' Alley."

Kaleb said, "I know that pipe den."

The light from the chobata lit his face; his weariness seemed to have fallen from him like a discarded shirt. "The owner's Asech; his name's Skandar. I know him. He wouldn't object if we wanted to speak privately with one of his patrons, as long as we didn't wake the others up. . . . He has private rooms, also."

Sereth beamed at the watch commander's words.

Paxe said, "Well, you're convinced." She rose, and walked around the room. The statue of the Guardian, in its place, seemed to watch her, and for a moment, it almost seemed to move.

"All right," she said finally, "let's try it." She wondered what Arré would say if Paxe brought her evidence proving that Isak Med was directly involved with smuggling swords.

Sereth accompanied them to the pipe den, of course. The two men waited in the Yard while Paxe summoned Dis, her watch second, and instructed her to make rounds in Paxe's place. Dis was a stolid, dependable woman, and a grandmother with six grandchildren at last count. "Whatever you're doing," she said, "have fun."

The farther south they walked, the thicker the fog. It smelled of fish. "Down by the docks, it must be thick enough to swim in," said Sereth.

Kaleb said, "I can't swim."

Paxe glanced at him. His face was somber. She tripped him. He took two quick steps forward and whirled on his toes.

"What are you so gloomy about?" she demanded. "A while ago, you were all joyful, now you're down a well!"

"I was thinking," said Kaleb.

"What were you thinking?"

"How to talk to Leth-no-Chayatha." His grin grew wolfish.

Paxe frowned. "He won't take much persuading," she said. "He's going to be cloud-high on heavenweed."

"True," said Kaleb. "Very true."

They were challenged three times before they reached the Street of the Whispers, twice by Med guards and once by a

Batto guard. The damp streets seemed to mute their steps. Kaleb, of course, was noiseless, and Sereth glanced at him enviously three or four times, and finally asked, "How can you move so silently?"

"Training," said Kaleb. "Practice. I was brought up in the desert, and learned to approach rats so silently that I could take them with my bare hands."

Sereth flicked an unbelieving look at Paxe. "It's true," she said. "I've seen him do it." Drops of mist rolled down her collar, and she thrust her hands in her pockets and cursed to herself, wishing she had remembered to wear her cloak with the hood.

The mist made the gray pitted streets gleam black in the lamplight. They passed few others: some late-night carousers, who barely knew it was raining, a girl let out late from her shift at a tavern, an old man plodding homeward beside a droop-eared donkey; appearing and then vanishing in the mist like ghosts. Many of the taverns they passed seemed half empty, and a few, that looked as if they ought to be open, were barred closed.

They came to the Street of the Whispers. "Why do they call it that?" Paxe asked.

Sereth answered, "Because there's a spot on the street, they say, where, if you stand there, you can hear every word anyone else is saying anywhere on the block. I've never found it."

"Have you tried?" asked Kaleb.

Sereth shrugged. "Once or twice."

They were two blocks from the House of Pleasant Dreams. Already Paxe could smell the strong, sweet scent of the drug. The heavenweed smoked in the pipe dens was a lot stronger than the kind one could find on the streets. Paxe preferred heavenweed as an intoxicant to wine, because it heightened the senses in a way she liked.

But she had stopped smoking heavenweed when Ricky had started to do nothing else. She wondered how he was, and if he had received the boots she'd sent him.

"Here," said the Gate Captain. "Here we are."

The house was long and low, built like a warehouse, with few windows. A banner flapped on a pole above the door. On it was a painted picture of a clay pipe and the serrated-edged leafe of the heavenweed plant. Under the picture was written: *The House of Pleasant Dreams*, in faded letters. The heavenscent was overpowering. "In this place," said Sereth, "even the mice are high."

He mimicked an intoxicated mouse. Paxe chuckled, and jerked her head toward the door. "Come on, actor."

"Let me talk to Skandar," said Kaleb. Paxe nodded. They pushed open the door.

The long room was in shadow: choba dishes on small tables sent tongues of light over the dreamy faces of the smokers. The room was hot and stuffy. The heat came from braziers standing at intervals in the corridor; smokers tended to feel chill more quickly than other people. The room was broken up into smaller rooms by half-screens, no higher than the height of a tall man, which gave the illusion of privacy. Voices murmured from the cubicles; laughter sounded from the back of the house. The air was heavy with heavenweed; almost at once, Paxe felt her body beginning to respond to the drug's allure. That, too, she told herself, was an illusion.

A man hurried to them down the corridor. He had a typical Asech face, dark, narrow, bronze, with blue jewels glinting in his earlobes. Kaleb went forward to talk to him and they had a whispered conversation. Kaleb came back to them. "Leth-no-Chayatha is in a back booth, high as the Tanjo dome. Skandar says he can put us in a back room and then bring the man to us, but he requests us, please, to keep this quiet, or it will disturb his customers."

"How much?" said Paxe, feeling for her money string.

"A trey."

Paxe worked the bonta from her pocket and gave it to Kaleb, who gave it to Skandar. They followed the man past the booths to another wooden door. Here the rooms were more solid, walled in wood. There were cushions on the mats and a table to lean on. Paxe took off her shoes and sat on a cushion. Sereth thrust his hands through his hair until it looked like a scrubbrush. She hit his leg to get his attention. "Sit down."

He sat. Kaleb leaned on the doorframe. In a moment, they heard a voice. "That's Leth," said Sereth. "Chea, he's high." The mumbled words were thick as glue.

Kaleb said, "When he walks in, I'll bring him down. Yardmaster, you hold his arms and shoulders. Sereth, get his legs. We'd better have something to stuff in his mouth."

Paxe said. "Use his shirt. You're going to strip him."

Kaleb said, "Good idea."

"Where should I—" Sereth began.

"There!" said Paxe, pointing to the end of the table nearest the door. Sereth scrambled to it. The door opened and a man walked in. "Now what's this?" he said, peering forward into the dim space.

Kaleb reached out, spun him, and threw him backward over the table in one crisp economical motion. Sereth grabbed his feet. Paxe locked his arms behind his head, immobilizing his torso. As his back hit the table, he cried out in pain. Kneeling, Kaleb caught his shirt in one strong hand and ripped downward. It came free, and he thrust the back of it into Leth's open mouth before the caravan master realized what was happening. As the cloth filled his mouth, he started to struggle, trying to buck and roll free of his captors. Kaleb put a hand on his throat, finger and thumb on each of the big arteries, and applied pressure. Leth gasped, and his eyes started to glaze.

Kaleb took his hand away. "If you yell, no one can hear you." he said. His hand snaked to his boot and came up with a knife. Sereth's eyes widened, and he glanced at Paxe, who shrugged. "All we want are the answers to some questions. You tell us, we go away. You don't tell us, we hurt you. Understand?"

Comprehension and the drug struggled in Leth's blue eyes. He tried to speak through the gag. Kaleb smiled, and laid the tip of the knife tenderly against the man's dark belly. "Don't yell," he said, and pulled the soggy gag out.

"Who the hell are—" Kaleb put the gag back over the man's mouth, but did not force it in.

"That's none of your concern, my friend. Now, here's the first question." He dug the knife in a little. Blood trickled down Leth's belly. He sucked in his breath to escape the probing steel, and Paxe pulled down on his arms, forcing his back to arch upward. Kaleb lifted the knife. "Who paid you to put the kyomos into Vanesi's caravan?"

He lifted the gag. Leth said, in a choked voice, "I didn't, I didn't. You've got the wrong—"

"Person," said Kaleb, clapping the gag back on. "You don't think I mean it. Hold him." Lightly, he began to draw the knife along the man's muscular torso, from nipples to belly button, making one line, two, three—He stopped and reached into his pocket. He held up a bag. Paxe recognized it. It was the bag she kept salt in; Kaleb had taken it from her kitchen.

She had not even seen him go there.

"Salt," he said. He laid the knife down and began to open the bag, slowly, drawing it out. Paxe looked at Sereth. The younger guard was pale, his lips tight together. Leth was trying to writhe free again and she clamped down hard on his arms. The salt would hurt but it would not damage. She only hoped that he was not too high to feel it.

Kaleb had the bag open. Casually, he pinched salt between thumb and finger and dusted it over the wounds. Leth squealed, through the gag, and tried to break free, but Sereth and Paxe held him fast. Tears rolled from his eyes. Kaleb waited until the man stopped fighting, and lifted the gag. "Who paid you to put the komys into Vanesi's caravan?" he said.

"Minto," said Leth. "The Lord Cha Minto."

"He's lying," said Sereth instantly. "He went nowhere near the Minto house."

"I'm not lying, I swear it—" Leth's voice rose. Kaleb stuffed the gag in his mouth and leaned on it. With his left hand he rolled Leth's trouser waist down over the man's hips to just above the genitals.

He picked up the knife.

"Wait," said Paxe. Leth had, indeed, a nice body; trim and tight and sleek as a wildcat's. "Lift the gag." Kaleb obeyed. "Tell me," Paxe said, "who *handed* you the money."

"Isak Med," said Leth.

"Where?"

"At his house. But he told me it was Minto money, that he was just the paymaster."

"Do you believe him?" said Kaleb. "If not—" He lifted the knife.

"I swear it's true," said Leth, and his voice broke. "Please—"

"Shut up," said Paxe. There was no reason for him to be making it up. Of course, Isak might have told him to say it, if asked. It was just the sort of thing Isak would do.

"Make sure," she said to Kaleb, and tightened her hold. Kaled nodded, his face resolute. Paxe looked away; so did Sereth.

Nothing that followed was pleasant. But at last, Kaleb lifted the knife and said, "I think he's honest." Through the gag, Leth sobbed, more in fear and humiliation than in pain. Kaleb drew the pants up over the cuts, trying not to scrape them. Leth had stuck to the story; that Isak Med had told him, casually, offhandedly, that he was paymaster for Cha Minto.

"One other thing," said Paxe. Kaleb lifted the gag. Leth gazed at her with swollen eyes. "Where did you get the swords from?"

"They were delivered to us just outside Mahita. I put them in the boxes."

"How did you know where to get paid?"

"I got a message."

"Weren't you afraid of the Ban?" asked Paxe.

Leth shrugged and winced. Paxe scowled, and he flinched away from her. "I thought—if the Minto house was bringing in the swords, it had to be all right," he said timidly.

Kaleb snorted. "Did you think that before or after you got paid?"

Somewhere in the den a woman's voice sighed aloud, in fear or pleasure—it was impossible to say. Paxe felt light-headed from the omnipresent smoke. Cha Minto, she thought, and Isak? She would not have thought Cha Minto capable of it—he had always seemed to her to be rather a simpleton—but if Isak had manipulated him into it—yes, she could believe it.

"Why did you agree to it?" she asked.

"For the money," said Leth-no-Chayatha, his voice a shade puzzled.

Paxe sighed, and released her grip on his arms. "All right."

Sereth let go of Leth's feet. He sat up, moving with care, and lifted himself from the table to the mat. Absently, Kaleb moved back to give him room. "Can I go?" Leth said humbly, to the second.

Kaleb looked at Paxe. His knife was still in his hand. "May he?"

"Yes, let him go. Give him his shirt," Sereth fished it from the floor and handed it to him. It was tattered, damp with saliva, and looked like a rag.

"Don't go shouting to the housetops that you were questioned at knifepoint about swords," Paxe said, "or you may find yourself in a guardhouse. Until the Council says otherwise, bringing swords into the city is still unlawful. There'll be someone watching you until you leave. When are you going north?"

"After Festival," said Leth.

"Make sure you do go," said Paxe. She stared hard at him, and filled her voice with menace. "You got off very easily, you know. It could have been worse. It still can be, if you open your mouth."

Leth shivered. "I won't say anthing."

"See that you don't. You sit here. We'll leave." She rose. Sereth stood, stretching his cramped arms. Kaleb swept the bag of salt from the table, and standing, made his knife disappear.

They put their boots back on, and went to the front of the pipe den. Skandar came from a room. "How have you left him?" he whispered.

"Whole," said Kaleb, "but shaken. Thanks, my friend. Your service won't be forgotten."

"No trouble." He ushered them outside.

Paxe sighed as the cool, foggy air swirled round them. Her head ached; she told herself it was from the smoke in the pipe den. She clapped Kaleb on the shoulder.

"Thanks. I couldn't have done that," she said.

Sereth shuddered. "Nor could I."

Kaleb shrugged with his hands. "Here." He handed Paxe the bag of salt. She put it in her pocket. The wind swept from the south, sending leaves rustling and knocking unlatched window screens against their frames.

Sereth said, "Shall I find someone to watch him?"

Paxe smiled. "No. But let him think you have. You know where he lives; you might wander by it sometime when he's there, to let him see you. You were wise to come to me about it."

Sereth tried to hide his grin of delight. "Now where are we going?" he said.

"You are going to your beds," said Paxe. "And I to work." And in the morning, she thought, I will talk with Arré. They walked slowly east and north, three ghosts, appearing and vanishing in the mournful darkness.

CHAPTER FOURTEEN

"Cha Minto?" said Arré. "Are you sure?"

"I'm sure," said Paxe.

They sat in the little parlor. Arré was waiting for Jenith, and for Morin, the tailor. In the early morning hours, the east wind had risen and blown across the city, sending the fog scudding west. The sun sat over an ocean sparkling like silver, and the sky was clear and blue and hot.

Arré had not been prepared for Paxe's tale, but the news that Cha Minto had paid for the smuggling of the swords into the city did not surprise her. "So that's what was wrong with him at the Council meeting." She turned the bracelets on her left arm. "I don't suppose I want to know exactly how you obtained this information."

"No," said Paxe, "you don't. But I guarantee you my informant believes it."

Arré wondered how Isak had enticed Cha Minto into this scheme. Were they lovers? she wondered. Somehow she did not think so. Her mouth was dry; she reached to the carafe of water that sat on the lacquer table and poured a second glass. Ever since her sickness, she had been taken, off and on, with a raging thirst.

Paxe's eyes followed her movements. "Arré, are you recovered?" she said.

"I seem to be," said Arré. "I've had no wine since that night." It was still difficult for her to believe that she'd slept for two days. "What are they saying in the city, now, about Ron Ismenin and the swords?"

"The news that the Ismenin Yard is teaching swordplay is all over the city."

"Are people connecting the Ismeninas with the smuggled swords?"

Paxe rubbed her chin. "Not yet. Oh, a few have. It's strange, Arré. Weapons just don't seem *real* to the city-born. They talk about them but they don't think about them."

"How are your soldiers reacting to the sword training?"

"They love it. But even they don't see swords as real, as tools that can maim or kill."

"I hope they never do," Arré said softly.

Paxe said, "Do you think there's a chance of it?"

Arré sighed. "I told you once, I don't know what Ron Ismenin plans. Maybe you can find out. Ask your friend Dobrin."

She had meant it half seriously. But Paxe's eyes narrowed, and then she nodded. "I may," she said.

Lalith tapped on the doorjamb. "Lady?"

"Yes, child, what is it?"

"Jenith is here to see you."

"Good." Arré set the glass down on the table.

Paxe rose. "I'll leave you to talk." She stretched her long arms above her head. "Guardian, I'm tired." She strode out. She halted a moment in the corridor to talk to Jenith: Arré heard their voices, Paxe's deep, the stranger's higher but husky. Then Jenith came into the parlor. She was small and dark, with an attractive, weathered face and gold rings in both her ears.

"Lady." She bowed, and looked about her with frank appreciation. "This is nice. I like the little lamps."

"Thank you," said Arré, amused and charmed. The lamps were white procelain, the finest made in all of Arun; on them an artist had painted grapes still on the vine, in tribute to that source of Med wealth. The colors were fresh and luminous. "So do I. Please sit." She pointed to the stool.

Jenith sat. "Do you mind if I smoke?"

"No." Arré watched, fascinated, as Jenith drew a pipe and a little kid pouch from a pocket in her robe. She filled the pipe from the pouch with a green herb, then drew tinder and flint from the same place, and lit the pipe.

"Ah." She tipped her head back and opened her mouth. A ring of soft gray smoke floated toward the ceiling. "That's better."

Arré had never seen anyone blow smoke rings before. She watched, fascinated, as the gray rings floated from the woman's mouth and headed toward the ceiling. Before they got there, they dissipated, and Arré wondered what it would be like if they hung together; she imagined a ceiling lined with hovering gray rings.

"Want some?" said Jenith, waving the pipe at her.

"No, thank you," said Arré. The scent of heavenweed filled the sunny chamber. "I'm sorry I was sick before, when you came."

"Ho, were you sick? They didn't tell me; they just said, come back. I would have come back the next day but that was the day the courier left town and of course I followed him."

"Left town," said Arré. "Kim Batto left town?"

"No. But his messenger did." Jenith pointed the stem of the pipe at Arré. "You know, Lady, your instructions weren't very good. Paxe said I was to follow Kim Batto, but you don't really want to know where Kim Batto goes every day, do you? Oh, I can tell you that. What you want to know is what he's *doing*."

Arré raised her eyebrows. "Go on," she said.

"A moment. Excuse me." Jenith took out a stick and poked at her pipe. She sucked it hard, until smoke came from the bowl in a thin steady stream.

"Anyway, I started by following Kim Batto, as I was told. First day last week I don't know what he did; I wasn't watching then; Paxe only came to see me that afternoon. Second day he went to the market and to the Tanjo. Third day he went to the baths, and then to the tailor, where he picked out fabric for some new clothes to wear to the Ismenin betrothal."

"How do you know what the clothes were for?" demanded Arré.

"I talked to the tailor. He's a neighbor of Shem, my second in the warehouse. *He* didn't know why I wanted to know."

"I see," said Arré. "Go on."

"Fourth day—" Jenith paused to blow a fat smoke ring— "fourth day he spent the morning in his house. I talked to one of the kitchen boys and found out that he was writing, and swearing a lot. That afternoon a courier came to the house, not a messenger but a guard wearing riding clothes. I got curious. I found a friend and told him to stay at the house and watch what the Batto lord did, and then I followed the courier. He left the house with a bag under his arm, and went to the stables to rent a horse. I knew someone in the Med district stable, so I borrowed a horse and followed. He took the river road. He put the bag and what was in it in his saddlebag, and whenever he stopped to eat, he took it with him, so I guessed it was important. He went to Mahita the first night, and I stayed in the inn with him, but he slept with the bag in his bed. In Warrintown and Elath, he did the same. In Elath, he talked to a girl at the Travelers' Hall and told her he was going to Nuath." She blew another smoke ring. Arré sat, entranced by the recital.

"On the road between Elath and Shonet, he got careless, or cocky. He left the bag in the stable when he went to an inn to eat. 'Course, he didn't know I was there. He did the same thing that night. So I went into the stable with a big rolled-up kava leaf, the biggest I could find, tied with a bit of string, and I put it in the bag, and I took out what was there." Reaching into her capacious robe, she withdrew a white scroll, sealed with the Batto crest, the running horse. "Then I rode as fast as I could back. It would have been impossible on the horse *he* was riding, but I was on an Asech horse, so it took me half the time to get back that it had taken him to go. Even if he discovered the leaf in the morning, he won't be back for two more days."

Arré took the scroll in both hands. "You astound me," she managed.

Jenith smiled. "It was easy," she said smugly. "The guard was a fool not to see to me. I'd've seen me. But then, after he started smoking heavenweed on the road, he'd not have noticed a pig if it had crawled into his bed."

Arré opened the scroll.

She scanned it quickly, automatically translating its formal language in her mind. It was to the Lord Tarn i Nuath Ryth, of the town of Nuath. It confirmed an agreement between Tarn i Nuath Ryth and Kim Batton "in recognition of mutual interest" and contained vague allusions to grain prices which might be lowered in response to the rendering of service having to do with the Council of Houses of Kendra-on-the-Delta. What, she thought, was going on? She had expected Jenith to provide her with some evidence of the link between Ron Ismenin and the Tanjo, not evidence of what appeared to be a treaty between Kim Batto and some upriver, Blue Clan barbarian!

She re-read the scroll. It told her no more the second reading. She wondered what the "services" (carefully unspecified in the scroll) were going to be. There were not, she thought tartly, going to be any such services done. The making of treaties by individual houses (except in the traditional way, by marriage) with other houses or clans was strictly forbidden. She grinned at the thought of what Kim Batto would do when his courier returned to say he had gotten as far as Shonet—or Sharon, or even Nuath—when he noticed the scroll was missing.

Jenith said, "Was it something you wanted?"

Arré looked up. "It was certainly something I wanted," she

said. "I hadn't anticipated it, that's all, and I'm not sure what it is. I must owe you some money." She went to her chest, hesitated, and then pulled out two tetras. She brought them to the small dark woman. "Is this sufficient?" she asked. "You must have had some traveling expenses."

"It covers them," said Jenith. "I didn't have many; I borrowed a horse, and I slept in the stables." She lifted her pipe from the lacquer table. "Do you want me to keep on at it, Lady?"

"I do," said Arré. "At least for another four days, till the Ismenin betrothal."

Jenith's capable hands hid the coins amid her robes. Her hair was pitch-black and scented with jasmine, and she wore a copper talisman with the figure of an ox on it around her neck.

"Don't those rings hurt?" Arré said, gesturing to the gold rings in Jenith's ears.

"Naw," said the Asech woman. "My aunt made the holes with a pin, when I was just a babe. My daughters have them, too."

"You have children?"

"Three of them; two girls and a son."

"How old are you?" Arré asked.

"Forty," said Jenith. She smiled. "I've worked for the Med house since I was twelve; in the fields, in the winery, and now in the warehouse."

Forty, thought Arré. Jenith was only four years younger than she. "Thank you for your service to my house," she said.

Jenith nodded. "You pay well. Good day to you, Lady." She marched out.

Borrowed a horse and slept in the stables, Arré thought; I could not do that. I couldn't've done it twenty years ago. The knowledge left her somewhat bemused.

That afternoon, Paxe went to talk to Dobrin.

She had planned to sleep until it was time for her to teach the first sword class. But she had not been able to sleep. At last, she had risen from her bed and opened the lid to the cedar chest.

She took the sword from it, and laid it to one side. Then she reached into the chest for the things she knew were there, though she had not seen them in sixteen years. She found the clove oil first; she unstoppered the bottle to smell the oil. It still smelled usuable. The powder was in a little box with its brush. She took it out. Last, her fingers encountered the piece of faded red cloth that she had brought back with her from the Red Hills. She lifted it from the depths of the chest and laid it across her knees.

Tyré had worn it. Dying, he had taken it from his arm and put it in her hand; his sharize, emblem of the cheari, given to him fifty years before by Doménia. Paxe tried to tell him she had no right to it, but he had not listened.

She stroked it. It smelled of cedar. She had never worn it and she was not going to wear it now, but she had needed to look at it.

She fixed her eyes on the red stone image of the Guardian. But nothing happened, no sense of relief or surcease of worry. She told herself that it was only a statue, and that the chea did not always speak. Rising, she wound the sturdy length of cloth around the base of the statue. Then she returned to her place and cleaned the northern sword.

When she finished with it, she put it back in the chest and left the house. The Ismenin mansion sat in massive splendor on its hillside; she climbed to it, wondering as she passed the gate what it would be like to live in. Damp, probably.

She walked to the Yard. The Yard gate had been replaced. No longer was it of iron, with bars that could be seen between if there were not a guard in front of it. The new gate was of red cedar planks, with a heavy latch, and it stood taller than she, tall as the top of the fence. The guard in front of it (a different man than had been there before) saw her and stiffened to attention, his spear horizontal, barring the door.

"Tell your Yardmaster that Paxe-no-Tamaris is here, and would like to speak to him," Paxe said.

He bowed. "If you will excuse me, Yardmaster—" Unlatching the heavy gate, he slipped within, holding it closed to prevent her from seeing anything. She listened to the cadence count floating over the walls until the guard came back. "The Yardmaster asks you to go around the Yard to his house."

"Thank you," Paxe said. She went round the Yard; the count grew louder. ("One—and two—and three—and four!") The river gulls hooted over her head.

The door to the cottage was open. She went it. Dobrin sat crosslegged behind his table. A spray of yellow blossoms sat in a copper bowl on the table, and a second branch stood under the statue of the Guardian. Instead of fetuch, there were apple slices in a plain blue bowl.

Taking her boots off, Paxe set them in the alcove by the door and walked across the mats to the waiting cushion.

They ate the apple slices.

Dobrin said, "It's good to see you again."

Paxe said, "You know where I live."

"Yes." He sounded apologetic. "I've been busy—and you're on night watch now, are you not? I don't want to interrupt your sleep."

Paxe smiled. "How goes your training?"

"Well," said Dobrin, "and yours?"

She had assumed he knew. "Adequately," she answered. "We've not had the sejis very long."

"Do you find the city-bred soldiers do worse or better at handling the blades?" he asked.

She scratched her chin. "About as well as the country-born—except that they forget to treat the wood as if it were steel. They don't think of them as swords; they think of them as sticks."

"Yes," said Dobrin, "I noticed that, too."

Paxe said, "Where did you get your weapons training, Dobrin?"

"From a woman named Sithi, in the Galbareth. She was quite old. She had trained with a chearas for a while, before the Ban, but did not herself have the shariza. Why?"

Paxe touched the soft yellow petals with one finger. They were butterweed blossoms; they grew all over the delta, and had almost no fragrance. "I've been thinking," she said, "about what you said to me of the witchfolk, and about other things. . . . Dobrin, do you trust Ron Ismenin?"

Stiffly, he said, "I don't know what you mean."

Paxe scowled. "Dammit, man, don't play the fool with me. We are colleagues, if not friends. You know what the Ismeninas have been doing; smuggling edged weapons in through the Gates. Where are they, in your weapons shed? Hidden in the house somewhere?" She discovered, to her astonishment, a great desire to shout at him. With effort, she kept her voice down. "What is Ron Ismenin planning to do with those blades?"

To her amazement, Dobrin smiled. He smiled, "I understand your suspicion, Paxe. But you are wrong."

"About what am I wrong?"

"It is true, the swords are here. But their smuggling was not arranged by the Ismeninas. Ron Ismenin has sworn it to me, and I believe him. It was another man's idea."

Isak's? thought Paxe. Cha Minto's? "Whose?" she asked.

"I don't know."

"What does Ron plan to do with them, now that he has them?"

"Nothing," said Dobrin. He held up a hand. "Nothing, until the Council meets after Festival. At that time, he tells me, he will approach the Council to suggest that short swords be once again permitted in the city, to the guard only, of course."

"And the White Clan?" Paxe said. "How do they come into this?"

Dobrin looked surprised. "In no way. The Ismenin house has no dealings with the Tanjo. My lord feels as I do about the witchfolk. He reverences the chea, but neither consults nor trusts the witches."

I rather doubt, Paxe thought, that Ron Ismenin has reverence for anything but his own wants. "What if you are wrong?" she said, leaning forward, and found that her voice was shaking.

Dobrin said gently, "But I am not wrong, Paxe." He laid both hands flat on the table. "I know the Ismeninas. I have served them for years; I was Colin Ismenin's Yardmaster, and I even knew old Rath Ismenin those few years before he died. The Ismeninas have always looked to what will serve the city."

"And themselves," said Paxe.

"Is the Med house any different? Do you think Arré Med does anything without first considering the interests of her house?"

It was a fair question. "No," said Paxe.

Dobrin nodded. "Believe me," he said earnestly. "If I thought Ron Ismenin was doing aught to harm the city, I would not remain his Yardmaster. On my skill as a swordsman, I swear it."

There was little more Paxe could say. "May you never have cause to regret your oath," she said.

"You will see," said Dobrin, "that my trust is not misplaced."

"Loose!" said Kadra.

Sorren let go of the bowstring. The arrow wobbled off the bow, skidded toward the target, and careened into a thornbush, leaving a gouge on the ground.

"Again," said Kadra. "Nock." Sorren lowered the bow to her waist, and, turning it horizontal, laid an arrow on the string. Her left arm ached, and she wanted to rub it. But the ache, Kadra said, meant that she was holding the bow too tightly, not that she was tired. Carefully, she relaxed her tense grip on the bow.

"Aim." Lifting the bow, she drew back the string, bending her elbow as Kadra had showed her, until the string touched the middle of her chin. She looked at the target, trying to find its middle. It was hard to see the middle of a hay bale.

"Loose." She opened her fingers. This time the arrow hit the edge of the target, stuck a moment, and then bounced off, to lie in the ground beside the tied bales. Sorren glanced at the dirt beside her right leg. She had four more arrows.

"Nock," said Kadra. "You're doing well. Aim. Don't look at the arrow, look at the target. It doesn't move. Keep your shoulders down. Loose."

They were in a paddock in the Batto district, streets and streets away from Plum Street. Horses and mules grazed in a pasture behind them. Blue flies buzzed frantically around the animals, the hay bales, and them; the ground was covered with old and new dung balls. It was hot, and Sorren wondered irritably how long they had been there. It felt like forever, though it was probably no more than an hour or two.

Tammo slouched up behind her; she did not turn around, but she could hear him and smell him. He shuffled, as if his feet were too heavy to lift off the ground. He asked Kadra a question in a whining voice, and she said something to him gently. Tammo was simple; his task was to keep the pastures free of dung pats; a never-ending task which he did not seem to mind, though it would drive a child crazy. But Tammo was not a child; he was grown, with heavy muscular arms and straight black hair thay fell in tangles over his brawny shoulders.

He was fascinated by Sorren, by her fair hair and skin. When Kadra first brought her to the paddock, he had reached out to stroke her. She stepped back in alarm. "Let him," the ghya said, "he won't hurt you. He's just curious." So Sorren stood still while Tammo ran his fingers through her hair as though she were a horse. But after that he had, indeed, let her alone.

"Nock," said Kadra. Sorren reached for one of her remaining arrows. Sweat stung her eyes. She took her hand from the arrow and wiped them. Archers had to see. She took the arrow up again, being careful not to crush the feathers. "Aim. Loose." This time the arrow flew right to the target and stuck there, quivering. "Good!" said Kadra, and Tammo let out a funny high-pitched crow.

Sorren flexed her fingers around the bow's center. The bow was made of wood and horn; it came up to her breasts when she put one end of it on the ground, and its tips were curved like wings. It was not hard to pull; Kadra said it was too light for her, in fact, but that it was better for her to a light bow then one whose pull was too strong for her. The arrows were cedarwood, fletched with gray turkey feathers. The bowstring was silk. "Nock," said Kadra. She had been standing just behind Sorren's left shoulder the entire time. "Aim. Don't squeeze your fingers together. Loose."

There was one more arrow sticking in the ground. Sorren sighed and reached for it. It had a blunt point, which meant that it was not an edged weapon, but when she thought about the fact that she was using a bow within the city walls, her heart began to pound. "Nock," said Kadra. Blunt points, she had said, were better for small animals than real arrowheads, because they stunned, so that the animal fell over. (Of course, that meant you had to sometimes kill it after you found it. Sorren didn't like to consider that. She disliked the smell of blood.) "Aim. Loose." The arrow flew true to the target and stuck there. Sorren grinned.

"Unstring your bow," said Kadra. Sorren stopped grinning. This was hard, even though she had been shown how to do it, and had done it twenty times. Bracing the bow against her foot arch, she held the bow steady with her right hand and flexed the bow away from her with her left, sliding the bowstring out of the groove. If she did it wrong, the bow would pop back and hit her. It came out easily. She laid the bow down. The inside of her left arm, below the elbow, stung, despite the cloth Kadra had told her to wrap around it, and the fingers of her right hand below the first knuckle were scraped and sore.

"Here," said Kadra, holding out her silver flask. Sorren took it and tipped it to her lips. The strong wine made her choke. She took one small sip and handed the flask back; Kadra drank it down as if it were water. "Guardian, that's good," she said. "Go get your arrows."

There were seven arrows in the target—one in the center— six on the ground in front of the target, and two in the thornbush. Sorren found a long stick and dragged them out. Her shoulders ached, and she worked them up and down as she had seen Paxe do after training. She wished she'd worn sandals to the field; not because of the thorns but because of the horseshit that lay everywhere.

She brought the arrows to Kadra. The ghya looked them over carefully, inspecting them for cracks. She found none. She offered Sorren the flask again. "No, thank you," Sorren said. Kadra drank. The sun glittered on the silver surface. "Where did you get it?" she said. "It's beautiful."

"It was a gift from a house whose messages I carried in Tezera." Kadra coughed, and put the flask away. She was not wearing her cloak, and the shape of her breasts showed clearly under her thin linen shirt.

"Shall I set the arrows up again?" Sorren asked.

"No," said Kadra, "that's enough for today. How do you feel?"

"My back hurts."

"You're using new muscles. Don't let it trouble you. You're very good with that bow, you know that?" The ghya smiled, a real smile, without the sardonic glint that Sorren had come to expect. "It must be the northern blood in you."

"Thank you," Sorren said.

She picked up the bow. Her arms were red; the sun had burned them. They would be painful tonight. She would have to brew some tea for compresses. A fly lit on her knee and she swatted it away.

Kadra said, "I still think you ought to have a knife."

"I don't want a knife," said Sorren.

"I'm not talking about a weapon! Guardian, girl, you can't travel without a knife. What are you going to gut fish with, your teeth? And an axe wouldn't hurt either. You'll need it when you have to build a fire."

Sorren said, "I'll think about it. I'm not leaving for another year." She held up the bow. "What shall I do with this?"

"Leave it here. Tammo knows where to hide it. Next week, we'll come and shoot some more." Tammo heard his name and shuffled over. Kadra said, "Tammo, put the bow and arrows away where no one can find them, all right?"

"Aaah, aah," he said, waving his hands toward the barn.

"Yes, good. We'll come back." Kadra patted his shoulder. "You've been very helpful, Tammo, very good."

"Aaah!" He beamed, and did a strange, antic dance. "Aaah!"

They left the pasture with Tammo looking after them and waving his arms. "Who is he?" Sorren asked.

Kadra laughed. "He's my brother. My mother was unlucky in her children. She bore two freaks and that was enough. The next time she got pregnant she took a potion." She laughed again. "How do you like archery?"

Sorren shrugged. "I like it, I guess."

"Shooting a hay bale is easy. Next time, I'll bring a target that moves, so you can see what it feels like to aim at something that isn't standing still."

"A live thing?"

"No. You'll see. But you'll have to shoot live things eventually, Sorren."

"I'd rather set traps."

"Traps don't always work. Believe me, I know." They came to the alley leading to the street. Garbage was piled at one end of it; corncobs and kava rind and pottery shards. At the entrance to the street, Kadra stopped, swaying, her face suddenly losing color. Thrusting a hand out, she leaned against the brick wall.

"What is it?" asked Sorren, alarmed. "Can I help?"

"Don't crowd me," snarled the ghya, and Sorren stepped back. Kadra continued to breathe deeply. Finally she straightened, and took her braced hand off the wall.

"I don't like to be touched," she said.

Sorren put her hands behind her back. "Sorry."

"I know," said the ghya, "you were trying to help. I don't want help."

Two women walking arm in arm passed them, and the nearest wrinkled her nose and said something in an undertone to her friend.

Sorren gazed at her muck-coated feet. "I can't go back to the house like this," she said. "Is there a bathhouse near?"

"Down this street and turn left."

"Will you come with me?"

"I'll walk you there," said the ghya, "but I won't come in. I bathe in private." *Where*, her tone implied, *no one but me can see.*

Sorren wondered what Kadra would do if they—whoever "they" were—did not take her on the ship. The ghya's drinking (and her manners) were surely enough to keep her off. Twice the ghya stopped and held on to the nearest wall, right arm over her stomach as if she had cramps, and Sorren wondered what she would do if she collapsed. But each time she straightened. They reached the red brick archway leading into the bathhouse. A statue of the Guardian sat just outside the entrance. Under the statue was a heavy, long-necked jar into which bath patrons were expected to put money.

Sorren bowed to the statue. Kadra did not.

Sorren wondered if she really had time to bathe. She had the feeling—it was probably silly—that Arré had begun to watch her, to notice when she left the house and what time she came back. But this morning Arré was busy with her tailor. Glancing at Kadra, she worked a wishbone off her string and dropped it into the jar's wide mouth. "You should come with me," she said.

"Why?" the ghya flared, suddenly, brutally. "So you see what's really under the clothes? Thank you, no." She turned and walked away before Sorren had a chance to say, no, I didn't mean that—oh, damn, Sorren thought. She started to run after Kadra, and then stopped. The ghya would probably just tell her to go away. She would wait a week. Perhaps in a week Kadra would have had time to cool off.

Every district of the city had a public bath. They had been built by the city after the plague years. They were paid for by tax money. The first room of every bathhouse was the changing room. It was a small room, usually lighted by a skylight, and lined with shelves. An attendant sat in it, ostensibly to guard people's belongings and give out balls of soap; but really to make sure that no one who shouldn't entered the baths. Some people were not permitted in the public baths: women during their blood-time, people with rashes or skin eruptions, and anyone with an open wound.

Sorren had just finished her blood-time. She went blithely into the changing room. The attendant at the Batto baths that day was an old woman, bent over and nearly bald. One of her shoulders was higher than the other.

"Want a robe, my sweet?" She pointed to the racks of cotton bathrobes, all in bright designs.

"No, thank you," said Sorren, peeling off her pants and shirt and bundling them into a cubbyhole. She put the money string and her bondservant's bracelet on top of them.

The attendant looked at her with lascivious appreciation as she freed her hair. "Ah, you're lovely," she said. Her nose wrinkled. "What's that smell?"

Sorren glanced at the mud caked on her legs. "Shit," she said. "I was in a pasture."

The attendant clucked between her teeth. "That'll have to be all washed up, ugh." She pressed a ball of soap into Sorren's palm. Sorren sniffed it; it was scented with mint. "Go right in, dearie. Hot room to the right, fountains and warm pool to the left, cold pool in the back."

The corridor to the bath chambers was tiled in white and yellow tiles. At the end of the hall, Sorren turned left, to the fountains. There were two of them, with water that ran continually from a pipe in the ceiling into the bowls of the fountains and over them onto the grated floor. The water came from the river, and was heated as it passed the furnace. There were wooden benches around the fountains for people to sit on as they washed. Three women sat there now, talking with great gestures to one another. Sponges littered the floor; by the near fountain, an old man solemnly washed his toes. A little girl, pert as a chipmunk, played beneath the second fountain's spill.

Sorren picked up a sponge. Standing beside the fountain she cleaned herself with the sponge and water to get off the surface dirt, and then soaped her whole body, starting with the pubic hair.

Her left arm and her right hand stung with the soap, but the sponge felt good, like a big friendly hand moving over her flesh. When she was all clean, she went to the warm pool. It was right beside the wash-room. People came to the warm pool to sit, to relax and soak and talk with their friends. The cold pool, beyond it, could be entered from both the warm pool and the hot room. The hot room was heated by hot stones. It, too, had benches to sit on. The benches were set up in terraced rows; the lower benches were cooler, and it was customary for people to sit first on the lower benches and work their way up to the hot ones. Sorren glanced at her reddened arms. She liked the hot room, but the heat would sting her sunburn.

She slid into the water of the warm pool, and her hair billowed out like kelp. Arching her back, letting her nipples poke above the water. She wondered idly what Kadra really looked like. It could not be anything too strange. How could anyone have a cock and balls *and* woman's parts?

After the wonderful feel of the bath, her clothes felt dirty and smelly and sticky. Gritting her teeth, she dressed in them anyway. She left her hair unbound, so that it could dry as she walked. She counted the bontas on the money string; they were all there.

The attendant saw her counting, and bridled. "Think I'm a thief?" she said.

"No, mother, but your back might have been turned for a moment."

"Mother?" The oldster showed her few remaining teeth. "I'm not *your* mother, dearie, not with that white skin and bright hair." She brandished her thin black arms. "Besides, I'm too old, or you're too young. Grandmother, maybe. You look like a lady I knew, a long time ago, in the Galbareth. Ah, now, *she* was a pretty one."

Refreshed, Sorren ducked through the archway and came out upon the street. The sun fell full upon her head, and she ran her fingers through her hair, separating the strands. Squinting, she hoped that Arré was still occupied with the tailor. She strolled north, searching for a street that ran from the Batto district to the Med district, and found one: the Street of the Tortoise.

She began to sing, very softly. *"Where did they go, the ones who were chosen? Where did they ride, the dancers so strong? With their long blades sharp, and their long hair flowing, Where did they go, what is their song?"*

From somewhere in front of her came a cadenced chant. "Ho—ho, and—ho—ho, and—ho—" It was not a litter-bearers' chant. Ahead of her, people were backing up against shop windows and entrances, the way they did for caravans. Sorren stepped back, and someone's elbow pressed into her stomach. People shouted from up ahead. A hot wind seemed to blow down the suddenly frozen street, and a horse whinnied, a musical sound like the challenge of a horn.

Like an apparition out of the past, soldiers came down the street. They wore leather and steel, and carried tall pikes on their shoulders. Their faces were obscured by helmets with tall gold plumes upon them. The chant came from them; they marched in time to it, in four straight columns, their arms swinging, the booted feet lifting to the chant. In their midst rode a man on a black horse, and he too wore armor. On his lap he hald a naked sword blade. Empty scabbards swung at the marching soldiers' sides.

They went down the Street of the Tortoise toward the middle of the Batto district. As they vanished, the astounded watchers poured into the streets. "They're from Tezera!" cried one woman, pounding her fist on a gatepost. Others insisted the soldiers were from Shanan or Mahita or Shirasai.

Sorren went home. As she passed the Northwest Gate, she saw a huge crowd gathered round it, and the folk from the public stables leading riderless horses. The horses' harnesses were rickly decorated with feathers and silver clasps. By the time she reached the Med gate, the news had raced ahead of her. "Heard about the soldiers?" said the dung collector by his cart.

Sorren shouted as she turned into the gate, "I saw them!" She wondered if they were really from Tezera. They seemed like beings out of the past, not chearis but like chearis. She felt that she had conjured them up with the words of her song.

She went breathless into the little parlor, and stopped short. Paxe was there. Arré looked at Sorren, and her mouth quirked. "You saw the soldiers," she said. "I can tell by the shine in your eyes." She turned back to Paxe. "Go on."

"They're from Nuath," said the black woman. "The Lord Tarn i Nuath Ryth brought them with him; they're his escort, he says, to the betrothal of his daughter. Kim Batto met him at the Northwest Gate."

"The Lord Tarn i Nuath Ryth!" Arré sounded half amused, half angry. "The effrontery of the man! And he has it wrong, it ought to be Tarn-no-something Ryth i Nuath. What was his mother's name, I wonder, and why does he discard it? How many soldiers did he have with him?"

"Forty," said Paxe. Her clothes were wrinkled, and Sorren guessed that she had been asleep when the messenger from the Gate had come to find her. "They gave up their horses and their swords at the Gate. He insisted on retaining his. He said—not to me, I was not there, but to my day watch commander—'I will sit outside the city wall, I and all my soldiers, and no one will get in or out this Gate until I am permitted to enter the city on horseback, with my sword.'"

Arré snorted. "He would have held up traffic as far north as Nuath!"

"That is why Ivor finally decided to let him in."

"Oh, it was the right decision. Kim Batto met him?" She grinned her urchin grin. "I wish I'd been there to see it. How was it explained? It should have been Ron Ismenin."

"Ron Ismenin was delayed," said Paxe. "He sent a message. As I was leaving, Col Ismenin arrived, so everything was proper. Tarn i Nuath Ryth is staying at the Batto house; it has more room than the Ismenin house. That's probably true; the Ismeninas have a houseful of their Blue Clan relatives."

"And the woman for whom all this has happened, where is she?"

"When I left the Gate, her litter was just entering."

Arré looked at Sorren. "What did *you* think of them?" she said.

Sorren cast about for an answer. All she could think of was the way they looked. "They had gold feathers on their helmets, and tall boots, up to the knee."

Arré said sarcastically, "They must have been hot, riding through the valley. Well, this is all very interesting. Tomorrow at the Ismenin house should be even more exciting. Double the watch on the Batto border," she said to Paxe, "until these folk have gone back to where they came from."

Paxe nodded, and left.

Arré said, "Did you get caught in the crowd? Is that where you've been?"

"Yes," said Sorren. "Did you get your clothes?"

"The tailor will bring them back this evening." Arré tilted her head to one side. Sorren tensed. "There is something on your bed for you, go look at it."

Sorren went upstairs. In the doorway of her room, she halted, gaping. A silk tunic and matching pants lay spread across the coverlet. They were blue, with scarlet braid on the cuffs and collar. She knelt and ran a hand over the fabric. It was heavy silk, twice as fine as anything she had ever owned. The sleeves were wide and full, like the mouths of bells, but they stopped at the elbow. She rubbed the cloth on her cheek, loving the feel of it. She held the tunic up to her chest.

She ran downstairs again. Arré was sitting in her chair. "Do you like it?" she said, smiling. "There's this, too." She held out her hand; in it was a thing that glittered. Sorren took it. It was a comb, the kind that Isak sometimes wore when he performed. It was red, with lapis lazuli inlay.

"It's beautiful." Sorren knelt by the chair, holding the comb in both hands. She could not even guess what the comb and clothes were worth. "They're too fine for me."

"Don't be silly," said Arré, "You will look splendid in them, and why should you not have expensive clothes for such an occasion?"

"What are *you* wearing?"

"A gown. You will see it tonight." She stroked Sorren's hair. "You smell of mint."

"I was at the baths."

"I see," said Arré. She rubbed her chin. "I don't want to know what your secret is, child. But—do you have another lover?"

"Another—" Sorren wanted to laugh. Was *this* why Arré had been watching her? "Oh, no. Nothing like that."

"Good. Paxe would mind, I think, though she might not say so. She has lost a son; it would trouble her to lose you, too."

"But Ricard wrote to her," Sorren said, "and I'm not going anywhere." Yet, she thought, thinking of Kadra and the bow and the map . . . yet.

"Are you all well?" she asked.

"Never better," Arré answered. "I must simply remember not to drink at the party."

CHAPTER FIFTEEN

The Ismenin house was even grander than the Hok house.

The walkway to the front gate of the big white house was lined with kava fruit trees. As Sorren came up the path, with her drums under one arm and her fine new clothes in the other, a butterfly spiraled from a tree branch to cling, for a moment, to her hair. She shook it gently off. The air was filled with Kava scent and cooking smells, as the Ismenin kitchens prepared for the party. The guard at the iron fence surrounding the courtyard had, flatteringly, recognized Sorren and let her through, with the instruction that she should go around to the side entrance. But it was obvious that the guard at the steps did not know her. He glared at her suspiciously as she approached him.

"I'm drumming at the party," she said, showing her drums.

He jerked his thumb at a path that headed off at an angle from the courtyard. "Kitchen door." He was wearing armor: a helmet, a leather and metal breastplate, and his sandal straps were wide and studded on the outside with metal. He looked very uncomfortable.

The kitchen at the Ismenin house was not much different than at the Med house, only bigger. The chief cook was a thin dark woman. Almost as tall as Sorren, darker even than Paxe, she spoke in choppy ferocious sentences to the six or seven assistants and apprentices who whirled about her. Slabs of raw fish sat on the boards, their odor overwhelming any other smells.

It was the chief cook who noticed Sorren first. "Yes?" she said.

"I'm drumming at the party," Sorren said. "The guard told me to come here."

The cook raised her voice. "Tokki!"

"Yo!" called a voice outside the kitchen, and a second person entered the kitchen. Sorren blinked. This person was tall and thin and black-skinned—and a man, she realized, staring at Tokki's hips and hands and at his dark born-curly beard.

He beckoned to her. "Are you going to stand there forever, girl? Come on." Sorren picked her way across the kitchen to him, feeling hostile. She hated being called girl. As she reached him, he said, "What's your name?"

"Sorren."

"Sorren. Well, you can stop wondering. We're twins, Tekka and I. She's cook and I'm steward. You're Isak Med's drummer, aren't you? He said you'd be here early." He was hurrying her quickly down a hallway; he took even longer steps then she did, and it was a new sensation to have to lengthen and not shorten her steps to someone else's. "Whoa, stop." She had started to outpace him. "Put your sandals here."

"Here" was a big alcove, almost a room, off the corridor. Sorren slipped off her sandals and put them on a shelf, wondering if she was going to have to go barefoot through the house. So far she had seen no mats on the stone floor.

Tokki pointed to a box. "There are shoes in there. Find a pair that fits you."

Sorren looked into the box: it was filled with all sizes of shoes. Each pair was tied together by a ribbon. They all looked alike: yellow and gray, the Ismenin colors. She hunted for a pair her size, found one that looked right, tried them on, wiggled her toes. . . . "These'll do," she said.

Tokki pulled up his pants legs to show her that he, too, was wearing them. "Guests get them, too." Taking her elbow, he guided her into another hallway. This was carpeted, with thick wool carpet in a bright geometric pattern in red and black. It matched the corridor's wall hangings. Tokki opened a door. All the doors in the house seemed to be wood, not screen, so that you has to pull them open and push them closed. "You can change here. The grand parlor is that way, that's where all the guests will come. The piss-room is that way—" He pointed to a door on the far side of the room. "I'll come warn you when the entertainment is about to start. Don't worry, you're not first. Are you hungry?" Sorren nodded. "You'll get food. Don't wander around; you're sure to get lost. This house is very confusing." He smiled at her, showing white teeth, and left. The room was as big as the little parlor in the Med house. The walls were stone, the floor was stone, even the ceilings were stone. The floor had a tan rug on it, and the walls were obscured by thick tan hangings.

There was a long, low cushioned seat against one wall. Sorren sat on it, wondering if she was to spend the whole of the party, when she was not drumming, locked in this room.

She kicked the divan with her heel. It would be very dull. She wondered how many people there were in the house. The Ismenin family was large, and like the Hok family, they all lived together, but unlike in the Hok house, she did not feel welcome, or warm, or like anything but a servant. She listened, but the stone walls and the fabric that covered them muffled most sounds. A wagon could be going past the door this instant, she thought, I wouldn't know. What if Tornor was like this, she thought, all isolated and quiet and cold.

At that moment, the door opened and Jeshim pranced in.

He carried a long box in his arms, and a shapeless bag dangled over his back. He swept across the room and plumped the box down on the seat beside her. "Sorren, my lovely girl, how are you? Isn't this a marvel? And I owe it all to you." He swept her a bow. "Thanks. How do I look?"

He was dressed in a long red and orange gown with bright blue splotches on it. The red and brown matched his beard.

"You're noticeable," she said.

"I think so." He opened the box. In it were his knives. They gleamed against the dark felt that lined the box. He drew a finger lovingly along one bright blade. "Oh, you beauties. Aren't they pretty?"

Sorren did not think they were pretty. "What's in the bag?" she asked.

He hauled it to the seat of the divan. Undoing the neck, he held it out to her. "My juggling balls." She glanced inside. There were close to twenty balls in the bag.

"Can you juggle that many?"

"No. But I always bring extras. I'm a professional, whatever I do." He let his left eyelid descend in a slow wink. "Remember that."

"What's the rest of the entertainment? Do you know?"

"A mime. You remember Saëdi? He was at last year's Harvest Festival. Three musicians. Me, then a break, then you and Isak Med."

"What musicians?"

"I don't remember." He sat on the divan and put his arm around her shoulders. His beard tickled her chin. He smelled of heavenweed. "Want to smoke?"

"No." She stood up. "And I don't want you to keep touching me, Jeshim. I don't like it."

He shrugged. "I was only trying to be friendly." He smiled

slyly at her. "How do you like Kadra? Tell me, what's he look like stripped? I never saw him without that cloak."

She stared at him, astonished and angry. "What do you mean?"

"Oh, come on, honey," he said, looking up at her with a leer. "You've been seeing him; half the city knows it. What's it like, fucking a ghya?"

Cold bumps rippled over Sorren's arms. "I'm not," she said.

Jeshim took a knife from the open box and dug at a callus on his palm. "Anything you say. I was just asking."

She snatched the knife from his hand. "You listen to me," she said, holding the knife low and flat, the way she had seen Paxe hold a niji. "Maybe you don't have friends, so you don't understand that you can like a person and not go to bed. But Kadra and I are friends, and I don't want to hear any more talk like that."

She was shaking, she was so angry. Jeshim didn't move for a moment. Then he extended his palm to her. "Sorren, give me that knife," he said softly.

She wrapped her fingers around it more firmly. It was tiny, smaller than a kitchen cleaver, and not frightening at all. "Are you going to leave me alone?"

"Give me the knife. Or I'll hurt you."

"You won't," she said.

"Don't try me." She felt him tensing to strike at her and stepped back, out of range. Suddenly, a hand dug into her shoulder, stopping her retreat and making her gasp with pain.

"That will do," said a voice—Isak's voice. He took his hand from her shoulder and walked into the space between her and Jeshim. "I don't care what started it, but it stops now. Sorren—" he fixed his dark eyes on her— "put that knife down on the floor. Now."

She knelt, and laid the knife down at arm's length. He knelt and picked it up, and gave it to Jeshim. "Juggler, put that box away."

The room seemed smaller with him in it. Sorren stood up, rubbing her shoulder.

Isak smiled amiably at her. "Well, how are you, child?"

She wondered if he had forgotten what he'd said to her last time they met. "I'm all right."

He gestured at Jeshim, and his tone grew teasing. "I thought you were friends. Friends don't fight, do they? You looked as if you were ready to cut his throat."

"I just want him to keep his hands off me," Sorren said.

"Juggler, keep your hands off her. And your tongue. My bag's in the hallway; get it." Jeshim, chastened and silent, went to do as he was told.

Isak sat on the divan, pushing aside the knife-filled box. "How is my dear sister?" he said, tilting his head to one side. He was dressed in walking clothes, but his hair was coiled on top of his head, pomaded and scented, so that he smelled like a garden.

Arré had said, that morning, "You may tell Isak anything he likes, except that I am coming to this party. If he asks you that, lie."

"She's better," Sorren said.

"I hear she was sick. I'm so sorry. I would have come to visit, but sick people are so easily exhausted." He saw her drums, and found the clothing lying beside them. "What's this? New clothes?"

"Yes. Arré got them for me."

He held them up. "Very nice."

Jeshim struggled in from the corridor with a huge bag in both arms. "Guardian, what's in it?" he said.

"Costumes," said Isak. He undid the lacing and took out the Stallion's straw prick.

Jeshim chuckled and took it up.

He pretended to tie it around his thighs. "Wouldn't mind one of those." His mouth curved lewdly. "Got any more?"

"No," said Isak.

His tone was chilling. Jeshim dropped the prick beside the bag and scooped up his own bag from the floor. "Excuse me," he said.

Isak smiled. He looked again at Sorren. "So my dear sister sent you here all prepared. How sweet. *Was* she sick?"

"Yes," said Sorren. She worked her fingers; the anger had drained from her, but it had left her tense and sticky beneath her clothes.

Isak opened the bag again, and took out his face paints. He had several different kinds of paint in little enameled boxes. "With what?" he said.

Sorren tapped her fingers up and down her thighs. "She drank too much."

Isak's mouth quirked. He took out the brushes he used to paint his face and smoothed their glossy tips. "It's ironic, isn't it? The Med fortune was and continues to be made by our vineyards and our wineries, and my dear sister can't drink the stuff."

Suddenly, the door to the room opened, and people poured in. A gray-and-yellow-clad servant carried in a platter of food. Saëdi the mime walked in, and his narrow brown face turned with an artist's interest from Isak (to whom he bowed) to Jeshim to Sorren. Three women in silver robes carrying long wooden flutes came in and instantly sat in a corner and began to play, trills and runs and bits and pieces of street tunes. Sorren's stomach rumbled. She went to the tray, which sat on the floor, and picked over the cheese and fruits and little sausages until she found the noodle pies.

She ate six of these. When she looked up from the tray, Isak was watching her. He had a brush in his hand and a brass mirror on his knees.

She blushed for her gluttony. "My lord, do you want some?"

"No. I ate." He beckoned. "Come here."

She crossed to his side. He pulled her face nearer to his. "Hold still. Close your mouth." She put her lips together and in a moment felt the light shivery kiss of the brush on her face. It skirted her eyes, and then withdrew. "Look." Isak turned the mirror so that she could see. She found herself regarding—herself, yes, but a self with thick black eyebrows and languorous eyes. She put up a hand to touch the strange black lines and he pushed her hand away.

"Leave it; it looks good. You can take it off after you've drummed." He cocked his head. "The guests must be arriving. Hurry up, dress, child. There will be a little food, then entertainment, then more food, and then the ceremony."

Sorren listened, and heard the soft din of people all talking at once in a large room. "Aren't you going?" she asked.

Isak shook his head. "After the performance, never before; it spoils the mood." He began to strip. Sorren pulled her shirt over her head. Somehow, in the week and a half since she had last seen him, her hatred of him had vanished, to be replaced by the odd cameraderie that, mixed with respect and a little fear, she had always felt. She watched him dress in Peacock's harness and feathers, admiring the way his muscles twisted under his skin, the grace of his lithe torso. . . . Across the room, Saëdi was staring too.

Suddenly, a sound split the air, silencing the musicians and freezing everyone in the room into immobility, even Isak. One

of the musicians dropped her flute. It was a horn blast, like
the sound of the ships' conches in fog, but louder, and much
wilder.

"What the fuck—" said Jeshim.

Isak laughed, and picked up the little mirror which had slid
from his knees. "That," he said dryly, "is Tarn Ryth."

"The man with the soldiers," said Sorren.

"The man with the soldiers," agreed Isak. "Did you see
them march into town yesterday? What did you think?"

Sorren smoothed the silk on her lap, remembering her own
reactions upon seeing the soldiers. She had thought of the
chearis. But now, after seeing the house guard close up, in that
ridiculous armor, she thought, the chearis were not like that.
Isak is more like a real cheari than that man on the horse.

"I think they're silly," she said.

Isak chuckled. "So do I," he answered, setting the feathered
crown of the Peacock on his head.

The door opened. Cha Minto walked in. "Isak!" His voice
was high and strange. "She's here! She came!"

"What are you talking about?" said Isak, lowering the brush
with which he was painting long thick eyebrows on his forhead.

Cha Minto—he looked very fine, in pale green silk—said,
"Your sister is at the door."

Isak paled.

The color flowed out of his face and into his hands, which
had locked together on the mirror. He squeezed it as if he
wanted to break it. . . . When he spoke his voice was icy. "What
did Ron do?"

"He's letting her in, of course. What else can he do?"

"Nothing," said Isak. His color was coming back, a little
at a time. "Nothing. All right. Go be pleasant. No," he said
sharply, as the other man started to speak, "I can't come, look
at how I'm dressed! Go."

Cha Minto went. Isak looked at Sorren. She swallowed.
Her hands were cold. There was no warmth in his eyes; no
feeling, none of the humor they had just shared. . . . She fumbled with the tunic and at last got it over her head. As it slid
to her shoulders, Isak said softly, "You knew she was coming."

Sorren nodded. Her mouth was dry as caked mud.

"Would you have told me if I asked you?" he said.

She licked her lips, discovered that she couldn't speak, and
shook her head. In his corner, Jeshim dropped a ball. It bounced
over her foot.

Isak nodded, once. "Put your pants on," he said, and rose, a jeweled and splendid fantasy, the image of an avian prince.

Arré Med was having a good time.

The look on Cha Minto's face—and his immediate departure for the interior of the house—and the look on Ron Ismenin's, when he realized that, under no circumstances, could he find any excuse at all for having her kept out—were balm to her soul. She accepted Ron Ismenin's stuttering greeting with a smile, and then stood back to let Marti Hok (older than she, infirm, and eldest of the Council) enter the mansion. The guard at the front door, with his armor and the beads of sweat dotting his brow, amused her. Cha Minto amused her. The blank looks on the faces of the most sensitive guests, who knew that something was amiss but had no idea what, made her want to laugh out loud.

She marched up to Kim Batto, who was chatting with a merchant. "Good day," she said to him. His back was to her; he turned, and she had the pleasure of seeing his jaw drop. "I know, you thought I wasn't coming. Sorry to disappoint you. How did your courier enjoy his little ride north?" Leaving him gaping, she moved on to greet Edith Isara and her tall daughters. The house, she admitted to herself, looked and smelled entrancing. The Ismeninas had spared no expense in their desire to satisfy, entertain, and please their guests. A long table with prepared meats, honeyed fruits, and other delicacies ran the width of the great parlor. The room was filled with fresh-cut lilies. Standing lamps with scented oils lit the rather gloomy chamber, and mirrors, both silver and bronze, hanging on the walls, reflected back more light. Arré caught a glimpse of herself in a mirror, and nodded at her image. The gown— which was red and long—was very becoming, and she was wearing, in addition to her silver bracelets, one immense sapphire, which lay across her throat in its silver setting like a great indigo eye.

She had bought the sapphire that morning at Smith Tian's. It was ostentatious, but so was this whole event. She wondered where Isak was: dressing, probably. She picked up a seaweed ball and ate it. In one corner of the parlor stood a huge knot of people, and she guessed that Tarn i Nuath Ryth was in the middle of it. He was the most interesting event to happen to Kendra-on-the-Delta since the Ban. He was the reason she'd purchased the sapphire, besides the fact that it was beautiful.

She wanted to talk to him, and to do that for long she would have to hold his attention. Barbarians, whether from outside Arun or from within it, were notoriously fond of jewels.

Cha Minto had returned. She went to him. "Good day, Cha."

He avoided her eyes. "Good day, Arré. This is an impressive spread, isn't it?"

"Introduce me to Tarn i Nuath Ryth."

He took her arm. "Look, the musicians are here!" He turned her so that she could see the three fluteplayers in their gauze gowns. "Shall we go and listen to them?"

"No," she said. "I can always ask someone else, Cha. You're being a fool, you know. Did my brother tell you to keep me away from him?" She took her arm out of his hold.

Helpless, he simply stared at her. The musicians began to play, a light dancing melody that made the more musically inclined guests bob their heads. "That's lovely music," said Arré. "Are you going to do as I ask?"

"I can't," said Cha. His eyes looked panicked.

"Don't, then. But when your servitude to my brother's plots begins to gall, come to me."

Karya Holleth Ismenin appeared at her elbow. "Arré, good morning. Isn't it a lovely day for a betrothal? It's been a long time since you were last here, may I show you the rest of the house? It's much changed."

"Thank you," Arré said. "Another time, Karya. Right now I want to talk to Tarn i Nuath Ryth. Will you introduce us?"

Karya said desperately, "Oh, he is not all that interesting, I assure you. Look at the musicians, aren't they talented?"

"Undoubtedly," said Arré. "Excuse me." She sidled past Karya and walked toward the corner.

Kim Batto intercepted her. "Arré, I should like to know the meaning of what you said to me when you walked in."

She looked him up and down, noting the sheen of sweat on his brow, and wondering if his bald spot was sweating, too. "You know what I meant," she said. "I know about the paper you sent north, and what it said, and I know, too, that it didn't arrive. Would you like the Council to know you have been making your own treaties with other clans? I doubt they would approve. I may tell them, if you keep getting in my way." Her temper was beginning to rise.

Suddenly, a bell rang. Everyone quieted. Unobtrusively,

the servants had been filling the room with soft folding calfskin
stools for people to rest on. The musicians began to play a
fanfare. The crowd in the corner grew silent, and the people
on the rim of it sat down. Arré glimpsed a brown-haired man
with a big beard, wearing a brilliant yellow tunic and a black
kilt. Gold chains, many of them, hung around his neck.

Kim slipped his arm through hers as she started to move.
"Listen to the music," he urged. "That's the music for the
mime. You must see him." He sat, carrying her with him.
Short of screaming or hitting him there was nothing she could
do about it, and, smoldering, Arré let herself be seated on the
stool. The mime appeared from behind a curtain. He was slight
and slim and remarkably fluid. He mimed, quickly, a woman
combing her hair at a mirror, a old man washing clothes in a
river, a sailor climbing rigging, a man in Sellers' Alley (this
was daring) waiting for a lover, and a bored soldier on watch,
trying not to fall asleep, keeping an eye out for her captain.
He was very good. Arré found herself laughing despite her
fury. He then did a longer piece about a drunk attempting to
urinate. Laughter filled the room, as he pretended to have lost
his prick, and went around the bedroom searching for it, chamber pot in hand. Finally he lost the chamber pot and ended by
pissing out the window, onto the head of an irate passerby.

"Isn't he wonderful!" said Karya Holleth Ismenin. She
leaned forward to tap Arré on the shoulder. "Isn't he good?"

"Brilliant," said Arré, noting that Ron Ismenin now stood
between her and the corner.

The mime finished, bowed, and went back behind the curtain. The musicians began again.

Arré was tempted to ask Karya Holleth Ismenin why she,
Arré, had not been invited to the betrothal celebration, just to
hear what she would say. But that would be both cruel and
crass. She smiled at Kim. "I'm hungry. Shall we go to the
tables?"

"I'll bring you a plate," said Karya, rising hurriedly. "Don't
move." She rustled to the tables.

"'Don't move' appears to be the theme of this gathering,"
murmured Arré to Kim. "You shall have to let me up eventually, you know."

He pretended not to hear her. "I am looking forward to your
brother's dance," he said.

"Oh, so am I," said Arré. She wanted to see Isak when he

saw her. His face would show nothing of his chagrin—he was, after all, a dancer and knew how to disguise his feelings until even he did not know he had them—but his body would give him away. She wondered what he said to Sorren when he learned she was present. She hoped he had not been too angry.

"Here we are!" said Karya. She laid a heaped plate across Arré's knees: on it were ten or twelve different things, fish cakes and little pastries and noodle pies and seaweed balls and fruits in slices. . . . Arré ate another seaweed ball. The musicians played a funny little tune and a man in red and orange and blue leaped into the chamber. Balls whirled around his head. He counted softly to himself as he balanced first on one leg, then on the other. Sliding behind the curtain, he reappeared with a handful of knives, little ones. He started to juggle them. The musicians stopped playing and everyone grew silent, leaning forward on their stools to watch the blades flicker through the air like pennies. . . . Arré found that she was holding her breath. Slowly she let it out.

"Let me see those!" boomed a voice. Everyone jumped, and the juggler dropped a knife. It tumbled to the carpet at his feet. The man in yellow and black strode across the chamber, one hand outstretched. "Give me that." He plucked a knife from the juggler's hand, and touched the point of it with his thumb. "Hunh. It's sharp. But that's no way to treat a knife. They aren't toys." His arm swung overhead, and a glittering object hurtled through the air. Someone shouted. The thrown knife landed in one of the Ismeninas' fine wooden doors.

Karya Ismenin shuddered. "That barbarian!" she said.

The juggler said, "You throw well for an amateur." Coolly, he selected one of the knives in his hand, and threw it in the same direction. It landed quivering in the wood, a handsbreadth from the first one.

Ron Ismenin quietly walked across the room and pulled both knives from the door. "You will frighten the guests, Tarn," he said. "Perhaps this could be saved for later?" He gave the juggler both knives. "Thank you, that was remarkable." He turned to the company. "The meal is ready, friends. Shall we proceed to it?" He gestured to a servant, who opened the doors to the dining room. Long tables with benches stood laden with food. The musicians started to play again and everyone got up.

The meal seemed interminable. Kim Batto and Karya Ismenin maneuvered Arré into a seat as far as possible from Tarn

i Nuath Ryth, with nothing to do except talk to them and eat.
She spoke with them as little as possible and ate as little as
she could. She drank no wine, though Karya said over and
over again that it was Med wine and how tasty is was. Normally, in events of this kind, there was a lull between the meal
and the next stage of the party, but she had the feeling that
this time there would be no lull. She wished she could make
one. Finally the meal ended, and everyone drifted into the
parlor again. The stools were still there but the table with the
food had vanished; instead, a wooden platform had been
brought in. It was a stage for Isak.

Arré caught her first sight of the rest of the Ryth clan: they
were gathered around Tarn i Nuath Ryth, talking to him, laughing with him, telling stories. . . . Was it to protect him from
people (like herself) that they were there, or was it to protect
the company from him, she wondered. Nathis Ryth and Col
Ismenin, of course, had not yet emerged. They would not join
the company until just before the ceremony. Now, she thought,
I have to do it now. After the ceremony, they will hustle him
out.

She smiled at Kim, who was still sticking to her like a
lover. "I must speak with Marti," she said.

"I'll come with you," he said promptly. Marti was sitting
with her children about her, very much the matriarch. As they
walked to her, Arré saw Boras Sul roaming the chamber, looking sad. Probably he was still hungry, she thought in disgust.
The embroidered slippers they had been given as they came
in the house whispered on the carpet. Marti's children—what
lovely manners they had—stood at her approach.

"What a nice party," said Marti. She pointed to the stool
beside her. "Arré, won't you sit down? The meal was wonderful."

"But long," Arré said grimly. "Marti, I have a fancy to
meet Tarn i Nuath Ryth, but I keep getting distracted. Will you
lend me your well-known imperturbability?"

Marti seized her silver cane in both hands and heaved herself
up. "Of course." She smiled at Kim Batto, who looked as if
a bird had just shat on his pate, and put her arm through Arré's.
"I have not met him, either. Shall we?"

There was no way for Kim or Karya or Cha or Ron Ismenin
to stop them. Marti Hok was the eldest member of the Council.
They strolled across the chamber, toward the assembled Ryth

clan, who melted away without comment. Kim Batto accompanied them halfway across the room and then murmured something and went away. The bearded man watched their advance with unabashed curiosity.

Ron Ismenin came to his side. "Tarn i Nuath Ryth," he said, "may I present to you the Lady Marti Hok and the Lady Arré Med? Ladies, this is Tarn i Nuath Ryth, from the town of Nuath."

The bearded man said, "The *Lord* Tarn i Nuath Ryth." He inclined his head in the bow of equals. "I am honored to meet you both." His eyes narrowed as he looked at Arré. "Forgive me, Lady, but I had heard you were not coming. Indeed, I heard that you looked with great disfavor upon this betrothal."

He can talk, at any rate, Arré thought. He sounds quite intelligent. "You were misinformed," she said. "It is very pleasant to meet you—I have heard a great deal about you." Casually, she let her fingers stroke the sapphire.

He looked at it, and then at her face. "With your permission, Lady?" he said to Marti Hok. "Arré Med, we should talk to each other."

"I would like that," Arré said. "Now and in private?"

"Certainly."

Ron Ismenin said, "We are about to begin the dancing, my friends."

Tarn looked at him. "Tell them to wait till we get back," he said.

He led her through the halls and chambers of the Ismenin house as if he had grown up in it. "You know this house well," she said.

He skirted a startled servant. "I do. My house in Nuath is very like it."

He opened a door and gestured her to go first. She walked out into the air, and caught her breath. They looked upon the delta, and beyond it, the ocean. It was the middle of the afternoon: the heat was at its peak, and the sun, shining upon the infinity of water, turned it every color, green and red and blue and silver and orange. . . . It looked like rucked and rumpled velvet. Below them on the river, the barges swarmed, tiny as toys.

"Guardian, how wonderful," she said involuntarily.

Tarn i Nuath Ryth nodded his appreciation. "It is. You have a beautiful city." He sounded regretful.

"If you like it so much, why don't you live here?" she said. "Your own clan would surely welcome you."

He smiled. "I have a house. A family. Children. Besides, Arré Med, there is as much likelihood of my moving to the city as there is of you moving upriver."

The gold chains glittered on his chest. Arré leaned on the balcony railing. "Why?"

He leaned beside her. "Because I am a lord there. In Nuath. Here I am an upstart, a merchant, a barbarian. I was born upriver; I know it well, and it knows me. I am not going to exchange what I have built for the privilege of being related to the Ismeninas."

"Did Ron Ismenin tell you I would not be at this party?" she said. He nodded. "That's because I was not invited. He did not want me here. They have been keeping me from you for the last four hours. What else did they tell you about me?"

"That you were obstructive, that you despised merchants, that you preferred the past to the present, that you were jealous of the privilege of governance and refused to share it—"

"Stop," said Arré. She opened her fingers, which were gripping the iron circlet of the railing.

He tangled fingers in the longest chain and looked at her from his great height. "False?" he said.

"Not true." She scratched her nose. "I am jealous of the privilege of governance, but that is because I think I do it well. I do not prefer the past to the present. I do not despise merchants. I don't think I am obstructive, but that always depends—"

"On who wants to get where," he finished. "Yes. Then why have you refused to support the membership of the Blue Clan on the Council?"

"I haven't been asked to support or reject it," said Arré slowly. "I have rejected the membership of the White Clan on the Council."

A gull swooped by them, imploring sustenance. Tarn i Nuath Ryth reached into a pocket and brought out a handful of seaweed balls, one of which he tossed to the gull. He ate one, and offered a third to Arré. She shook her head.

"They told me you had refused to grant membership to the Blue Clan."

"It has not come up," said Arré. "Not in the last ten meetings."

"Would you support it?" he said.

"I don't know. I would listen to the arguments." She put her hand on his arm. "You puzzle me, Tarn i Nuath Ryth."

"To my friends I am Tarn Ryth, or Tarn."

"Tarn. You speak like a man of schooling, of breeding. Yet you throw knives in a betrothal party, you ride a horse through the streets, you bring soldiers and weapons into the city—"

He laughed. "Chea, woman, I threw that knife because I was bored out of my mind, as you would have been if you had to listen to my cousins rattling and whispering. As for the horse and the soldiers—I am a lord in my own territory. If the Lord Santh of Anhard rode to the city, would you tell *him* to get off his horse? I don't think so."

"Are you not being—forgive me—a little presumptuous? I realize you are a power in Nuath—"

"You don't know what you are talking about," he said flatly. "I am not 'a power.' I am *the* power. From Shonet to Septh, the river is mine. Every barge pays my tolls, every tollhouse pays my taxes, with money that has my face on it. My soldiers keep the country free of thieves and evildoers. The aqueducts and irrigation sluices are built by my builders. The wagons ride over my roads."

Arré was silent. Finally she said, "I do not doubt you. But how is it I do not know of this?"

"How would you know?" he said. "*Your* money comes from your vineyards, which are well south of my borders. You pay my taxes without knowing it, through the Blue Clan. Every time a Med wagon rolls north, say, to Tezera, laden with wine for that city, the Blue Clan family whose wagon it really is pays toll to me, and you are charged accordingly for that service. You don't leave the city, though I understand your brother does. The same goes for the houses whose fortunes are built through the sea. Now, Ron Ismenin, he deals with me all the time. I buy ore from him. In return, well, his brother is marrying my daughter."

"And Kim Batto?"

"He has been my voice on the Council—I thought."

"He has not," Arré said firmly. "I will swear it by any oath you choose. No mention of the Blue Clan has been made in the Council. Guardian, don't you think if it had, it would be in the reports of each meeting, which are a matter of public record? There is one in the Black Clan archives, and another in the Blue Clan hall."

"I see." He took another seaweed ball from his pocket and chewed it reflectively. "These are good, you know? We do not have them upriver. Maybe we can get them. So you say you *would* support the Blue Clan's membership on the Council."

"I don't say that. Don't put words in my mouth. I said I'd listen. What have you to do, by the way, with swords in the city?"

If she had thought to surprise or shake him, she was disappointed. He scratched his beard. "Nothing. Oh, I have heard about the Ismeninas training their soldiers in sword techniques. I know nothing more than that. Though I think it a good idea."

"Do you? Why?"

He snorted. "Your ancestors would not have asked that."

"But I have said," Arré said, "that I do not prefer the past to the present."

He grinned. "Ah, you are quick. You have twice the brains of that skimpy Batto person, and you smell better. Look. Civilization is a building, like this house." He thumped his fist on the iron balcony, which creaked. Arré repressed the urge to step back from it. "The foundation of the house is the oldest thing built, but it is also the strongest, because it carries the rest. When it is weak, the house crumbles. Our foundation—the foundation of Arun—is not weak. Many things make it up: our noble families, the wealth of our cities, the fertility of our soil and the beauty of our lavish rivers, without which the soil would crack and blow away, our songs, our dances, our truths, our trust in the chea—and our weapons skills are part of it! Without our courage and skill in weapons, Anhard would have run over us four hundred years ago. You say you refused membership on the Council to the White Clan. I agree with that. The witchfolk are useful but no more useful than farmers or merchants—or soldiers. Peace is valuable, necessary, longed for—but not at the expense of digging out a cornerstone of our foundation and tossing it away. The Ban was wrong, Arré Med. A country needs its warriors. I am *not* talking about armies. The Ban was wrong, and the witches were wrong. They should—*you* should—never have driven the chearis away."

His passion was impressive. The hairs on the back of Arré's neck lifted at his eloquence. She said, defensively, "People still learn sword arts outside the cities, don't they?"

"No, why should they? Arun is at peace. They don't *need* to. The chearis gave them a reason to: any child, anywhere, if she were good enough, quick enough, graceful, and disciplined, could be a cheari. But when you forbade the chearis the cities, you destroyed them, you cut them off from their greatest audience. The city—" he waved his arm at the river, its docks, its barges, its people—"you have always lived here, so you do not know what it means for a boy from the Galbareth to come to the city. The city is the center of all that is alive ane exciting and different and creative. The chearis—well, it's said they came from the Red Hills. Maybe. Maybe. But—" his hands lifted in the air—"the city is a fountain. Water feeds it from all over Arun, and it sends its life-giving spray back all over Arun." His hands made a great circle in the air, being a fountain.

Arré felt battered, beaten, drenched, drowned. He folded his hands across his chest, watching her with intensity. She rubbed her hands across her face. "Tarn Ryth," she said, "you are extraordinary."

He bowed, and stayed silent.

"I—I need to consider what you have said. Your ideas—" she hesitated; chea, where did the man get them? she thought— "astound me. I have no idea if I can trust you."

He grinned and was silent.

"But if you are what you seem to be—and I have not decided what that is and I do *not* want you to tell me!—then let me say, we are *not* enemies."

"Are we friends?"

"I don't know."

Meditatively he said, "I think we could be friends. That is, if you could bring yourself to be friends with a barbarian from upriver."

"If Kim Batto can," Arré said, "I can."

"Kim Batto—" his face twisted, as if he smelled something rotten—"is a chaba'ck."

"What does that mean?" asked Arré.

He grinned again. The smile through his great beard made him look like a bandit or a river pirate. "A pimp," he answered.

Arré laughed. "He *is* a pimp," she said. "But it is you who are having secret dealings with him, not I."

He stroked his beard. "If you know of them, they are not secret, are they?"

"Tell me," she said, "what do you hold over Cha Minto?"

"I do not know him," Tarn said. "Should I?"

She did not know whether to believe him or not. The door to the balcony opened and a woman's face looked around the door. It was Karya Ismenin. "Excuse me," she said, with extraordinary timidity for a woman in her own house, "but the dancing is about to begin—"

"We'll come in a moment, thank you," said Tarn. Karya vanished. He caught Arré watching him and smiled sourly. "You think I have no manners? You think I am a barbarian? So do they. I merely live up to their expectations."

"They are your hosts."

He shrugged. "They are getting what they want, an alliance with the man who controls the river. Col Ismenin is a puppy, but when I've finished with him, he won't be."

"What must your daughter be like!" Arré marveled.

His face kindled. "She is a wonder. Wait until you meet her. Shall we go and see this famous dancer brother of yours?"

She turned her bracelets on her wrists. "Do you know Isak?"

"I met him last night, at the Batto house. He was very quiet."

The sun, moving west, was beginning to leave the balcony some shade. Arré stepped to the railing again. She beckoned to Tarn, and he came to stand beside her. She pointed down, to a barge heaped with grain sacks. "Is that yours?" she said.

He smiled. "Uh-huh. And that one, and that one, and that one . . ." He pointed them out to her.

She nodded. "I understand why the Ismeninas need you," she said. "But I do not understand why you need the Ismeninas."

"Metal," he said. "Their mines are very close. The Tezeran mines are far away, and most of those have been dug out until they're empty."

"The Ismenin iron deposits are in the Red Hills, near Shanan, which is farther from Nuath than Tezera," she said.

He blinked at her. "You are well-informed." He tangled his left hand in his longest necklace. "Hmmm. Well, there is another reason. It will seem silly to you." He glanced sideways at her.

"Try me," she said encouragingly.

"I was born in Nuath. I came to the city when I was a child, on a visit. I came down the river. . . . I was ten, or so. I am forty-seven now. Old Rath Ismenin's house was fifteen years old, and a magnificent thing. I saw it from the river, at sunrise, with the sun breaking off these white walls—I was almost blinded by the glory. It seemed to me then that the Ismeninas must be the wisest, strongest, finest family in the city, to have such a house." He stroked the white marble side of the building. "When I built my house in Nuath, I sent for the plans of this one and made my architects and builders copy it as best they could. That is how I know my way around it. And when Ron Ismenin came to me to suggest the marriage—how could I refuse? Nathis wanted it." He smiled. "And there were good economic reasons for it."

A breeze blew at them from the river. Out on the ocean, a light blue mist was forming. How long had they been talking—an hour? More? The Ismeninas, Arré thought, must be frantic.

She laid a hand on Tarn Ryth's bare arm.

"Come," she said. "Let's go inside."

CHAPTER SIXTEEN

Isak's dance was breathtaking.

Arré saw little of it. She sat beside Marti Hok in the large parlor, thinking, thinking. . . . Whenever she glanced up from the carpet, she saw Tarn Ryth looking at her. The drumming went on until she seemed to feel it in her bloodstream, like a fever. Sorren's hands moved so fast they could not be seen. She looked lovely, with the silk gleaming round her pale face and the hair piled on her head like burnished gold wires, infinitely flexible. Arré caught sight of Boras Sul's face. He was gazing at the girl as if she were a dish of food—say, berries topped with cream.

Isak's jeweled loincloth shimmered as he moved. He was Swan now, regal and seductive. This part showed off his body best of all. The third Ismenin brother, Berd, was staring at the dancer, lips parted, eyes shining. His wife, beside him, looked resigned to her husband's open adoration. Isak's hair, on top of his head, made his long slim neck look even longer than it was. The dance was (supposedly) the dance the male swan performs to lure the female, and it was erotic without ever being vulgar (as was the dance of the Stallion) or comic (as was Bear). The drumming crescendoed as Isak whirled, back arching, in what seemed to be an impossible position, and then it softened, smoothed, rippled outward, and the ecstatic Swan furled his graceful wings and glided, with elegant hauteur, from the stage.

Everybody breathed again. Berd Ismenin smiled wryly and patted his wife's hand. There was a smattering of applause from the Ryth family, which stopped when they realized no one else was clapping. True art was best appreciated in silence. A few people stood to smooth their clothing or order drinks from the servants. Marti Hok left the room on the arm of her son, Sironen.

Now would come the ceremony. Arré wished she could leave. Rituals bored her. On the other hand, she wanted to see Nathis Ryth. In the rear of the chamber, there was a sudden commotion. Arré turned to see what it was.

Soldiers—wearing the yellow and black of Nuath and holding drawn swords in their hands—were filing in.

Tarn Ryth's voice cut smoothly through the hubbub. "Friends, family, guests," he said, standing. "Please don't be alarmed. This is entertainment, that's all, nothing to frighten you. If the servants will remove the stage—" he looked at Ron Ismenin, who after a moment of total immobility gave hurried orders to the servants—"my guards have prepared a treat for you. The swords they carry are wooden, and may be freely handled, but that must wait until after the show. Please sit down." So compelling was his manner that everyone, even Ron Ismenin, sat. The soldiers walked to the front of the chamber and stood in two lines, facing each other, with their swords out in front of them, each facing pair of weapons barely touching at the tip. "Dennis, my son, will explain to you what you are about to see."

Tarn sat down, and the man on the left-hand end of the line with his back to the audience turned around. He looked like Tarn. "We will show you three things, family and guests," he said, his voice a light copy of Tarn's resonant tones. "First, you will see the warm-up strokes that every guard does in training. This is the simplest exercise there is. Then you will see the first naïga, that is also a training exercise which two people do, consisting of specific strikes and parries. Lastly, you will see a real bout between two soldiers, with wooden blades of course." He stepped back in line. The soldiers tensed. "One—and two—and three—and four! One—and two—and three—and four!" The blades sliced down and sprang up again with the count.

With each stroke, the guards stepped forward; with each retraction, back. The floor shook. Arré watched the soldiers' faces. They were young and intense and wholly concentrated. Their precision was very beautiful. "Yai!" Dennis Ryth's shout halted them. They bowed to each other, to their audience, and to him, and then marched around the open space, to seat themselves around the edge of it. Dennis stood where he was, to the very left of the chamber.

"Now the naïga." He barked two names and two of the guards rose from their seated positions and entered the space. They bowed to the audience and then to each other. One of them was a woman; her breasts showed clearly under the cotton of her tunic. She had a broad face and brown hair with streaks of gold through it. The guard facing her was older than she was, a man, with a heavy yellow beard. He had the pale, somewhat yellow cast to his skin that suggested he had Anhard blood.

"Yai!" said Dennis, and the two lifted their swords. "Ha!" The blades whistled through the air. Everyone jumped. Arré closed her fingers on the hard wood seat of her chair. The strokes—going for the head, the legs, the belly—looked terribly real. The fighters breathed in great deep puffs, huff, huff. They stamped and leaped and attacked and retreated.... Arré began to see form through the apparent formlessness. Certain strokes and parries reappeared. Just as she was beginning to see the pattern, Dennis shouted, and it was over.

Col Ismenin appeared in the chamber; he was sitting beside his brother, smiling a bit nervously. Arré turned around, but if Nathis Ryth had come in, she was hidden among the myriad Ryth cousins. The two guards marched to their places. Dennis shouted again, and another guard rose from the circle.

Dennis strode inside it to face him.

They bowed to the audience and to each other. Then, without a sound, Dennis attacked. The crack of blade on blade made everyone start. Arré remembered what Paxe had said. "You can kill with a wooden sword, if you know how." These blows looked as if they could kill. If one of them slipped, she thought, if one parry came too late—she glanced at Tarn Ryth. He was smiling, leaning back against the cushions, seemingly unworried. His left hand toyed with the chain around his neck.

She had no skill to see which man was the better swordsman. They advanced and backed and turned in the circle. Once in a while, a heel came dangerously close to stepping on the seated men and women guards, but no one moved, not a handsbreadth; they remained impassive and disciplined. Suddenly, Dennis Ryth knocked the other man's sword to one side and lunged forward. The tip of his wooden sword halted a knuckle-length away from the man's unprotected throat.

The man dropped his sword. One of the guards caught it. Then Dennis lowered his to his side. Both men bowed, to the audience and then to each other.

Tarn Ryth rose from his seat. "We hope you have enjoyed this demonstration," he said blandly. Oh, yes, Arré thought. The faces of the watching guests reflected shock, appreciation, and not a little fear. You have indeed demonstrated your power, Tarn Ryth, and I, for one, am very, very impressed.

"I like to think my guards are skilled," continued Tarn, "though of course, their skills do not compare with the skills

of the chearis that were. I have one more surprise for you."
He grinned. "In case you have not noticed, I enjoy surprises.
I should like to present to you—" he paused, and the woman
guard who had performed in the naïga rose and came to stand
beside him—"my daughter, Nathis-no-Iryllen Ryth."

Col Ismenin grinned from his seat. Nathis Ryth smiled.
Boras Sul said, "What?" very loudly. Then Col Ismenin rose
and stood beside his betrothed.

The ceremony did not last long. From the way Nathis Ryth
and Col Ismenin looked at each other, Arré could see that
though the match might not be a love match, neither party had
any regrets. Nathis Ryth was not beautiful but she was well-
made and healthy and would have no trouble bearing children.
The terms of the betrothal were of course not stated aloud but
Arré could guess at some of them and knew at least one of
them: Col Ismenin agreed to give up his family name and
become Col Ismenin Ryth, and his wealth (whatever portion
of the family fortune he was entitled to) went with him to
Nuath.

The ceremony closed with Tarn Ryth saying, "And you
must all come to Nuath for the wedding." Not likely, thought
Arré. The wedding was traditionally held three months after
the betrothal, and a journey upriver at the end of autumn, in
the rains, would be unpleasant at best. She stretched, and found
Tarn Ryth at her elbow.

He extended a hand to help her up, which she ignored.
"How did you like *my* entertainment?" he said proudly.

"Very much," said Arré. She cocked her head. "Tell me,"
she said softly, "was the first staged, too?"

He laughed, and bent his head to hers. "Of course," he said
in a rumbled whisper. "Do you think I'd risk my son just for
a game?"

"No," Arré said. "In fact, I would say you don't take many
risks."

He straightened. "You are right," he said. His hand toyed
with his chain.

The farewells were being said. Tarn Ryth said, "I must join
my cousins and my new relatives now."

"I would not keep you from them," said Arré, and saw him
grin. "You have been frank with me: may I ask yet another
question?"

"Ask," he said.

"Have you made marriage plans for your son?"

He nodded appreciatively. "Not yet. I have approached the ruling house of one of the northern Keeps. An alliance north would certainly be useful to me. On the other hand, the Isara house of this city boasts of four daughters."

"Would you wish your son to become an Isara?"

He tangled a hand in his neck chains. "No. But if the Isara could see beyond tradition, they might be willing for an Isara daughter to become a Ryth. . . ."

Arré frowned. She did not particularly approve of that. "When do you leave to return to Nuath?"

"Almost at once. Day after tomorrow." He smiled grimly. "I shall spend the next two days avoiding the company of Kim Batto."

"It was most instructive to talk to you."

"I hoped you'd find it so." His huge hand closed over hers, dwarfing it. "You have said we are not enemies, Arré Med," he said. "I hope you meant it. I am a bad enemy. On the other hand—" he smiled, like a pirate—"I make a very good friend. Farewell." He released her hand and strolled off, cleaving through people like a ship under full sail.

Arré went to find Marti Hok. The old woman was in the Ismenin courtyard, looking at the flowers. "I shall have to ask Ron Ismenin who does his gardening," she commented. She leaned on her cane with both hands. "You spent a long time with that man."

"It was worth it," Arré said. "He is—quite remarkable."

Kim Batto, gown flapping, walked across the granite flagstones to them. "Arré," he began, "I think you had better listen to me."

"I think I had better not," Arré said. "You will lie to me, as you lied to Tarn." His eyes widened. "Did you think you were using *him*? You are a fool, Kim Batto, a worse fool than Boras. Go away."

He backed from her as if she had suddenly turned into a bear or a snake. Marti Hok said, "That was wonderful. Will you tell me what happened? I detest ignorance, especially my own."

Arré said crisply, "Kim Batto has been playing a game with us. He has told Tarn Ryth that we have refused to permit the Blue Clan on the Council, thus maneuvering Tarn into making alliances with separate houses of the city, namely the Batto and Ismenin houses."

"But who *is* the man, and why should Kim Batto and Ron Ismenin care what he does?" demanded Marti.

Arré told her. "All the grain supply to Kendra-on-the-Delta passes through his hands. He has drawn the cities of the river together, making of them a little district of Arun, like our city districts. He has money, a lot of money, and influence, and military skill, as he took pains to show us."

"What does he want?"

"To be treated as a ruler, as an equal of any member of a noble house."

"Indeed," said Marti, and her eyes narrowed. "Arré, can you possibly support this man's ambition? He is a barbarian! If once we show weakness to him, we are lost. He can extort anything he wishes from us by threatening the grain supply."

"He can do that now," Arré pointed out. "He does not threaten."

"Then what do you call that performance in the parlor?" said Marti. "Entertainment, indeed."

"I do call it entertainment," said Arré firmly. "I think the Council could do worse than consider an alliance with Tarn Ryth."

"And, doing that, how do we avoid listening to the Ismeninas?" said Marti.

Arré scowled. "I don't know. But Marti, I would rather know what Ron Ismenin is doing than *not* know."

"Do you think Tarn Ryth will tell you?"

"I think he might."

Sironen Hok strolled to his mother's side. "The litter is here, Mother," he said. "Lady Arré. You look beautiful."

He was a handsome man himself, with a fine thick black mustache and a firm, sensual mouth. He was also married, with five children, and quite faithful to his wife. "Thank you," Arré said.

"He is so tactful," said Marti. "That is his way of telling me we must go home. Well, Arré, was it worth coming to, this party?"

"Most definitely," Arré said. "I enjoyed myself tremendously and you are a wicked old woman."

Marti chuckled, and whispered, "I practice." Her son rolled his eyes expressively and tucked his hand through her arm.

"Wait," Marti said. "Arré. Send that Sorren child to me this week."

Arré smiled. "With so many grandchildren of your own

blood, Marti, I fail to see why you need a stranger to tell stories to. But I shall do as you ask, of course."

"Mother, come." Sironen tightened his grip on his mother's arm.

"You see how they treat me," said Marti cheerfully. She kissed Arré's cheek. "I am coming, my dear."

Grinning, Arré watched them go. Her own litter was somewhere out in the street with the others, but she felt no desire to go to it. A tall spear of purple lilac caught her eye, and she stooped to smell it.

When she straightened, Cha Minto was beside her. He looked very unhappy. He said, "Arré—I just want you to know that what I did was not done out of malice. I—I had to do it. At least, I thought I did."

Arré was torn between pity for his distress and contempt for his weakness. "Cha, we cannot talk here," she said. "Come and see me."

He wet his lips to answer. At that moment, a soft voice said, "My dear sister. Did you enjoy the dance?"

It was Isak. His face was still painted with the outline of the Swan's feathers. He wore street clothes, and under them his muscles showed, hard as metal, tensile as wax. He put his arm through Cha's, holding the other man to him like a lover. "You had a lot to say to our merchant guest. Did you find him cultured?"

Arré said, "We talked politics, not art. Did you find him cultured when you met him last night?"

"He did not talk to me," Isak said. "I am not the head of my house. *Did* you enjoy the dance?"

"Yes," she said. "You always dance well. Isak, why did you tell Ron Ismenin to keep me out?"

"To irritate you." said Isak, smiling. "And because I felt that Kim Batto's games might be spoiled if you had an opportunity to speak directly to Tarn Ryth. You managed, of course. How resourceful you are. Poor Kim looks like a drowned hen."

Yes, thought Arré, that is the end of this alliance. I shall have to tell Jenith to return to her job at the warehouse. "Did Ron know what Kim Batto was doing?" she said.

Isak said, "Ask him, my dear."

"Did the L'hel?"

The dancer shrugged. "I don't know. I have as few dealings with the Tanjo as possible; it is the one thing you and I agree on. Cha—" his voice grew barbed—"come with me. I have something to show you."

"You interrupted us," Arré said tartly.

"I know," said Isak. Locking his hand through Cha Minto's elbow, he dragged the weaker man away.

Arré went to find her litter. She located it by the red and blue streamers on the poles. Sorren sat beside it, holding her drums and her new clothes.

"The dance was beautiful," Arré said to her. "You looked lovely." Sorren smiled faintly and did not speak. She looked haggard. "Come, ride in the litter with me."

Sorren said, "I can walk."

"I know you can walk! Get in." Sorren sighed. Rising, she entered the litter. Arré followed her, and the bearers stood. The girl's long legs crammed the tiny aisle between the two seats, and she drew them up beneath her. Arré thumped on the side of the box, and the litter lurched up and forward.

"Well?" Arré said, "what happened?"

Sorren rubbed her face with her hands. She was still wearing her hair in its coil, and the lapis lazuli comb winked and shone in the smelly box. "Isak knows I lied to him," she said.

"Was he very angry?" Arré said gently.

Sorren dropped her hands in her lap, and nodded. "He didn't say so. But I know he was."

"He doesn't have to say it. His body speaks for him. Child, you needn't drum for him again. He can get another drummer for the Festival."

Sorren bit her lip. "He probably will. He won't want to see me again. But—I *like* drumming for him!" The last sentence was a wail. Arré reached across the tiny space and took hold of one of Sorren's hands. The girl gulped, and breathed hard. "Marti Hok was right, I think. He is evil."

"When did she tell you that?" asked Arré.

"When I went to her house."

Arré was reminded of Marti's last request. "Would you like to go see her again?"

Sorren said, "Oh, yes." Some of her usual animation returned to her face. "May I? She wants to see my Cards."

"Certainly, she must see them." Arré let go of Sorren's hand. Briskly, she said, "And you must not let Isak distress you. He is not worth your pain." My little brother, she thought. I suppose he loved me once.

But the pleasure in Sorren's face vanished at the mention of Isak. She bowed her head.

Arré hunted for something to distract the girl. "Sing something," she said.

Sorren's head came up. "I can't sing."

"I can," said Arré. "Sing, and I will help you."

Automatically, Sorren drew her drums into her lap. "Anything?" she said. Arré nodded, hoping the girl would not choose something too ribald.

The litter swayed as the bearers climbed the hill. Sorren sang softly: *"Where did they go, the ones who were chosen? Where did they ride, the dancers so strong?"*

It was a song Arré knew; she joined in, thinking of Tarn Ryth, of his children, and of his visions. *"With their long blades sharp, and their long hair flowing, Where did they go, what is their song?"*

The next afternoon, Jenith came to the Med house. She sat in Arré's study and blew smoke rings and talked about Tarn Ryth. "He's camped with his soldiers in the Batto Yard," she said, "and the servants say that he and Kim Batto are not talking to each other." Sorren saw Arré's wide grin as she went down the hall.

The following day was laundry day. Sorren and Lalith soaked and scrubbed all the household clothes (even the cook's aprons) and hung them out to dry in the rear courtyard. Arré left the house early. (She always did, on laundry day. She said the smell of soap made her gag.) There was a well at the south end of the district that people complained was bad, and she had gone to look at it. Sorren was feeling virtuous. She sauntered down the hill with the box of Cards in her hands. There were piles of froth in all the alleys; it seemed as if the whole city was doing its laundry. The smell of roasting walnuts filled the air. She loped across the Minto district to the Hok district, following the Street of the Weavers into Lerril's Street. Someday she would ask Arré who Lerril was.

Tomorrow she was going to the pasture in the Batto district to shoot more arrows. She flexed her hands, feeling the muscles move under her skin. In her room, where no one could see, she had been exercising her arms and shoulders the way Paxe did, lifting herself from the floor while keeping her body straight. The first time she'd tried it, her arms had collapsed after five upward pushes, but this morning she had done ten.

The Hok guards waved her into the house without question, and she was ushered to Marti Hok's room like a real visitor. Marti was sitting with a pile of scrolls on her lap, and she looked very tired. As Sorren entered, she smiled and put the scrolls on the little table at her elbow.

Sorren said, "I can come another day if you're busy, Lady."

"Marti. No, I asked you, remember? Did you bring the Cards?"

Sorren held the box out.

"Good." Marti took it from her. Sorren sat on the mats. A girl in white brought a tray of sherbet, lemon sherbet this time, with honey swirled in it. Marti took all the Cards from the box and looked at each Card. "These are very beautiful," she said. "Were they in order when you got them?"

"Yes. The Dancer first, and then the Weaver, the Sleeping Woman, the Lady—"

"Yes, I see." Marti shuffled through the Cards, putting them in order, and then handed them to Sorren. "Let's go to the library, shall we? You can bring your sherbet."

They walked to the library. On the way, the girl-child who had wanted to keep the butterfly ran out of a room. "Abu, where are you going?" she said.

"To the library, sticky-hands, where thou canst not come."

"I'm going to the water," said the girl, puffing out her chest. "Da is taking me to see the ships!"

The library was just as Sorren remembered it, and she said so.

"Of course, child," said Marti, sitting in the big wood chair. "No one comes here but I. Do you remember which case holds the red binder?"

Sorren pointed. "Thy memory is better than mine," the old woman muttered. "Take it out."

Sorren laid it on the desk. The brittle paper flaked on her fingers, though she touched it as lightly as she could. She recognized her own name, and pointed to it. "That is my name?"

"Yes. That tall letter is an 'S' character. This is the story I read you before. Now, what did I do with those papers? Ah. Here." She lifted the small pieces of paper from the binder. "Now, you hold the Cards while I read the names. Let us see if you have the complete deck, or if there are more you do not

have. The Dancer. The Weaver. The Dreamer, yes, that one.
The Lady. The Lord. The Scholar; that is the man in the black
robe, of course. The Lovers. The Archer." Sorren drew that
Card out with a sudden jolt of recognition. "The Messenger.
The Horseman. Surely these are from the north, child. Look
how in that one it is snowing, and in that the man is riding
across the steppe."

"Have you been there?"

"To the steppe? No. But I have heard it described. Great
plains, going on and on endlessly until they reach the mountains. A desolate countryside. The Stargazer. That is the
woman in blue. The Illusionist." Marti looked at the paper and
then at the Card. "How interesting. The man in the Card is
wearing the same color clothing as did the juggler at the Ismenin
betrothal."

Sorren looked at the Card again. Marti was right, except
that Jeshim had worn no ruff.

"The Eagle," said Marti. "No, the Wolf, then the Eagle.
The Phoenix. The Mirror. Look how cleverly that is painted.
If there were no number on the Card, you would not know
which way to hold it. The Tower. The Wheel. The Demon.
What an ugly creature that is. Death. The Moon. The Sun."
She paused. "Is that all of them?"

"That's all," said Sorren.

She had spread them out across the dark wooden table, in
two lines of eleven.

"Look at the detail," said Marti, marveling. "Look how the
picture shows the tree on the tapestry that the Weaver is weaving, and the faces of the people trapped in the spokes of the
wheel. And you cannot use them?"

"No."

"A pity."

"But it is ni'chea to use them."

Marti snorted. "No, it is jealousy on the part of the White
Clan that made them declare strawcasting and stargazing and
other seeing arts ni'chea."

Sorren wondered how that could be true. Surely it was
weakness that made people jealous, not strength.

"Arré said I should learn to use them, but she could not tell
me how."

Marti nodded. "I agree," she said. She touched the Card
of the Scholar with one finger. "The Black Clan might have

the knowledge of their use locked somewhere in their archives. But even if they did, I doubt they would share it with you. They would probably try to take the Cards away from you."

"But the Cards are mine!" Sorren said. She reached to them, ready to gather them up.

"Of course they are. *I* am not going to take them from you." She leaned on one hand, gazing at the pictures. "The White Clan would know. You might ask them."

Sorren bit her lip. "I can't."

Marti smoothed the sleeves of her pale cream-colored jacket. "I don't see why not," she said. "The L'hel may be venal, but not every witch is. You might have to swear not to use them, but a promise is only as binding as you believe it is. They might want to take them from you, but you are bonded to the Med house and they would have to ask Arré's permission to do anything, and I am sure Arré would tell them to let you keep them. Why, then, can you not ask them?"

"I can't!"

"Tell me why not," said Marti.

Sorren told her.

Midway through the telling, Marti began to smile. When Sorren finished, she reached out and took the girl's hand in her own. "You have never told Arré this, have you?" she said. Sorren shook her head. Her throat was dry. She had never told anyone, except Paxe. "And this is your reason for not taking the Cards to the witchfolk, because you are afraid that they will force you to stay in the Tanjo, and become a witch, and never leave the city?" Her fingers were warm. "You poor child. Sorren, you cannot be forced to do anything you do not desire to do! You are a witch, yes. But there is no way, *no* way you can be made to exercise your talent, your far-traveling, if you don't want to use it. *Tanjo* means school; that is what it is, a school. I think you *should* go to the Tanjo, tell them what you are, and let them teach you. You may find that, after all, you don't wish to go north."

"No," said Sorren. "I want to go."

"I assure you," said Marti, "they would not keep you. They can't."

Sorren gazed at painted pictures. You tell me, she thought. Tell me what will happen if I do it. But the Cards remained mute. Her hands were shaking, and she clenched them at her sides. The thought of going to the Tanjo terrified her. But what if Marti Hok was right? She thought of Sorren the warrior, the princess, Sorren who looked like her, Sorren whose name and (perhaps) blood she carried. What would that Sorren have done?

She would have gone wherever she wished, and no one would have dared to touch her.

But I am not that Sorren, she thought.

Marti said gently, "Sorren, why have you never talked to Arré of this? I am sure you have not, because I know she would have told you the same thing."

Sorren rubbed her cheek. It was hard to explain. "She would have wanted me to go," she said.

"She would never force you to."

"No. But she would talk about it and ask about it and make me feel foolish if I chose not to."

Marti nodded. "That is true," she said gravely. "Arré does not seek power, but when it is offered her she takes it, and she would not understand your not taking it. But what does your lover, the Yardmaster, say?"

"I haven't asked her," said Sorren.

"Why not?" said Marti. "She is a wise woman; she must be, to have Arré's trust. Perhaps you should."

It was good advice. Sorren thought about it on her way up the hill. As she reached the Yard, she glanced through the gate bars to see if Paxe was there. The guards were training with their new wooden weapons, but Paxe was not among them. Sorren hesitated, and then went to the cottage. She knocked on the door very softly. If no one answered, she would leave.

"A moment," called Paxe's voice. Footsteps strode across the mats and the door opened. Paxe looked out, face stern. "Oh," she said, "it's you. Come in."

Sorren said, "If you're busy—"

"If I'm busy, I say so," said the Yardmaster. "Come." She stepped back. Sorren went into the cottage, carrying the Cards. She sat on the mats; Paxe threw her a cushion and she put it under her buttocks. She put the box of Cards beside the table.

"I haven't seen you in a long time," she said to her lover.

"I'm on night watch," Paxe said. "And you've been busy. Whenever I see you, you're on your way down the street."

Sorren started to say, Arré keeps me busy—but the words stuck in her throat. It was not Arré who kept her busy. She remembered Arré asking her if she had another lover. Did Paxe think she had another lover? She looked hard at the older woman, seeing the new lines of worry on her face. She seemed thinner, too. That could be from the sword practice, but it could be from a question she did not want to ask. When Paxe was angry or upset or troubled about something, she did not speak of it: she worked.

Sorren said, "I've missed you."

The Yardmaster held out a hand. "Then why are you all the way over there, where I can't reach you? Come here."

Sorren moved. They hugged lightly. "That's better," whispered Paxe. She traced Sorren's eyes with her tongue. "Is something troubling you, chelito?"

Sorren put her head into the hollow of Paxe's shoulder. "There's something I have to tell you," she said.

"Tell me," said Paxe. She twined her fingers in Sorren's hair.

"You remember weeks ago, at the Council meeting, when Isak first asked me to drum for the betrothal?"

"I remember," said Paxe.

She was not going to think about Isak. "Well, the next morning, Arré asked me to find out for her who the Ismenin boy was marrying."

"Was she surprised when you told her?"

"Yes—but that's not what I want to tell you. I asked Jeshim, the juggler. He was on the Jalar slipway, juggling for the sailors and fishermen. Anyway, I met this—this person on the docks. Her name is Kadra. She told me she had been a messenger, and then she hurt her leg and couldn't ride."

"Kadra. Does she live in this district?"

"No, in the Jalar district—sort of. I talked to her. She's a mapmaker. I asked her if she had heard of Tornor, and she said yes. She said she'd make me a map, to show me the towns I would have to go to, and the roads. . . ."

Paxe said, "How long has it been since she was hurt? They've changed."

"I don't know," Sorren said. "She never told me. A long time, I think." She pulled herself out of Paxe's embrace. "If you keep asking me questions, I'll never tell it right," she said.

"I'm sorry," Paxe said. She crossed her legs and folded her hands in her lap. "I just like to hold you."

"Hold me after. Kadra—Kadra's strange. She's a drunk. I've never seen anybody who could drink so much and still stay on her feet. She was a messenger until she hurt her hip, falling. She wants to go on the ship—the *Ilnalamaré*." She said the strange word carefully, so as not to miss a syllable.

"What ship?" said Paxe. Sorren told her about the ship. She shook her head. "The things I don't know about this city. Now I've interrupted you again. Go on."

"Kadra's been marking the map for me, and she's named me all the towns between here and Tezera. I know them, all the names, I mean."

"Really? Show me."

"Terzi, Mahita, Warrintown, Elath—I'm *not* going to Elath—Shonet, Sharon, Nuath, Yfarra, Morriton, Septh, Kup-on-the-Marsh, Tezera."

"Very good," said the Yardmaster.

Sorren took a breath. "There's more." There was a loose straw on the mat; she teased it with her fingers to make it break off. "Kadra's teaching me the bow."

Paxe's back straightened. "Whose idea was that?" she said.

"Hers. She said I have to learn to hunt if I'm going to go north alone." The stubborn straw finally came loose in her hand. She lifted her head to meet Paxe's eyes. "I know it's unlawful for me to learn a weapon art, but I just want to learn how to shoot animals, fish, nothing more."

Paxe shook her head. "Chelito, you're taking a chance," she said gently. "Where are you learning this?"

"In a pasture in the Batto district. The bow is hidden. I was there this week and I'll go next week, and the week after that, and the week after that, until the ship leaves."

"Then what will you do?"

"I don't know," Sorren said.

Paxe said abruptly, "Bring it here." She rose suddenly. "I'll keep it for you, in my chest." She pointed with her chin to the carved wooden chest. "I'll set up a target in the Yard for you to practice with. What are you shooting at now?"

"Hay bales. I'm not very good." Sorren's pulse leaped in her throat. "Do you mean it?"

"I don't say what I don't mean," said Paxe. She half smiled. "Chelito, you've grown."

"My clothes all fit."

"That's not what I mean." She came across the floor and, leaning, fitted her mouth to Sorren's. They kissed, bodies making a circle of light and dark in the sunlit cottage. Paxe was the first to move her head. "Chea," she whispered, "I'm going to miss you when you go north."

"I'm not going for a year," Sorren said.

"It'll take me a year to get used to it," said the Yardmaster. "Come, I want to show you something." She brought Sorren to the chest. The carvings on the lid were in the shape of a great tree with spreading branches. Birds peered out of the branches, and the brass clasp on the chest was shaped like a bird, with great extended wings.

Paxe opened the chest and took out a sword.

It was spotted with rust, but the edge looked sharp, and the hilt and the piece of metal that protected the user's hand were bright and shiny. Paxe lifted the scabbard from the chest as well. "It's very old," she said. "I don't have it in the scabbard because the scabbard is so worn that the leather's falling apart. The silk keeps it safe." She held the blade to the light. "You wanted to see it," she said. "Would you like to touch it?"

Sorren nodded. "Hold your palms out, flat," said Paxe. Sorren obeyed, and Paxe laid the sword across her palms. It was not as heavy as she thought. Paxe took it back. "Do you want to grip it?"

"May I?"

"Put your right hand on the hilt."

Sorren reached her right hand out. Paxe was holding the hilt in her left hand. Sorren closed her fingers around the hilt and Paxe took her hand away. Sorren tightened her fingers. "Is it—is it old?" she said.

"Very old," said Paxe gravely.

Sorren wondered if it had ever killed. The thought made her shiver. She closed her eyes, willing herself north with all her strength, as if the presence of the sword made a magic that would help her be there.

She was there. She was the bird, flying over the mountains— except these were not her mountains, not the great gray hills she had come to know. These were red. They reminded her of the Tanjo, except where the Tanjo stone was shaped and polished, this stone was rough and scoured by wind and rain and frost. There was snow on the peaks. Sorren-the-bird swooped lower and realized it was summer. She glimpsed green, houses, a windmill—she was riding the currents between two tall ranges, and below was a village.

She dropped lower, until she was hovering above the village. Slowly she drifted, invisible as music, down what seemed to be the main street of the village. At one point was a large dirt square—a Yard, she thought—with people in it.

They were speaking to each other, but their accents were strange; she could not understand them. Some of them had weapons, wooden knives of the type she had seen Paxe use with her soldiers. One man stood out. He was in the center of the space, with his hands on his hips, a teacher's pose, she thought. His hair was tricolored, and he tied it back from his forehead with a red scarf—a shariza, thought Sorren—and then the vision snapped.

She returned to the present to find that Paxe had taken the blade from her hand. Her knees buckled, and the Yardmaster caught her and lowered her gently to the floor. "What did you see?" she said. "The Keep?"

"No." Sorren swallowed. Her throat and lungs ached, as if she had truly been breathing the air of the mountains. "No. Mountains—but different mountains. Red ones." She described them.

Paxe listened, her arms around Sorren. "It sounds like the Red Hills," she murmured as Sorren described the color and height of the snow-capped ranges. "What else did you see, chelito?"

Sorren said, "A place. A village in the mountains. And a man, teaching in a Yard. He wore a shariza." Again she closed her eyes, trying to dredge detail from her memory. "He wore clothes like the ones you wear in the Yard, and his shirt had a pattern on it, a running horse—like the Batto crest."

"What was he teaching?"

"I saw wooden knives." She struggled to call it back, frightened at the same time that she would turn again into Sorren-the-bird. "I've never seen this place before. What made me go there? What do you think it was?"

Paxe said, "I don't know. It could have been anywhere in the Red Hills—Tor's Rest, perhaps. Even Vanima."

Sorren jerked around. "Vanima?"

Paxe half smiled. "I didn't mean it, chelito. I think the sword took you somewhere it's been, but I can't guess where."

"I *did* see a cheari."

"Probably you did," Paxe said. She slid her thumb down Sorren's spine. "But there's no way you can know for sure."

Unless I ask the witchfolk, Sorren thought.

Lifting the sword from the mats, Paxe wrapped it in silk and laid it in the chest. Sorren watched the practiced motion. Paxe had known a cheari once. A question leaped to her lips.

She hesitated, and then said, "Do you think there are any left?"

Paxe understood. "No," she said. "I hope not. The world has passed them by. It's changed."

No, Sorren thought, and her hands clenched. It hasn't changed that much!

She picked up the Cards from where she had put them, near the table. "I brought them to Marti Hok; she wanted to see them," she explained.

"What did she think of them?" Paxe asked.

"She said I should go to the Tanjo and learn to be a witch. She said they could teach me how to use the Cards."

"Do you want to?" said Paxe.

I don't want to go to the Tanjo, Sorren thought. But what if everything Marti said was true? She remembered the moment in the street, when the black-haired witch had—touched her. She shivered with the memory. It hadn't really hurt. What if she took the Cards to the Tanjo? Fortunetelling was ni'chea; they might take the Cards away. But what if they didn't; what if they taught her how to see what was to come? It might not be so terrible to be one of them.

"What would *you* do?" she said.

"Were I you?" said Paxe. "I would go."

"And if I do go, and become a witch," Sorren said, "will you still be my love?"

Paxe's mouth twisted, as if the words hurt. Crossing the space between them, she bent and kissed the top of Sorren's head. Her voice husked as she answered, "I will love you always, wherever you go."

Arré went to bed early. The excursion to the well had tired her; she did not eat, much to the cook's disgust. Climbing to her chamber, she leaned heavily on Sorren's arm. "Did Marti like your Cards?" she asked from her bed. Sorren nodded. "Good."

After putting Arré to sleep—like a worn and cranky child, she insisted on talking until she fell asleep in mid-sentence—Sorren went to her room. But the silence disturbed her. She was restless, too restless to sleep, but she did not want to drum. She went downstairs to the little parlor. Elith waddled in and noticed her. "What are you doing here?" said the old woman. "Go, go." She made shooing motions with both hands. It was futile to argue; Sorren left. She went into the kitchen. Toli was cleaning a sturgeon for breakfast, the fish smell made her flinch.

Finally she went outside. They sky was moonless; the crescent moon that had roamed the afternoon sky was down beneath the world. Sorren walked through the rear courtyard. The tiles were cold on her bare feet. If she went to the Tanjo. . . . The thought dried her mouth. She walked to the Yard fence and passed a hand over a plank. If she was truly a witch. . . . She bit her lip and continued to walk, fingers trailing lightly on the wood.

She walked by the Yard gate, and stopped. Someone was in there. The sound of heavy, deliberate breathing reached her across the fenced-in space, as even as the sound of the sea. She looked through the gate and her heart pounded. Paxe stood in the Yard. That tall silhouette was unmistakable. She held a sword as if she faced an enemy, and she was moving a swift pattern, back plumbline straight. Sorren curled her hands around the chill bars of the gate and stayed very still. The sword gleamed; it was metal, not wood.

Paxe had not seen her. The Yardmaster wore the clothes she usually wore on watch, but in the starlit night she seemed more like a shade than a human being. Her movements reminded Sorren of Isak's movements in the dance, but where Isak was graceful, Paxe was deadly. Suddenly, Isak seemed like a child, playing at art. This is the true art, Sorren thought. Her eyes began to ache, and she blinked to ease them. In the blur, Paxe's outline changed, and Sorren saw not Paxe, but the teacher of her vision. . . . She blinked again, and saw her lover. This was a Paxe Sorren did not know, perhaps had never known. The girl shivered. And, tall and slim and deadly, Paxe danced; thrusting, leaping, thrusting again, a dark and fluid shadow against the pattern of stars, the whites of her eyes glittering like quartz.

CHAPTER SEVENTEEN

The fourth day of the week, Sorren went to the house on Plum Street to meet Kadra.

Now that she had told Paxe about Kadra and about the bow, Sorren found it easier to simply do her work and leave the house. Elith grumbled, but as long as Sorren did the shopping and the cleaning, she could not complain. Arré did not seem to mind.

On Plum Street, the Asech children were playing Catch Me in among the houses and gardens. Sorren looked for the girl with the blocks who had first directed her to the goat hutch, but could not find her. All the children, with their dark eyes and brown skins and narrow faces, looked alike.

Kadra was not in the goat hutch. Sorren looked everywhere behind the house. She even went to the windows and put her face against the screen, trying to see through the silk-flecked paper, but saw nothing. She called. Only the high laughter of the children answered her. Finally she left Plum street and went to the pasture.

Tammo was delighted to see her. He went at once to the place where the bow and arrows were hidden and pulled them out. "No, Tammo, I'm not going to shoot today," Sorren said. His face wrinkled in disappointment. "Tammo, have you seen Kadra?" He whined, and wriggled, and then shook his head. "You haven't seen Kadra, Tammo?" He waved his hands in the air emphatically. "If you see her, tell her Sorren is looking for her. Sorren. Can you remember that?" The child-man nodded and waved his hands. "Sorren," she repeated, and picked her way across the littered pasture.

She no longer had to ask directions to the Jalar slipway. Hurrying across the city, she strode through the Sul district to The Silver Fish. Shards of blue glass from the front casement glittered on the cobbles like the lapis lazuli of her comb, and the tavern's heavy swinging door had been torn right off its hinges. A man festooned with carpenter's tools was measuring the casement. "What happened?" she said.

He grunted. "Some fool of a wagon driver tried to drive along the street and rammed into the building. Door gone, windows gone. Norres is so mad she's pickled." Sorren could hear the tavern owner screaming within the inn. Turning from the refuse, she walked toward the pier, glad that she had worn her sandals. A dog growled at her from a doorway, and she shied a pebble at it.

The guards in yellow let her stand on the pier for a long time. She gazed at the ship. It looked finished. The sides sloped smoothly up to the deck. The stern was square, the bow pointed. Three tall masts towered in the air. Ropes hung all over them, and there were more ropes coiled all over the ship. Where the sides of the ship curved inward, at bow and stern, cabins had been built, and in several places on the deck there were square holes with covers beside them. Ladders slanted down into the darkness. The deck was white, and so were the ship's sides, and the cabins were yellow. As Sorren watched, a black and white cat marched across the deck, agile as an acrobat amid the clutter of ropes and rolled canvas and boxes.

"Can I go down there?" she asked. The mud seemed deserted. But Kadra might be there, near the ship she loved. The guards frowned but waved her on, and she scudded down the slope of the slipway in a clatter of pebbles.

Near the ship, the stink of fresh paint almost overcame the sea smell. Clay pots peppered the beach at odd angles. In places the shifting mud had thrown the pots to one side. A red-shelled crab waved its claws at her defiantly from a pot rim. She went to the next one; not even a crab greeted her.

She called, her voice mingling with the ocean's. "Kadra!" No one answered. At last she gave up, and climbed back to the street. She went to the inn. Two women were maneuvering a plank through the doorway; Sorren waited until they were inside, and then followed them.

Hammering sounds were coming from the kitchen. Norres stood in the middle of the tavern's common room, arms akimbo, telling the carpenters that if they wasted any more time she was not going to pay them. Her staccato voice, like rain, beat on Sorren's ears. The tavern owner saw Sorren watching and swung around. "What d'*you* want?"

"I'm looking for Kadra," Sorren said. "We were supposed to meet today, at a house on Plum Street. But she wasn't there."

Norres glared. Her hair was ragged and short; it barely touched her shoulders. "I don't know where that one is."

"When did you last see her?"

"Two days ago, drunk." She swung on the carpenters again.

"And you'll pay for the beer you're drinking, too. D'you think it's free?"

Sorren tried again. "Don't you want to know where she is?"

"Why should I?" snapped Norres.

"I thought—"

"I don't care what you thought," said the innkeeper. She looked Sorren up and down. "Gawky, aren't you."

"No," Sorren said. "I'm not gawky, I'm tall. And I want to find Kadra. She's sick. She could be sick, somewhere in the city, lying in the road—"

Norres' eyes fastened on hers. She had green eyes, green as jade, and smoky. Quietly she said, "I know that. And I've learned not to see, over the years."

"Years?"

"Eight years we've been lovers. *You* wouldn't know. That one never says. Eight years—and I've watched the drinking and the fighting, knowing that someday they'll come to me and say, 'You know Kadra-no-Ilézia, the ghya. Better come to the guardhouse, there's a body you might want.' When a person wants death as much as that one does there's little to do to keep her from it. I've done my best. But after a while, you just give up."

Sorren felt as if she had suddenly stepped into a morass. "I don't understand," she said.

"No, how could you?" said Norres, and Sorren saw that her incredible eyes were filled with tears. "Go home, girl, to wherever your home is, and find your lover and hold her, and be happy. Did you look by the ship?" Sorren nodded. "So did I, last night. Did you go to Tammo's?"

"Yes."

"I couldn't. But if that one was dead, I think I'd know." Scowling, she dashed the tears from her eyes. "Ai, now you've made me weep, and I swore to give up weeping for that one. Get out of here, girl. You're in the way."

At that moment, they heard the conches blowing.

"But there's no fog—" said one of the carpenters.

"That's the danger signal!" said Norres. "Fire or flood or fight." She cocked her head. "Where's it coming from?"

"North," said the carpenter.

"No, west," said the other.

Sorren said, "I'd better go." She slipped out the door, listening to the bellowing horns. Slowly she began to trot north,

across the Jalar district into Isara territory. An Isara guard ran
across her path, carrying a pike and a sling with three weighted
balls on it, for throwing. She yelled something incomprehen-
sible as she raced by.

As Sorren turned into the Avenue of the Pines, she heard
the conches blowing. "Awoo," they howled, like wolves across
the plains. "Aawhooo!" A man loped by, carrying a piece of
wood with iron nails sticking out of it. He saw her and yelled
wordlessly, and swung the makeshift club over his head in a
circle, but did not stop. Frightened but determined, Sorren left
the avenue and headed toward the Tanjo. She heard a dull roar,
like the sound of the sea in a rainstorm. She froze, heart thumping, trying to decide where it came from so that she could go
the other way.

As she hesitated, it caught up with her. Suddenly the street
was filled with people, all shouting. She saw a man with a
knife, and another man trying to wrest it from his hands. There
was blood on their clothes. A woman crouched in a doorway,
gripping the bottom of a broken bottle.

"Jalar—Jalar—Jalar—Jalar—" The chant came from the
south. "I—sar—a, I—sar—a—" Sorren looked for a place to
hide. All the people in front of her ran backward with a rush,
and she had to run with them or be trampled. There was a
scream as somebody fell. A knife flashed, then another. The
Jalar guards were trying to drive the people into the Isara
guards, and the people were fighting back. Under and around
and over the din, the conches blew. *Get off the streets!* they
said.

Sorren's throat felt as if she had been breathing sand. She
backed into a shallow doorway, and realized that it was the
doorway where the woman with the bottle had crouched. Sorren
looked around for her but she was nowhere to be seen. A
woman in a Jalar guard tunic ran past, limping. Blood streamed
down her leg.

The street seemed clear. Sorren stepped from the doorway,
trembling. Suddenly, it filled again. People spilled into the
alley like water pouring into a tide pool. Sorren pressed into
the doorway. A woman tumbled backward out of the knot of
people fighting, and her head hit at Sorren's feet, an ugly,
pulpy sound. She did not move. Sorren stretched her hand out
and touched the woman's mouth, and felt nothing. The pale
face stared upward, unseeing. Sorren fisted her hand in the
woman's shirt and tried to drag her into the shelter of the

doorway. The head bumped on the stones.

She let go. More chanting echoed down the street, coming from the north. She heard marching. "Is—men—in, Is—men—in!" Soldiers in gold and gray, the Ismenin colors, blocked the mouth of the street. They held swords in front of them. Slowly they began to march forward, toward the brawlers.

Sorren flattened into the hard wood of the door. She watched the swords advance. The soldiers' faces were set, intransigent. A man tried to club at one of them; the sword slashed his throat. He rolled away, with blood running down his chest and back. A small dark man appeared to be giving the orders. She turned her face away so that she would not see a sword coming at her. The street shook. Then they were past her, leaving the smashed and sodden dead behind.

She crawled into the street. The conches had ceased; there was no sound from the city. It took her a long time to pull the dead woman's body into the doorway. Her hands and arms shook, and she wept. When she finished, there was red on her hands. A door opened, across the street, and a man looked out. When he saw her, he shut it quickly. She wondered who lived behind it, and if they were home, and if they had known she was there. Dragging herself up, she made herself walk past one dead body, then another. The sound of the wind blowing up the avenues, sharp and fresh as pain, seemed to her to be the sound of the city, crying.

The din had stopped.

Arré stood beside the window of the parlor, waiting for the messenger that Paxe had sent to return.

Her stomach churned with tension. The first guard had reported breathlessly that the Jalar and Ismenin guards were fighting with live swords in the city streets. The next guard said no, it was not that; a fight had broken out in the Jalar docks and the Isara and Jalar guards had together been unable to halt it. "If the Ismenin soldiers hadn't come, it could have spread into the Hok district and maybe even farther!"

"I doubt it," Arré said. But the sound of the conches frightened her. The last time the conches had been blown a fire had threatened to engulf half the Sul district, and it had taken the combined forces of three districts and the mindlifters from the Tanjo to extinguish it. In the kitchen, the apprentices were chattering about the fight. Arré's nerves screamed. She wanted a drink. She clenched her fists and walked back and forth across the parlor. I should have known, she thought, and was answered, Don't be silly, how could you have known? Are you omniscient, can you see into the future? Such things happen.

I do not believe this fight just "happened," she thought, and no, I am not omniscient. Nevertheless, *I should have known.*

Paxe came in. She was wearing armor, overlapping scales of leather and steel, and carrying a pike. "Twenty-two dead," she said softly. "They are clearing the streets now."

Arré groaned. Last report had said twelve dead, why was twenty-two so much worse than twelve? "Is Sorren back yet?" she said.

"Not yet," said Paxe.

Lalith came in, eyes bright. "Two more responses, one from Boras Sul, one from Kim Batto," she said. "They both say they will come. The cook wants to know what he should fix for dinner."

"I'm not hungry," said Arré. Lalith bowed and went out.

Paxe said, "It's better to eat."

Arré said, "The dead don't eat."

Paxe shook her head. "Arré, you are not responsible."

"I feel responsible."

"Feelings are not fact."

"And patience is a virtue," snapped Arré, turning from the window. "Don't cant at me. Have your guards managed to get one of those swords, yet?"

"Not yet."

"I want one. And I want someone, anyone, Paxe, who saw this riot start. It can be someone who was in it, who fought in it, I don't care, I want her. Get her to me."

"I will. Be patient." Paxe's calm was infuriating. The Yardmaster went to the doorway, called for Lalith, and gave her instructions. Then she came back into the parlor.

She leaned her pike casually inside the door. The cook·came in. He put his hands on his hips. "What do you mean, you won't eat?" he said. "You'll get sick." Lalith slid through the doorway with a bowl of apples on her palms, and he gaped at her.

"Go away," Paxe said to him. He reared his head back, offended. "Make food. She'll eat it."

The scent of the apples made Arré's mouth water. She said,

between her teeth, "Don't talk about me as if I were invisible!"

Lalith put the bowl on the table, bowed, and left the room. Paxe picked up an apple and turned it in her palms. Sorren walked in. Paxe put the apple down.

Arré said. "Where the hell have you been? The Council meets tonight, here!"

Sorren went to the bowl of apples. "I was there," she said softly.

Her face was pinched and white. Arré went to her. She was hunting intently through the bowl of apples as if it were the most important thing in the room. She picked a soft yellow apple from the bowl, and cupped it in her hands. There was red around her nails, and dirt on her clothes, and her eyes were odd.

"You were where?" said Arré.

"At the fight. I saw it."

Arré grew cold. "What were you doing there?"

"I was on the docks, I heard the conches—" She bit into the apple and began to shake. Her mouth worked. "I hid in a doorway. A woman died in front of me. Her head was all soft, like mud." She swallowed, shaking.

Paxe took the apple from her hand. "Go and wash," she said crisply. Over her shoulder to Arré, she said, "Best to keep her occupied." To Sorren she said, "There's a Council tonight, and you will be needed. Lalith!" It was her Yard voice. Lalith shot into the room as if kicked from behind. "Take Sorren to the laundry and help her get clean. Stay with her."

"But—the kitchen—"

"Go," said Paxe. She pushed Sorren's shoulder. The blond girl went out. Arré looked at Paxe and saw that she was trembling with fury. "If something had happened to her—" the Yardmaster said.

"Nothing did," Arré said. Paxe took a deep breath and calmed herself, but her eyes were obsidian.

Heavy footsteps sounded in the corridor; both women turned. A guard came to the doorway, holding a sword. "You wanted this Yardmaster."

Paxe took it from him. "Thank you. Dismissed." He bowed and clumped away. "Look, Arré." Paxe held the blade to the light; sun shimmered on the steel. Arré shuddered, wondering if it had killed anyone.

"Where did it come from?" she said. "Can you tell?"

Paxe nodded. "This is Ismenin smithwork. The steel is lighter than Tezeran steel. This is one of the swords Cha Minto brought east."

"If it was Cha Minto," said Arré.

Paxe said, "Leth-no-Chayatha was *not* lying, Arré."

"Oh, I believe you." But I know Cha Minto, Arré thought, and even with Isak's connivance, I cannot believe he has anything to do with the presence of swords in the city. It *has* to have been the Ismeninas. "Would you swear to the origin of the sword?" she asked.

"In the Tanjo," said Paxe.

Arré's eyes stung. I shall have to tell her, she thought. "Paxe—" She drew a deep breath.

Paxe interrupted her. "I know what you're about to suggest," she said. "You're about to say that Dobrin lied to me. Don't say it."

Arré sighed. "No," she said, "that is not what I was about to say. If you say Dobrin was telling you truth, I must believe you. I do not know the man. Only—someone might have lied to *him*."

Paxe frowned. "Y-y-yes. But he was so certain, Arré."

Arré said, "Tonight after the meeting, I will speak to Cha Minto. I will tell him what you have told me about the swords, and his part in it. Do you wish to be here?"

"Yes," said the Yardmaster. "Is that possible?"

"It can be arranged," Arré said.

Paxe sighted down the sword edge. "I would like that," she said softly. She reached for the pike. "I must put this away. If you want me, I will be in the laundry for a few moments, then down the hill, near the Tanjo guardhouse. The gate guard will know where to find me." She edged sideways out the door, carrying a weapon in each hand. Arré's throat ached; she wanted to weep. We shouldn't have waited, she thought; we should have searched the Ismenin Yard and taken the swords from it, we should have stopped the sword training the week it started, twenty-two dead, I should have known, I should have been able to avert it, damn Ron Ismenin; O mother, *I should have known. . . .*

When Paxe got to the laundry, after putting the weapons within the Yard gate, Sorren was alone. She was drying her hair with a towel, and the strands ran like spun gold between her palms and the cloth. The laundry was dingy; once it had been painted bright saffron, but over the years, steam from the tubs had peeled the paint from the walls. Sorren's pale skin was scarlet. As Paxe entered, she dropped the towel and ran like a deer between the tubs.

"You'll scratch yourself," Paxe said, holding her gently off from the armor.

"I don't care," said Sorren.

Paxe glanced around the damp building. "Where's Lalith? I told her to stay with you."

Sorren said, "Cook needed her, so I told her to go. I'm all right."

"Are you?"

"Yes," said Sorren. With her hair slicked back across her forehead, she looked like a pale and furless seal. Paxe stroked her face.

"Did you come here naked?"

"No. Lalith took my dirty clothes and brought me clean ones." Collecting the clean clothes from a hook, she put them on. She pulled the drawstring of the trousers tight. "Paxe, what made it happen?"

Paxe said, "I don't know, chelito." But I can guess, she thought. Ron Ismenin made it happen. She thought of Dobrin, with heartache.

Sorren wound her hair around her hands and twisted it, like cloth. Water dripped on the floor. "Is there really a Council tonight?" she asked.

"Arré said so," said Paxe, envying the resilience of youth. They forget so quickly, she thought; horror passes through their minds like a bad dream. "Will you feel well enough to serve?"

Sorren frowned. "I'm not a child." She held her hands out in front of her, scrutinizing them, knuckles, nails, palms. Paxe looked at her quizzically and she blushed. "They were bloody."

Paxe took the immaculate hands in hers, and kissed them. "If you had been hurt—" She could not complete the sentence. She had a brief, harrowing vision of Sorren sprawled lifeless in the street. A terrible anger surged through her muscles, shivering her like a leaf.

Sorren said, "Paxe?"

"Never mind," Paxe said. "Chelito, I'm on duty; I must go." She pushed the laundry door open. They went outside. The breeze felt cool after the steamy heat.

The west was turning lavender, as the falling sun hastened in its flight to the mountains. Paxe drew Sorren to her and kissed her mouth. The girl's lips were soft, and they tasted of soap. "Drink some wine before you sleep tonight," she suggested.

"I'd rather smoke heavenweed," said Sorren. They walked toward the house.

"Yardmaster!"

Paxe turned. Sekki was hastening to her across the courtyard. "Yardmaster, we found him."

"Who?" said Paxe.

"The one you wanted. Someone who saw the fight start. He's a fisherman. He saw everything begin, he says, and ran when the guards came. He hid in a privy. He stinks to the moon but he's willing to talk."

"Where is he?" said Paxe.

"In the Yard. Kaleb's got him."

Paxe said, "I'll come right away."

The fisherman's name was Luki. He was young, a scant sixteen, with an adult's breadth of shoulder and the bow-legged stance of one who spends most of his time braced against a boat's pitch and roll.

They took him to the laundry and cleaned him up, but he still stank. It was Paxe's idea to have Arré talk to him in the kitchen. After some prodding, he admitted shyly that he had not eaten since the dawn. Paxe cut him some bread and cheese. Arré sat on a stool, he sat on another, holding bread in one hand and cheese in the other and taking alternate bites.

He wore the coarse cotton clothes of a poor man, and his arms and hands were covered with scars—"From th' skinnin' knives," he said, when Arré asked what made them. He started out slowly, obviously in awe of her and somewhat frightened of Paxe, who was a head taller than he. But in a short while, the story took him, and he forgot his listeners.

"I was comin' off the ship—we had a load of spot fish an' the' cap'n wants 'em put in the tubs so we can run to the outer banks, it was a real good haul, they were near leapin' into the nets—an' I saw a crowd o' dockies—what *you* call dock workers, m'lady—all standin' about in a circle, laughin' and pointin'. I went to see what was they laughin' about. What it was, they tied Granny Cat in one of her own nets, bein' funny they thinks."

"Who is Granny Cat?" asked Arré.

"She's an old woman mends nets for the fishers. She's a bit silly, you know, but she can still tie nets with the best of 'em, my ma says. . . . She was mad as fire, spittin' and yellin' and clawing at them through the net, and they was all laughin' and pointin' and some was pokin' at her to make her madder the way you might poke a dog to tease it. . . . I wouldn't even poke a dog. They wasn't all dockies, neither, some o' them was swanks—"

"What's a swank?" said Arré.

He grinned shyly. "You're a swank, m'lady. The house-folk."

Arré nodded. "Go on," she said gently. "Who were these swanks?"

"Ismeninas," he said succinctly. "The two young ones."

"How many dock workers were there in the circle?" said Paxe softly.

"Oh, maybe fifteen. But there was plenty of 'em just standin' 'round watchin'. An' then the res' of the crew comes up. Medi, she's the second mate, she sees what's doin' and goes storming out there, bein' as Granny Cat is some kind of aunt of hers, and she starts yellin'. So they start to tie her up, too, in one o' Granny's trawl nets, an' she starts to fight with 'em, and then the rest of the crew sees it and they all pile in."

"Who drew the first weapon?" said Paxe.

"Medi pulled her dirk to cut the net off Granny, and someone got in the way. She didn't mean to cut him. Then the crew o' the *Eel* hears the noise—the *Eel's* in dock while they scrape her—and they come fallin' out. Then the Jalar guards was all over an' I ran." He shivered. "I saw m' cousin get stabbed across the throat. The blood—I'm a coward about blood m'lady, I can't help it, it makes me go all sick and queasy. I ran clear off the dock, and stayed there. When I came out, there was two folk dead and three more bloodied like fightin' seal—Medi was one o' them, and her face was all slashed—"

Paxe said, "That's enough." She put a hand on his shoulder. "Where do you live?"

"Jalar district. Sam Street."

"Can you go home, or will the Jalar guards pick you up?"

"Dunno." He hunched his shoulders.

"I'll send a guard with you," said Paxe. "Here." She laid a largo in his hands. He gazed at it, unbelieving.

"Jus' for talkin'?" he said.

"That's right. And for not talking about this," said Arré. "Forget you ever saw this house."

He grinned slyly. "What house?" He ran his thick fingers over the bonta. "I never held one o' these before." He rose, and bowed awkwardly. "I won't say nothin', m'lady."

He followed Paxe to the door; Arré heard her hail a guard. Then she came back in and stood with her hands on her hips. "It was the Ismeninas," she said.

Arré nodded. "I thought it would be." She rose. "The Ismenin soldiers had to know that the riot was happening. They were there, ready, and armed. The only way they could have known it was happening so quickly was if they knew before it started, which meant they had to start it—" She found herself calling down old curses on Ron Ismenin in her mind; may your harvest fail and your seed be barren, may the winter demons devour your soul. . . .

"Will Ron Ismenin be coming to the Council?" said Paxe.

"No," said Arré. Not now or ever, she thought. Her stomach lurched at the picture of the woman on the dock, face bloodied "like fightin' seal."

The cook tramped back in. He sniffed. "Stinks," he said.

"Never mind," said Arré.

"Don't blame me if the food smells strange." He began to chop meat with great sweeping strokes of his cleaver.

Arré went to her study and sank into her chair with knees that shook. Lalith entered. "The Lady Marti Hok says she will attend the Council meeting, Lady."

"Good," said Arré. "Let me know when Cha Minto responds."

At last, the vivid images faded from her mind. She called Lalith to find out what the cook was fixing.

"Soup, Lady."

"Bring me some."

Lalith returned with a bowl filled with pea soup. It smelled wonderful. "Where is Sorren?" Arré asked.

"Dressing, Lady. Do you need her?"

"No. Later I will."

All through dinner, guards came to the door with news. There were, on final count, twenty-three dead and forty-one wounded. Of the dead, six were Jalar guards. Seven Isara

guards and three Hok guards were hurt badly. If the Ismenin
Yard had casualties, it was not admitting them; after clearing
the streets, the Ismenin soldiers returned to their posts and,
armor and swords out of sight, resumed their normal duties.
Someone, in the confusion of the day, tried to start a fire in
the Isara district, but the Isara guards put it out and arrested
the man, who was nearly killed on the way to the guardhouse
by his infuriated neighbors. Besides the deaths, there was property damage: slashed and broken screens, torn nets, overturned
barrows. There were also complaints of theft; in the aftermath
of the riot, the abandoned streets became a target for half the
city's thieves. Forty-three people were arrested. It seemed
likely that there had been more involved in the riot, (near one
hundred, Paxe said) but the others had melted away, into alleys
and gardens and houses and pastures. The men and women
arrested were staying stubbornly silent, but Arré thought that
their silence would last no more than three or four days, until
the core of them realized that no one was going to break or
buy them from the guardhouse. Then they would begin to talk.

Marti Hok was the first to arrive. Arré met her at the front
door, and kissed her. "My dear," said the old woman tremulously, "what a terrible thing."

"Come." Arré brought her to the big parlor and settled her
in a chair. She had ordered the wine to be heated. She rang
for it now, and Sorren came in with a tray. She brought Marti
a mug of steaming wine, and questioned Arré with her eyebrows and a pointing finger. Arré sighed. She wanted wine.
"Tea."

Cha Minto and Kim Batto entered together. Arré gazed at
Cha with contempt, and at Kim with venom. Welcome to my
web, she thought. Cha was nervous and silent. He took the
mug Sorren brought him in both hands, and drank half the wine
straight down, ignoring its heat.

Kim was more deliberate. He settled himself in his armchair
before speaking. "Marti, I understand that three of your guards
were injured in this incident. I am so sorry."

"Thank you," said Marti. "That is kind of you."

Boras Sul came through the doors. "Terrible!" he exclaimed. "Shocking!" He sank into a chair. "Ghastly!"

Marti said, "Boras, can you only say one word at a time?"

He gazed at her with an injured expression. "I—"

"Because if you cannot speak in sentences, I beg you to be quiet."

He flushed an unlovely red, and took the wine from Sorren's hands without seeing her. "Very sorry," he said stiffly.

Kim said, "Our scribe is not here?"

"She will be," said Arré. "Patience is a virtue, Kim."

Sorren brought Arré her tea in a cup with the red and blue fish. The fishtails swirled in the ceramic sea. They reminded Arré of dancers. We are all dancers, she thought, especially Isak, who is not here tonight. And Ron Ismenin. But this is my house, and I will contrive this dance. She sipped the tea. Sorren had dropped honey in it, and the sweet taste was soothing. The lamp flames flickered in their painted prisons as the south wind rattled the window screens.

Azulith came in. In subdued silence, she seated herself at Arré's left, and set up her brushes and ink. Arré waited until she had the first scroll in her lap.

"Councillors," she said, "I have something to declare. I wish to discuss the manufacture, smuggling, and use of the short sword, the kyomos, by the Ismeninas."

Kim Batto said, "Is that really the question before us? I beg to differ with you, Arré. I believe that the event that brings us here tonight has less to do with the presence of swords in the city than it does with who keeps order in the city streets. It is clear to me that the Jalar soldiers failed badly in their attempt to keep the riot from spreading. I think the Ismenin house deserves, not censure, but commendation for having sent their soldiers so promptly to the aid of the Jalar guards."

Kim Batto being pompous, Arré thought, would set even a ceramic fish's teeth on edge. She wondered if he had helped to plan the riot. She doubted it. She imagined Isak and Ron Ismenin together working out the movements of the troops the way Isak arranged the steps of his dances.

Marti Hok said, "Kim, do you *really* want to discuss order in the city?"

Kim twisted in his chair to face the old woman. "I don't know what you mean by that tone."

"The riot started in the shipyards, Jalar territory. It spread to my district when the rioters fled from the pikes of the Jalar guards. What prompted the Ismenin soldiers to come to the 'aid' of the Jalaras, as you put it? Did they ask for help? I do not think so."

Kim Batto said angrily, "Perhaps they should have! I have no idea why the Ismeninas were there when they were needed, but I think it was lucky that they were."

Marti smoothed her sleeves. "I doubt that luck had anything to do with it."

Boras Sul, with one of his rare flashes of intelligence, said, "How did they know there was going to be a fight, eh?"

Cha Minto was so pallid as to be almost white. He said, "You think the Ismeninas knew about the fight before it happened?"

Arré said, "Cha, I think they planned it. But that should come as no surprise to *you*."

He shook his head; his hands trembled. "I did not know," he stammered. "How could I know?"

Could he really have been so oblivious? thought Arré.

Marti Hok lost her temper. "Cha, don't be more of a dolt than you are!" she said, "Who gave you those words to say?" She mimicked him savagely. "*Why would anyone do that?* For power! You are near forty and you cannot see the strongest motive of all at work? Arré, explain it to him."

Arré said, "It *was* the swords that cleared the streets, yes. But the Ismeninas knew about the fight; perhaps hired the people who began it. Kim, here, is the Ismenin voice on the Council." Kim started to protest and she rode over him. "It is the Ismenin wish to create a market in the city for the short sword. This incident was staged, to make it look as if the sword is needed to keep order in the city."

Kim said, sulkily, "You have no proof of any of that, Arré."

Marti said, "We have no proof of *your* involvement. But twelve of the rioters are in the Hok guardhouses, not the Ismenin guardhouses, and though the ones in the Ismenin guardhouses will no doubt stay silent, the ones in my guardhouses will speak, or I do not know my Yardmaster. Three Hok guards were injured, as you pointed out, in the fight." She clutched her cane, as angry as Arré had ever seen her. "They *will* speak."

Kim's manner lost some of its assurance. He gulped his wine. "Since when is creating a market a crime, Marti? If it is, then Arré Med must answer for the drunks and derelicts that haunt the wine shops, and we must all claim responsibility for the heavenweed addicts."

"Perhaps we must," Arré said. "There were twenty-three people killed in Kendra-on-the-Delta today. If people die to serve someone else's political ambition, then I believe that ambition to be a gross and evil thing. At best, we must call it a mistake. If we are no better than our ancestors who used the sword, then we should go back to killing people by planning and fighting wars. War at least is an open evil." Her voice shook, and she stopped speaking, astonished at her own passion. "I didn't know I was going to say that," she said.

Marti raised her wine mug in silent commendation. But Kim said, with fury. "You are a fine one to talk, Arré Med. Your own Yard is training in the komys."

"And how did you learn that?" murmured Arré. "From Ron Ismenin, or from the Tanjo?"

Cha said loudly, "What of the Tanjo?"

"Nothing," said Kim coldly. "Arré was joking."

Arré said, "There is nothing about this that I find funny, Kim. And you are quite wrong about the absence of proof of my charges. There is proof. I can put my hands on it." She stared hard at him. If you fight me, Kim Batto, she thought, I will make public here and now your dealings with the Nuathan.

The message seemed to reach him; his lips tightened, and he stared hard into his cup.

Marti Hok said, "What is your proposal, Arré?"

The room seemed to contract. Arré said, "I propose that this Council officially ban the making, import, and use of the komys, the short sword, in Kendra-on-the-Delta. I further propose that the Ismenin family be censured for having brought the sword into the city, and fined for the entire amount of the damage done in today's riot." Marti Hok nodded. "I also suggest that at the next meeting of the Council, next month, we consider extending the Ban to the kyomos. Considering today's events, I feel sure that the Tanjo will support it."

"I agree," said Marti."

"So do I," said Boras. "Shocking."

Since three votes were all that were needed to pass Arré's resolution, neither Kim nor Cha spoke. Kim looked shrunken, like a bladder with the air pricked from it.

"I will ask you all to leave now," Arré said. "I'm tired."

Azulith was first to rise. She packed up her cases in silence, bowed to the Councillors, and shuffled from the chamber. Kim stamped out without farewells. Boras mumbled something about the wine and left in the care of his servant. Sorren brought Marti's cloak to her.

Marti said, "Arré, do you still think that this Council should treat with Tarn i Nuath Ryth as an equal? He is a man who delights in weaponry. We would have more blood in the streets."

"That's exactly what we would not have," Arré said. "Tarn Ryth is open about his weapons." Cha Minto was fumbling with the slits of his cloak like a man struck blind. Arré touched his arm. "Cha. Will you stay a moment?"

His eyes were pits. "I—I should go—Arré—you remember what I told you at the betrothal—"

"Before Isak dragged you away? I remember. Do you remember what I said? You should have come to me." Pity stirred in her for him; he looked so desperate. "Stay," she said gently. "Stay and we will talk."

She walked Marti to the litter. The horned moon sat over the ocean like a boat. As they reached the foggy courtyard, the thoughts that had been burning in her since she first heard the toll of the dead burst from her lips. "Marti—did *we* make this happen, with our rumors and our plans? Suppose we had left Ron Ismenin alone, might not the city be at peace tonight?"

Marti shook her head. "No." Behind her, the bells jangled as the litter-bearers rose to their feet. "No, my dear, we did not make this happen. We did not bring swords into the city. What if this had taken place at Festival, Arré? I think that was when it was planned for. More would be dead, and in the outcry of horror it is possible that the Ismeninas would be looked upon as saviors." She laid her cheek against Arré's for a moment. "I think it is very likely that in doing what we did, we saved some lives."

CHAPTER EIGHTEEN

Arré listened to the diminishing sound of the bells. When she could hear them no longer, she walked across the courtyard to where the gate guard stood, leaning on his pike. The scent of fallen kava fruit blew toward her in the mist. Autumn is here, she thought. "Idrith," she said.

The guard came to attention. "My lady."

"The Yardmaster said that you would know where she is. Would you send for her, please?"

He pursed his mustached lip and whistled, a two-note, piercing call. In a moment, the same call was repeated, farther away. "That's the signal, my lady," he explained. "She'll come when she hears it."

"Thank you," said Arré. She went into the house. Sorren was standing in the hall. "What are you doing, hanging about?" said Arré. "Go to sleep."

"Cha Minto is still here."

"I know that! Bring a pitcher of tea to the parlor and then leave us. Do you think I cannot pour a cup of tea? Who do you think served at the Council meetings when my mother was alive? I did, when they were here."

"I know," Sorren said. "You've told me."

"Go," Arré said. "I can't make you, you're too big."

Sorren smiled. "I'm going." She walked toward the kitchen. Arré returned to the large parlor. Cha Minto sat huddled in his armchair like a little boy anticipating punishment. Arré brought the lamp from the mantel and set it on the table between them. Sorren opened the door with her shoulder and came in with a tray. She put it on the table.

"Thank you," Arré said. "Leave the door open when you go out." Sorren nodded, and put her fist to her mouth to hide a yawn.

Arré poured the tea, watching the black leaves swirl to the bottom. Cha Minto leaned from the armchair and took the nearest. "Marti was right, wasn't she?" he said. His face twisted. "I have been rather a dolt."

"A dupe," said Arré. She cocked her head, hearing footsteps. Like a large shadow Paxe slipped through the open door

271

of the parlor. Soundless as a shadow, she went behind Cha's chair, and vanished. "For how long has my brother been treating you as if you were his property, Cha?"

He rubbed his eyes. "Does it look like that?"

"Yes."

"It didn't start like that."

"When did it start?"

"Around Midsummer Festival, I guess. I watched him dance. After the dance, I went up to him, just to say—you know, the things one says. How beautiful I thought it was. He—he was charming to me. Witty, complimentary—how can I describe it?"

"You don't have to," Arré said dryly. "I know Isak. Go on."

Something creaked in the big dark room; the wind on the screens, or Paxe, stretching in her concealment. Arré tensed, but Cha did not seem to hear it. "He invited me to his house. I reciprocated. We talked. It was pleasant."

"What did you talk about?" said Arré.

"You, mostly. Not at first. But after a while, the talk was all about you." He flushed. "I—I'm sorry. But I must say I believed most of it; that you were jealous of Isak's beauty and talents; that you gave him only nominal responsibility, that you ran everything, even the grapefields, and that even though he was your heir, you told him nothing of what was happening at the Council, nor asked his opinion or advice—"

Arré drank, and watched the tea leaves settle again. "Some of that is true," she said. "I don't invite Isak to the Council, nor ask his opinion. I don't trust him. As for the grapefields— he hates them. His wife runs them. And I suppose I am jealous of his beauty. But I would not let that jealousy interfere with my judgment." I don't think I would, she amended privately. I hope I would not. "So you became friends."

"We became friends."

"Lovers?"

Cha shook his head. "No. Oh, I will admit it crossed my mind—but no." He hunched forward in his chair. Arré sipped her tea, savoring the sweet minty flavor.

"And then what happened," she prompted.

"I lent him money," said Cha.

Arré's eyebrows lifted. "There is no reason for my brother to be short of money," she said.

"He told me a long story—I won't repeat it. It had you at

the center of it. It was not a lot of money."

"How much?"

Cha looked wretched. "Four hundred largos," he said.

"I would call that a lot of money," said Arré. "Guardian, Cha, one of my guards might earn half that in a year! Was it a personal loan?"

"Yes. But Isak insisted we sign a note for it. I barely looked at it."

"And then what happened," said Arré.

"Then the Council meeting happened," said Cha. He rubbed his eyes again. "Isak came to visit me beforehand. He started talking about a proposal to admit the Jalaras and Ismeninas to membership. I was stunned that he knew about it. I told him I could not talk Council business with him—and then I asked him who had told him about the proposal. He said Ron Ismenin had. I said: Who would make it? He laughed, and said: *I* would! I told him not to be ridiculous, that I thought the Ismeninas were irresponsible. He changed the subject, and started telling me all about the swords the Ismeninas were bringing into the city. When I expressed my horror, he said not to worry, that the Ban did not apply to short swords. I asked him how he knew all this, and he said he had helped Ron Ismenin to plan it, and had contributed part of the money to pay for the smuggling." The words, which had been flooding from him, dammed suddenly.

"Yes," said Arré, "go on."

"I asked him—I was angry, outraged—how he could afford to lend Ron Ismenin money when he had just borrowed from me. He smiled, and took out the note, and made me read it. It said, *For the transport of short swords to Kendra-on-the-Delta*. And there was my signature and seal at the bottom!" Cha's voice broke.

"Drink your tea," murmured Arré. He gulped it back. She refilled the cup. "That must have been terrible for you."

Cha's mouth twisted. "I don't deserve your sympathy, Arré. I would rather you named me the fool I was. I didn't know what to do. I said no one would believe it. He pointed to my signature and said that everyone would believe it. He said, moreover, that the smugglers as they were paid were being told it was my money. I told him a Truthfinder would be able to tell what had happened, and he laughed, and said that the Tanjo knew all about the smuggling, and that the White Clan had its own bets to place. He made me believe that somehow he, or Ron Ismenin, had subverted the White Clan."

Arré listened for some rustle of reaction from Paxe. She heard nothing. Her heart was beating like Sorren's drum. She leaned back in her chair and sipped her tea, forcing herself to be still, to breathe, to relax.

"So you made the proposal to the Council," she said.

"I did. And then, at the betrothal, I simply could not stand it anymore, and I tried to tell you—"

"And Isak stopped you."

Cha whispered, "Perhaps I should not be my house's representative. I could give it up. Gwyneth could do it."

Gwyneth was his sister and his heir. Arré thought, she would probably do no worse.

But there was no guarantee she would do better. Arré made her voice sharp. "Self-pity will get you nowhere, Cha. I see no reason why you should abdicate your position. Use your sense, man. You were trapped, but you are not trapped now. You do not have to support the Ismeninas. If Kim should bring the proposal up at the next Council—" she paused—"well, I doubt he will, but if he does, you can vote against it, if that is what you want to do. And if Isak threatens to use your note against you, tell him you will go to a Truthfinder, and don't let him scare you with what he says about the Tanjo."

"It was a lie, then?" said Cha eagerly. "He sounded so certain."

Arré took a deep breath. "No, it was not a lie, exactly. The L'hel, and Senta-no-Jorith, his Truthfinder, and maybe others of the White Clan, have known from the beginning about the smuggling. They tried to use the presence of the swords to extort a membership in the Council—the L'hel said to me, the Tanjo would support the Council's extending the Ban to short swords if the Council admitted the White Clan to membership. Kim Batto has been the link between the L'hel and the Ismeninas; he sees them both."

"So that is what you meant," said Cha, "when you asked Kim if he had learned about the Med Yard training from the Tanjo."

"That is what I meant," Arré said.

Her arms were knobby with cold bumps; the evening had grown chilly. Arré thought, I should have asked Sorren to make a fire before I sent her to bed. The waxing moon, riding the horizon, shone its silver beams into the chamber. Arré looked behind Cha's chair. Paxe's shadow lay long on the carpet. Arré tried to see her face but could not find it. She turned back to Cha.

"Go home, Cha," she said gently. "Go home, and don't worry. It will be resolved." The platitude made her flinch. "Do you wish an escort? I will have one of my guards walk with you."

He shook his head. "I am not a child, to start at shadows," he said and added wryly, "I make big mistakes, when I make them. I see shadows and think they are the sun." He rose. "I should have come to you."

"I understand why you didn't," she said.

She walked him to the gate. The damp made her shiver. He walked through it, and then turned back to say, "Why do you think Kim will not bring up the proposal a second time, Arré? Has he said so?"

"No," said Arré. "I just think he will not."

"There's something you will not tell me," said Cha. "Well, you're right not to tell me." He squared his shoulders and walked off, and the mist swallowed him.

His disappearance gave Arré a sudden start of panic. Even his footsteps, muffled by the wet, could not be distinguished from the other night sounds. She turned to the guard. "Send someone after him."

"My lady?"

"He has no escort. Send someone after him, and tell them not to let themselves be seen. I want to be sure he gets home safely, after what happened in the city today."

The guard pursed his lips, but he was not about to argue with her. He gave a three-toned whistle. In a few moments, a hooded figure came up the hill. They talked; the figure nodded, and walked east, toward the Minto district.

"Hani will follow him, my lady," said the guard. "Nothing'll bother him."

"Thank you." Shivering with the chill, she hurried inside.

Elith stood there. "Foolishness," she muttered, shutting the door. She started to lock it.

"Wait," said Arré. She hurried into the parlor. The moon shone directly through the window, silvering the porcelain chobatas on the mantel, the brass tongs by the fireplace, the gray wood of the big carved doors.... Arré went to the armchair Cha had vacated, expecting to see Paxe sitting in it. It was empty.

Elith stood in the doorway. "Who are you looking for?" she

said. "There's no one here. I'll lock up."

"Wait!" said Arré. Lifting the chobata on the table, she took it into the corner where she had last seen Paxe's shadow. "Paxe?" she said.

But there was no one in the corner—nor in the hall, nor, when she looked, in the kitchen. Paxe had gone.

The Tanjo dome shone in the dying moonlight. Paxe stood just outside the gate. The wind tugged her hair like a peevish child, calling her to go indoors, it was cold out.... She did not feel the cold. The chill moonlight fell across the country, from the choba groves of Shirasai to the western mountains. In Tor's Rest, she thought, Tyré's grave lies bathed in moonlight. The granite flagstones of the Tanjo courtyard glittered like water. What if she were a bird flying over Arun, what would she see? Towns and farms, travelers huddled around guttering fires ... The wind tugged at her again, flapping her cloak, and she laid her cheek against the gate's iron bars and whispered to it, "Go away."

A boot clicked on stone. "Is someone there?" The figure came nearer; it was a Med guard. "Yardmaster, let me open the gate."

"No," said Paxe, "I'm leaving." The guard stared after her; she glanced back to see his pale silly face like a little moon in the darkness. I must sound very strange, she thought, or look very strange. Or both.

She walked south, to the mouth of the boot that was her district, and back around the Batto border. The guards saluted her but did not speak. Maybe they were ghosts. She caught herself thinking it and told herself not to be a fool. She turned down the Street of Small Pears, and the next post she passed, she hailed it. "How goes the night?"

"Quiet," said Nekko, a tall dark woman who at twilight was sometimes mistaken for Paxe, and Paxe for her.

She walked up Broad Row, the street between the Batto and Med districts. It extended almost the entire length of the border. She walked to the Northwest Gate. The city wall sat solidly in the incantatory moonlight; a small figure, dwarfed by the masonry about him, paced slowly up and back the gatehouse wall. The flickering light of a brazier illuminated his face a moment as he halted to warm his hands. He turned his back on warmth and resumed walking. Outside the wall, a dog howled.

She rounded the toe of the boot. Passing a Minto guardpost she saw a lantern swinging from a moving hand; Darin-no-Sara, the Minto Yardmaster, was making *her* night rounds, going north, toward the Gate. Paxe stayed in the shadows until Darin passed her. She was walking slowly—how long had it been since she left Arré's parlor? An hour? The light had been growing increasingly dim. She glanced over her shoulder but could not see the shape of the moon, only the glow shining on the horizon. It was past midnight, then. Leaves rustled in the wind beneath her feet. The fog blew from the south and tore itself to shreds against the Tanjo dome. A watcher standing on the docks in this weather would see a wall of cloud reaching into nowhere, and no stars.

By dawn, she had gone five times around the district. At sunrise, she returned to the Yard to exchange her command. If she looked or sounded odd, Ivor chose not to remark upon it. The sun rose like a great blind eagle out of its nest in the fog.

She was weary; she wanted to go home, and sleep. But she couldn't, not yet; she had an errand to do. She crossed the Minto district (past Three Fountain Street, where Vanesi the merchant stayed when she was in the city) into Ismenin territory.

There were no signs here of the carnage of the day before. All was peaceful. The fisherfolk stood by the river, watching their lines; barges piled with grain sacks sat at their moorings, tugged by the current and the great river's tide. Smoke and cooking odors streamed from the houses as the people of the district woke to go about their business, and the smell of roasting nuts began to steal through the alleys. The Ismenin Yard was filled with people; behind the tall red fence, Paxe heard them shouting an exercise count ("One—two: one—two!"). A woman in Asech robes strode west with a net of snails over her shoulder; snails, Paxe remembered, were an Asech delicacy.

She did not bother to stop at the gate. She went around the Yard to Dobrin's cottage. The curtains were drawn (she had expected that) but the door, unexpectedly, was wide open, and all the mats lay in the dirt in front of the cottage.

It was the custom in the Galbareth, when someone died, for the mats to be picked up and the houses all through the village to be swept and cleaned . . . Dobrin came from the Galbareth. . . . Snail-like, the thoughts crept into Paxe's mind. She gasped, as if someone had struck her from behind, and then started to run.

She skidded into Dobrin's cottage without taking her boots off. The table stood on end; the statue of the Guardian lay on its side, and the petaled branches lay ground into the floorboards. The room was not empty. Gavriénna, the watch second, stood in the middle of the chamber. There were tears on her cheeks.

She said, "He said you would come. Here." She held something out; a letter. Paxe took it.

"Is he dead?" she said.

Gavriénna shook her head. "Gone. The letter will tell you." She walked outside. Paxe opened the letter.

Paxe, it read. *You were right. I was wrong. I have done my duty to the house I served, and now I am leaving. I shall go into the Galbareth, and be a farmer, and lay my weapons aside. I have asked Gavriénna to take my place as Yardmaster; please help her, if you can bring yourself to do so. She was innocent of the Ismenin intentions, as I was. Farewell, friend. Dobrin.*

Arré sat in her workroom.

She had not slept well that night. By the time Sorren brought the hot wash water to her bedroom, she was awake, sitting on her bed. Now she was trying, but not very successfully, to read the plans the surveyors had sent her by courier that morning—as if she did not have more important things to think about! She tossed the scrolls from her; they landed on the floor and curled like leaves. Lalith, entering with a bowl of fish cakes, regarded them with trepidation, as if the papers had teeth.

"Lady, do you want me to pick those up?" she said.

"No. Leave them." Lalith shrugged, handed her the bowl, and left. Arré nibbled a fish cake and scowled at the floor. She wanted to talk to Paxe—not that she had anything to say, what could she say?—just to be sure that she was all right.

Sorren tapped on the doorjamb.

"Come in," said Arré. "Pick up those scrolls for me, please."

Sorren scooped the scrolls up and put them on the table. "I'm going shopping," she said.

Arré gestured toward the chest. "You know where the money strings are. Help yourself."

Sorren went to the chest. Lifting a string out, she closed the lid and stood by the chest, rubbing the string through her fingers. The bontas clinked.

"Have you seen Paxe this morning?" Arré asked. The girl shook her head. There were dark circles under her eyes; they showed up like bruises on her pale complexion. She didn't sleep well, either, Arré thought. None of us did.

"Where are you going to shop?" she asked.

"Where I usually shop," said the girl. "The river markets."

"Hok district. Good. I want you to take a good look and tell me how extensive the damage is. You can go to the Isara and Jalar districts, too."

Sorren nodded. She moistened her lips. "Could the witches have stopped the fight yesterday?" she said.

"I don't see how," Arré said. "Short of throwing themselves in front of the rioters, and that might not have worked."

"What if they had known about it beforehand?"

"Then I suppose they could have said something—but how could they have known about it beforehand if it did not happen?" Arré remembered the story the L'hel had told her in the Tanjo, of the various futures the Tanjo seers had seen. She wondered if this was one of them. "I don't know, child. You could go and ask them," she added, gently, so that Sorren would not feel her fear was being made fun of.

Sorren simply nodded. Sliding the money bracelet over her arm, she left the chamber. "Don't forget to order sweet berries!" Arré called after her. Lifting the scrolls from the table, she unrolled them across her knees. They were not too bad.

Lalith spoke from the doorway. "Lady, the Yardmaster is here and would like to see you."

Arré started, and the plans slid to the floor. "Tell her to come in, and pick those up, please." Lalith looked at her as if she were mad, and put the papers on the table. She went to the hall; Arré heard murmured words, and then Paxe's firm step. She came into the room with both hands wedged into her pockets. Arré tilted her head to look at her. She looked tired, and her boots were caked with mud.

"Was it a quiet night?" Arré said.

Paxe nodded. "Dobrin's gone. He left me a letter."

"The Ismenin Yardmaster? What do you mean, gone?"

"He's gone back to the Galbareth to be a farmer. Gavriénna-no-Nusuth is the new Ismenin Yardmaster." Her voice was bleak with grief. Arré hunted frantically for words.

"What a waste," she said.

Paxe nodded. "I met Sorren on the way here; she said you asked for me."

"Of course I asked for you!" Arré said. She held out her hand. "After last night—Paxe, please sit down."

Paxe shook her head. "No. I want to sleep."

Arré sighed. "I wish I could comfort you," she said sadly. Where had her skill in words gone? She rubbed her eyes. "You know," she said slowly, feeling her way like a sailor walking a spar, "you know I do not believe in the chea. But if it exists, if there is indeed some great harmony to which we all dance— its existence does not depend on the honor, or lack of it, of the White Clan."

Paxe did not respond at once. But after a while, she said, "Yes. You are right." Suddenly, she stepped beside the chair, and, bending, laid her cheek against Arré's. "Arré—*why* did you wait all this time to tell me about the L'hel's treachery?"

Arré said steadily, "Because I am a coward, Paxe. I did try once, yesterday, but you thought I wanted to say something else, and I couldn't, I *couldn't* speak. Fault me for it, if you will."

"I do, a little," whispered Paxe in her ear. "But I am equally to blame, for not listening." She straightened and went from the room before Arré could call her. Arré lifted her hand to her cheek. She did not know if she had said the right thing or the wrong thing. After a point, she told herself, the words do not matter. What matters is the trust. Her stomach rumbled, wanting cream and berries and honey.

She could not think about the plans. Rising, she went down the hall to the kitchen and into the rear courtyard. The trees arched overhead, leafy and full. Little sour apples dangled from the branches, but Arré was not tall enough to reach them, and besides, they tasted terrible. She walked into the garden. The flowers stook like pikes, orderly. The last bees of summer buzzed at the dry blossoms. She bent, passing her hand over the grass; the texture was drier. The year was ending. Soon the rain would beat the leaves from the trees and the scentless heads from the flower stalks, and the city would celebrate. She imagined the L'hel raising his fine, strong voice to thank the Guardian for the year's bounty....

Her fists clenched. Had he known Ron Ismenin's plan?

She paced along the flower beds. There was no way she could touch him; the Council had no authority over the White

Clan. But she could insure that he did not get what he wanted: a Truthfinder on the Council. And Isak? she thought. What do I do about Isak?

Maybe, she thought, maybe it is my fault that he is what he is, a liar, and irresponsible. I have not treated him as my heir. *I* attended Council meetings when I was seventeen; maybe I should do for him what my mother did for me, let him be present, if only to listen. Maybe because I do not trust him, he does what he does. Were I to invite him to the Council, ask his advice, give him the power he so desperately desires, might he not grow, and change?

I should give him a taste of what I do daily; let him govern the district for a month or two. He would find there's nothing exciting in sewers and petty theft and ditch digging.

And you, Arré Med—where would you go? she thought. To the vineyards, to keep company with Myra? You would be bored to tears by three days in the vineyards.

Where, then?

It came to her; she grinned. Walking briskly through the courtyard, she halted in the kitchen to ask Lalith to bring her a dish of water, before going on to her workroom.

She knew where she could go. Had she not been invited? She laid her writing materials out on the table, and, dipping brush in ink, wrote: *From the Lady Arré Med, Kendra-on-the-Delta, to the Lord Tarn i Nuath Ryth, Greetings....*

Sorren went to the market.

Walking through the avenues in the Hok district, she saw the scars of destruction left by the riot: smashed screens, broken glass, and the less overt effects: the sad-faced men and women, the guards' angry mutters. Thrice she passed houses in which the curtains were down and the windows back. She could hear weeping through the wide open doors. In places the streets were wet, where the sweepers had scrubbed blood from the stones.

In one tangled garden, three children were playing. One of them had a stick and was chopping at the others with it, as if it were a sword. Sorren wanted to scream at them, to tell them that swords were not toys—but then a man came out of the cottage's rear door and saw them, and started shouting. She went to the fishmonger's. Thule was there, his red face redder than usual. He took her fish order listlessly. "What's wrong?" she asked.

"Soketh was caught in the riot," he said. Soketh was Mirrim's husband. "The Healer at the Tanjo says he may lose an arm."

Going back to the hill past the Tanjo, she saw the families of those who had been hurt patiently waiting to hear when mother or father or uncle would be coming back. The question she had asked Arré thudded through her head. Surely, she thought, surely the witches would have found a way to halt the riot, if they had known.

You might have known, whispered a voice in her head. The Cards might have told you, had you been able to read them.

But I don't know how to read them, she answered.

The witchfolk could have told you. You should have brought them the Cards, weeks ago.

They would have taken the Cards away.

You don't know that. Perhaps they would have taught you how to use them. You, Sorren of the fields, might have been the key to the Tanjo's knowledge of the future. But they did not know about the riot to stop it, and now twenty-three people are dead, and Mirrim's husband may lose an arm.

"No!" she said, aloud. A few people turned to gaze at her, and then looked away. It isn't my fault, she stormed silently. You cannot say it's my fault.

But the nagging voice would not stay silent as she returned to the hill.

She went into the house. Arré was writing. The statue of the Guardian in the hallway caught her eye, and she went to it. The black vase on the table beneath it held white and purple blossoms: gardenlace, and autumn roses.

She stared at the carved face. Are you speaking to me? she thought. She waited for it to answer. But the eyes did not look at her, beneath graven lids, and the stone lips did not open.

At last, she went upstairs and got the Cards from under her pillow. These are mine, she thought. The witches cannot have them; they are mine, my inheritance. That was Arré's word. My mother gave them to me, and hers to her, and hers to her. . . . She imagined a line of women, some tall, some short, some fair, some dark, passing the Cards on to daughters and sons. She wondered how far back the line went. She gripped the box so strongly that the edges hurt her hand. Perhaps it was the ghosts of those women who spoke to her now. If you cannot use the Cards, you should not have them, said the interior voice. You have no right to them. You must either give them up or learn to use them.

Step by reluctant step, she walked out of the house toward the Tanjo.

The guard on duty at the Tanjo gate did not even question her. "That way," he said, pointing to the attentive throng. Walking across the white pavement to where the acolytes stood, keeping people back, she reminded herself of what Marti Hok had said, that the witches could not force her to do anything she did not want to do. She whispered excuses to the others as she pushed through the crowd. An acolyte with skin so dark it looked painted thrust a hand out to keep her from going any further.

"Name of the person," he said.

"What?"

"Name of the person you want to inquire about."

"I don't want to inquire about anyone," Sorren said. "A Truthfinder told me to come and see her."

"Really?" he drawled. "Which one?"

"I don't know her name. She has long black hair and a beautiful voice."

His eyebrows climbed his forehead. "What would the L'hel's Truthfinder want with you?"

His disbelief made her temper flare. "Why don't you go and ask her?"

He snorted. "Fine fool I'd be. She's Healing."

"You'll look a worse fool if you don't let me in," Sorren said. "Tell her that Sorren of Arré Med's house has come." She turned so that he could see the bonding bracelet on her left arm. "Or do you think she won't mind if she finds out that you've been keeping me waiting?"

He scratched his chin. "Wait," he said gruffly. "I'll be back." Robe flapping around his legs, he went toward the dome. Sorren cradled the box in her arms. Her throat was dry. The people near her stared, and some whispered. Sooner than she had expected, the acolyte was back. He beckoned to her. "Come."

"How come she gets to go in?" called a stout woman with a tattered straw hat on her head. "I been waiting since sunup."

The acolyte answered. "A lehi wants her."

She followed him, expecting to have to walk through the Tanjo. She had been in it only three times, and the thought of going inside the dark, incense-scented place made her shiver. But the acolyte steered her around the outside of the building.

They went in a door, crossed a blue-tiled hall, and came out inside a garden. "These are the apartments," he explained. "All the witches, even the L'hel, live here."

The garden was lovely, with high banks of flowers and a shallow pool in which Sorren saw red fish swimming back and forth. A pink granite bench stood below the flower beds. She held the box, and waited. A door opened in the side of the building, and the Truthfinder came out.

The acolyte bowed low. Sorren bowed, too.

"Thank you, Jomi," the witch said, her voice melodic and seductive. "You may go."

The acolyte left. The Truthfinder sat on the bench. "So you came at last," she said. "I have been hoping you would conquer your fears enough to come to me. I asked Árré Med to send you, but evidently she chose not to. Your name is Sorren, I know. Do you know mine? It is Senta. Senta-no-Jorith." She tilted her head to one side. "What brings you here today, child?"

Sorren licked her lips. How to explain the internal turmoil that had driven her here? She held out the box. "I had to," she said. "I had to bring you these. Marti Hok said you would teach me to use them."

"So," Senta said, "you have spoken of me to Marti Hok?" She did not sound displeased. She took the box in both hands. Sorren waited for her to open it, but she did not. "How is the Med house, child, in the aftermath of these sad events?"

Sorren guessed that she meant: How is Árré Med? "Angry," she said.

Senta grimaced. "She should be. Ron Ismenin is a fool. Has the Council met already?" Sorren nodded. "Don't worry, I won't ask you what was said." She opened the box and turned over the first Card, the Dancer. "Oh, my." Gently she laid that Card on her lap and took out the second and the third. . . . "Where did you get these?"

Sorren said, "They belonged to my mother, Kité. She left them to me."

"They are beautiful," said the Truthfinder. "They are for seeing the future, are they not? One lays them into a pattern?" She swept her hand in a half circle.

"I think so," Sorren said.

Senta nodded firmly. Her hair dipped over her face. It was glossy as a raven's wing. "I wonder what this means. Sorren—" she looked up—"you know you are a witch, do you not? That afternoon we met beside the well, when I walked with Kim Batto, I touched you, and you felt it. Was that why you ran away?"

Sorren nodded. Her heart was pounding in her chest and throat.

"How old are you?" the witch said.

"Seventeen. I'll be eighteen in the spring."

"How old were you when your mother died?"

"Thirteen."

"And when did you first feel the gift in you?"

"The day I came back to the city from my mother's burial," Sorren said.

"Was your mother a witch?"

"I don't know," Sorren said.

"Did you ever see her use the Cards?"

Sorren shook her head. "No."

Senta said, "Let me tell you right away, Sorren-no-Kité, that I cannot help you learn your witch-gift. You are not an inspeaker—what you call a Truthfinder. You are, I think, a far-traveler. Tell me, do you ever have visions, or vivid dreams, of places you have never seen?"

Sorren said, "Yes. I see a Keep in the north, named Tornor. I want to go there, after I am free."

Senta looked pleased. "Then you have already explored your gift! Why did you not come to Tanjo before?"

Sorren said, "I don't want to be a witch."

"It is not a thing you make a choice about," said the Truthfinder. "Any more than you can choose not to be tall." She stroked her white gown. "But I assure you, it is not so bad."

Marti Hok had said they could not keep her. "I want to go north."

"North, east, west—who would stop you? Go where you choose."

"But—if I am a witch, mustn't I stay here?"

"In the Tanjo? In Kendra-on-the-Delta? Sorren, you will do what you wish with your gift. I would hope that, once you learn it, you will stay here, or, since you wish to go north, perhaps go to the Tanjo in Tezera. But that's up to you."

Sorren swallowed. "Promise," she said, knowing it was childish but needing to hear it said.

Instantly, Senta said, "I swear by the chea that whether you learn your gift or no, you may do what you like, where you like." She brushed her hair back from her face, smiling. "Are you satisfied?"

Sorren nodded. She was still frightened, but less.

Senta said meditatively, "I was a fisherwoman's daughter when I began to hear other people's thoughts with my mind. I was terrified. No one in my family was a witch, I thought. I finally told my mother and she, clever woman, brought me to the Tanjo. Once a year, I go back to my village on the coast and go fishing with the folk of my family, so that I will not forget what the day-to-day life of my sisters and brothers is like. . . . Sometimes I miss it." She half turned on the bench, looking toward a door. In a moment, it opened, and a man came out. He was brown and small, like an acrobat. "This is Rinti," said Senta. "He is a far-traveler."

Rinti wore bright blue beads in a chain around his neck, and he bounced when he walked. He rubbed his hands together in a way that Sorren found unpleasant. "What's this, what's this?" he said.

"This is Sorren," said Senta, "who may be one of us. She is bondservant to Arré Med, and I think she is a far-traveler."

"Ho." Rinti grinned. His teeth were big, and very crooked. "Really. Do you see places, girl?"

Sorren was getting tired of being called "girl." She said tightly, "My *name* is Sorren."

Rinti stared at her, and then laughed. "I beg your pardon." He sat unceremoniously on the grass. He smelled of garlic. "Sorren. Do you see places?"

"Sometimes."

"Tell me about them."

"I see the steppe—sometimes it's green, and sometimes brown, and sometimes covered with snow—I see the mountains—"

"What do they look like?" said Rinti.

"Gray. Icy. There are trails through them. Goats live in the crags. The streams are very cold. . . ."

"Go on," said Rinti. "What else do you see?"

"The castle."

"What does it look like?".

"It changes," Sorren said. "Sometimes it looks very old and broken, and sometimes new."

"Do you see people?"

"Not often. I saw a man with one arm writing in the tower.

I saw a cheari." That was different, but she did not feel like going into detail. The questions were making her uncomfortable.

"How do you get there?" said Rinti.

"I just do. In dreams, or when I am awake."

Rinti frowned. "You don't need to touch an object to go there?"

"No. Once—" she was thinking of the sword—"I did. But I didn't go to the castle that time."

"When you travel, are the seasons you see the same as the present season?"

Senta said, "In fall, do you see the castle in fall, and so on?"

"Sometimes, sometimes not."

Rinti nodded. "Go now," he said.

Sorren didn't understand. Was he telling her to leave? She looked at Senta. The Truthfinder said, "He wants you to travel, Sorren, so that he may link with you and follow you. Can you take your mind to Tornor where there are other people about?"

"I don't know," Sorren said. "I've never tried."

"Try," said Rinti. "Here." He swept the box of Cards from Senta's lap and deposited it in Sorren's. "Do it now."

His brusqueness offended her; she wanted to balk, like a stubborn mule. But Senta nodded at her, encouragingly. "Go ahead," she said, aloud, and then her voice said, in Sorren's mind, *Do you still distrust us, Sorren? Mind to mind cannot lie. You are one of us; in no way would we trap you or trick you or hurt you.* The soft words held the unmistakable ring of truth. Sorren laid her hands on the box, and thought of Tornor, the castle walls like armor against the gray northern sky. . . .

The garden dissolved. She hovered over a bed. In it a woman lay; her hair was white as milk, with streaks through it of a darker color which showed that it had once been gold. On each side of the bed another woman sat: one was young, with amber hair; the second woman's face was hidden from Sorren's eyes, but her hair too was white, and her hands were gnarled and old. The younger woman was weeping, and the woman in the bed patted her hand. Then she tried to pull a ring from her finger, but her joints were so swollen she could not take it off. Suddenly, Sorren saw that there was a fourth person in the room, a man. His hair was tawny, streaked with silver, and his face was lined like an autumn leaf. Gently he reached forward to help the woman in the bed take the ring off. . . .

"Sorren!" For a moment, Sorren could not tell if the voice was coming from inside or outside the dream. "Sorren!"

The vision vanished.

She blinked. She looked at Senta. "I went," she said.

"What did you see?" said the witch.

"A woman in a bed, and two other women, and a man—" She described the vision slowly. Senta looked at Rinti, who was twisting his beads in both hands.

"What's the matter?" she asked. He scowled ferociously.

"Don't know. I tried to link and follow her, but it was like running into a wall. The link severed. She was gone—but damned if I know *where* it was."

"I told you," said Sorren. "It's Tornor Keep."

"Try again," said Senta. "Try somewhere else. Give her your beads."

"What?" Rinti covered the beads protectively with one hand.

"Rinti, let her hold the beads," said Senta. "She can use them to travel."

Rinti played with the catch of the beads. "I won't hurt them," said Sorren. He let her hold them with some reluctance. She wondered if they would really take her somewhere. The sword had—why not little blue stones? She ran her fingers over them lightly, and closed her eyes.

. . . *She was in a field. The corn was all around her, towering over her head. She lifted from it, Sorren-the-bird, and found herself looking down a great rolling plain, covered with gold. Below her was a tiny house with a white roof, and a windmill beside it. The mill turned lazily in the sunlight. In one corner of the sky, the crescent moon floated like a wraith. Suddenly, a little boy ran from the house, running into the corn as if a demon were chasing him, only he looked glad, not afraid. She swooped lower, to try to see what he was so happy about, and the corn and house and boy went away. . . .*

She blinked. "I'm back," she said.

Rinti slammed his hands on the grass. "Damn. It happened again." He took the beads back. "Where did you go? Describe it."

"It was a farm. There was corn all around I saw a boy—" She described him, his clothes, his hair. Midway through the description Rinti held up a hand.

"Stop," he said. His voice was hoarse. "I don't know how you did that—but that was me you saw."

"What?" said Senta. "Are you—"

"Sure? I'm sure. I remember the day. I was running because my mother had just told me we were going to Shanan to see my father. I ran and ran until I fell down. I was wearing the beads. Guardian, Senta, no wonder I can't follow her! The girl isn't far-traveling, she's *seeing*. But she's not seeing the future, she's seeing the past. It isn't I who should be here, it's Tukath!"

A red bird flew down from the Tanjo dome and came to rest on Senta's shoulder. "Not now, Leeka," she said. With a mournful toot, the bird flew away. "I have never heard of such a thing," she said. "A far-traveler who travels to the past."

"She isn't a far-traveler. If she were, I would be able to go with her. She's a seer."

Sorren scowled. She hated being talked about. Senta said, "Sorren, forgive us. But you are—or rather, your gift is—like nothing we've encountered before. Have you ever had the feeling that you know what was going to happen, and had it come true?"

"No," said Sorren.

"No premonitions of pleasure or disaster?"

"No."

"Definitely we should ask Tukath if he has ever heard of this." Senta rose.

Rinti scrambled up from the grass. "Come on," he said.

Sorren folded her arms. "Where are we going?" She was not an acolyte and she was not going to be pushed and prodded and taken places. "Who is Tukath?"

Senta said, "Tukath-no-Amani is our seer, and very wise. If you are a seer, he will know it. Will you come meet him?" She held out her hands. "You are free to leave anytime, Sorren. But if you wish to learn to use your Cards, you should stay."

CHAPTER NINETEEN

Tukath-no-Amani lived in a room in the back of the Tanjo. The blue-tiled hall was clean and quiet and reminded Sorren a little of the Ismenin house. She could not imagine feeling at home there but she was no longer frightened; mostly, she was curious, wondering how many people lived there. She had no idea how many witches there were in Kendra-on-the-Delta.

The halls smelled of some faint scent she could not place. Senta strode on ahead of her, while Rinti jogged beside. "How old are you?" he said.

"Seventeen."

"How long have you lived in the city?"

"Seven years."

"Did the gift come to you about the time your blood-time started?"

Sorren looked down at him, astonished. She had thought only women talked about the blood-time. "Yes."

"Why didn't you come here sooner, then!" he almost shouted at her.

Senta turned, long hair flying like a black cloud. "Rinti, let the girl alone. Her reasons are her own affair."

Rinti scowled at the rebuke. Sorren said, "What difference would it make?"

His brow furrowed. "What do you mean, what difference? You have a gift none of us has ever seen before. You see into the past. Think how valuable such a gift would be, developed. You could go back through the history of Arun, tell us what *really* happened, show us the mysteries we do not know. From you we could learn how the first Teacher died. No record of it was ever made."

"Who was he, and what did he teach?" asked Sorren.

"He built the first Tanjo in Elath," said Rinti reverentially, "and his name was Sefer. You could see the old wars, see how they happened, so that we can be certain to avoid them. You could see your family; would you like that?"

Sorren swallowed. "Could I see the Red Clan?"

"Certainly. Why would you want to?"

"I—just want to know where they went."

"They died, my dear," said Rinti. His sandals, which were loose, flapped on the tiles. "They died."

"Here is Tukath's room," said Senta. She slid the door back, and gestured to Sorren. "Go on, Sorren. Go in."

Sorren went in. The room was screen on all four sides. As Sorren entered, a white cat which was sprawled on the tiled floor leaped up and stalked under a table. A man at the table looked up and smiled. He wore the white robe with the hood; beneath it his hair showed silver-black. On the table in front of him lay a piece of clear glass, curved in a strange way, and several jars, and some pieces of fine cloth. He looked at Senta and moved his fingers in a signal.

"Tukath is deaf," said Senta, in her wonderful voice. "He has been deaf from childhood. He knows how to speak but because the sounds he makes are so unpleasant, he prefers not to. He has developed a sign language which we here in the Tanjo know and use. With me he can speak directly, since I can hear his thoughts in my head, and he mine in his, but for you I must translate. If you can, imagine that he can hear you, and speak to him as if he could. I will tell him what you are saying and he will speak to me."

Sorren looked at the table and the glass. "What are you doing?" she said.

Tukath beamed. He picked up the glass and showed her that both of its sides were curved. Senta said softly, "This glass can make small things appear large. Tukath has made it and is polishing it so that the image is as perfect as it can be."

"What kinds of small things?" said Sorren.

The inventor beckoned to her to look. He held the lens against something on the table. Sorren bent down. At first, she could not see anything, but as Tukath moved the lens slowly up and down, a blur appeared to her vision, sharpened—she caught his wrist to hold it steady. Now she could see the thing clearly: it was milky-white, with a great curved tip like a monstrous horn. "What is it?" she said, awed.

Tukath took the lens away and beckoned to her to look. She could not even see what she had been staring at. He laughed without sound, and, picking up something, held it close to her eye. It was a piece of the sheath around a cat's claw.

"Tukath wants to know if you have ever looked at stones underwater, and then lifted them through to the air and found them to be smaller than they seemed."

"Yes."

"The glass works in the same way. The surface of the water is curved, too, just a little, enough to distort what we see."

Rinti said, "This is a marvel but it gets us no closer to what we need to know. Tukath, listen to what this girl does. She sees backward! Senta thought she was a far-traveler but I have tried to follow her and absolutely can't, it's like trying to see through fog. I'm sure she's not a far-traveler because she doesn't use a link, she just goes. Go with her and see if I'm right."

Tukath looked at Sorren with question in his eyes.

"Tukath wants to know if you are too tired to try one more time."

"I'm not tired at all," said Sorren.

"There's another thing," muttered Rinti. "Why isn't she tired? She ought to be a little tired."

"Tukath says he is ready to link with you whenever you are ready to go."

"All right," Sorren said. "Shall I hold something?"

"No," said Rinti. "Do it without. If you can do it without you are not far-traveling."

Sorren stared at the lens. . . . *The chamber went away. She hovered over a stream. A little boy knelt beside the stream, his small face intent. He was looking at something. Sorren went lower to see what it was. It was a leaf, with a drop of water on it. He was looking at the veins of the leaf through the water drop. He opened his mouth and went, "Huh, huh!" It was a sound of triumph.*

Then she was back, and Tukath was staring at her, eyes wide in wonder. He lifted his hand, pointed to the lens, and then, slowly, to himself.

Sorren understood. She had seen him. He was the small boy at the side of the creek. Beside her, Rinti was dancing, hopping from one foot to the other in excitement. "Did you follow her?" he shouted. The seer nodded. He grinned. "See, I told you," he said to Senta, "she *is* a seer. But she sees the past!"

"I think you are right," said Senta. She laid a hand on Sorren's shoulder. "Child, do you understand what this means? You have a rare gift. Tukath says he has never heard of a seer going into the past. You must come to the Tanjo, truly you must. We need to understand this thing."

Sorren stiffened. "You said I could go."

The Truthfinder dropped her hand. "I did, and you may. But Sorren, think what you will be giving up if you leave. Oh, you may go and come back, but think. The place you have seen in your dreams, Tornor—it is still there, certainly, but it is nothing like what you have seen in your visions. All that is in the past. You cannot go there."

Sorren knew it was true. Tukath was watching her, nodding to emphasize the Truthfinder's words. She wondered who the people she had seen were, the three women, the man with one arm, the many others she had seen over the years. . . . She squared her shoulders. "I still want to go," she said. Rinti groaned and thrust his hands through his hair.

Senta nodded. "I thought you would," she said. "But if you change your mind, Sorren the aftseer, come back to us. The door will always be open."

It seemed like a farewell. Rinti was shaking his head and making noises under his breath. "What about my Cards?" Sorren asked. She picked them up from where she had placed them, on the table.

Tukath's long, delicate fingers took them. He glanced at Senta for explanation. Meaning passed between them. Then the inventor opened the box and looked through the Cards. He stopped at the picture of the Stargazer and again at the picture of the Wheel. "What do you know about these Cards?" Senta said.

"They're old," said Sorren. "They're from Tornor. Marti Hok has pictures of them in her records. My mother had them and she knew how to use them, but I cannot. I want to know how."

Tukath folded the silk around the Cards and laid them in the box. He pushed it across the table to Sorren, and his pale, lined face was suddenly sad. Senta said, "Tukath says the Cards are indeed fortune-telling Cards, Cards to see the future with. He says he can feel the pull of them in his mind. But he does not think they will work for you, or if they do, they will never be able to tell you the future. For you they will only tell the past."

Even Rinti was silent. In the quiet, Sorren could hear the singing of the Tanjo birds, and she suddenly realized that Tukath, with all his power, could not, just as he could not hear Senta's beautiful voice, or the sound of water racing through the gutters after the rains, or the wind in the trees, or even his cat.

She pushed the Cards at him. "You have them," she said. "You can use them. I can't."

But the seer shook his head and slid them gently back to her. "Tukath says, they're yours, even if you do not wish to use them. If you choose to give them up, it should be for your own purposes, not another's."

Sorren took the Cards. "Thank you," she said to Tukath. "Thank you for telling me about my gift."

The seer lifted a finger. "Tukath says, Be careful."

"About what?" Sorren asked.

"The past is calling you, surely, and it is a seductive call. Do not be trapped by it."

Marti Hok had said something like that, once. "Then am I not to use my gift?" Sorren said.

"Use it, use it," muttered Rinti.

"Use it as you like," said Senta. "But do not fill your life with it. Remember, the past is gone, and it cannot come back. Even if you want it to."

Rinti said, "Why does she not get tired? She should be tired after her journeys."

Senta looked at Tukath for the answer. "Because," she relayed, "she is traveling in the past. The past is frozen, unchangeable; hence it presents no resistance."

"Then I can use the Cards to go to Tornor whenever I like!" Sorren said. "I don't have to wait for a vision."

"You don't have to," said Senta for the seer. "But perhaps you should. It is not wise to overuse a gift. They have been known to fade. And when you come close to the place of your dreams, Sorren, do not be surprised if the gift diminishes, even vanishes entirely. The nearer you are in this world to the object of your sight, the less of it you will be able to see. This is true of the future; it must be true of the past."

"Why?" said Sorren.

"We don't know," said Rinti. "Come to Elath, and help us find out."

But Sorren did not want to go to Elath. She shook her head at the insistent witch. "No." She looked at Senta. "I want to leave now." Tukath smiled at her, gray eyes warm.

"Well," said a strong voice, "what's this?"

Everybody turned. All three witches bowed. Tukath covered his lens with one long hand. *Kneel*, Senta hissed in Sorren's mind. She dropped to one knee, and lifted her head to find a man with fair hair and broad shoulders gazing at her. He wore a long white robe. A white pearl dangled from a chain around his neck.

"Who is this?" he said.

"A servant of Arré Med's," said Senta. "She came to us with a deck of fortunetelling Cards. Knowing they are ni'chea, she desires us to have them." *Give them to me*, she said. *Leave them with me and I will get them back to you.*

"A servant of Arré Med's? How convenient," said the man. "Stand up, girl."

Sorren rose, and passed the Cards to the Truthfinder.

"You look intelligent," said the man. "Can you remember a simple message?"

His tone made the muscles in Sorren's back knot. "Yes, my lord," she said, knowing that one did not call witches "my lord," but not knowing what else to call him.

"I am the L'hel, girl. I have a message for your mistress. Tell her that our war is not over, that she has merely won a skirmish. Say it." Sorren said it. "Good. Tell her also that it is always regrettable when lives are lost. But it is not always possible to choose one's tools."

She repeated it.

"Excellent," said the L'hel. He gazed at the other witches. "Lehi, there is Healing to be done, and your services will be needed."

"Yes, L'hel," said Senta, her lovely voice submissive. He turned and left. The three witches exchanged glances. Sorren leaned on the table. Marti Hok had said the L'hel was venal. Sorren did not know what the word meant, but it sounded cruel.

Senta put a hand on her arm. "Sorren," she said, "I will take you out. Let me keep the Cards; he may want to see them later, and I cannot say I destroyed them. I will get them back to you, I promise. Come." She was moving as she spoke.

Sorren turned once in the doorway to say farewell to Tukath, but the inventor was bending again over his bit of glass, and did not see her. She followed Senta through the blue-tiled hall to the little door which led to the garden, and through the garden to the street.

The sun glistened on the white pavement. The sun was strong; Sorren shielded her eyes.

Senta laid both hands lightly on her shoulders. "Sorren,

may I burden you with a second message?" she said. "This one is also to your mistress."

"Yes," Sorren said.

"Thank you. When you give Arré Med the L'hel's message, tell her also that I was with you, and heard it. And tell her this from me." She paused. "Tell her that the L'hel's ambitions are shared, by some at Elath, and by others. She will soon be approached to approve them. Tell her to be strong, and tell her, if she has people she trusts outside the city, to warn them. She will know what to warn them of."

Arré was in the study when Sorren returned. The letter to Tarn Ryth, sealed, sat on the table, and she had decided to ask Jenith if she would deliver it to the Nuathan ruler. She heard Sorren come down the hall and stop. A tapping made her lift her head. "What is it?" she said.

Sorren said, "I have a message for you from the Tanjo."

Arré's eyebrows went up. "From the Tanjo?" she said, amazed. "What were you doing at the Tanjo?"

"I went there, with my Cards."

"You went there?" Arré said. Sorren nodded. There was no terror in her face; she looked calm and collected and determined.

"What did you do?" Arré said.

"I spoke with the Truthfinder, Senta," said Sorren. "And with two other witches. They were kind to me."

"Did they show you how to use the Cards?" Arré said.

Sorren frowned faintly. "Yes and no. My—my gift looks to the past, not to the future, so I cannot read the patterns of the Cards."

Arré said, "So you left them."

"Senta will bring them back. She said so. I have a message for you from her and from the L'hel."

A chill lifted the hairs on Arré's neck. "Give them to me."

Sorren repeated them, first the L'hel's, and then Senta's. The L'hel's message brought Arré from her chair, too angry even to speak. So the L'hel thought that the deaths of twenty-three citizens was "regrettable," did he?

Rage flowed through her, swifter than the blood beneath her skin, and she felt herself darkening with anger. "That—that monster!" she said.

"Is he?" said Sorren.

"Oh, he is," said Arré.

But the second message cooled the anger quickly. "Did the Truthfinder say who she wanted me to warn?" Arré asked.

"No. People you trust, she said, outside the city."

Tarn Ryth, Arré thought. Yet what can I tell him? "Thank you, child," she said absently to Sorren, who bowed and vanished. Perhaps I should wait until I am "approached." She wondered who would approach her—the L'hel? Kim Batto? Both? The L'hel could not be happy with Kim Batto. Nor could he have been pleased by the news that his puppet, Ron Ismenin, had been formally censured and fined by the Council.

She did not have to wait long to learn the L'hel's mind. The next afternoon, Kim Batto came to the Med house. Sorren announced him. Arré regarded Kim coldly. She had not forgiven him for his part in the killings; she thought perhaps she never would. "I shall not offer you a chair because I don't want you to stay," she said, and had the pleasure of seeing him flush.

"I bring you a message from the L'hel," he said.

"Do you find it an interesting occupation, being messenger?" she inquired.

His lips clamped together as he strove not to answer her. She decided to stop baiting him, and folded her hands.

"Jerrin-no-Dovria i Elath would like to see you," he said.

"I will not go to the Tanjo," Arré said.

"He will come here."

Arré wondered if she dared refuse. She thought that would be too open a challenge. "When?" she said.

Kim named a day in the next week.

"I accept," Arré said. "Let it be the afternoon. A visit from him in the morning would sour the rest of the day."

The day the L'hel arrived, it was raining slightly. He came in a litter, escorted by a brace of acolytes. Arré watched from the study window as he emerged from the litter and strolled bareheaded along the path. Hearing the front door open, she went swiftly to her chair. A second armchair had been set up facing it, and a long table formed a barricade between them. The study door slid aside. Jerrin stood framed in the doorway. Actor, Arré thought contemptuously. He made a fine picture. She took a breath—he was imposing—and said, "Welcome, L'hel."

Smiling, he crossed to her and seated himself in the cushioned armchair. The air around him seemed to shimmer faintly.

The shimmer faded, leaving Arré wondering if she had imagined it, but as Jerrin's robes swirled she saw that the white silks were dry as glass, unspeckled by the rain. She clenched her hands, and then released them so abruptly that her bracelets clinked.

"May I offer you refreshment?" she said. "Wine? Tea? Water?"

"Wine," he said. Arré rang the bell on the table. Lalith stuck her head through the doorway.

"Bring a carafe of wine for the L'hel, and water for me."

The scars on his cheeks creased. "You won't drink what I drink, is that it?"

"No," Arré said, "that is not it. I have given up wine. It makes me sick."

"Have you consulted a Healer?"

Arré said, "No. But others of my family have. It is not an ill that can be cured."

"That is unfortunately true of other ills besides the ones of the body," Jerrin said softly.

Lalith came in with a tray. She looked awed and frightened. As she knelt to put the tray on the table, her hands trembled. Jerrin, leaning forward, caught the tray from her hands and set it down. He smiled at the girl warmly. "Thank you, child." Lalith rose. Eyes glowing at the words of thanks, she marched out. Once again, Arré had to admit the man had charm.

She took her glass of water from the tray and drank. Her stomach twisted around the cool liquid. Jerrin poured wine into his glass and copied her. "Let us drink to our fair city," he said, in that eloquent, measured voice, "that she may soon recover from her ills."

Arré set her glass down with a thump. "Ills which *you* are, in large part, responsible for!" she said.

The L'hel spread his hands. "That is unjust," he said. "I assure you, Arré Med, I had no idea that Ron Ismenin was going to plan so destructive an approach to power. I do not support it, and I agree wholly with the Council's judgment upon him."

This was not at all what Arré had expected him to say. "Kim Batto voted against it," she said.

"Kim Batto takes too much upon himself," said the L'hel dryly. His tone cheered Arré considerably.

"He does tend to overreach himself," she said. She could

not help the sarcasm that crept into her tone. "I am glad that the Tanjo approves the Council actions."

Jerrin ignored it. He glanced around the study. Toli had lit a fire in the hearth that morning, and the pine logs had given the room a pleasant smell. "This is a lovely room," he said.

"Thank you," said Arré. She took a sip of water. "If you are not here to convey the Tanjo's disapproval of the Council's action, L'hel, then why *are* you here?"

Jerrin leaned back in his chair. "To make a compact with you, Arré Med."

"To make a tool of me, you mean," she said.

He frowned. "That was a message framed in anger," he said. "I regret it. It seems clear that neither of us wishes to turn this city into a battleground for our ambitions. I offer you a partnership, Arré Med. The old order of governance in Arun is changing—must change, for change is the essence of life. New forces are arising to the north, and this city must be strong to meet them. I think you have such strength, and I think you know that I do. You run the Council—but it is to me, to the Tanjo, that the people of the city look for guidance. Together, we might make a great power." He was leaning forward now, his blue eyes blazing into hers with almost physical force. "If *we* do not, then someone else will. Do you wish to see this city governed by such as Kim Batto and Ron Ismenin? Or see it fall into the hands of Tarn Ryth?" He said the name with a sneer behind it. "Time moves in a circle, Arré Med, but it is never the same circle." His blunt left hand, with the gold ring on it, described a spiral in the air. "A chance once missed never returns."

Arré swallowed. "If you speak of the White Clan seat on the Council—"

"I do not! That is unimportant. If it comes, that is well, but can you not see, Arré Med, that the Council is doomed! All the old forms and orders are changing, must change, and we must change with them. The Council has served its purpose. Now a new time comes. Join me in fashioning that time, Arré Med. Better that we should be allies than opponents. Please believe me, I have nothing but the good of the city in mind. It is not just Kendra-on-the-Delta that I am concerned for, but all the land of Arun. This land has functioned like an island for centuries. It is time now for us—for Arun—to reach out, to become the heart of something bigger than ever has been dreamed of before. It has already begun. The Isara ship is part of it. So is the founding of Shirasai and the alliance with the Asech. They, too, are part of Arun, though they know it not." He drew a breath. "This, too, our seers have seen."

Arré said, "But you told me that the Tanjo seers see different futures."

"Yes. But knowing that the one we wish to come is in fact possible, we can work and plan for it with hope."

He was eloquent. Despite herself, Arré found herself moved by his words. She leaned back in her chair, deliberately putting space between them. Some of what he said reminded her of Tarn. Indeed, she thought, they are very alike. She was impressed that he could so humble himself as to come here and ask for help. "Do the L'helis of the other cities feel as you do?" she said.

He flapped a hand. "I have not discussed it with them. They, like most who hold power in Arun, cling to the old forms. They would keep each city, each region, separate from the other, autonomous and isolated, connected only by trade."

"And you?" Arré asked.

His voice strengthened. "I see it united, brought together, made whole."

"Whom do you see governing that whole?"

"I do not know," he said. "That choice may not be in human hands."

Arré said, "Could it be you?"

"If the chea wills." He spread his arms, as if embracing the possibility, and then closed his hands together on his lap. "Or you."

Arré felt trapped in her chair, pinned to it. Rising, she slid between the table and chair and walked round the back of it. She leaned on the wooden rim. Governing a city was one thing, she thought. But how could one person govern Arun? "I have enough trouble running one district of Kendra-on-the-Delta."

"You underestimate yourself," Jerrin said.

Arré closed her eyes, trying to feel her way into the picture the L'hel's words drew. She wondered how this dream of a country united under one ruler would come about. By force? It would not be easy to persuade the individual city councils to relinquish power. "Have you shared this vision with Kim Batto?" she said.

The L'hel snorted. "Kim Batto is weak, and a fool."

"That does not answer me."

Jerrin frowned. "Yes," he said, biting off the word. "We spoke of it, at a time when I thought better of him than I now do. The next thing I knew, he was off making a private alliance with that northern barbarian." Scorn infused his words. His face hardened. Arré nodded slowly. She wondered: was that the choice? Did the future demand that she align herself with Tarn Ryth or with Jerrin-no-Dovria i Elath? She measured Jerrin with her eyes. She did not need a Truthfinder's gift to see the depth of his desire for power. He was hungry for it, lustful as a hunting wolf. There was no warmth in him, no compassion, and no room for equals. He had come to make a compact, he said, but what he had truly come for was to make her his creature: a thing that would do his work and would not break, like Ron Ismenin or Kim Batto.

She rested both forearms on the back of the chair. "L'hel, you are wasting your time."

He met her eyes, and she felt the strength of malice in him. "How so?"

"I will not join you."

"Then you are a fool," he said.

"Then I am a fool." Straightening, she came round the chair and stooped to the table. She range the bell. "What you do, you do without me."

He stared at her, and then rising, pointed a finger at her glass. "A time will come when you will wish you chose otherwise," he said. He clenched his fist, and the glass shattered. The pieces flew; a few of them embedded themselves in the fabric of his chair. The water puddled on the table and dripped slowly to the floor. "You will be less to me than this glass." Lalith appeared in the doorway, and stared in surprise at the scattered shards of crystal.

"The L'hel is leaving," whispered Arré. He turned and followed the girl. She watched him go. Her skin felt icy cold, and her hands were trembling. Gathering strength, she reached with both hands to the L'hel's glass and lifted it to her lips. The wine burned her stomach. For an instant, she felt compassion for Kim Batto, who had trapped himself between the rock that was Tarn Ryth and the hammer that was the L'hel. The litter bells jangled. She put the glass down. She wished with painful intensity that she had someone now to run to, to be held by, to hide behind: a friend, a sister, a lover. . . .

She took a step, and her foot crunched a piece of glass. She was not alone. She had Marti Hok. She had Paxe. She had poor Cha Minto, who at least might learn from his mistakes. She even had an ally within the Tanjo: Senta, the Truthfinder, whose warning had proved accurate. It was clear that she would have to trust the Truthfinder, despite her dislike of the Tanjo.

Lalith came to the doorway with a brush in her hand. "Lady, shall I—"

"Yes," Arré said. She went to the record case and pulled out her writing materials. Sitting in her chair, she tugged the lacquered table close to her and began again to write: *From the Lady Arré Med, Kendra-on-the-Delta, to the Lord Tarn i Nuath Ryth. . . .*

The week before Festival, the watches grew frenetic. Paxe transferred four night guards to the day and late watches, leaving her with only twelve soldiers under her command, the bare minimum for her district. Night watch hours lengthened as sunrise grew later. The guards grew tired, and Paxe went from post to post, relieving those who needed it so that they could go into the guardhouse, eat, perhaps nap.

She was standing watch on Jasmine Street, at the border of the Sul district, when she heard the whistle call that meant the Yardmaster was needed on the hill. Quickly, she went to the guardhouse and shook the drowsy guard awake. "I've got to leave." Praying there was no emergency, she loped north.

It took her half an hour to get there. A torch was lit in the Yard. She went through the gate and found Idrella, the gate guard, waiting for her.

"Who's on the gate?" she said.

"I called Rak over from Oil Street." She lifted the torch from its pole and led Paxe to the weapons shed. The door had gouge marks around the lock. Paxe rattled it. It was intact. "Look," said Idrella. She walked around the shed to its one small window. The thick opaque glass had been broken inward. There were footmarks in the dust.

"I heard noise, and came to look. I got here just in time to see someone running. Whoever it was scaled the fence as I arrived; I saw a leg vanishing over the top. No way to tell who it was, or if she got in."

Paxe felt for the weapons shed key. "Let's look," she said. Opening the shed, she ducked under the lintel. Idrella handed her the torch. Holding it at arm's length to keep from losing her eyebrows, Paxe edged toward the back of the shed. The pikes, normally kept in orderly rows along the sides of the shed, were tumbled so that she had to step over them. "Someone was in here," she said.

The smell of grease tickled her nostrils. She took another step into the small crammed shed and halted, as the torch glinted off metal. "Oh, damn," she said.

"What is it?" said Idrella.

Paxe knelt. "Someone's been at the swords." The silk lay in disarray on the hard earthern floor. Slowly she counted the swords, eleven, twelve, thirteen, fourteen—there were supposed to be fifteen. Of the thirty-five swords that had come through all the Gates, the Med Yard had—was supposed to have—fifteen of them, the Hok Yard six, the Minto Yard ten, and the Sul Yard four.

There were only fourteen swords. She held the torch out, looking into the cobwebbed corners, hoping that the thief might have dropped it in flight. But nothing shone out of the darkness. She backed out. Handing the torch to Idrella to hold, she shut and locked the door.

Idrella said, "I'm sorry, Yardmaster."

"You can't be everywhere," Paxe said. "Give me the torch a moment." She took it to the garden shed where Toli kept his tools, found a board and a hammer and some long iron nails, and brought them back. She hammered the board across the open window. "We'll have to call the glazier and put a new window in," she said.

A light trembled in the kitchen and Toli called, "Who's there?"

"It's me," Paxe said. "Never mind." She walked around the inside of the Yard, just in case the thief had not in fact gotten out and was hiding somewhere, but the big quiet space was empty.

She wondered who the thief was. It took nerve to break that window, she thought. It might have been anyone who saw the wagon with the swords arrive from the Gate, and guessed what was in it. . . . But it bothered her, and not only because it meant that a live blade was loose in the city, in her district. It seemed too big a risk to take for something that could not be openly used, that had to be hidden from family and neighbors.

The following evening, she went to the house at dinnertime to tell Arré about the theft.

They had eaten early. Paxe went upstairs, to find Arré sitting on the bed. She had just bathed, and her short hair was clumped in tight curls; they were almost as tight as Paxe's. She was sipping tea. "I've turned into a tea drinker," she said, and sent Sorren for a second cup.

Paxe watched the tall girl leave the room. Something was troubling her; Paxe wondered what it was. Arré coughed, and she turned her attention to the matter at hand. "I've stopped the sword training classes, as you ordered," she said.

"Good," said Arré.

I miss them, thought the Yardmaster. But she did not say it. "So have the Ismeninas."

"So I would hope." Arré leaned back on her pillows. "Ron Ismenin may have to melt his swords down and sell the metal to pay the fine the Council levied on him."

Sorren came in with a green cup in her hand. She gave it to Paxe. "Thank you," Paxe said.

"Shall I bring anything else?" said the girl to Arré.

"No, that's all. Leave us." Sorren left. Arré turned the cup between her palms. "The L'hel was here last week," she said.

Paxe said, "I know. The gate guard told me."

Arré said, "He asked me if I wished to join him in uniting the country, making it one thing, under one rulership."

"What did you say?" Paxe said.

"I said no. The land of Arun may unite, or not, I don't know. My concern is the city. I might even wish to see it united. But the L'hel wants to do it now, in his lifetime, and he wants to be its ruler. I told him that I would not work with him."

Paxe nodded. The thought of the L'hel—what he was, what he could do—sickened and angered her. She did not want to talk about it.

Arré said, "Have you heard from your son?"

"Not since I sent him boots. The scribe must be busy now, writing Festival greetings for everyone in the fields. I'm not worried." It wasn't true, she was worried, but only a little. She would always worry about him. She put her cup down. "Something happened last night that you should know about, Arré." Hands on her knees, she told Arré about the theft.

Arré scowled. "Drink your tea," she said. Paxe picked up the cup from the table and sipped the bitter liquid. She didn't really like tea, unless it had honey in it. "What have you done?"

"Put up notices across the district with a reward for information, and had the window of the shed boarded up from inside."

Arré nodded. "It can't stay hidden for long. The thief will show it to a friend and boast, and next day you'll hear all about it."

"I hope so."

There was a little pause. Then Arré said, "I'm glad you came tonight. I've been meaning to talk to you about my brother. I want advice."

Paxe shifted on the stool. She hated giving advice, and what could she say to Arré about Isak that Arré did not know? "What about him?"

Arré said, "I'm thinking of going away for a while."

The stone figurine that looked like a bear sat on the table. Paxe put down her teacup. Picking up the statue, she stroked the cool stone. "Where?"

"Upriver. Last week I wrote to Tarn Ryth, to tell him the result of the Council meeting and some other things, and to ask him if I might visit him. He desires my political support. We got along rather well at the betrothal party, and he is too powerful to be ignored. I received his answer this morning."

"That was fast," Paxe said. Normally it took at least eight days for a letter to go and come back between Kendra-on-the-Delta and Nuath. "What did he say?"

Arré smiled. "A lot of things. He said Ron Ismenin was a fool and a knave for arranging the riot. He said we should throw Kim Batto off the Council. He told me to beware of the L'hel; it did not need telling." The smile grew to her urchin grin. "He said yes, of course I might come, and stay as long or as little as I like, and he would take me fishing. I've never been fishing."

Paxe said softly, "You like the man, don't you."

Arré shot her an oblique glance. "Yes. I do."

"When would you go?"

"After Festival."

Paxe gazed at her steadily. "And who would rule in your stead?"

Arré looked at her hands. "I thought of asking Isak to be my steward."

"Why?"

Arré sighed. She turned her cup between her palms. "Because—because some of the things Cha Minto said the other night were true. I haven't given Isak much responsibility. I've never asked his advice, or invited him to attend Council meetings. . . . He is my brother. It may be—" she paused—"it may be in some sense my fault that he is conspiring with the Ismeninas and playing nasty games with Cha Minto. Perhaps none of these things would have happened if I had treated him as what he is, my heir."

Paxe said, "It is your privilege to do that, of course."

Arré put her cup down. "Must you be formal with me, Paxe? I want to know what you think."

Paxe sighed. She put the figurine on the table. "I think Isak hates you," she said. "I don't think you can change that."

Arré grimaced. Inconsequentially she said, "Do you remember him when he was small, Paxe? He was a beautiful child. If I did go, and name him steward, would you serve him?"

The lamplight trembled in her hair; the gray tips were turning silver. Paxe said, "I serve the Med house."

"You would do it," murmured Arré, "but you would hate it." She leaned back in her cushions. "So would I; I would worry every moment of my absence. Nevertheless, I think I will do it."

"You must do as you think best," said Paxe.

Sorren was worried about Kadra.

It was easier to think about Kadra—where was she, what was wrong?—than to think about the Tanjo. Nevertheless, it was not Kadra that she first thought of when Lalith came to her bedroom to say, "There's someone here to see you. She's at the kitchen door."

Sorren leaped from the bed, tumbling her drums from her lap. "I'm coming." She wondered if it were a messenger from Senta, bringing back her Cards. She hurried downstairs, nearly tripping on the last step. Toli said, "You have strange visitors," and jerked a thumb toward the rear courtyard.

It was Kadra. She was sitting on the tiles. She was very pale, and her eyes were closed. Frightened, Sorren knelt beside her. As her knee touched the tile, Kadra's eyes opened. She coughed, and said, with familiar acerbity, "Don't look at me as if I were a sick cow!"

Sorren sighed. "I was worried about you."

"I know. Norres told me. Did you think I'd run off with your map?"

"I wasn't thinking about it at all," Sorren said.

"Well, I didn't." She moved, grimaced, and flipped the fold of cloak covering her lap to one side. "Took me long enough to do it, I wouldn't want it to be wasted. Here it is."

Sorren took the paper cylinder in both hands. Unrolling it, she traced the route north with her eyes, saying the names of the villages in her mind. She knew them all. When she got to Tornor, she grinned. Instead of writing, which she couldn't read, Kadra had drawn for her in red ink a castle with a tower. Beside the tower was a red, eight-pointed star.

Carefully, she rolled the precious paper up. "Thank you," she said.

"Here," said the ghya. "Tie it." She pulled a ribbon from her belt. It was a bright green, messengers' color, and the sight of it made Sorren feel strange. Taking it from Kadra's hand, she tied the scroll.

"Is your bow still at the pasture?" she said.

"I guess," said Sorren. She had not been there in nearly two weeks.

"Haven't you been practicing?"

"I've been busy," Sorren said defensively, "and when I looked for you, I couldn't find you. I was afraid you were in the fight."

"I was."

"Were you hurt?"

Kadra shook her head. "I got hit in the stomach with a pike butt."

"I was in it, too," Sorren said.

"Were you?" said the ghya. "What were you doing?"

"Mostly hiding." Sorren told what she had seen. The fear and horror had diminished to where she no longer felt sick, telling it. Kadra listened and nodded.

"Glad you got away," she said. "A lot didn't." She coughed. "I came to say good-bye."

"Good-bye?"

"Damn it, girl, are you an echo today? I'm going on the ship. I got my papers this morning."

"But what—are you going to be a sailor?"

Kadra laughed, and coughed, "I'm a mapmaker. They'll need my skills, to map the new lands they find."

Of course. "But how can you go? You—" Sorren broke off, remembering how the ghya hated to be fussed over.

"Oh, I'll go. One way or the other. But I probably won't

see you again. I've got some things for you, little things. They're at the inn. Listen, the ship leaves the day after Festival. Will you be there? If you come to the dock you may even be able to see me board. I shall look for you. Will you do it?"

"Of course I'll do it," said Sorren. "But won't you be at the inn? I can come and say good-bye to you beforehand."

"Maybe I will, maybe I won't," said Kadra. She rose; as she straightened, Sorren saw her put a hand to her right side. She took a limping step. "All your friends are watching me from the kitchen windows. What will they think?"

"I don't know and I don't care," said Sorren. "Have you eaten? There's fish cakes in the kitchen, I can get some for you."

Kadra laughed, but the laugh ended in a terrible spasm of coughing. Finally she hawked and spat into a flowerbed. "I'm fine," she said, wiping her lips with her hand. "I'll look for you when the ship leaves, remember. With the tide, the day after Festival." She lifted one hand in farewell and limped slowly away, toward the street.

Toli leaned out of the window. "Psst!" he said. "Who was *that*?"

"I'm not going to tell you," Sorren said. "Leave me alone."

CHAPTER TWENTY

In the courtyard, Arré and Myra Med were talking. Sorren stuck her head into the kitchen. Lalith grinned at her amid the litter of pots and pans. "We're leaving now," Sorren said. "See you later!" She hurried down the hall, past the parlor, which was strewn with the leftovers of dinner: fishbones and clam shells and peach pits and kava rinds.

There were two litters in the front courtyard. It was a perfect night for Festival. The witchfolk had promised good weather and they had kept their promise: after days of heat and mist the fog had withdrawn to the south. The twilight bristled with excitement; crowds of people swirled up and down the dusky, glittering streets, talking and laughing and singing together. The sky was clear, spangled with uncountable stars.

Isak's two youngest children were scrambling in and out of first one and then the other litter, shouting. Sorren had forgotten how noisy young children could be. Riat, the eight-year-old, the oldest and the heir, stood beside his mother, looking grave and adult in his new silk clothing. Sorren took a deep breath. Her feet twitched to be moving. She went over the preparations in her mind. There were blankets in each litter. Myra and Arré each had cloaks. The lead litter held a basket of food; she hoped there was enough of it. She bit her lip, wondering if Arré and Myra were ready to leave. She rather liked Myra Med, who was a buxom, pleasant woman with a kind manner and a great deal of sense. She rarely hurried, and she was in no hurry now, standing on the steps, talking to Arré about the administration of the vineyards.

Sorren glanced around for Paxe. The Yardmaster had come in earlier to speak with Arré about the details of the watch. But she had vanished, which was not surprising; the night watch had twice the number of people on it than was usual, and she had to keep an eye on all of them. Kaleb stood at the gate, swinging a lantern in one hand, talking to the litter-bearers, and Sorren heard a chinking sound as bontas changed hands. The gate guard shifted his feet, looking bored.

Arré looked very fine tonight, in a red tunic and trousers. She had washed her hair and scented it with jasmine, and it stood out from her head in soft curls like a peacock's crown. Myra wore dark, dark green, so dark it was almost blue. She and Arré got along perfectly as long as they did not spend too much time together. The day and evening of Festival "is about as much as I can stand," Arré had said that morning. "She talks about the harvest and about her children, and after a while I want to run screaming from the chamber." A piercing sound came from the second litter, and everybody jumped. The little girl (who was three) was sitting in it, blowing a reed whistle.

Sorren went to the litter and leaned in the entrance. "Why don't you wait to blow that until we get to the park?" she said. The girl smiled sweetly and shook her head. Sorren plucked the whistle from her hand and brought it to Myra.

"Thank you," said Myra, and continued to talk. Inside the litter, the girl howled. Finally she realized that no one would come to her; she clambered from the litter and ran to her mother's side. "You can have the whistle back when we get to the park," said Myra calmly. "Stop sniffling."

"Shall we go?" said Arré.

That afternoon they had gone to the Tanjo precincts, to hear the L'hel invoke the Guardian's blessing and favor upon the land and upon the city. All that afternoon, tents had been going up in every district. The Blue Clan tent, in the Ismenin district, was the biggest, but the Jalar pavilion was the finest and most gaudy. Twelve days after the riot there were no signs of damage in the Jalar district, except in the places where walls and windows and screens had had to be replaced. The Med pavilion sat in the park at the foot of the hill. It was red with blue triangles on it, and was big enough, Arré said, to hold several thousand people. Arré had spent the last four days at the park, watching the engineers decide where the pavilion would be, and arguing with them about it. Two great pits had been dug for garbage, and two roads had been smoothed into the bare ground, and great tubs of water had been set near the site, in case there was a fire. One year there had been a fire in the Sul district, and the pavilion burned, and many people were hurt. Now all the districts took precautions.

Sorren thought it was a wonder there were not more fires. All the street lamps were lit, and all the house lanterns, and people walked about with candles until moonrise. "Here," said Arré, thrusting the cloaks at her. "Are you sure you know where we're going to be?"

"By the big trees, I'll find you. There's a guard there, right?"

Arré scowled. "I wish it were over," she said. "Are you sorry not to be drumming this year?"

Sorren sighed. "A little."

Isak had engaged another drummer for his dance this year. Sorren had expected him to do so, after the betrothal, but it still felt strange to be a spectator and not a performer.

"Don't think about it," said Arré. She went headfirst into the litter. Myra smiled at Sorren and followed her.

In the second litter, the three-year-old was screaming, "Want go Mama!" Sorren hoisted her from the litter and carried her to her mother's arms.

"Be hush," said Myra, rocking her.

"Me, too," said Kathi, the middle child, starting to climb from the litter. Riat sighed and folded his arms in lordly disdain.

"No," said Sorren. "You stay there, or I'll make you stay in the house with Lalli and wash all the pots." That silenced her. The litter-bearers took their places. In no time at all the litters vanished down the hill, bells tinkling. Sorren waved at Kaleb and went after them at a slower pace, carrying the cloaks in her arms.

The street din was tremendous. At every corner, it seemed, a little performance was happening. There were jugglers everywhere, tossing pears and apples, sickles and spoons; there were dancers and mimes, there were tumblers standing on their heads and on each other's shoulders, there were people selling fish cakes and noodle pies and heavenweed and wine. Children rode their parents' backs, wide-eyed at the spectacle; men and women in headbands and doisse and in the flowing robes of the Asech clumped on the corners watching the performers. An old man was telling fortunes in the middle of the street. The smell of roasted quail drifted from a vendor's barrow. There were guards everywhere, watching for thieves, for Festival was a pickpocket's holiday. They stole purses; many carried sharp knives with which to cut the strings of carelessly handled money bracelets. Sorren's bracelet (it was truly her own, Arré had given it to her as a Festival gift) reposed securely in the pocket of her pants. It had one of each kind of bonta on it, except a largo.

Sorren kept an eye out for friends as she strolled. Tani and Simmy and Nessim would be in the Isara district most likely, and Jeshim—who was not a friend anymore—was juggling at the Blue Clan tent. But people she knew from the markets might come around; it was traditional for people to go all over the city, from district to district, looking into every tent.

Clouds of heavenweed smoke eddied around the lanterns, and people carried wineskins over their shoulders. A hand snaked in front of Sorren's nose with a pipe in its grip. She glanced down. An Asech boy grinned at her. She sucked on it; before she had time to say "Thank you," he was gone. The drug made her limbs tingle pleasantly. The full moon's glow was spreading into the sky. Sorren did not know which she liked more, this feast, or Spring Festival, when people danced in long snaky lines through the streets carrying torches. In the grapefields, she remembered, they danced through the fields over the sown seed, pounding it into the earth with their bare feet.

She entered the park. The night watch guards were all about. Children tumbled everywhere, cavorting like puppies. Sorren looked for the big tree. It was near the tent, but not too close to the pits, which stank, or to the roads, which were dusty.

She saw it, and started toward it. Suddenly, everybody shouted. The moon was rising. It came up almost directly south; it was yellow as a daisy's heart, and huge, and bright enough to see colors by. People jumped and stamped and yelled. Sorren tossed her head back and cried, "Yip-yip-yip-yip!" It was the pickers' call. Half a hundred voices answered her. She hugged the cloaks and shivered with excitement at the joyous sounds.

She weaved through the throng to the tree. The three-year-old was blowing her whistle with great solemnity, marching up and down as if she were leading a band. Arré was sitting on a blanket, the open basket beside her. She was munching a seaweed ball. "Sit." She pointed to the blanket. Sorren sat, feeling shy. Myra was telling Kathi all about the Festival, what it celebrated, how old it was, and so forth.

The guard near the tree was showing Riat his pike. Sorren lay back on the blanket with her head pillowed on one arm and watched the moon rise. It whitened as it went higher in the sky, but it was still huge and brilliant and beautiful. The three-year-old grew bored with her whistle and came to sit beside

her mother. She looked like Myra, with brown hair and skin,
and light eyes.

Sorren wondered where Paxe was. Technically, the Yardmaster was not on duty until midnight but in fact she was here,
somewhere in the crowd, making sure that everything ran
smoothly.

"Sorren!"

She jumped. Riat was at her elbow. "You startled me,
chelito. What is it?"

"I want to go see Papa. Will you take me?"

The year before, he had come to the little tents where the
performers dressed to see his father before the performance.
"Ask your mother," Sorren said.

Riat went to Myra's side and whispered urgently. He came
bounding back to Sorren. "She says I can go." He seized
Sorren's hand. "Will you take me?" He smiled trustingly at
her. His dark eyes reminded her of Isak. She did not want to,
but there was no one else to do it. She glanced at Arré, who
spread her hands.

"Come on." She started to walk toward the big tent.

Kathi set up a jealous wail. Myra took her in her arms and
fed her a seaweed ball. Riat raced ahead of Sorren to the tent.
He was like a little Isak, all dash and fire, but without Isak's
cruelties. The guards at the pavilion looked at them sharply,
and she turned so that they could see her bondservant's bracelet.

At the entrance to the little tents, they were stopped. "Sorry,
no one goes in there but performers."

"But he's Isak Med's son," she said. Riat bounced up and
down on the end of her hand.

The guard frowned. "I got orders," she said.

"Papa!" shrieked Riat. Sorren looked up, to see Isak saun-
tering around the corner of the pavilion. Riat tugged free of
her and ran to his father, who picked him up and swung him
in the air.

He settled the boy on his hip. "What are you doing here,
eh?" There was true affection in his voice. Sorren stared at the
ground. He strolled up to her. "And Sorren. My wife and sister
are here, then."

"Yes, my lord."

"Papa, I want to see the fire-eaters, will you take me,
please?"

"I'll take you. Sorren." She looked up. Isak was smiling

at her. "I forgive you," he said. "I wish you were drumming for me instead of Itaka, but it's too late now."

Damn him, she thought, he always knew what to say to bring her back. "My lord, I wish I were, too."

The moonlight glittered on his sequined cloths. He held Riat firmly. "I'll take Riat with me. You needn't stay." Riat gazed at his father with worshipful eyes. "You might return for him in a bit."

"I will, my lord."

"So formal!" he said teasingly. He tousled his son's curly hair. "Come on, youngling." The boy slid to the ground and pranced in Isak's wake to the little tent.

He would get tired of the boy quickly, she knew, but it gave her a few moments to be by herself. She strolled around the park. The guard who had stopped her before nodded to her. The moonlight made all the colors into pastels. She wandered into the tent; it was as thick with people as a honeycomb with bees. On the big stage, two women tumbled while a third played a wooden flute.

She heard Paxe's name from behind her, and turned. Two Med guards stood by one of the tent supports, talking. They were swearing praisefully about Paxe. "Handle one of those blades as if it were wood and she'll take your fuckin' ears off. Tough as a smith, she is." They saw Sorren listening and shut their mouths. She grinned at them.

She went back into the park. She crossed her arms on her chest, covering the enameled bondservant's bracelet with her cupped palm. Now she was nobody, anybody, a stranger. She went by a vendor selling pigsfeet. She felt in her pocket for a deuce, and gave it to him. He gave her four fingerlings and a pigsfoot. It was hot; she juggled it from one hand to the other until it cooled off.

She went back toward the little tents. A man in red and orange and blue loped by her. They recognized each other at the same time. He spun around.

"What are you doing here?" she said.

Jeshim grinned. "Talking to me again, are you?" He reached forward and, before she could stop him, pretended to pull a red ball out of her left ear. "Oh, things. I'm off now. Come and see me."

She frowned after him. She had no intention of going to see him. She bit into the pork; the juice ran down her chin.

Riat was with Isak in the little tent, watching the dancer

make up his face in front of a silver mirror. The tent was hot with candles. Isak's robes were green and gold and patterned like a serpent's scales: he was dancing the Serpent and the Wise Witch. He drew lines around his eyes to make them stand out. Sorren's fingers tapped on her thighs as she recalled the beat of the dance. Riat's mouth was open in wonder at his father's transformation.

Itaka sat in the corner, practicing the rhythm of the dance. She smiled at him, wishing she could steal his place. "How much longer?" said Isak.

Sorren glanced at the hour candle to the right of the mirror. "Half an hour."

"Ah. Take this imp off my hands."

"Riat. Come now, you papa's busy."

"I want to watch," protested the boy. But he let Sorren detach him from his stool.

"Can you find your way back to the big tree by yourself?" she asked him.

He puffed his chest at her and strutted. "Of course!"

"Why don't you go and tell your mother that your papa is almost ready to dance? She might like to watch him." The boy tossed his head like a colt and galloped off.

Isak grinned at her in the mirror. "You've a way with kids. Why don't you find a man, and have some?"

She laughed. "Arré wouldn't like it."

It was the wrong thing to say. She wished futilely that she could call it back.

But Isak simply smiled. "Are my dear sister's wishes so important to you, then?" he said.

She said, "Of course."

"Of course. Now, I have never had that problem." He drew a final line across his face, and put the brush down. "Tell me, do you think she will come to watch me dance?"

The question was rhetorical; they both knew she would not.

She went into the pavilion. The three tumblers were lighting the torches around the stage, making an act of it, riding each others' shoulders and clowning, pretending to lose their balance, drop each other, and fall off. People were whispering Isak's name. A hand thrust into Sorren's; she looked down. It was Riat. "They're coming. I found them," he said. Sorren turned, wondering if Arré had decided to come after all. But no; "they" meant Myra and the two little ones—and Paxe.

Sorren's heart thumped. Paxe was carrying the three-year-old.

Riat was looking at Paxe with some of the same reverence he reserved for his father. She was wearing the Med colors, and high soft boots. She looked very splendid. Paxe saw his gaze, and grinned. "Sorren, will you hold the baby?" she said. Sorren took the baby from her, and she picked Riat up in two hands and threw him onto her shoulders. Myra was holding Kathi. "There, now you can see," said Paxe.

Myra said graciously, "Yardmaster, you mustn't let my children keep you from your duties."

Paxe said, "They won't, my lady; they give me an excuse to watch the dancing." And to see you, her eyes said to Sorren. She moved so that their arms brushed each other. Around them, the crowd had recognized her and was keeping its distance. "We can go closer if you wish."

"This is fine," said Myra. She saw her son's face, and smiled. "Well, perhaps a little closer." Paxe stepped forward, and people moved out of her way. Sorren followed, shifting the three-year-old from one arm to the other. The little girl had grown sleepy. She laid her head on Sorren's breast. Sorren rocked her gently. She was very nice, Sorren thought, when she wasn't yelling; plump and soft and sweet-smelling. She rubbed her cheek gently against the child's neck.

Now the tumblers were tossing flaming torches at each other, pretending to drop them, while the crowd went Oooh. Sweat coated Sorren's sides. She shifted the baby to the other side, canting her hip to take the child's weight. Itaka walked onto the stage. Everybody cheered.

Riat leaned to talk to his mother. "Papa's coming!"

"Oh, how nice," said Myra. "Kathi, Papa's coming soon. Don't pull my hair, chelito." Riat was bouncing up and down on Paxe's shoulders, both arms windmilling in his excitement.

Isak came onto the stage.

He had whitened a ring around his eyes, to make them stand out. His robes gleamed like the Serpent's scales. The drummer was a pounder; *pom-pom, pom-pom*. After the first burst of cheering, the crowd had grown silent, awed by the dancer's magic. Isak *was* the Serpent; sinuous, subtle, and brutal. He hissed, and the people in the front row stepped back. Sorren shuddered at his artistry. He glided behind the screen, and when he came out he was wearing a white robe over the green and gold costume. Now he was the Wise Witch. Slowly the story unfolded. The Serpent coveted the Witch's wisdom. He came to her cottage and danced about the house. She did not know he was there. She mixed a potion in her cauldron, and when she was not looking, he glided inside and lay down beside the cauldron. When it was all mixed, she tasted it. The Serpent lay in wait for her to look away. (By now, the children in the audience were crying, "Watch out!" while their parents tried to hush them up.) The Witch left the house, and the Serpent reared up, ready to steal the potion. The Witch came back and found him with it. The drumming reached a crescendo. She made a spell, and the great beast cowered, belly to the ground, and crawled out, unable to stand, armless and legless.

At the Serpent's punishment, the children cheered. Isak came from behind the screen, first as the Serpent and then as the Witch. Sorren went "Yip-yip-yip!" and he looked toward her, and smiled.

"He is good, isn't he?" said Myra, her voice soft and sad and lonely. She misses him, Sorren thought. She must love him.

"The crowd thinks so," said Paxe. Reaching over her head, she swung Riat down. "I'm sorry, chelito, I must go." She looked toward Sorren and smiled. Sorren mouthed a kiss at her.

"Will he do another dance?" said Riat. "I want to see it!"

"No," said Sorren. "He always does just one."

They went back to the tree. Arré smiled at them. "Well?" she said.

Myra sat beside her. "The people liked it," she said. "I hope you were not too bored out here. Your Yardmaster was very kind; she came and stood with us while we watched the dance."

Riat said, "Can I go and see Papa again?"

Myra took the three-year-old from Sorren's arms and settled her in the blanket. "The children miss him, you know," she said to Arré.

"I'm sure they do," Arré said gently. "Sorren, would you take the boy back behind the tent?"

Sorren bowed, and beckoned to Riat. "Come on," she said.

If anything, the crowd was getting louder. It took them a long time to work their way back to the pavilion. Riat stayed close to Sorren, a little frightened by the mass of strangers, all taller than he. They stopped a while to watch a woman with a snake. The snake had green scales. "Like Papa," Riat pointed out.

"Not as big," said Sorren, which made him laugh. The

dancer was not as agile as Tani.

As they went on, Riat said, "Is my father a good dancer, Sorren?" The note of love in his voice was so naked, it was painful.

"The best," Sorren said firmly.

Riat repeated it to himself all the way across the park; "The best, the best."

They came around the corner of the pavilion and were face to face with Borti. He greeted Sorren with a smile and a hug. "How are you, girl?"

She was delighted to see him. Now that he was Ivor's second he was never around the house. "I'm well."

"Come with me," he whispered. He took her behind a tent. Riat tagged after her. "Look what I've got." He had some heavenweed in a water pipe. He handed it to her.

"You shouldn't have this—what if Paxe sees you?" she said, but she took a pull at the pipe anyway. The water bubbled.

"She won't. Don't worry about it." He sucked on the pipe, filling his big chest. "That should have been you up there, drumming for Isak Med, not that other fellow."

Riat's head turned at the mention of his father. "I'm going to find Papa," he said. Before she could grab him, he set off, running lightly over the trampled grass.

"Oh, hell," said Sorren. She pushed the pipe into Borti's hands. "I have to go after him."

"Who is he?" said the old guard.

"Isak Med's son, you fool."

"Then he's perfectly capable of taking care of himself."

He was probably right. "He's my responsibility. What if he gets lost?"

"It's light. He'll find his mother."

"I'd better look for him."

She called him as she walked. "Riat. Riat!" In the babble of people about her, she could barely hear her own voice. She went to Isak's tent, but it was empty. The costumes hung on hooks in a corner. Her heart began to beat painfully hard. Nothing ever happened to children—but what if something did? He could fall into the garbage pit, he could eat something bad and get sick, he could get bitten by a dog or kicked by a mule.... "Riat!" Only her own voice answered her.

She would have to tell the guards soon if she did not find him—and Arré, and Isak. Guardian, she said in her head, help me find him. She wanted to weep, and knew it was the heavenweed. She stopped one of the tumblers. "Have you seen a little boy, about this high, wearing blue silk?"

"No, sorry."

"If you do, will you grab him and take him to a Med guard?"

"Sure. Is he yours?"

"In a way. Riat!" she called.

She could not find him anywhere. She combed through the pavilion, looking on the stage, under the stage, in every corner and fold of cloth. She thought of the snake dancer and raced outside to look for her. Guardian, let him be there. . . . She pushed her way to the front of the snake dancer's audience. Riat was not there. She swore, trying to keep panic down, and forced her way out of the circle, ignoring the caustic comments directed at her back.

A silken voice said, "Troubled again, Sorren?"

Sorren whirled. Senta the Truthfinder was standing beside her. She had put her white robe aside, and her clothes were ordinary: a red cotton tunic, dark pants, boots. But there was no mistaking her voice, or the fall of hair that gleamed like ebony in the moonlight.

She smiled. "Why so astonished? Even witchfolk enjoy festival. I come to tell you; your Cards are in your house. I left them with an old fat woman who wheezed at me. I instructed her to put them with your belongings. What's the matter?" Her voice grew very gentle. "Perhaps I can help."

Sorren said, "I'm looking for someone, lehi."

"We are colleagues, are we not? Call me Senta. For whom do you search?"

"A little boy in blue. He's lost. He's—he's Isak Med's son."

"He was in your charge, and you lost him? That is ill. Would he stay here, or might he wander from the park?"

"I don't know. No, I think he would stay here."

"Then let me see if I can find him. Be still." Her brows drew together. "Ah. Yes. There he is, by the tents." She drew a sharp breath. "I would go very quietly and carefully there, Sorren the aftseer. Isak Med is occupied, and he will not take kindly to interruption."

Sorren's knees felt weak with relief. She went down on one knee. "Thank you, lehi."

Senta pulled her upright. "Don't thank me, child, just go, but quietly, quietly. And remember me to your mistress."

Now why—but she did not have time to wonder. Remembering the Truthfinder's admonition to go quietly, Sorren hurried to the rear of the pavilion.

The grass was taller here, less trampled; a small child could easily lie in it and be lost to sight. "Riat!" she called softly. She walked around the first tent, and the second. "Riat?" Thinking she heard a giggle, she turned—but saw nothing. "Riat; please," she said. It was hard to distinguish shapes from shadows; moonlight dappled the grass and the tentfolds with streaks of silver.

Suddenly, a man strode from the second tent. He was tall; as the moonlight broke over his hair, it gleamed red. Despite his swift stride, there was something furtive in his manner. Without thinking, Sorren shrank against the tent side, where the varnish of moonlight confused the eye.

He looked all around in one swift gesture, and then twitched the hood of the cloak over his face and walked away. The cloak had no insignia on it. But in the moment he turned her way Sorren had seen his face clearly, and known him. It was Ron Ismenin.

Sorren almost forgot her worry over Riat in surprise. What would the head of Ismenin house be doing here, in the heart of the Med district? A rustle in the darkness recalled her errand to her. "Riat!" she said, and pounced.

Her fingers closed over a fold of cloth.

Chagrined, she rose. But now she did hear a giggle, clear in the silence. "Riat, come here at once," she said, still softly.

A voice spoke from within the tent. "That's a lot of money, my lord. You must want you sister dead very badly."

Sorren turned around, as Isak's voice answered, half amused, half threatening: "That's right. Badly enough to pay for it—and if it's botched, to pay someone else to find you."

"Oh, I won't botch it," said the second speaker confidently. "I have my own score to settle with the Med house. You want it tonight?"

"It's a good time; the guard is busy. You know who your accomplice is—the juggler."

"Say 'partner,' my lord. It sounds better." There was a chink of coin. "Nuathan money, my lord?"

"You want to have to stop at the gate to change your bontas?"

"No."

"Then don't ask stupid questions. You have weapons?"

"I have a sword. Stolen from the Med Yard just this week."

Isak chuckled. "Ai, I like that. Your partner—" the light voice grew ironic—"will get you both out of the city before the alarm is raised. Do you mind the Asech?"

"I can stand them."

"You'll live with them for a while, until I'm named to succeed her. Then you'll come back to the city."

"I may not, my lord." The other man's voice was dry.

"Suit yourself."

"Papa!" cried Riat. He leaped from the grass. Sorren saw him silhouetted against the moonlight as he sprang through the entrance to the tent. "Papa, can I go, too? I like the Asech!"

Within the tent, both men exclaimed. Isak said, "Riat, what are you doing here?"

"Hiding from Sorren. I wanted to find you. Papa, there's a lady with a snake out there who looks like you!"

The other man said, "Sorren—who the hell's that?"

"Watch your mouth," said Isak. "She's my ex-drummer, my sister's servant. The northern girl."

"Ah. The Yardmaster's doxy. I'll go look." Sorren loosened her hold on the tent and dropped flat, into the grass. She squirmed as close to the tent as she dared and pulled the loose cloth over her. A man came out of the tent and walked all around it.

His boots crunched on the pebbles a handsbreadth from her chin. She held her breath. "I don't see her," he called. He went back inside the tent. Instantly, Sorren rolled away from the tent and scrambled to the shadow cast by the one next to it. She was shaking.

She drew breaths until the trembling stopped. If I had my bow . . . she thought. But she did not have her bow. Rising, she stepped firmly forward, and called, "Riat!"

Riat crowed from within the tent. The entrance flap opened outward and two men walked into the moonlight. One of them was Isak, his son in his arms. The second man swung around the tent and disappeared toward the pavilion. His walk looked familiar, but that was all she could see of him. "The Yardmaster's doxy," he had called her. She made herself pretend not to have noticed him, but her heart seemed to stick in her throat as Isak strolled toward her.

He was wearing soft blue cottons, and his face was bare

of paint. He was smiling faintly. "Riat," he said, "it isn't kind of you to worry Sorren. She's responsible for you." He put the boy on the grass.

"Papa, who was that man?" said Riat.

"Someone I know. Don't worry about him." He looked at Sorren over the child's dark head, and she steeled herself to meet his eyes.

"My lord, he terrified me. I've been looking for him for nearly an hour." Her voice shook, despite her care. Would he notice it?

"Have you?" Isak put a hand on his son's shoulder. "Riat, that was ill-done. Apologize to Sorren for making her worry."

"I'm sorry," said Riat. "Papa, come and see the lady!"

"No. Sorren, what did you think of the dance?"

"It was beautiful," Sorren said. "But your drummer was too loud."

"I know," said Isak. "It should have been you. Where are you going now?"

She reached a hand to Riat. Mischievously, he skipped away from her. "I'm going to take this imp back to his mother, if he'll let me."

"He'll let you." Isak's hand shot out and caught his son's wrist. "You come with me, youngling." They walked away, toward the tent mouth. Sorren put her palms to her cheeks. She was icy and feverish all at once.

She tried to think who the man could be. Someone she knew—or who knew her. She knew who the juggler had to be—Jeshim. That was easy. Isak was talking to the boy softly; Riat nodded his head. He was probably telling the boy not to say anything about "the man" to his mother. Guardian, be with me now. She had to get back, to find Paxe. Isak and Riat returned.

"Here you are," said Isak. "Chelito, I'll see you tomorrow." He smiled again at Sorren and strolled away.

"Good-bye, Papa," called Riat. He looked as if he wanted to run after Isak, and Sorren caught his shirt. "I won't run. Let me go." She let him go. He stood staring after his father. "I have a secret," he said with jealous pride.

"Well, don't tell me what it is," said Sorren. She picked him up and put him on her shoulders. He wound his fingers in her hair.

"Giddap, horse!" he commanded. She let him pretend she was a horse, and loped through the park toward the tree, looking for Med guards. Her heart drummed in her chest. Her knees felt weak. She told herself there were too many people about, that nothing would happen in the park.

The baby was crying. Myra walked up and down, joggling her. Sorren put Riat down. "Where've you been?" said Arré crossly.

Riat said, "I ran away. I saw a lady with a snake, and Papa!"

Sorren said, "He ran away from me, and it took me a long time to find him."

"I'm tired," said Arré. "Go get the litters, child. Myra, I'll drop you at Isak's house."

Myra nodded. "Riat, it was very naughty of you to run away so long."

Kathi was asleep, curled on the blanket with her whistle in her fist. She looked like Arré, sleeping. Sorren went to the entrance to the park to get the litters. She had to find Paxe. She saw a Med guard and seized his shirt. "Where's the Yard-master?" He shrugged. "Please, it's important. Arré Med wants her."

His expression altered. "Why didn't you say so?" He gave a two-note whistle. In a moment, it was repeated from the direction of the pavilion. "She's that way," he said pointing.

"Thank you," said Sorren. She watched, waiting for the crowd to part, for Paxe to walk through it. . . . Her breath rasped in her throat. The words she had heard in the tent were burned into her memory like a brand. "You have a good memory," said Kadra's voice in her head.

"Well, there she is!" said the guard in her ear. Sorren blinked. Paxe was walking toward her, smiling and brisk.

Guardian, let her know what to do, Sorren thought, and then her self-control shattered. With a sob, she flung herself into Paxe's arms.

CHAPTER TWENTY-ONE

"I don't believe you," said Arré.

Paxe said nothing. Arré walked from wall to wall in the darkened bedroom, sliding her fingers over the screens and holding on to the furniture with unsteady hands. Sounds of revelry blew up from the street on the night wind. Paxe waited for Arré to stop moving. She could hear the soft *pah-pah-dum* of Sorren's drumming, coming not from her room but from the head of the stair. In the kitchen, Lalith was scrubbing the already clean pots. Arré walked to the window. The screen was open, looking on the garden. Paxe went to her and put both arms around her. Arré was shaking. The moonlight poured down upon her rigid face.

"I'm all right," she muttered, resting her forehead against Paxe's breast. "And I do believe you." She sucked a deep lungful of air. "My little brother. My murderous, stupid little brother. What do I do now? What have you done?"

She was coming out of her shock. Paxe pulled her away from the window. "Sorren is playing the drums on the stairway where she can keep an eye on the front door. Lalith is in the kitchen, making noise. The kitchen door is barred from the inside. The guards—what few of them are still around the house—are in their usual places."

"Do they know? Have you told them?"

"No. I had to tell you first. Give me half an hour and I'll have a fence of bodies about this house." Arré's heartbeat was rapid as a bird's. Paxe turned her face up and kissed her gently. Her mouth was salty; she had been crying so softly that Paxe had not heard it. *"Nika*, don't," said Paxe. "Nothing will happen to you, I swear it."

"I can't help it." Pulling herself lightly from Paxe's embrace, Arré walked around the room again. "I didn't know you could pay people to kill."

"What do you think an army is?" said Paxe. She rubbed her hands over her face. Her skin felt tight. "You can pay people to do anything."

Arré said, "That's not what an army is." She turned around. "Can you pay people to do anything? Can you pay them to be loyal—to love you?"

"No," Paxe said. "Not that."

The revelers had stopped beneath the window to argue where they would go next. Stand there and fight, thought Paxe. Go ahead. But the proximity of the big house made them nervous, and they staggered away, still talking. *Pah-pah-dum*. That was Sorren, on the stairs. After that first fit of tears, she had grown calm and thoughtful—it was she who had suggested getting Lalith to make noise in the kitchen.

Arré said, "How many of them will there be?"

"We know of two, the knife thrower and one other. There might be more."

"I don't want any of the household hurt."

Paxe said, "Someone has to stop them, Arré."

"Can we frighten them away?"

"And have them try again, some other night, or day? You want to live your life looking over your shoulder?" The words rang loudly in the still house. Sorren's thumping halted, and then resumed.

"If they are going to kill me tonight, they'll have to come to this room," Arré said. "Can we let them come into the house, and capture them when they get here?"

"You want to trap them in the act."

"Yes. And I want them alive, so that they can say who hired them."

Paxe turned it over in her mind. "I think it can be done," she said. "But you must make me a promise."

"What?"

"That you will leave it to me to decide how it is to be done, and that if I tell you to do something, you will do as I say."

Arré laughed shakily. "It's hard for me to do things any way but my own."

"I know how you are."

"I promise," said Arré. "Though I reserve the right to carp afterward."

"You would anyway."

Arré sat on the bed. A shaft of moonlight fell across her hands as she twisted and turned her bracelets. "I suppose I shall not go north after all."

"I think not," Paxe said. "Your brother isn't fit to rule, Arré. His mind is poisoned."

Arré tried to smile, and shivered instead. "Tarn Ryth will be disappointed."

"I think he'll understand when he learns why you stayed."

Arré thumped her fist on the bed. "No one is to know! I want this to be private, Paxe. Shall I tell the whole city that my brother is trying to kill me?"

"I will keep it as quiet as I can," said Paxe. "And I will try to see to it that no one is hurt. No one should know, except you and me, and Sorren, and the people you choose to tell."

"And the Truthfinder," said Arré. "I wonder—" But she left the sentence unfinished. "And my brother."

Paxe sent Arré down the hall with Sorren to Sorren's bedroom. "You are not to come out until I come for you," she instructed them. "Even if you hear noise, stay still. Don't talk above a whisper."

Sorren said, "Should I pretend to be here, or to be gone?"

"Be here."

"Should I play the drums?"

"Do you, at night?"

Sorren blushed pink. "Sometimes. I try to do it quietly."

Paxe smiled at her. "Then play for a little while, and then stop."

She went about Arré's bedroom, arranging the room to her satisfaction. She put the stool in front of the door, where anyone entering might trip over it. Then she went to the kitchen. Lalith was a tiny pigtailed shadow in the moonlight.

"My arms are tired," she complained. Fretfully, she kicked a pot.

Paxe said, "I'm going out. I want you to make noise a little while longer, and then go to your bed, and stay there. Leave this door—" she gestured to the kitchen door—"unbarred, and then don't get up for anything until I tell you you may. You understand?"

Lalith's eyes were wide as plates. "What are we doing?" she said.

"Never mind now. You'll hear later." Paxe walked around the room, piling pots in strategic places under the windows. They looked too small for anyone to climb through, but it was better to be safe. Lalith watched her, sporting a disapproving frown.

"That's not where they go," she said.

"Leave them," Paxe said. "They can go back in the morning." She tugged gently on one of Lalith's ebony braids. "Remember, to bed, and no noise." She went back into the front room, through the two parlors. The moonlight reflected off the tall glass of the scroll case, and in it she saw the room, herself, printed on the image of the rolled-up scrolls.

Then, as she had every night since change of watch, she went out to walk her district.

The night was still brilliant, but in the south the fog was clumping thicker and thicker. Little clouds scudded like birds across the star-wreathed sky. The door guard under the kava fruit tree was a shadow, the tree a thicker shadow. She made herself walk slowly, evenly, the way she always did. Late-night celebrants staggered from a nearby alley and trudged up the hill, laughing. As they passed the house, they quieted, warning each other owlishly not to disturb Arré Med. She pressed against the garden wall; they went by her without seeing her. They smelled of heavenweed and cheap wine. She went east, into the toe of the boot, and then north, along the border of the Minto district. She walked past a corner that should have held a guard. It was empty. Where was he? She cocked her head, listening, and heard nothing, no raised voices, no sounds of argument, no footsteps.

She located him in a thicket, smoking heavenweed, hands cupped around the glowing bowl of the pipe. Quietly, she came upon him from behind. Catching him at both elbows, she dug her strong fingers into the nerve. The pipe pitched from his shocked hands. Bracing herself, she lifted him out of the air and slammed him, hard, down on the street. The jolt jarred him from toes to crown. "Five strokes if I find you smoking again," she whispered into his ear.

He staggered as he turned to face her. "Yardmaster—"

"Don't make excuses. Get back to your place." He stiffened, and went to the corner. She hunted until she found the fallen pipe. Picking it up, she threw it with all her strength; it gleamed in the moonlight for a moment before it clattered down into someone's garden.

Outside the Tanjo, she stopped, as was her custom, to exchange words with the guard there. The red dome's edges looked as if they were cut out of paper. A shadow of a bird cut across the face of the full moon. "They're restless," said the guard. "Hear them cooing? The light keeps them awake." She looked for the lights in the L'hel's chambers but they were dark. Again she wondered why the Truthfinder had warned Sorren to go quietly to the tents. The warning had probably saved Arré's—and possibly Sorren's—life.

Paxe wondered if Isak would have killed the girl right then, had he thought she'd heard his deadly intrigue. Perhaps he would not have done it with his son looking on, but surely he would have done it. She turned north. She hesitated at the park, and then went on. By now Lalith would have ceased making her racket in the kitchen.

She completed her circuit swiftly. Her muscles felt stiff; she had been on duty a long time, since the pavilion had gone up, and she was very weary. She waved to the gate guard and spoke loudly, hoping that it would be heard. "I'm going to be in my cottage for a bit. Wake me if you need me."

Before she went to her cottage, she made one brief stop at the Yard. The moon threw her shadow in sharp relief on the walls. Then she went to her cottage. The cat greeted her with a puzzled "Meow," and she stroked it until it purred. She went up to her bedroom and lit the lamp, hoping that the killers were outside and would see the light and think she was making ready for bed. She walked across the chamber, clattered the basin and the pot, made the noises they would expect to hear, and finally blew the lamp out.

Then she lay down on the bed in the uncertain moonlight, and made herself lie still.

Sweat ran from her. She was afraid. She tried to guess at how many there would be; two, three, four, five? They have to come tonight, she thought. O Guardian, let them come tonight. Arré will never consent to live behind an army, always guarded, always frightened. . . . She listened for the sound of Sorren's drum, but could not hear it. She was too far from the house to hear it, anyway. Her bed felt as if it had rocks in it, and she forced herself to lie still, watching the moonlight travel over the floorboards. Let them come tonight. She felt herself growing chilly and she began to exercise, flexing her muscles, keeping them warm for the work that lay ahead.

In a little while, she heard a distant clamor. She had expected it, thought she did not know what it was, a staged quarrel, a pretended theft, a distraction to call the attention of the guards. Flexing fingers, thighs, and neck, she rose from the bed. Silently, she went downstairs. Opening the cedar chest, she took out the northern sword. She had managed to get most of the rust off. Light gleamed on the newly polished edge. She imagined Tyré watching her from wherever he was, and tried to silence her mind, in case his soul was calling to her—but she heard only the silence and her own thunderous heartbeat. Nothing spoke to her across the desolate plain of death.

She put the sword into its sheath, and, holding it firmly against her, she opened the cottage door. The moon sailed in a web of cloud. She waited until its vast light faded, and then, closing the door, she ran across the courtyard to the rear of the house. The eave of the roof cast a great shadow over the entrance. The pots sat on the kitchen floor where Lalith had left them. Paxe piled them in front of the door so that its opening would knock them down. Then, leaving it unbarred, she climbed the stairs to Arré's bedroom and lay down on the bed.

They came in the back door as she meant them to, and fell over the pots, giving her the warning she had hoped for. Rising, she unsheathed the sword. They were coming down the hall to the stairs, coming fast; she heard a voice, and the sound of something falling. She wondered what it was. She was not angry yet. She prayed for anger as another might pray for peace—Guardian, make me angry—she kicked the sheath under the bed and tried to conjure up past hurts, old hates, anything to start the necessary, killing rage.

They came upstairs. They were wearing boots, and she counted every step. One man whispered, she couldn't hear the words, but the voice sounded familiar. The blood pulsed in her veins. They came closer, and she flattened herself against the wall, counting—one, two, three, four; *four to kill one small woman*, she thought, and the red anger began to rise in her head like a fire, as she had prayed and hoped it would, otherwise they might kill her—they came through the door, one, two, three, the fourth outside, and she leaped at them and ran the first one through the throat as he lunged with his drawn knife toward the empty bed.

He fell across it in a gurgle of blood. Paxe jerked the sword from his body and swung at the second man. He tried to beat her blade away; she swung back under his stroke and cut him across the belly, feeling the blade slide on the ribs. He screamed like a pig and folded over with his hands clutching the wound. The fourth man leaped into the room. The lamp tottered on its base and fell from the table, spilling oil over the floor. She recognized him. It was Seth. He grinned at her across the room. "I thought it was you, you cunt," he said. He was holding a sword. Paxe recognized it; three nights ago it had been in her weapons shed. The other man was holding a long knife by the point. "Hold off, partner. I want this one."

"Do you?" said Paxe. Pointing the sword at them, she circled to the bedroom door and knocked it closed. "Well then, come on."

The knife thrower held back as Seth lunged for her. He sliced at her, tearing through a screen. She ducked under the blow and felt it whistle over her head. She stabbed upward at Seth but he evaded it, scrambling to the other side of the bed. Now the dead man on the bed lay between them.

"Now!" called Seth. The knife thrower swung. Paxe saw the knife come glittering through the air. It hit her in the upper arm; the pain seared through the flesh. She grunted and then closed her mind to it. As the knife thrower felt for his second blade, she stabbed him. He screamed. "Damn you," said Seth. Her feet slipped in the oil as he swung at her, and her sword fell from her grip. The slice missed. His own feet slid and he overbalanced, his sword waving wildly. She caught his wrist with her left hand, ignoring the pain that wrung a cry from her lips, his elbow with her right, and forced him backward against the wooden wall.

They struggled. He snarled at her. She brought her knee up between his legs as hard as she could, and he shrieked. The sword dropped from his hand. She let him fall to his knees, and then, with a brutal twist, broke his right elbow. He collapsed, unconscious, or near to it. The room door opened. Sorren was standing in the doorway, holding a candle in her left hand and a monstrous kitchen cleaver in her right. Paxe leaned on the wall and swore at her. "I told you not to leave your room!"

"I had to," said Sorren. She held the lamp up. Orange shadows wrestled with the moonlight. Her eyes went from one to the other of the motionless men. "Are they dead?"

"Three of them are."

"Is Jeshim there?"

"The juggler? That he is."

Her guards came leaping up the stairs, now fully aroused. "Yardmaster, what—" Paxe picked up the sword. She glanced at Seth, who was moaning, hands between his knees.

"Get the bodies out of here. Mind that lamp!" she warned Sorren. "There's oil all over the floor."

Reaction hit her. The pain from her arm rocked her where she stood. The corpses' feet bumped on the stairs as the guards carried them out. She felt Sorren move aside. The light swung in a circle—"You're hurt," said Arré. She stood in front of Paxe, peering into her face. "There's blood on your shirt. Do you have to stand there, or can you walk?"

"I can walk," said Paxe. She let them lead her down the hall to Sorren's room. She dropped on the bed and laid the sword at her feet. The house was noisy with people; Lalith, Toli, the outraged and angry cook.

Sorren went to get water. Arré sat on the bed beside Paxe, an arm around her waist. "Who were they?" she said.

"The juggler, Jeshim, the one who threw the knives at the betrothal party," said Paxe. "Seth, a guard who ran away. Two others. I don't know them."

"Are any of them alive?"

"Seth is. You said you needed one." The blood was running down her arm. "Get me a pad." Arré looked around, and then took her own shirt off and thrust it at Paxe.

"Is it bad?" she asked.

"I can't tell." She pressed the shirt against the slice, and swore. "Serves me right," she muttered. She had been stupid, she should not have given them that chance to rush her. "Five years ago, they never would have touched me."

The cook came in, carrying a basin of water. Lalith pattered behind him with a white cloth. "Let me see that," he said to Arré. Obligingly, she moved from the bed. He sat down, laying the basin on the floor. "Fine mess that is," he said to Paxe, plucking Arré's shirt from the wound. "Put that here," he said to Lalith, pointing his chin at his own knees. Lalith laid the cloth down and unlapped the sides; in it was a bag of green powder and thread and a long curved needle. "Where are those cloths I told Toli to bring?" Lalith scampered out the door, returning a moment later with an armful of strips of cloth.

Dipping a cloth in the water, he cleaned the blood away from the gash. Paxe set her teeth against the heat. "Needs stitching," he said.

Arré said, "Can you do it?"

"No different than stitching up a goose." He peered into Paxe's face. "Lalith, does that numbskull Toli have any heavenweed?" She nodded. "Bring it, and a pipe."

Lalith soon came back, with a clay pipe filled with the strong greenish drug. Sorren lit the pipe and held it to Paxe's lips. She took the smoke gratefully into her lungs and leaned back against the wall, while the cook cleaned and powdered and finally stitched the long ugly gash. "The knife should have stayed in the wound," Cook muttered.

"He was moving when he threw it, and so was I. It spoiled his throw." Paxe grinned. She was floating now. "He was aiming for my heart, or my throat."

Cook tied a final neat knot in the strip of cloth that held the bandage on. "You could take that to a Healer," he said.

"I may" said Paxe. "Thanks. Neat job."

"Easier than it looks," he said, suddenly embarrassed. "I'll make you broth for the next few days." He gathered up the basin and the bloody cloths and needle. His eye found the cleaver. "What's that doing here?" He jerked his head at Lalith. "Come on, it's over." He tramped down the hall, his big feet shaking the floor. The room seemed to sway . . . Paxe smiled. That was the effect of the heavenweed.

Sorren said, "Is it over?"

Arré said, "No. Only this part is over." She picked Paxe's right hand from her lap, and kissed it. "I don't know what to say to thank you."

"You asked me to do it," said Paxe. She straightened. Pain shot through her left arm, and the floating sensation receded some. One of the guards was standing in the doorway and she said, "Yes?"

"My lady," said the guard. Arré looked up. "My lady, I'm sorry—will you come?"

"What?" said Arré. She looked at Paxe. They all followed the guard down the stairs.

Someone had lit the lamps. By the light they could see Elith lying half in, half out of the doorway to the large parlor. The guards had covered her with an ancient blanket. It smelled of the stable. Paxe knelt beside the old woman. The guard drew back the cloth from her face, and Paxe touched the dry lips. The old woman's eyes were glazed and still. She lifted the flaccid weight of one fat hand.

"She must have heard them come in, and gone to see what it was," said the guard. "She never had a chance."

I forgot, thought Paxe. She stood, feeling sick. I forgot to warn her.

"I forgot," said Arré. "She wanders—wandered at night. I didn't think of her. Why didn't I think of her?" Her face twisted with sudden tears. The guard drew the cover over the dead woman's body.

Paxe put her hand on Arré's arm. "It was my fault," she

said. "It was my job. Blame me." Arré gulped like a child, and was silent.

"It was Isak's fault," said Sorren suddenly. "Blame Isak."

Arré looked up. "Yes," she said. "Isak. Where is that man, the one who lived?"

"In the guardhouse."

"Take—take Elith's body away. Bring him here." She tugged one of the big armchairs nearer the lamp, and sat in it. "Paxe, can you stay? Sorren, bring me wine."

"Should you?" said Sorren.

"Guardian, girl, just a little. Have some yourself, too." She tilted her head. "Paxe, do you know him?"

"I know him," said Paxe grimly.

They brought Seth into the parlor. Paxe saw to her satisfaction that he was having considerable trouble walking. Someone had bound a rough pad around his elbow with cloth and twine. Sorren brought two glasses of wine, one for Arré, one for herself. Seth stared at Arré; he could not seem to keep his eyes away from her bare breasts. Paxe said to Sorren, "Get a shirt." Walking to Seth, she closed her right hand over his hair. Very softly, with her face quite close to his, she said, "You can be dead very soon. Remember it." His face grayed, and his eyes contracted. She let him go, and stepped back. Her arm throbbed, but the heavenweed kept the pain from being too real.

Arré said, "You were a guard of mine, the Yardmaster says. Why did you leave?"

"I didn't like the way I was treated," he said, looking at his feet. Sorren brought Arré a shirt. It was huge, one of hers.

"I couldn't get into your room," she said. "The oil—Toli's cleaning it up."

Arré put the shirt on. "How did my brother find you?" she said.

He rubbed his chin with his good hand. "I found him. I heard he didn't like you much. I thought he'd take me on."

"And did he?" said Paxe.

"I've been working for him for nearly a month."

"That's why we couldn't find you," said Paxe.

Arré said, "After you'd killed me, what were you supposed to do?"

"Run," said Seth. "To the Asech country. The juggler was going to arrange that part."

"Who were the others?" said Paxe.

Seth started to shrug and thought better of it. "Oil Street thugs," he said.

Arré sipped her wine. "You know what can happen to you now," she said.

Seth drew his thumb across his throat in the universal gesture.

"Yes," said Arré. "But I'm not going to do that. I'm going to keep you alive so that you can speak against him. After that, we'll see." She beckoned to the guards to take him, and looked at Paxe. "You *could* sit down," she said. Sorren leaped to one of the armchairs and turned it so that it faced Arré's. Paxe sat. The cushion felt so good that she was afraid she might fall asleep right there.

She moved her injured arm so that the pain would keep her awake.

Arré rubbed her eyes. "Now what?" she said.

Paxe said, "Let me go get him."

Arré said, "He's a member of a noble house. You need a Council order or he doesn't have to come." She had not needed to be told who Paxe meant by "he."

A spurt of some of the rage that had possessed Paxe in the bedroom made her shiver. "I would like to see him try to fight me," she said harshly. "Arm or no arm."

Arré said, "No. He—Myra is there. And the children."

The sky was paling in the east. Beneath the windows, the rumble of carts began. "He doesn't have to know," Paxe pointed out. "If his plan had succeeded, wouldn't I be going now to his house, to tell him of your death and ask him what to do? Let him think it worked, until I get him outside his house."

Arré pulled Sorren's shirt around her as though it were a blanket. "All right," she said. "Do it like that."

"Good," said Paxe. She ached, and wished that she did not have to move. Sighing, she made a conscious effort, and rose.

"What will you do to him?" Sorren said.

"I don't know," said Arré.

"And to Ron Ismenin?"

"Ron Ismenin?" said Arré. "What of him?"

"He was there," said the girl. "I saw him leave the tent before I heard the voices. He didn't see me."

"Ron Ismenin," said Arré. "That—that—" words failed her. She worked one of her silver bracelets—the big one, with the blue stone—over her knuckles, and handed it to Sorren. "Here, child, take this with you: it will get you through the guards. Go to the Hok district, and bring me Marti Hok."

An hour later, Arré faced her brother across the little parlor.

She was not alone with him: Paxe and another guard were present. Arré's knees were shaking, and she firmed them with an effort. My little brother, she thought. She gazed at him, trying to find in his handsome, evil face the face of the little boy she had played with and loved. She kept seeing Riat in him. He was hastily dressed, without the jewels he usually wore; Paxe had told him that she was dead, and he had pulled on the clothes to hand and left his house, leaving Myra and the children sleeping in peace and ignorance. He rubbed his wrists with an absent gesture, his eyes never leaving hers, and she saw the red marks of a rope on them. Paxe said that he had not fought; why had she bound him?

"Well?" he said, and she wondered what it meant to him to see her alive and know his plot had failed.

"Why?" she asked him. "Why that way?"

"It was a last resort," he said. "I would never have done it if you had agreed to accept the Ismeninas on the Council."

"They knew of it, then?"

"Not precisely," he said. "They paid for it without knowing what it was they paid for. At some later time, I might have told them, of course."

It was the same tactic he had used with Cha Minto. "How did you get Ron Ismenin to give you money?"

"We made a bet," Isak said blandly, "and he lost."

"What was the bet about?"

"Something trivial."

She doubted it. But she could—and would—deal with Ron Ismenin later. "Should the Council have disrupted the city, to serve your ambitions?"

A smile flickered across his face. "You have never understood," he said.

For a moment, in her weariness and pain, Arré hated him. He was always beautiful; quicker than she, softer than she, graceful and illusive as moonlight. Then hatred died, and she was only weary. She spread her hands. "Explain to me, then."

"I suppose I might as well. What if it had been you in my place, sister; confined to the country, to overseeing the harvest, to raising children and vines—would you be content with that life, Arré?"

In the garden, a bird trilled. Someone—Lalith?—tiptoed past the parlor door. "I don't know," Arré said. "No, I doubt I would have been content, Isak. But I would have tried to do it as best I could!"

He said, "I did. It was like living in a cage."

Arré said, "There are people in this city who would give their souls for such a cage!"

"They're fools." He reached a hand toward her. Paxe moved sharply, and he drew it back. "Arré, you cannot blame me for desiring power."

"I blame you for trying to take it by killing me."

"If you had given it to me another way, perhaps I wouldn't have tried to have you killed."

"So you admit it," she said.

He shrugged, a beautiful dancer's motion that rippled over hands, arms, neck, shoulders. "I understand you have two witnesses." Arré nodded. "I am a realist; why should I deny it? But you have only yourself to blame for it."

Arré shook her head. "Isak, you are not going to convince me to blame myself for your ambition. Why not lay the blame upon our parents, who begot me first?"

"Oh," he said, "I do."

She did not want to stand any longer. Her chair stood at her side; she sank into it, and looked up at Isak. "Now what am I to do with you?" she said.

He smiled. "I know what I would do were I in your place."

"What?"

He drew his thumb across his throat from ear to ear. Paxe, her eyes on Arré's face, nodded her agreement.

"No," said Arré. "I don't want you dead, though people keep telling me I should."

His eyes narrowed.

"But I don't want you here, in Kendra-on-the-Delta. You'll scheme and pry and trouble me."

"If I—"

"Give your word? I don't trust your word." She watched the sunlight sift through the window, wondering when Marti would come. "I want you gone."

Isak said, "An order for exile must be signed by every Council member."

"It will be. At sunset today, your outlawry will be proclaimed, you will be stripped of rank, and taken outside the city Gates. I don't care what direction you travel in. The vineyards are no longer yours; I will give them to whomever I decide should have them."

He swallowed. "And Myra?" he said. "And the children? Shall they be outlaws?"

"Would Myra follow you?"

He shook his head. "No. Why should she? It's a hard life without a roof, without friends, without money. I don't want my children to live like that."

Arré turned her bracelets on her wrists. He wants me to give Myra the vineyards, she thought. "You know you will not be permitted to see her. If you are found on Med land, the Med soldiers will hunt you like a wolf."

He smiled. "There are no wolves in the grapefields, Arré. Myra's ambitions are less exalted than mine. She would rather live in comfort without me than follow me through the wild."

"Where will you go?"

He spread his hands. "Not upriver. Tarn Ryth will not want me on his lands. And not the Galbareth, I would die of boredom. Shirasai, perhaps, or farther. There are other lands."

"Anhard?" said Arré.

"Too cold."

He was taking it well. Perhaps he was counting on Cha Minto or Ron Ismenin to send him money. She didn't care. She hadn't slept in more hours than she cared to count, her eyes felt like sand, her mouth like wax, and she was very, very tired. "As long as you are out of Kendra-on-the-Delta, I don't care where you go. Take him." Paxe stepped forward and seized his arm. For a moment, all his muscles stiffened, and then he smiled, and relaxed, and let her take him. Arré closed her eyes. She suddenly could not bear to watch him walk away.

When she opened them, Marti Hok was standing in the door. The old woman limped to her and laid a hand on her hair. "When Sorren came for me this morning," she said, "I was awake. I wake early; I lie in bed listening to the birds and to the merchants passing through the streets on the way to their shops. When Sorren asked me to come to the house, I did not think, something is wrong. I thought, how original of Arré, a morning party. I was charmed."

"And then she told you."

"And then she told me," agreed the old woman. "My dear, I am sorry."

Arré nodded. Reaching for the bell, she rang for Lalith.

Sorren came in. "Tell Toli to bring in another chair." She rose. "Sit, Marti. You are older."

"But I suspect you are the more tired," Marti said. Nevertheless, she sat. Toli, his eyes still crusty with sleep, brought a chair from the big parlor. Arré sat in it.

"Do you want tea?" she said.

"I do."

Arré rang again. Sorren came in, her hair half braided. "Bring tea, child."

The tea was brought, and they sat sipping it. Arré yawned. Marti said, "What do you want me to do, Arré?"

Arré said, "Two things. I want you to help me obtain the Councillors' signatures on an exile order for my brother."

Marti sighed. "Have you talked to him? What does he say?"

"He is unrepentant."

Marti shook her head, not in negation but in sorrow. "I will help you, of course. What of Myra and the children?"

"I shall give Myra the vineyards. Riat is still my heir."

"I approve," said Marti. "And the second thing?"

"I want you to be present when I speak with Ron Ismenin."

Marti said slowly, "Did he know of this?"

Arré said, "He paid for it. Isak says he did not know what he was paying for."

Marti snorted. "Ron Ismenin is stupid but I cannot imagine him paying for something without knowing what it was."

"Nor can I," Arré said. "But only he and Isak know the truth."

Grimly, Marti said, "I would be pleased to be present when you speak with him."

Sorren tapped on the door jamb. Arré looked up. "Come in, child," she said.

The tall girl entered. Her braid was coiled on top of her head, held there by the lapis lazuli comb. Her eyes were red, and Arré wondered if she had been weeping for Isak. She dropped her knee to Marti Hok and then faced Arré. "May I go down to the docks?" she said.

"Down to the docks? Why?"

"The ship is leaving today, and I promised a friend that I would go to the docks to see it leave. She's on it."

"The ship—oh, the Isara ship. Who is your friend?"

"Her name is Kadra. She's a mapmaker."

The thought of the Isara ship made Arré think of the L'hel. Could *he* have known of the plot? Could Kim Batto have known? Perhaps she could find a way to ask Senta-no-Jorith about that. She scowled at the floor, and glanced up to find Sorren waiting patiently for her answer.

"I'm sorry, child. I was thinking. Yes, you may go. Promises should be kept. Do you know when the ship leaves?"

Sorren shook her head.

"High tide today is four hours before noon," said Marti Hok. "The ship will leave on the rising tide."

Arré grunted. "How do you know that?"

Marti said, "Arré, don't be silly. My district borders the delta; of course I know the tides. So do half the folk of this city."

"Yes," said Arré, "I suppose they do."

She could not help thinking of Isak. She wondered if they had bound him when they returned him to his cell. "Ron Ismenin," she muttered, and seized a piece of paper. *"Please come to my house the first hour before noon today."*

"It sounds like a magistrate's summons," said Marti.

"I mean it to." He would come; she was sure of it. She thrust it at Sorren. "Give this to a guard to deliver to the Ismenin house."

Sorren bowed.

"Go, go!" Arré ordered. The tall girl turned and vanished though the doorway. Arré heard her stop and speak to the guard.

Marti leaned forward. The sunlight gleamed on her hair. "Arré," she said, her voice somber, "let that girl go."

Arré was still thinking of Ron Ismenin. After she spoke with him, she would write to Tarn Ryth again. "What?" she said. "I did!"

"No," said Marti. "Let her *leave*. Can't you see—she's grown, she's ready? She longs to go north—oh, yes, she told me. You know it, too. How much longer is she bound to you?"

For a moment, Arré could not recall. "A year, I think," she said. "Yes, a year."

"Give her the year. If for nothing else, then for her service to you this night; she has earned her freedom." Marti lifted her teacup to her lips. Arré remembered the longlegged, tawny child she had first noticed in the grapefields, bending over weeds. It's true, she thought. She *is* grown. The child is gone.

CHAPTER TWENTY-TWO

Ilnalamaré was leaving.

She sat upright on the slipway, great angled timbers holding her balanced, while the friendly tide swirled around her bow. A work crew stood by, waiting to pull the timbers free of her with ropes. In the water, two sturdy boats waited to haul her into deep water; they were linked to the larger ship by lines ending in claw-shaped hooks. Sorren squinted into the sunlight. Her eyes hurt, and her mouth was fuzzy with lack of sleep. She wondered if they had told Myra yet what Isak had done. The whole of the events of the night seemed like a bad dream which she had not had to go to sleep to remember.

She had expected there to be a crowd on the boardwalk. More guards than usual paced the street. As she approached the walk, a guard signaled her to halt. "You can't go there," he said.

"Why not?"

"It's reserved." He stepped aside a moment to let her see. A small group of richly clad people stood at the walkway's tip; she recognized Edith Isara.

"Can I go down to the shore?" she said.

He glanced from one side to the other, and then shrugged. "You didn't ask me. I didn't see you."

"Thanks."

As Sorren slithered down the pebbly bank, a noise began. It froze her. "Awhoo! Aawhoo!" The alarm! she thought, in useless panic. But the work crew lounging in the mud merely pulled on their gloves and looked toward the ship. From this perspective Sorren could see again how big it was. But compared to the ocean, it was no bigger than a toy, no bigger than a floating chip of wood.

"Awhoo!" The sound came again, from the south.

"It's the fishin' boats," said a man. He was sitting in the shade cast by the boardwalk. Sorren shielded her eyes. Twenty or so people stood or sat along the walkway's length. "They'm greetin' they new sister." He turned his head, hawked, and spat into the mud.

"Is all the crew on board?" Sorren said.

"Ya. You know someone?"

340

She nodded. He jerked his thumb toward the others. "So do they. So do I."

Around the ship's white hull, the tide was sliding up. Sorren sat in the mud beside the friendly man. He smelled of fish. She listened to the people telling stories about the ship's building and its captain. Her name was Ruth-no-Tania. She had been raised west of the city, in a fishing village, and had been at sea, as deckhand, mate, and skipper, for sixteen years. She was one of the most respected shipmasters in Kendra-on-the-Delta, and when Edith Isara had first conceived of the ship, it was to Ruth-no-Tania she went, before anyone.

"How old is she?" said Sorren, imagining a strong, lean woman with iron-gray hair.

The fisherman told her, leaning sideways again to spit. He had a huge purple birthmark in the shape of a hand on his left thigh. "Thirty-one."

More people came down the bank and settled into the shade. Sorren drew her legs up and put her head on her knees. A girl in a ragged shirt said, "I think they'll go west."

"East," said someone else.

"South, into the mist." They argued desultorily. Someone passed a waterskin; it landed in Sorren's hands, and she drank gratefully. The strong smell of unwashed bodies was making her queasy. She wished she could get higher. Kadra would never see her here; never know. She wondered where Norres was. Suddenly, a shiver went through the little crowd, and everyone stood up. Sorren craned her neck like a seabird, as people around her went "Aah!"

"I see Jemmy!" cried the girl in the ragged shirt. She waved both hands frantically.

"There she rides!"

"She's lifting!"

The lines linking the ships tightened. The rowers in the small boats strained at their oars. The work crew began to walk backward, pulling the propping timbers from the big ship's sides. . . . Suddenly, with a great shudder and a jet of spray, *Ilnalamaré* slid into the ocean. The yellow-sailed fishing boats blew their conches again, and the muddy hollow beneath the boardwalk struts resounded to cheers.

A small boat cleaved to the white ship's side. A rope dangled from the larger ship's deck down to the small one. A figure in blue caught it and climbed it, hand over hand. Sails blossomed from the spars; they, too, with blue, a deep indigo, nearly purple. The fisherman beside Sorren said, "Them'll fade. Two months in the sun and salt and they be the color of wheat."

"Kadra," whispered Sorren. "Safe journey—" The words stuck. There was a great surge forward, as people ran toward the hole where the ship had been to pick up bits of wood, scraps of sailcloth, nails, pieces of net, anything from the ship before it, too, floated out on the tide. Sorren stayed where she was. The east wind bellied the sails and she saw the white ship turn to catch the breeze. She glimpsed a carving on the bow; it was a great-beaked bird, like the Eagle, fierce and strong and powerful enough to fly day and night across the world. She hoped it would be strong enough to guide the ship to land, and then to turn around and bring it safely home.

"Good-bye," she said, more to the ship than to her friend. She had already said farewell to Kadra. Recalling the ghya's instructions, she turned her back on the scrambling people and climbed the bank to the street. When she turned once more to look at the ship, it had grown noticeably smaller. She saw the guard who had let her go onto the beach, and waved her thanks at him.

The inn's new door was propped back with a stone, leaving the common room open to the sun. She stepped inside. The room was empty. "Hello?" she called. Nothing answered. She called again. The kitchen door slid back. Norres stood there.

"Oh," she said, "it's you. She said you would come."

Her voice was dull, and her face was gaunt. Sorren wondered if she was sick. "Are you all right?" she said.

Norres ignored the question. She pointed behind her. "Through that door," she said, "in the storeroom through the kitchen. She's there."

"Who's there?" said Sorren.

"Kadra."

Sorren blinked. "What?"

"Go look yourself," said Norres. Slowly, Sorren walked past her, into the kitchen. A girl scrubbing an oven did not even glance up as she walked by. The kitchen smelled of grease and fish. Dried herbs dangled from the roof beams. Sorren looked for a storeroom, and saw a door standing half ajar in the rear of the kitchen. She went to it. Pushing the door open the whole way, she stepped into a dim and musty room.

She thought it was a storeroom; it had shelves and bins and

tall jars standing about on the floor. It was lighted by one netted window. In the light, she saw a pallet, raised off the floor slightly, and a human form on the pallet, covered by a sheet. She went to it. The face was not covered. It was Kadra.

"But—she was going on the ship," Sorren whispered.

"That one was never going on the ship," said Norres from the door. "*You* heard the cough. The drink and the fighting and the sleeping in the road and on the beach killed that one, just as it was supposed to. I said, Come sleep in the inn. '*No.*' Come sleep in my house. '*No.*' So I learned not to ask. The ship—the ship was a dream, girl. Maybe you believed it. That one never did. Here." She walked to a shelf. "These things are for you. That one said I was to see that you got them."

Sorren said, "When did she die?"

"This morning, before dawn. Hurry up, take your leave. I'll make the grave when you go." She left abruptly. Sorren stepped closer to the bed. Kadra looked peaceful. Sorren wondered where Norres would bury her. You were supposed to tell a magistrate when someone died, so that they could come and examine the body and make sure the person had not died of plague.

"I thought—" Sorren stopped, and swallowed. Why was she speaking to the dead? She looked down at the corpse's face. The skin was beginning to lose its moisture, it was stretched tight over the bones, and the room smelled strange. Sorren reached out and laid her fingers lightly on the yellowish lips. The sheet hung loosely over the body. It was just a body now, the soul was gone, wandering wherever souls went. Soon the wrappers would come and wrap the body in strips of coarse linen and put it in the earth. Sorren slid her hand to the sheet. What if she rolled it back? No one was there to watch her. She had never seen Kadra naked in life. She would never get another chance to discover what made a person a ghya.

As she stood there, the tears spilled. She lifted her hand. "Damn you!" she cried. The earthen walls absorbed her shout and did not even give back an echo. "Why?" The dead ghya's chin jutted at her. A thread round her head held her jaw closed. She could not say in death what she had chosen not to say in life. Sorren lifted her hand and rubbed her eyes till they smarted. "Go with the ship," she said to the dead. Perhaps the soul lingered, and would hear her. "Go with the ship, and bring it home."

She went to the shelf Norres had pointed out at her. A

leather case lay on it, like a flute case, but much longer. She opened it. Her bow and ten arrows lay inside it. Beside the case was the silver flask, and the curved knife, and, folded small, the patched and ragged messenger's cloak.

She took the bow case from the shelf. The leather was supple as cloth and inlaid with a design of flowers. She hesitated, and then picked up the sheathed knife and the flask. Lifting the cloak from the shelf, she shook it out and wrapped flask and knife within it. No one would stop her for the cloak. If some guard asked her what was in the case, she would say she was carrying it to the hill for Paxe.

Cradling the cloak and case in her arms, she walked into the common room, leaving the door as she had found it.

Norres was swabbing the tables. She saw Sorren and nodded. "That one said you were going north," she said. "I wish you safe journey."

"Thank you," said Sorren. She hesitated, and then walked to the street. The wind rattled the pebbles over the cobblestones. She looked toward the ocean—the ship was there, sailing south, small now as a child's toy.

As she passed the courtyard in front of the house, she saw that Marti Hok's litter had vanished. Another litter, with blue and red streamers on the poles, sat in the dust of the street. The gate guard was peeling a kava fruit. The green rind curled around his forearm like Tani's tame snake.

She went to him. "Whose litter is that?" she asked.

"Myra Ishem Med's," he answered. "She's seeing her husband."

"Is the Yardmaster about?"

"In her cottage. Captain Ivor's got the watch command." He had the over-bright gaze of a man who has been awake too long. Sorren wondered if they all looked like that. She flexed her fingers and walked toward the cottage, hoping that Paxe was asleep.

She pushed the cottage door open very softly. The sunlight gleamed on the straw. The cushions lay in ordered piles. Beside the chest an oily rag lay where Paxe had dropped it. Sorren put the cloak and the bow-case down beside it. She heard a thump from the kitchen, and the one-eyed cat sauntered into the room and came to rub its head against her leg. She stroked it, listening. After a while, she heard Paxe breathing, and the soft interruption of a snore.

She wanted to tell Paxe about Kadra—but not now; not yet.

She gave the cat's head one last caress. Carefully, she left the cottage. She went into the house through the kitchen door. The cook was there alone. "Here," he said as she passed him, and held out a piece of kava fruit. She ate it absently, leaning on the cutting board. Litter bells jangled faintly from the front of the house, and she went to the corridor to see who it was. The front door opened and she heard a woman's voice and then the sound of Marti Hok's cane. She stayed in the doorway to listen as the old woman moved down the hall.

She finished the slice of fruit and wiped her hands on a rag. As she passed the study she saw Marti Hok give Arré a paper. She slowed her step to listen.

"Kim signed it without an argument," said the old woman. "Something has changed that man; he looks defeated. Boras was outraged—mostly that I would dare to wake him before noon. Cha Minto did not want to see me. When I told him what had happened, he wept. His tears, at least, are on the document. I brought one copy to the Black Clan and told the scribes I wanted copies enough to post in every district, by sunset."

So others had wept for Isak too, Sorren thought. The stairs creaked as she went up them and she remembered sitting in the thick darkness on the top step, weeping, drumming her practice rhythms over and over again.

Ron Ismenin arrived at the Med house at the first hour before noon. He came on foot, not in a litter. Arré had given orders that he be shown to the small parlor, where she and Marti awaited him. Lalith announced him, and he entered the chamber with long impatient strides, as if he were walking across a street.

Arré clasped her hands in her lap. She always forgot how fair the Ismeninas were. Ron Ismenin was as light-skinned as Sorren. He was dressed in his house colors, gold and gray, and he wore a huge gold ring on his right hand. He looked wary and annoyed.

"Ladies," he said curtly, inclining his head in the bow of equals. He glanced around for a chair, saw none, and frowned. "I hope this is important; I have work to do. I do not appreciate receiving invitations that sound like orders."

Arré said, "It is important, and you didn't have to come, you know."

Stiffly, he said, "I assumed this was Council business."

"Part of it is," Arré said. Her eyes felt gummy, and her mouth was thick as felt. Marti sat like a statue in her chair. Only her eyes shone. "You must excuse my shortness. Last night, four men entered this house and tried to kill me."

Ron Ismenin's long jaw dropped. "What?" His light blue eyes did not meet hers. Arré watched his gaze skitter from one corner of the room to the other. He coughed to clear his throat. "I'm glad to see that they did not succeed."

Arré thought coldly, He's no actor. "You don't ask who they were," she said.

"Who were they?"

"Thugs," said Arré, "hired by my brother, Isak. One of them is in prison; the others are dead. My brother is in captivity, and the Council has ordered him exiled from the city. The sentence will be carried out at sunset. I thought you might want to know before the notices go up on the street corners."

Ron Ismenin's face paled so that his freckles seemed to burn. "That's—that's dreadful," he muttered.

"Which," said Marti Hok softly, "is more dreadful: the attempt on Arré's life or Isak Med's banishment?"

"The attempted killing, of course." Again he looked for a chair. "I—I cannot quite believe it."

Arré said evenly, "You are a liar, Ron Ismenin. You knew about it."

He took a step backward. "You're mad!" he said. "How would I know of such a thing?"

Arré ticked the sentences off her fingers. "One. You gave Isak the money with which he paid the assassins; he says so. Two. You were seen in the park last night. Three. One of the killers was the juggler who entertained at your brother's betrothal feast. Four. Another used a sword made in the Ismenin smithies, brought to the city by *your* contrivance. All the evidence points to you."

Ron Ismenin swallowed, and his throat moved beneath the collar. "You cannot prove I knew about the act," he whispered. "I didn't." His voice rose. "I didn't!"

He is a coward, Arré thought. She wondered if Tarn Ryth knew it. She rang the bell, gazing at him, and did not trouble to hide her contempt. Lalith came to the door. "Tell Toli to bring another chair."

The kitchen apprentice staggered through the doorway with one of the parlor armchairs, and set it beside Ron Ismenin.

"You may sit," said Marti Hok.

Slowly, Ron sat. He was fighting visibly to regain his composure. He took a deep breath, and blew it out. "I cannot believe you mean to outlaw your own brother, Arré Med."

Fool, Arré thought. "It's done."

The color had come back to Ron's cheeks. "It must be convenient to have the Council in your pocket," he said. "But I do not think you will find it easy to do the same to me."

Arré made her voice languid, though her muscles were tense as steel. "I would not try. The Councillors agree that you are something of a fool, to let Isak play you like a drum, but we prefer dealing with you to dealing with your younger brothers."

He scowled at the insult, but Arré saw his shoulders relax. "Did you invite me here to tell me what you are not going to do?"

As if in counterpoint to the question, the sound of the flute floated through the doorway. *I am a stranger in an outland country; I am an exile wherever I go....* Arré shivered. She would never be able to hear that song without thinking of Isak. Sweat rolled down her temples, and the sun glinted off the glass of the scroll case into her eyes. She moved her head. "Do you gamble, Ron Ismenin?" she said.

His eyes narrowed suspiciously. "I'm not a gamester," he answered.

"But you've been known to place a bet," Arré said.

"Yes."

"Has it ever occurred to you that politics is like a game?" She saw him stiffen. "No."

"Then think on it," Arré said. She leaned forward. Out of the corner of her eye, she saw Marti Hok nod slightly. "It *is* like a game, Ron Ismenin, and the stake in this game is power. But this game is complex, and in it you have already made two major errors. Twenty-three lives were lost this year because of your ambition. You are a tool, Ismenin. You have been used by my brother, by Jerrin-no-Dovria i Elath, even by Tarn Ryth. You know little about politics and nothing about power." His face had gone chalk white with rage. Arré smiled. "You are angry now. But I assure you, I speak truth. It is only because you have lost your stake, and are not now a danger, that you are here, and not in prison. Do you wish to keep what you have, Ismenin? Then leave the game. A smart gambler knows when to pull his bones from the pot."

Ron Ismenin glared at her. "That's street talk," he said.

"So it is," Arré agreed. "The choice is yours, my lord. Pull, or go hungry."

His chest heaved as he looked from Arré to Marti. Finally he rose. "I pull," he said, and whirling, went through the door, nearly knocking the screen from its track. Arré exhaled. She was dizzy from tension.

Then she said, "Did I do well?"

Marti Hok smiled, and picked up her teacup from the lacquer table. "My dear, your mother could not have done it better," she said. "You did better than 'well.' You were magnificent."

At sunset, Paxe took Isak Med to the Northwest Gate.

She did not have to; Kaleb had made it very clear that he would gladly execute the exile order. But Paxe had insisted that he wake her. He came upstairs to do so. From the bedroom doorway he called her name, but she had already heard him and started to rise. Her arm pained her and she grimaced as she leaned on it.

Kaleb stepped forward. "Let me look at it."

She shook her head. "It's all right."

He scowled at her. "Stubborn woman. You're not twenty now, you know."

"Cook sewed it. Let it be." She swung the arm, testing its range of motion. It hurt but that was to be expected, and the hurt was clean, with none of the unpleasant dry burning that would mean the wound was infected.

Through her window, she could see the lavender sky; it was streaked with orange like a summer rose. The moon, with just an edge dulled, swept blazing out of the sea. "How is he?" Paxe asked. "Have you seen him?"

"The prisoner, you mean? He's fine. His wife brought him some gold, and Arré Med said to let him keep it."

"Are the notices up?"

Kaleb shook his head. "Not yet."

Paxe went to the basin and splashed her face with the tepid water. Then she looked through her chest for a shirt without insignia. "Does the Gate Captain know we're coming?" she said.

"Yes. There'll be no questions asked." Kaleb was edgy; Paxe could see it in the restless way his hands moved.

As they went downstairs, she said to his back, "What's the matter?"

He flicked a dark look up at her without missing a step. "I don't understand why we're doing this," he said.

"Doing what?"

"Letting him live," said the Asech. "If it were my decision—"

"But it isn't," Paxe said. "Nor mine, either. It's Arré Med's."

She understood what Kaleb was feeling about Isak. The Asech tribes were organized around family; such treachery as Isak had shown toward Arré was only handled one way according to the desert codes. She remembered Isak's sleek, feigned horror as she woke him from sleep in the early morning and a part of her, too, wished for his death. But killing was not the way. She imagined Jerrin-no-Dovria i Elath saying it in his persuasive, resonant voice. Listening to him make the Invocation to the Guardian at the Festival, she had felt sorrow and a stinging contempt. What happened, she wondered, after the body's death, to the soul of one who so perverted the chea?

She went by the chest, and stopped. A gray bundle and a leather case lay beside it. Kneeling, she pulled the case flap open. Inside it was an unstrung bow and a cluster of arrows.

"Turning archer?" Kaleb said.

She closed the case and rose. "No."

They went down the hill to the guardpost. The guard at the jail snapped rigid when she saw them. "Yardmaster. Commander."

"How's your captive?" Paxe said, taking the jail key from the woman's hand.

"Very quiet. His wife was here earlier, but she's gone now."

Paxe inserted the key in the lock and turned it. It made a grating noise, the door opened, and the smell of old wine, shit, and vomit leaked out.

Deliberately, Paxe had put Isak in one of the small cells which were attached to each guardpost. The buildings were no more than brick sheds. They were not designed for comfort; they had no water and no light. For a chamber pot there was a hole in the earthen floor. Straw and a coarse blanket made the only bed.

"Out," said Paxe.

Isak came out, squinting. His face looked pinched and tired. Paxe wondered if he had rested.

"Good evening, Yardmaster," he said.

His voice was flat; the bravado gone. Paxe tossed the key

to her guard, who shut the door. "Give him his money," she said.

Kaleb pulled a small pouch from his belt. From the way he handled it, Paxe saw that it was heavy. Isak brought both hands up to take it. He had no choice; they were linked together by a loose rope around both elbows and a tight one around both wrists.

"Thank you," he said. He glanced at his hands. "Could I be freed now?"

"At the Gate," said Paxe.

She glanced at Kaleb, expecting him to leave. He didn't move. "Commander," she said, "I don't want to keep you from your duties."

His face was impassive. "I'm coming with you."

Paxe stiffened. "Kaleb—"

Quietly, he shook his head. Isak, missing nothing, chuckled. Imrath, the late watch guard, was studiously looking the other way.

Paxe found her fists tightening. Pain ran like a flame up her injured arm. She swore and relaxed her hands. The pain faded to an ache. She gripped Isak's arm with her right hand. "Walk," she said. Obediently, he moved. They walked north, arm in arm, as close as lovers; Paxe could smell the stench of the jail on Isak's clothes. Noiseless as ever, Kaleb paced on Isak's right. After a while, Paxe grinned at him.

"I could order you beaten for insubordination," she said.

He smiled. "You won't," he said. "I'm a watch commander. Besides—who would you get to do it?"

A chestnut vendor swaggered past them, and the smell of roasting nuts filled the air. Isak sniffed. "I shall miss that," he said.

Paxe frowned. She wanted to tell him not to talk. But that seemed cruel.

The traffic thickened; they were coming to the Gate. Paxe had never realized how short a walk it was. A runner weaved between the carts, his arms filled with paper, and she wondered if he carried the exile order. Behind them, the sun still lingered, but ahead of them the sky had darkened to blue. The traffic flowed inward, as people from outside the city pushed to get inside before the Gate closed.

Paxe could feel Isak's tension through her grip on his arm. He was looking from side to side. Was he looking for someone?

she thought. Some accomplice, who might help him? But as she watched his head turn, she decided, no, he was not looking for anyone. He was looking at the city.

"Yardmaster," he said abruptly. "Please. Can we stop?"

"Why?" said Kaleb sharply.

But Paxe halted. "You hold him," she said. Kaleb caught Isak's right arm. She flexed her fingers. Isak looked at the crowd. A tall Asech woman led a string of goats through the Gate; she caught sight of Kaleb and shouted something in the Asech tongue.

He called back in the same language, and the woman grinned. "You know her?" Isak said.

"We're of the same tribe," answered Kaleb.

A pack of children chased each other around the side of the guardhouse. Isak squared his shoulders. "Yardmaster," he said, in the same abrupt tone, "would you carry a message for me, to Sorren?"

Paxe took hold of his arm again to start them walking. "That depends," she said.

"Oh, she'll want to hear it," said the dancer. "Tell her I'm sorry she was part of this. And tell her she's a much better drummer than Itaka."

Paxe nodded. "And to your sister?" she said suddenly.

Isak smiled sardonically. "I have nothing to say to Arré Med that was not said last night."

"I see," said Paxe.

Kaleb muttered something under his breath.

They were nearly to the gatehouse. The guards were letting the last few travelers through. The Gate Captain saw them and pointed to the little Gate. It stood a slight distance from the main entrance and was not strictly a Gate at all, but a door, wide enough for one person, much too narrow for a horse or cart.

Decades ago, the city had used the little passage to send scouts into territory held by the Asech. Before Paxe's time, it had fallen into disuse, and it hinges had been allowed to rust. Paxe's predecessor Kemmeth had ordered it repaired, and by Paxe's order the hinges were kept oiled. It even had its own grate which the guards lowered every once in a while for cleaning, though normally it remained up.

"Good idea," Paxe said to Kaleb. "Yours?" He raised one shoulder in the Asech gesture of embarrassment. A guard detached himself from the main Gate and strode to the little entrance. Kaleb joined him; together they pulled the door inward and propped it open with a stone, just wide enough for a slender man to slide through.

Outside the wall lay the caravans of the folk who had come too late to enter the city. Cooking smells rose from braziers and campfires. A band of gray cloud patterned the horizon, and above it the northern stars glittered. Isak's breathing grew swift and shallow as he gazed into the darkness.

"Loose him," Paxe said.

Kaleb bent, and came upright holding his knife. He sliced through Isak's ropes with an upward cutting motion. They fell to the dirt. Isak rubbed his hands. "That's better." He put the pouch of gold in his pocket. At their backs, the assayers were closing their tables. The wind shifted, bringing them the scent of the stables; Paxe heard the high wailing of the lamplighters' calls.

In the mingled torch and moonlight, Isak's face was pale and determined. He drew his shirt collar around his neck. Then, as if he were about to perform, he loosed his hair. It fell about his shoulders in a black cloud. "Good evening, Captains," he said, and the lilt was back in his voice. He gazed at the starry sky. "It's a fine night for walking."

In three long gliding strides, he was through the door. Bending, Kaleb put his knife in his boot sheath. The guard kicked the stone from the door and shut it.

Paxe shivered. Kaleb linked his left arm through her good one, and they leaned together in the darkness. After a while, she rested her head against his. "It's a fine night for walking," she said. "Let's go home."

Sorren woke late.

The smell of food, rising up the stairs from the kitchen, made her stomach growl. She sat up slowly. She could not remember falling asleep. She had dreamed, but, staring at the dark behind the silk-flecked windows, she could not recall them. Her clothes were sticky; she wriggled out of them and found fresh ones in the darkness. She wondered who else was awake in the house. It was odd to be dressing, combing her hair, sniffing food: so much had happened in one day that she felt as if everything should be changed.

Her hand encountered the box of Cards beside the bed. She

touched it, wondering. Somewhere in the pattern of the Cards, were she to lay it out, was everything that had happened since sunrise of the day before; the Festival, Isak's treachery, Paxe's wounding, the edict of banishment. Where would he go? She rubbed one finger along the box's corner. Even Kadra's death and the launching of the ship might be somewhere in the Cards.

In the kitchen, she found the cook playing the pebble game with Kaleb. It was late watch; she wondered what he was doing there. Perhaps he had come in for warmth. Toli was carving a goose under the cook's watchful eye. "Slugabed," he said to her.

"Shut up," said the cook, moving a pebble. "We're all tired."

Sorren wanted to ask Kaleb about Isak. Instead, she said to Toli, "Is Marti Hok still here?"

He shook his head. "She went home. But the Yardmaster's in the study." He smirked at her.

"Oh."

Kaleb moved a pebble and took four of the cook's stones off the board. "Game," he said. "Sorren, the Yardmaster has a message for you."

"For me?" Sorren snatched a piece of goose from under Toli's knife. "Thank you." Nibbling bits of goose, she loped to the study.

The door was closed. Before knocking, she licked the juice from her fingers. She tapped on the study door; Arré called, "Come in!" She pushed the screen to one side and entered. The room was warm; the porcelain lamps on the mantel were lit, and by their light she saw Arré in her armchair, and Paxe, booted feet stretching across the floor. A teapot stood between them on the lacquered table.

Paxe looked rested; there was a clean bandage on her arm. She tilted her head as Sorren came in, and smiled. But the smile was odd. Sorren tensed. "Yardmaster," she said, "K-K-Kaleb—Captain Kaleb—said you had a message for me."

Arré held out her hand. "Come here, child," she said. She patted the side of her chair. Sorren curled up with her legs crossed. "Do you know that you are still wearing my bracelet?"

Sorren looked at her own wrists with astonishment. There was no bracelet—"Oh." She ran her right hand up over her left elbow. She had pushed the silver bracelet up against the other, and forgotten it. She started to take it off.

"No," Arré said, "keep it. I want you to have it. It's a gift."

"But—" Sorren looked from Arré to Paxe.

Paxe said softly, "Keep it."

Sorren slid the bracelet down to her wrist and stared at it. Its thick silver was tarnished with wear. The blue stone gleamed in its setting. "Thank you," she said. She rubbed the stone with the ball of her thumb.

Arré said suddenly, "Isak's gone, Sorren. Paxe took him to the Gate at sunset. He's now an outlaw in the city."

Sorren swallowed. "Forever?"

"Forever," said Arré.

"Alone?"

"Alone. He did not want company. Myra said farewell to him. I let her give him gold."

Sorren shuddered. It seemed cruel to thrust someone outside the city, just like that. But then she remembered the men on the stair, and Elith. "Where will he go?" she said. "North?"

Paxe stirred in her chair.

Arré shrugged. "East, perhaps, to Shirasai. Or that may be what he wanted me to think. I don't know. I have written a letter to Tarn Ryth of Nuath, letting him know of the exile order and asking him to keep watch. If Isak is seen around Nuath, I shall hear about it." She leaned her head back.

Lalith came to the door. "Lady, do you want your meal now?" she said.

"In a moment," Arré said. "I'll ring." Lalith bowed and withdrew.

Paxe cleared her throat. "Isak asked me to give you a message."

The hairs on the back of Sorren's neck curled.

"He said to tell you, He's sorry you were part of this, and that you are a much better drummer than Itaka."

Sorren bit her lip. "That was kind of him," she said. She wondered if he had sent Arré a message too.

There was a little silence. It was broken by the sound of Toli's flute, running up and down the scales. Arré said, in a voice from which warmth had fled, "Sorren, go and stop him. I don't want music."

Sorren leaped up. Racing down the hall, she skidded into the kitchen, avoiding the cook's elbow by a hairsbreadth. She yanked the flute from Toli's lips.

"Hey!" he said. "What are you doing?"

"Arré said to stop you. She doesn't want to hear music."

He looked hurt. "She's never said so before," he grumbled, but the cook frowned with such ferocity that he winced, and grabbed for the instrument's velvet case. "Tell her the goose is drying," he warned. The smell of it made Sorren's stomach sizzle. Sneaking a hand under the cloth that covered it, she stole a second piece and ate it on the way back to the study.

Crossing the room, she saw herself reflected in the scroll case: a ghostly figure superimposed over the landscape of chairs and tables and tapestries. The tension in the room was stronger than ever. Was Arré angry at her? She could not think what she had done. Troubled, she returned to her place by Arré's chair. The lamplight touched the older woman's hair with silver. In the other chair, Paxe was nearly invisible, eyes closed, a dark and brooding shadow.

Arré put her hand on Sorren's left shoulder. Then she let it slide to the bonding bracelet, and fumbled with the catch. It sprang open; the bracelet fell off. It clattered on the floor. Arré said, "Sorren of the vineyards, I hereby release you from your service to me. You are no longer bound to me or to my house. Your time of service is over. You are free to go."

Free—what was free? Sorren could not speak. She stared at the bonding bracelet. Reaching out, she picked it up, turning it between her hands. The red and blue triangles shimmered. She flipped the catch with her finger. It looked broken.

"Why?" she said.

"Because it's time," said Arré. She leaned forward. "You are welcome to remain in my service, if you wish—but as paid servant, not as bondservant. There is money waiting for you. Or you may go to the vineyards. I will give you a horse."

Sorren touched the pale ring of flesh on her upper arm. "I can't ride," she said. She looked at Paxe. The Yardmaster's eyes were open. "I don't want to go to the vineyards."

Closing her eyes, she saw before her the map that Kadra had made her, with the line of her journey laid out. At the end of it was Tornor. She could no more not go there than she could cease to dream, or to speak, or to love. Rising, she went to Paxe, and knelt beside her chair. The Yardmaster leaned over her; her eyes glittered with unshed tears. Sorren put her hand out; Paxe clasped it and brought it to her lips. Her breath was warm. "Chelito." Gently, she laid her other hand on Sorren's hair.

Sorren leaned against her, careful of the bandaged arm. She said, "Will you come with me to the mountains?"

Arré stirred, and did not speak. She looked away from Paxe.

Paxe said, "I made my trip to the mountains years ago, chelito." She looked over Sorren's head at Arré. "I will miss you, with every breath I draw. But—my son is here; my responsibilities are here; my friends are here. I don't want to leave Kendra-on-the-Delta." The lamplight illuminated the curve of her face. "My journey is made; yours is beginning. This is your starting place. But this is *my* home."

CHAPTER TWENTY-THREE

The city walls were behind her now.

The bright autumn sunlight cast her shadow to the left. Tall one, small one, Sorren thought, looking from her own laden shadow to the smaller one of Jenith. Through the hanging branches of the willow trees, the river glistened to her right. The bargefolk were out on the river—she could hear them, exchanging stories, news, greetings. On the other side of the river lay the cotton fields, white with bolls still. The pickers moved through them, carrying their sacks. Sorren wondered if they had heard the news about Isak Med.

She shifted the pack straps on her shoulders. Her bow case and arrows bumped at her right hip. It was three days since Isak's exile. Myra Ishem Med was still in Kendra-on-the-Delta. Sorren remembered the rumors she had heard, that Isak Med, despite the exile order, was still in the city. But she knew it was not true. She wondered where he was. It was strange to think of him as just another traveler, somewhere on the roads. When she thought of Elith, she still grew angry at him. But when she thought of him, Isak the dancer, her feelings of anger faded, giving place, even now, to admiration and sorrow and to still another emotion which, she realized, was simple pity.

"Hungry yet?" said Jenith.

"No. Are you?"

"No." Jenith whistled softly. Arré had asked her to carry word of Isak's banishment to the vineyards, and Jenith had assented happily for the chance to see her daughters. She strolled at Sorren's side, a small pack slung from her shoulder, seemingly tireless.

Sorren recalled the moment she had walked through the Northwest Gate. She had expected it to feel portentous. But it had not. Stealthily she glanced back over her shoulder, but there were too many carts and horses and travelers on the road. All she could see between her and the city was dust.

She thought of Paxe, and a little pain thudded in her heart. They had said farewell that night. Paxe would not come to the Gate with her; she did not want to make a spectacle of herself before her soldiers. "Besides," she said into Sorren's hair, "I hate prolonged good-byes." Her parting gift to Sorren had been practical: ten hunting arrows with broadhead points. Arré's gift had been similarly useful: she had given Sorren boots. She had said farewell that morning almost casually. At the last minute, she held out a letter and asked Sorren to deliver it to Tarn Ryth of Nuath.

"If you don't go to Nuath," she said, "give it to a caravan going north." But when she turned away, Sorren saw the glitter of tears on her cheeks.

Seven Asech riders trotted past them. One of them saw Jenith and called a greeting in the Asech tongue. She said something back, and they laughed.

Sorren said, "Do you mind very much not riding?"

Jenith shrugged. "Arré Med asked me to walk, so I walk. Don't concern yourself."

At midday, they halted by the roadside. The grass was dry and fragrant. Jenith drank from her waterskin and leaned back, looking as fresh as she had at sunrise. Sorren sat heavily, grateful for the pause. Her stomach fizzed, warning her that it needed attention, and she drew the sticks of jerky from her pack.

Her fingers slid over the cool hardness of the flask. She thought of Kadra. She wondered where the *Ilnalamaré* was now. "Have you ever been on the ocean?" she said to Jenith.

The Asech woman shuddered. "No, and I don't want to," she said, grimacing. "It moves too much. I like surfaces that stay put beneath me." Her brown hand reached out and eloquently patted the dry brown earth.

A woman rode by on a small red mare. The turn of her head made Sorren think of Paxe. She wondered what the Yardmaster was doing now. Sleeping, perhaps, in the yard low bed, the one-eyed cat beside her. Or teaching in the Yard. . . . The thrust of memory was like a physical pain. Sorren wound her fingers in a grass stem and pulled, hard. The tall stem gave and she tumbled back onto her elbow.

"We should go," Jenith said.

They walked. Sorren's legs began to ache. Her feet felt fine; she had spent the last two days tramping about the city, breaking in the boots. But her calves ached. She closed her mind to the hurt and concentrated on the sights and sounds and smells of the road: the caravans passing, the barns and fields, the hot sweet smells of harvest, the cicadas hidden in the grasses, singing. Jenith glided smoothly beside her, hands at her sides, a straw between her teeth. "When were you last in the grapefields?" the Asech woman asked.

"When my mother died, four years ago," Sorren said. "Why—is it different?"

Jenith shook her head. The rings in her ears caught the light and glittered. "Naw," she said. "It'll never change."

It was the smell Sorren remembered first: the strong, heady smell of the grapes. She sniffed. "I think—we're close, aren't we?"

"We're there," said Jenith. She pointed her chin toward the west. "You know a grapevine when you see it?" Sorren squinted into the reddening sunlight. She saw deep furrows and tall green plants wrapped about wooden trellises. The plants were set in the rows at an angle to the road, and she remembered—how had she remembered it, after all these years of absence?—that the grapes were sweetest when they caught the full strength of the southwest light.

Jenith pointed across the field to a peaked roof half hidden by vine leaves. "That's a treading shed," she commented.

Sorren shifted her pack. "Is this all Med land?"

Jenith spread her hands; the Asech way of nodding.

At a gap between the furrows, they turned from the road. "Where are we going?" Sorren said.

"To find my daughters," said Jenith. "They'll be with the work crew." Sorren gazed over the silent fields. As far as she could see, there were vines.

She followed Jenith through the maze of furrows and ditches. Beneath her boots, the earth was crumbly. The grapevines brushed her chin. She forced her mind back, trying to remember back seven years, to a time when she had been much smaller.... I was smaller than the vines, she thought. Dimly she recalled tugging at weed stalks. She had worn a straw hat— her hand touched her hair—a straw hat with a blue band on it!

"There's the house," Jenith said.

Sorren saw the gleam of cedar planks in the distance. Isak's house, she thought, and corrected herself; it was not Isak's any longer. Suddenly she stiffened, listening. *Pah-pah, pah-dum-pah*. The drum sounds spoke into the sunset. *Pah-pah-dum*. Her fingers tapped the rhythm on her thigh. It was the pickers' drums, spreading the news of their arrival.

"They'll be waitin' for us," Jenith said. She pointed. "This way now." Sorren followed her, and the drum beats went on, blending with the wind and the sounds of the insects, until Sorren imagined that she could feel the pounding through the soles of her boots.

Suddenly the vines cut off. They were in a pickers' clearing; a small circle of tents and shacks. Smoke from a fire blew in their direction, smelling of roasted corn. People sat around the fire in a semi-circle. Slowly Sorren followed Jenith toward them. The drums had stopped.

"Come on!" That was Jenith, telling her to hurry.

"Coming," Sorren answered. She gazed at the shacks. Dark-skinned people watched her from the narrow doorways. Many of the women had gold rings in their ears. Their faces were secretive, impassive, but Sorren sensed their thoughts as if she had a Truthfinder's skill. . . . Stranger, they said to her. You are a stranger, not one of us.

Defiantly, Sorren squared her shoulders and marched to the fire.

A woman raised a hand. "I am Nado," she said. "Be welcome."

"Thank you," Sorren said, sitting beside Jenith. Even seated, she was taller than anyone in the circle by half a head.

Nado said, "Jenith says you were once of the fields."

Sorren slipped her pack from her shoulders. Drawing up one leg, she dug her knuckles into her aching calf. "I was."

"You were born here?"

"Yes. My mother was a picker. She died four years ago. For the last seven years, I have been bondservant in the city to Arré Med."

Nado clapped her hands softly. "Ai, you are *that* child. I remember. I knew your mother. You like her, but taller."

"You knew her—well?" Sorren leaned forward. It had not occurred to her that anyone in the fields would remember her or her mother.

"No, not well," said Nado. "She was always—different."

Sorren thought, I should ask about the Cards. But then she might have to take them out. She did not want to do that. Suddenly, Jenith leaped to her feet, as voices called out of the furrows.

"Iaah!"

"Yip-yip-yip-yip!" she answered. Two women strode into the clearing. Jenith beamed, and went to meet them. She brought them to the fire. They were brown and sturdy, and they looked like her; the elder was named Jezi, the younger, Aisha. Aisha wore gold rings in her ears, like her mother, but Jezi's left earlobe was missing, and if there was a hole in her right ear, it had closed over. Their shirts had bead circles sewed on the front and sleeves.

"Greetings," they said together, and then laughed, showing white teeth. Aisha made a hand signal.

Jezi said, "I will talk." She grinned. "We would be pleased if you would accept our hospitality for as many nights as you wish to stay with us." Aisha poked her and said something in the Asech speech, and the older sister shook her head, no. "Our tent is not far from here."

"Thank you," Sorren said. "I would like that."

Nado clapped her hands. "Wa'hai," she said. "Now, the meal is ready. We will eat; and after you will tell us your news."

The rest of the pickers gathered around the fire. The food was simple: corn, roasted in the hot earth near the firepit, strips of goat's meat, slabs of melon, wine. There were no plates and no knives with which to eat, and the meat came out of a common pot; you dipped your fingers in and took what you wanted. There was butter for the corn and honey for the melon. Most of the talk around the fire was in the Asech tongue. Jenith sat with her daughters; she looked very pleased with them. Sorren ate slowly. Her legs throbbed, and her eyes were heavy with weariness: it's the traveling, she told herself. All too soon, they were finished with the food.

"Now," said Nado, as around them the picker children scurried, collecting the cobs and gristle to feed the pigs. "What have you to tell us?" And Jenith told them; that Isak Med had paid four men to kill his sister, that he was now an outlaw, that Myra Ishem Med was in Kendra-on-the-Delta and would be returning, in a few more days, to the grapefields.

Sorren did not join in the telling. She had taken her boots off, and sat, yawning. In the darkness, she did not look so much like a stranger, she thought. Jenith waved her hands as she talked. On the other side of the fire, the log drums waited. When the talking was over, they would speak.

"Excuse me," a man's voice said, and a shadow stooped beside her. Automatically Sorren moved over to give the newcomer room.

"Sorren?" he said.

She stared at him. The fireglow bounced off his face. "Ricky?" she said. "It is you?"

"Yes—I hope you don't mind." His voice had deepened. "I won't stay. I heard the drums and thought I'd come to the telling. I didn't know the messenger would be you."

"It isn't. Jenith's the messenger."

He settled beside her. She saw the glint of red in his ears and realized that he had gotten his ears pierced. She waited for him to question her. But he did not; he sat quietly, listening to Jenith weave the story of Isak's treachery.

At last, Jenith fell silent, and folded her hands in her lap. Nado said a few words in the Asech tongue. The pickers moved from the fire, some to their tents, others to the waiting drums.

Ricky said, "Are you going back to the city?"

"No," Sorren said, "I'm going north."

She saw him nod. He seemed leaner, more muscular. He licked his lips, and asked diffidently, "Is my mother well?"

Sorren took a breath. "Yes. Her arm was hurt in the fight, but it's healing."

"What fight?"

"The fight with the assassins. She captured them."

Of course she had to tell him everything.

The telling took longer than she thought it would; when it was done, she could scarcely keep awake. Ricard walked with her to Jenith's daughters' tent. He had changed; the sullenness she had remembered was gone. At the tent entrance, he mumbled something at her, before ducking into the darkness. It sounded like: "Safe journey."

Yawning so hard that her jaws cracked, Sorren went into the tent. It was just big enough for four. Sorren took the gray cloak from her pack, and wedged the pack into a corner. Kneeling, she spread the cloak out, putting a layer of cloth between herself and the ground. Jenith brought out her pipe. She held it up; Sorren shook her head. "I don't need it," she said. "I'm already dreaming."

"Sweet dreams," Jenith said. She said something in the Asech tongue to Aisha, and the younger woman, giggling, brought Sorren a blanket.

"This is enough for me," Sorren said, patting the cloak. But Aisha simply dumped the blanket at her feet and went back to her pallet.

"Thank you," Sorren said. Lying down, she wrapped the

blanket around her and put her head on her boots. A patch of
blue sky glowed in the space between the tent poles, and the
smoke from Jenith's pipe rose toward it in a steady stream.

The drums spoke.

"Are you comfortable?" said Jenith gently.

"Yes," Sorren said, "I'm fine."

Jenith yawned. "I wonder where Isak Med is tonight?" she
said.

She would not think of Isak. . . . Instead, she wondered if
Arré had gone to bed yet. Lalith would have to do for her the
things Sorren was used to doing. The cook would need another
scullion, someone new to keep Toli company. . . . Paxe would
be asleep, perhaps alone, perhaps with someone else. . . . Her
eyes stung. She turned over, back to the sky, and rested her
head on her arm. She could not go back to Kendra-on-the-
Delta now, she thought. There was no place for her to return
to.

In the morning, she thanked Jenith's daughters for their
hospitality. To Jenith she said, "How far is it to Nuath?"

"A week and a half," said the Asech. "Six days to the
Shanan crossroads, and six more to Nuath from there."

The first day was not so bad. She walked on the side of the
road, watching the carts pass. At sunset, she came to Terzi,
but she did not go in; instead, she did as she saw many travelers
doing; she made a stone ring and built a campfire. The pickers
had insisted on giving her food: corn, goat jerky. She sat beside
the fire and ate it, and drank water from the silver flask. She
thought about taking her drums from her pack. But here in the
open the drum sound would be barely noticeable. Realizing
that, she decided to sing. She sang all the love songs she could
remember. She started to sing "I am a stranger" and halted,
thinking of Arré and Isak.

The second day grew more difficult. The fields unrolled in
front of her, featureless as Kadra's map. Carts and horses
clattered by her, raising dust. At midday she finished off the
last of the jerky. The sky was blue, with mushroom puffs of
clouds in the distance, the fields were brown, and no one
seemed to notice her, one small traveler alone on the high-
way. . . . She was bored.

That evening she shot a coney for dinner. She skinned and
gutted it, using Kadra's knife. Frugality made her scrape the

fur clean and tack it down to dry away from the fire; the meat
she sliced, seared, and ate. A berry bush provided her with a
savory dressing. It had only taken her the one shot to kill the
coney, and she was proud of it. It was that pride that made her
take the drums out. *I killed a rabbit,* she pounded. *Pah-pah-
pah-dum-pah.* She made a little song of it, imitating the rabbit's
scurry and the thump of the arrow. Behind her the river sang
its deeper music. At last, she burrowed into a nest in the dry
grass and rolled the cloak about her, listening to the crickets
and the water, wishing she had someone to talk to.

Midday of the third day, she reached Mahita. Her pulse
quickened as she approached it: here was a real town, not a
village. The hubbub outside the Gates drew her. She wanted
to go in.

But there was nothing she needed from the markets. If she
entered Mahita, she would only waste time. Sternly, she forced
herself to skirt the roads that led to the Gates. That night she
slept by the roadside again. Lying wakeful, she watched the
embers of her fire glow, and thought of Kadra. The ghya would
have been proud of the way she had learned to make a fire,
to hunt, to live off the land.

It took her four more days to reach the Shanan crossroads.
When she got there, it was raining. The intersection was really
a small town in itself: it had a stable, a baths, eleven taverns,
and a market where travelers could purchase food and supplies
and even horses. Sorren used some of her money to buy a straw
hat, a parasol, and a string of smoked fish. Past the Shanan
crossroads, the landscape altered. Though the road still went
beside the river, the fields had humped themselves up into
brown hills. Fat sheep grazed on the hillsides, and low stone
walls separated the farmers' fields from each other. Slat-armed
windmills turned on almost every rise.

Her map told her that she would be coming up soon to the
road that led to Elath. As she watched the hawks hunting
through the harvested fields, she wondered: Should she go to
Elath? Should she not go to Elath? She was a witch, one of
them, and a freewoman, no bondservant. They would not keep
her if she chose to leave them. Curiosity stirred in her. She
wondered what the town looked like, who lived in it—only
witches?—what the Tanjo—the *first* Tanjo, Rinti had said—
looked like. She imagined it of stone, twice as big as the one
in Kendra-on-the-Delta. Suppose she went there: how long

would they want her to stay? Two weeks, three weeks, a month. . . . She turned the silver bracelet on her wrist, caught herself doing it, and giggled.

If she stayed in Elath for any length of time, it would be winter in the north, too late to travel. She would have to delay the rest of journey until the spring. She did not want to do that. And anyway—what did Elath have for her? They would turn her into Sorren the aftseer. But she did not want to spend her life traveling through visions of the past; she wanted to go to Tornor.

Senta's voice, saying Tukath's words, spoke in the back of her mind. *One cannot so easily give up a gift.*

Outside Shonet she saw her first armed patrol of soldiers. They rode in a group of six; on their shoulders they bore gold and black badges, and they carried swords in scabbards on their backs. Sorren wondered if they would stop her. If they did, she planned to show them Arré's letter. But they rode past her with barely a glance. Later that day, she passed a second patrol. Their captain, whose helmet bore a gold plume, was listening to the master of a Blue Clan caravan.

As she neared Nuath, the road widened. At one point, it ran beneath an aqueduct. An hour's walk from the city Gates, the traffic clogged. Word filtered back that soldiers had blocked the road. Sorren learned from the comments of the travelers around her that this was a not infrequent occurrence; once or twice a week, the soldiers would stop every traveler on road and ask where each was going and coming from. The rest of the time they seemed content to make only random checks.

When she got to where the soldiers stood, she was holding the letter in her hand. "Name?" asked a fat, mustached man. He reminded her of Borti.

"Sorren-no-Kité."

"Starting point?"

"Kendra-on-the-Delta."

"Destination?"

"Nuath."

"For what purpose?" the soldier droned.

She extended the letter. He was looking beyond her and did not see it. "Business, pleasure, family concerns—"

"This is why," Sorren said, waving the letter under his nose.

"Huh?" He looked at it. His eyes narrowed. "Uh." He stepped back and nudged the guard behind him. They spoke in whispers. The second guard put two fingers in his mouth and whistled a shrill call. A woman wearing a plumed helmet strolled to the wooden barrier. She had light hair, and the yellowish cast of face of one of Anhard blood. At Sorren's back, someone yelled.

"Hey, what's holdin' up the line?"

"Move it!"

The woman in the helmet ignored the shouts. "What is it?" she said. The soldiers showed her the letter. She turned it, looking at the superscription, and then looked at Sorren. "When did you leave Kendra-on-the-Delta?" she said.

"Thirteen days ago," Sorren answered.

She nodded. "Pitor!" she called. Down the row of soldiers, a man turned. "Take this girl to the Lord Tarn Ryth's house."

They put her up behind the soldier. "Wrap your arms around my waist," he said. He was young, with a cheerful smile. He wore a badge on his right shoulder, and an axe at his hip, but no armor and no sword. He rode a chestnut gelding which made small work of the extra weight. "My name's Pitor-no-Ellita." he said.

"Sorren," said Sorren.

"You must be important, hey?" He slanted a look back at her. "Never mind, I'm fishing. Ever been to Nuath before?"

"No," Sorren said.

From the outside, Nuath reminded her of Kendra-on-the-Delta. It was a city, not a town. Dark stone walls made a defensive ring around it. Within the city streets, though, Sorren could see the differences between them. Kendra-on-the-Delta smelled of fish and salt; Nuath smelled of iron and meat and horses. The houses were of stone, not wood, and their windows were thick, opaque glass, not screen. All the soldiers carried swords, and Sorren saw many people openly wearing sheathed knives on their belts.

The people looked different, too. They were taller and broader than the folk of the south. Many of them were fair-skinned, with yellow or russet hair, and Sorren, for the first time in her life, began to feel inconspicuous.

Approaching the lord's house from the front, Sorren wondered for a moment if she had stepped into the past. The house was big and white and it overlooked the river. "Grand, isn't it?" said Pitor, seeing her face. When the great front doors opened, she half expected to see Tokki the steward. But the inside of the Ryth house was nothing like the Ismenin house: bright hanging lamps lit the wide stone halls; fur rugs covered the floor, and the walls were hung with immense pictorial tapestries. Scented braziers warmed the hallway.

A woman in a yellow dress greeted Sorren at the door.

"Welcome to Nuath!" she said. "My name is Widra; I am the steward of the house. The Lord Tarn i Nuath Ryth is occupied now but as soon as he is free, he will see you; meanwhile, he has instructed me to offer you food, clean clothes, and, if you wish, a bath."

"I wish it," Sorren said. Her last bath had been in Kendra-on-the-Delta, and the grease of the journey caked her skin. The woman brought her to an inside chamber; in it was a tub filled with hot water, a table piled with food, and a canopied bed.

"If you need anything, ring the bell, and someone will come," she said. She closed the door. Sorren took her pack off. Stripping, she sighed as she entered the water. A ball of orange-scented soap sat waiting for her. She lay in the wooden tub while the dirt of the road floated from her hair and skin; when she stepped from it, the skin on her fingers was wrinkled and white. She dried herself in a towel bigger than she was, and dressed in the clothes she found lying on the bed. They were practical, traveling clothes; brown quilted pants, a blue wool tunic, light, fur-lined boots.

The food was strange to her southern eyes: there was fish, of course, but there was also much more meat than she was used to, and vegetables that she had never seen before. Experimentally, she picked at them. She had barely cleaned her hands when Widra opened the door. "The Lord Tarn Ryth will see you now," she said. Sorren followed her down a hallway to another chamber, holding her letter. "Go in," said the steward, and Sorren walked in alone to what she realized was Tarn Ryth's study. It was lined with scroll cases, many more than in the Hok library. Tarn Ryth was standing in the center of it, waiting for her. He was bigger than she remembered; with his big curling beard and the gold splendor of his clothing, he looked like more than the lord of a city. Not knowing what else to do, Sorren went to one knee before him, and was astonished when he caught her under the elbow and stood her upright.

His teeth glinted through his massive beard. "We are not so ceremonial yet as you southerners," he said. "You have a letter for me?"

"Yes, my lord," she said, holding it out.

He took it from her hand and ripped the seal with his thumb. "Huh," he said, eyes going across the page. "Ho." His eyes narrowed. At the end of it he grinned. "Do you know what this letter says?" he asked, looking up.

"No, my lord," said Sorren.

"It informs me of Isak Med's exile—and other things. When did you leave Kendra-on-the-Delta?"

"Three days after Isak's banishment, my lord."

"On foot all the way?"

"Yes."

His lips pursed, but he did not ask her why. Instead—"Tell me how Arré Med is," he said. "Was she badly grieved by her brother's action? Is she recovered? Is she well? Has she had aught to do with the L'hel since she wrote to me?"

Answering his questions took several hours. At last, satisfied, he said, "I shall write to her this evening, and send the letter on the morrow. Shall I give her your greeting?"

"That would be very kind of you, my lord."

His deep voice grew gentle. "You love her, do you not."

Sorren nodded.

"She asks me, in this letter, to offer you whatever you need. She says that she looks upon you as the daughter she does not have."

Sorren was silent. Arré had never said that to her, not in words. Finally she said, "My lord, I have money. I will buy what I need in the market."

He snorted. "Will you at least take a horse from my stable?"

"No, my lord. I'm not comfortable on horseback. I would rather walk."

He tugged at his beard. "She said you would say that. But—" he leveled a finger at her—"you will take the clothes you now wear with you, as a gift. You will need them soon; the weather is harsher here than what you are used to. And you will stay in this house tonight. You will be better served here than at some tavern."

Sorren bowed her head. "Thank you, my lord."

"For what purpose do you go north, Sorren?" he asked.

"My—my family came from the north, my lord."

He moved restlessly; the light from the hanging candles glittered off his gilded clothes. "Where in the north?"

She did not want to tell him. "A Keep. Tornor."

"Indeed." His eyes narrowed. "I have had some dealings with the folk at Tornor. They are—independent. But admirable. I wonder: would you take a message to Tornor Keep for me?"

"A letter, my lord?"

"No, not a letter. Simply convey my greetings to the Lady Merith, Tornor's ruler. *And*—" he held up one hand, to emphasize the next part of the message—"my son Dennis' greetings, to her daughter. That is all. Can you remember it?"

"Your greetings to the Lady Merith; your son Dennis' greetings to her daughter," Sorren said.

"Thank you." He touched a bell hanging on a cord. In a moment, Widra appeared at the doorway.

In the market the following morning, Sorren bought an axe, travel furs, a sharpening stone for her knife, and a sliver of lodestone. The purchases took almost a third of the money she had with her. Strolling through the market, she saw a statue of the Guardian. It looked like a soldier, with a helmet on its head, and a carved stone sword at the foot of block, where its feet would be. The image disturbed her, and she went quickly by it.

From Nuath she walked to Yfarra, to Morriton, to Septh. Thrice she was stopped by the patrols. After the third time, she unfolded the stained messengers' cloak from her pack and wore it over her travel furs. To her delight and astonishment, the patrols passed her through without question. In Septh she spent more money, and bought passage to Lake Aruna from the riverfolk clan that poled up and down the river on their long, high-sided barges. They asked her where she was going, and she told them, "North."

"'Ware outlaws," they told her. The word made her think of Isak.

"What outlaws?" she asked, and they explained that lately, in the last few years, bands of outlawed men had started to roam the countryside above Tezera, stealing sheep from the villages, robbing unwary travelers, and raiding the occasional late autumn caravan.

"They won't trouble her," said the second-in-command of the barge, a man named Rok. "She's armed."

"Don't they carry weapons?" Sorren said. The thought of meeting an armed band of robbers frightened her.

But the captain of the barge, a woman named Tovi, shook her head and spat over the side. "Naw. Who'd sell them weapons, when the next day they might come in and cut your throat?"

"They might steal them," Sorren said.

Tovi shook her head. "From where?" she said quietly. "Except for the swords Tarn Ryth's soldiers carry—"

"And our knives—" Rok interjected.

"And our knives," said Tovi—"except for those, there are no weapons left in the north."

Sorren promised to be careful. By Lake Aruna she hunted in the moonlight, and shared her meal with a passing fisherwoman. The land grew marshy and treacherous, even near the road. Geese darkened the air above the marshes, flying in low monotonous circles. With her axe, Sorren cut herself a staff. She kept a wary eye out for outlaws, but saw none. Above Tezera, she traveled for three days with a trader who was going to Zilia Keep. He let her off where the road forked. Her road lay northwest; he was going northeast.

Now she was almost there. The straps of her pack cut into her shoulders, and her calves ached, as they had not since below the Galbareth; for two days she had been walking uphill, through a country strewn with stones. Ahead of her, the mountains cut the sky like knives. The days were short and sullen, and even at noon the sun only rose a little way over the peaks. The crescent moon sat in the west. Sorren trudged over the savannah. Four days back, it had snowed. Sorren had never seen snow, and the shimmering white lamina enchanted her, until she tried to travel through it, and discovered that it was both wet and cold. The next day in the dawnlight she saw her first gray fox. She thought it was a wolf and froze, heart racing, until she saw that it was small with a fox's muzzle and a wide, brush-like tail. A red tongue lolled between its jaws. It stood poised beside a boulder until the wind shifted. The next night the temperature dropped to colder than anything she had ever experienced: she burrowed among fallen pine boughs like an animal, as her breath froze, turned icy, and fell.

Ahead of her stood a cluster of dwarf pines; she planned to stop and rest within its shelter. The night before, she had slept in a woodcutter's hut. He had found her walking and offered her a ride in his wagon. It had been hard for them to understand each other, for she still spoke in the swift accents of the city, and his was a slow, thick speech, buttery and soft. She asked him if he knew where Tornor Keep was, and finally understood his answers to mean that it was one day's journey. He let her stay the night; she slept on the floor, beside his fire. That morning he gave her some strips of dried meat. She left him her rabbit skin, hoping he would find a use for it. The meat was a greater gift than he knew, for she was down to two hunting arrows.

In the shelter of the copse, the wind grew less bitter. Gratefully, Sorren shrugged out of her pack. Feeling in it for the silver flask, she dragged the cork from the top with her teeth and drank a mouthful of water. She took a strip of meat out and chewed it, relishing the taste on her tongue. She smelled her own stink. She wondered what it would be like to bathe again. The last few nights, she had dreamed of hot water, hot food, hot weather. She swallowed, letting a sliver of meat slide down her chilled throat.

Something moved in the pines: a bird, perhaps, or a weasel. Sorren watched curiously, wondering if it would show itself, but it had seen her head lift, and vanished into nest or burrow. She worked her pack onto her shoulders again. She took a breath of the cold, dry air: it smelled of pine, and rock, and silence. Ahead of her, the mountains waited.

Boots crackling on the frostbitten earth, she moved from the copse, narrowing her eyes against the glare.

CHAPTER TWENTY-FOUR

At midday, Sorren came to Tornor.

Stark against the icy landscape, the castle glowered at the day. It was larger than the Tanjo, larger than the Ismenin house. The plain before it was covered with patchy snow and seeded with round, smooth stones, as if a giant had tried to use the barren land to plant a second mountain range.

Sorren picked her way among the stones, staff in hand. The castle enlarged as she drew closer. She saw the gate of the outer wall, broken, and a flag flying from the battlement, showing a red, eight-pointed star on a white field. Tornor. Unfastening the ties of her hood, she pushed it back, ignoring the bitter wind, looking for the stuff of her visions: guards, sheep, the tower. Where was the watchtower? She could not see it. She gazed until her eyes teared.

A fat string of smoke steamed upward from the castle. Grasping her staff, Sorren headed for the wreckage of the gate. She crossed the wooden bridge spanning the frozen river. Its planks were coated with ice, and she had to use her staff. In the center of the bridge she stopped to gaze downward at the river. The ice over it was hard, lumpy, and discolored, but through it Sorren saw the living water running, black and pulsing with life, running the way she had come, through the Tezeran marshes, through Galbareth, past hills and orchards and cotton, into the southern sea.

She moved closer to the gate.

"Halt!" a voice cried.

Sorren stopped moving. Slowly, she scanned the entrance, trying to see the person who'd spoken. A figure rose out of the jumble of stone around the broken gate. As it came nearer, Sorren saw that it was a boy. He was slender, his fair skin reddened by the weather, and his eyes were blue, blue as lapis lazuli, blue as the stone in her bracelet. His hair was a tangled mane. He wore furs with the skin side out. His hands were gloved, and empty.

"Who are you?" he demanded. "Where are you going?"

"My name is Sorren," she said. "I come from the south."

"I can see that," he said. "Your boots are Nuathan. Are you a messenger?"

Sorren thought of the message she carried in her head from Tarn Ryth. "Yes."

"I thought so. Are you alone?"

Sorren grinned, and pointed a thumb at the tracks she had left on the field. "Do you see anyone else?"

He chuckled. "No." He combed his hair with both hands. Sorren wondered how old he was—she guessed eleven or twelve, no older. "Can you use that?" he asked, pointing to her bow.

She nodded. The wind snapped, and she shivered as the warmth began to leave her muscles. "Are you the guard of the castle?" she said.

He grinned in turn, delighted. "Yes! Sometimes," he amended. "Have you seen my sister? She's riding."

"I haven't seen anyone," Sorren said.

"Lauf is with her. Come this way," he said, beckoning. "The gate's up." Sorren followed him, stepping cautiously around the detritus of the broken gate; bits of wood and rusted pieces of iron.

Even doorless, the arch in the outer wall was formidable. "My mother's in the ward," the boy said. He strode toward the inner gate. It was flanked by two small gatehouses. The gate had rusted up, and it reminded Sorren, as she passed beneath it, of a mouth, filled with jagged, iron-tipped teeth.

She followed her small guide into the inner ward. A woman was sweeping the courtyard. The boy loped toward her. "Mother!" He whispered urgently in her ear. She picked up her broom, and stepped around her pile of leaves and dung pats toward Sorren. She was small herself, her body thickened by quilted cottons and a fur vest. She had a broad face, pale skin, pale eyes.

I should speak, Sorren thought. I am the stranger.

"Greetings," said the woman. "Welcome to Tornor Keep."

She had a pleasant, throaty voice. Her hair was long and light brown, and she wore it unbraided, tucked between the back of her vest and her shirt.

"It is an ill season for traveling in the north."

"I know," Sorren said. "When I left the south, it was summer."

"You come from the south?"

Sorren leaned on her staff. "From Kendra-on-the-Delta," she said. The boy's mouth opened in surprise.

"You didn't tell me that!" he said.

"Ryke," said the woman, with gentle reproof, "it is ill-mannered of you not to let her tell her own tale."

The boy blushed berry-red.

"Did you come on foot?" said the woman.

"Mostly," Sorren said. "Sometimes I rode in carts. I've been mostly on foot since Lake Aruna." The wind blew, nudging the pile of leaves.

"And what is your destination?" said the woman.

"Here," Sorren said. "Tornor Keep." She let her eyes look away from her interlocutor to the courtyard. It was empty, empty as a shell when the sea creature has found another home. The banner flapped against the wall with a sound like mourning.

"Few travelers from the south choose to come this far north," the woman said. She leaned her broom against the wall. "Ryke, go tell Meg that we have a guest. And ask Innis to heat some water." The boy nodded and loped away. The woman gazed after him, her face suddenly soft.

She coughed; a harsh sound in the Keep's stillness. "What is your name, traveler?"

"Sorren-no-Kité."

The woman's brows went up. The gesture reminded Sorren of Arré. "Sorren. That is a famous name; famous in Tornor, at least. Forgotten, perhaps, elsewhere. Like Tornor."

Sorren said, "I didn't forget."

"Many have," said the woman gravely. "After, all what is a Keep with naught to guard? There is no garrison here. It's been a long time since the north has held anything that Arun needs, or wants. Though that may change," she added cryptically. "My son said you bear a message."

"Yes," Sorren said. "It is from Tarn Ryth of Nuath, for the Lady Merith." She glanced toward the inner buildings, wondering where in them the Lady of Tornor lived. She pictured her as a small, pale woman, sheltering somewhere behind the thick walls.

The woman smiled. The creases deepened around her eyes. "I am Merith."

Sorren gaped. "I thought you were a servant!"

The Lady of Tornor laughed. "Because I wield a broom? I work here. Everyone works here." She picked up the broom, and Sorren noticed for the first time the ring she wore on her left hand. It was a deep red jewel set in a band of yellow metal, and it looked very old.

Sorren put her palms together, and bowed. "My lady," she said.

Merith coughed again, a wet and tearing sound. It reminded Sorren of Kadra. "Come inside," she said. "Come inside, and you may talk to me. I suppose I must hear your message. I'm curious to know what brings you here from Kendra-on-the-Delta. I'm sure it was not so that you could bear a message from Tarn Ryth."

Staff in hand, Sorren followed the Lady of Tornor across the courtyard. To her left rose dark stone buildings, checkered with shuttered windows. A few of the shutters were ajar. More hung loose, twisting in the wind; scraping the stone. Directly ahead of her rose a hall. To her right lay a well, and another building which, Sorren guessed, had once been a smithy. She could not tell what it was used for now. Beside the smithy there was an open space. The Yard, she thought. No footprints disturbed its dust. Smoke rose from the building to the right of the hall. She stared at the inner wall, wondering how old it was. Kendra-on-the-Delta was older than the Keeps, she knew, but the homes and shops and halls in Kendra-on-the-Delta had been rebuilt a hundred times. Wood rotted or burned; screens tore; bricks crumbled. The walls of Tornor were older than anything left standing in the south.

She sensed the weight of the past in the granite, saw it in the dark, implacable stone. My kin walked here, she thought. They entered the great hall. The windows of the hall were narrow, letting in scant light, but she could see the high arching beams of the ceiling, and the lines of the monstrous hearth, and the tapestries. They were grime-encrusted, weighted with the dirt of centuries: here a horse reared, nostrils flaring; there a man's arm lifted, brandishing a scarcely discernible sword.

A fire bloomed in the hearth. Merith walked toward it, boot heels echoing on the stone floor. In front of the hearth, before the hearthledge, there was a long table. An old man stood beside the table, setting out crockery. His back was twisted, so that one shoulder was higher than the other, and his hands were gnarled and knobby. He looked at the two women from under massive gray eyebrows.

Merith said, "This is Sark, Tornor's steward."

The old man grunted. It might have been a greeting. "That girl is still out," he said in a deep grumble.

Merith's lips tightened.

Sark gazed at Sorren, taking his time. "Where didst tha come from?"

"Kendra-on-the-delta."

"Thou't'll need a wash."

"That's being attended to," said Merith impatiently. "Tell Meg to hurry with the food." The old man snorted. Laying a dish down, he walked toward the kitchen. "You may take your pack off, Sorren," said Merith, sitting on one of the long benches. Sorren leaned her staff against the table and loosened the straps of her pack. She let it slide as she sat. Taking her gloves off, she rubbed her face with both hands. The heat from the fire reached her, making her shiver.

This desolate place was not what she had dreamed of. She had pictured Tornor as a little city, bustling and busy. Closing her eyes, as weariness seeped through her bones, she tried to summon up a dream, any dream. Surely here, in the heart of Tornor, a vision would come. But nothing happened; the reality—the cold, the dirt, the lifelessness—obliterated her link with the past. What am I doing here? Sorren thought. Why did I come here? Painfully, she found herself thinking of Paxe, listening for Paxe's step, waiting to see her come around the corner. . . . But Paxe was not here. Paxe would not be here.

She lifted her head, fighting back tears. Merith was watching her. "I can see that you are tired," said Tornor's ruler.

Sorren nodded without answering. Merith, too, looked tired. Her eyes radiated wrinkles; not the lines of age but the deeper ones of worry and work. She unfastened the vest, and Sorren saw patches on her quilted shirt. The table was seamed with nicks and dents. The plates and dishes were metal, but so discolored that Sorren had to look hard to see that there was a pattern under the tarnish. She traced the relief with her thumbs, and found first an animal—a goat, she thought, since it had horns—and then a hunter, carrying a bow in one hand.

"How old are these?" she asked.

"Two, three hundred years?" said Merith. "I don't know. The records are gone; they were destroyed when the tower fell."

"When did the tower fall? How? Why?"

"It was years ago," said Merith. "Forty years ago, perhaps. I was a child. I was told the wind blew it down. But that cannot have been true. It must have been the cold, cracking the stones."

"What happened to it?"

"The stones were carted to the village, and used for building. The records—" she paused—"many were burned. Some were taken south to be sold. The Scholars' Guild in Tezera bought many."

Remembering the records in Marti Hok's study, Sorren felt a pang of guilt. She told herself not to be a fool. *She* had not sold those records to Marti Hok's grandfather. "Why were the records sold?"

Merith's look grew quizzical. "For money, of course," she said. She waved a hand at the hall. "Can you not see, Sorren— Tornor is poor. Once most of the wool in Arun came out of the north. But the herds have moved west, and east, and south. The Anhard traders no longer come by Tornor. They prefer the lower passes near Pel and Zilia Keeps. During the War Years, the Keeps never had to pay for meat or grain or cloth or leather—now the villages provide for us, not out of gratitude but out of charity. I am the twenty-fifth ruler of Tornor, and perhaps the last. Tornor is a ruin. Would you bequeath a ruin to your children?" Her voice rose, and echoed in the hall.

Sorren cupped the silver bowl in her palms. "I don't know," she said. "My mother was a grapepicker. When she died, she left me a shirt and an old straw hat, and a box of Cards."

A door opened at the kitchen end of the hall, and a woman entered. She was carrying a platter of food. Sorren's stomach growled at the smell of meat. The woman brought the platter to the table and thumped it down in front of Merith. She was short and stout, with muscles like a dockworker's. She wore a stained leather apron. "There's not enough fresh meat," she announced. "We shall have to ask for something from the village."

Merith said, "Sorren, this is Meg. Sorren came from the south."

"Huh," said Meg. "She got here just in time, then. There'll be snow in two days."

"How can you tell?" Sorren asked.

"From the smell o' the sky. I was born here."

Sorren said, "I was born in a vineyard, I think. But my family came from Tornor."

"I'm not surprised," said Meg. "I can tell Sark to kill one of the pigs," she said to Merith.

"Do that," said Merith. There was a carafe of wine on the platter and three goblets. She poured wine into two, and pushed one at Sorren.

Sorren took a sip. It was white wine, harsh as winter, but it left a glow on her tongue and in her stomach. The goblets were yellow crystal. Merith spooned meat into her dish. Sorren ate some; it was spicy, peppery. "It's good," she said.

Meg was standing at the table, brawny arms folded across her chest. She nodded. "Of course it is," she said. She marched off.

Merith said, "Meg and I are the same age. We grew up together. She brought both my children out of my womb." She wiped her mouth with a cloth. "I suppose I must hear your message."

Sorren said, "It is greetings, for you from the Lord Tarn Ryth, and the greetings of his son, Dennis, to your daughter."

Merith frowned. "How did you come to be Tarn Ryth's messenger? There is a Green Clan Hall in Nuath."

"I was coming here anyway, and I had brought *him* a message, from Arré Med."

"Arré Med—aye, the Med family in Kendra-on-the-Delta. It was a rebel of that family who built Tornor Keep." She smiled at Sorren. "You are shocked that I must think to recognize the name? Tornor is isolated, Sorren-no-Kité. I have been to Tezera, to Nuath twice, but never south of Nuath, and no one in this household has ever been to Kendra-on-the-Delta."

"How many are there in the household?" Sorren asked.

"Ten," said Merith. "Counting the horses. Myself, Ryke and Kedéra, Sark, Meg, Juli, who helps Meg, Innis, Meg's sister's daughter, who cleans, and Embri, who lives over the stable. Once a year, my sister comes to visit us from Elath."

"Your sister is a witch?"

"Aye. Thirty years Miella has lived in the witch town. She is a weatherworker."

Ryke raced into the hall from the kitchen. "Sark says I can help him kill the pig!" he said.

"Come here," said his mother. He went to her side. She smoothed his hair with her palm. "Mind you do as he says."

"Yes, ma'am," he said. The moment she lifted her hand he leaped toward the door.

"How old is he?" Sorren asked, when he was well out of earshot.

"Eleven."

"He does not seem to mind the isolation."

"No. He spends much time in the village. It is Kedéra who suffers most. She is—discontent. I do not know what would make her happy." Merith's voice grew soft, until Sorren could hardly hear her.

She ate more of the meat. It had a strange taste to it, as if it were almost, but not quite, spoiled. Arré would never eat spoiled meat. She saw the castle suddenly through Arré's eyes, as a vast cold comfortless relic. Arré would never stay in such a place.

"Why are you here?" she said.

Merith said, "Because I was born here, and this is my charge." Her voice grew brisk. "Why are you here? Your mother was a grape picker but your family came from Tornor, you said. How do you know that?"

Sorren put her elbows on the table. As simply as she could, she told of her visions, of her visits with Marti Hok and with the witches, and of her own resolution to come north when her time of service ended.

Merith listened, and sipped her wine. When Sorren fell silent, she said, "It is like a story of legend." She half-smiled. "Were it truly legend, I would now be making a speech, welcoming a long lost daughter to her home. But there is not much welcome here. I am afraid your visions have deceived you, as such things are wont to do. Whatever you are looking for— glory, heroism—are no longer here, if they ever were, which I doubt."

Sorren said, "But I wasn't looking for glory." She ran a thumb over the tarnished bowl, wondering if her namesake had ever sat on this bench or held this bowl in her hands.

"May I see your Cards?" said Merith.

Sorren felt strangely reluctant to bring them out. But she dug into her pack and set the box on the table. Merith took the lid off, and peeled the silk from the Dancer. As she gazed at it, her face softened, as it had when she looked at her son. "Yes," she said. She lifted the Dancer to stare at the card beneath it. "The colors—how fresh they seem. How old did you say they are?"

"I don't know," said Sorren. "Old."

Merith coughed, and cupped the box in her hands. "Strange to think of such flimsy bits of parchment having the power to cause visions." She glanced sideways at Sorren. "Have you had any visions since you stepped beneath the gate?"

"No," Sorren said. "The witchfolk said that might happen."

"And you cannot read them at all?"

"No."

"Then they are not much use, are they?" said Merith. She coughed again. "If they had been left to me," she said, "I would have sold them."

Sorren was horrified. "Why?"

"What good are they?" said Merith. Her voice grew strident with pain. "Can they feed a hungry child, or mend a broken leg, or save a man from drowning? And if they had been left to me and I could not sell them, I would burn them." Her face set, she stared at the tapestries with their fadded glitter. "The past is a hobble, a chain. Better to forget it, and start fresh if you can. I would haul those tapestries down and burn them, too, if they were not needed to keep the room warm!" She thrust the box into Sorren's hands.

A horse whinnied from the direction of the courtyard. Sorren heard the jingle of harness, and the sound of hooves on pavement. A youthful voice shouted, "Hoy! Embri!" Someone ran across the courtyard. A dog barked.

Merith folded her hands in her lap. "Kedéra is home."

The door opened. Sorren felt a little shock run through her nerves, as if someone had pinched her. Kedéra stood framed in the doorway. She was small, like her mother, and fair-haired, like her brother; she wore stained riding leathers, and a fur vest over a coarse brown tunic, and russet boots. She strode toward the table, moving lightly, like a dancer. Merith watched her coming with a set, unyielding face.

She said, "Kedi, this is Sorren-no-Kité. She comes from the south. Sorren, this is my daughter, Kedéra."

"Greetings," said Sorren.

"Hello," said Kedéra. "Welcome to Tornor Keep." Her face was narrower than her mother's.

"Sorren comes from Kendra-on-the-Delta," said Merith. "She bears a message for you from Dennis Ryth of Nuath."

Kedéra scowled. "I don't want to hear it." Her voice was hostile and passionate. She sat on the bench beside Sorren, swung her legs beneath the table and reached for the wine carafe. Pouring wine, she gazed defiantly at her mother. "I know what it is."

Merith said, with an undertone of anger, "It is greetings, that's all."

Kedéra put the carafe down heavily. "I don't want greetings from Dennis Ryth. I don't want *anything* from Dennis Ryth." She scowled, and her gray eyes seemed to darken. She yanked a piece of meat from the platter. A few drops of sauce spattered the wood.

Merith said, "That is no way to speak to a messenger. And your manners are disgusting."

Something's wrong here, Sorren thought. The words had held rancor. Kedéra flushed. Merith sighed, and her expression softened. "We must not quarrel in front of our guest," she said.

"No," said Kedéra.

Her hair was cut short; it just brushed the nape of her neck. It looked sleek and soft as feathers. Sorren wondered what it would feel like to touch.

"Why do you look at me like that?" Kedéra said.

Sorren realized that she was staring. Embarrassed and confused, she said, "You look like someone I know." Now why did I say that? she thought. It isn't so.

A black shadow came slinking to the girl's side. It was a dog. Sorren stiffened; she was not overly fond of dogs, and this one was lean and hungry-seeming, with scarred ears and long, curved claws. "What kind of dog is that?" she asked.

The dog's claws clicked on the stone. "A wolfhound," said Kedéra. "His name is Lauf." She fondled the narrow head with casual authority. "Tell me about your journey," she said. "How long did it take you?"

"A month and a half," Sorren said.

"Riding?"

Sorren grinned. "Walking."

Kedéra's eyes widened. Her lashes were very fair, but long. Their length made her face look fragile. "That's a long way. Were you alone?"

"Not at first. But after."

"I'd like to do that," Kedéra said. She shot a look at her mother. "Make a journey like that, someday."

"Where would you go?" asked Sorren.

Kedéra's chin jutted defiantly. "West. To the mountains."

Merith said dryly, "You would do better to go south, to Nuath." She rose, and slipped from the bench. "Sorren, I am sure your bathwater is hot. Let me show you to your chamber."

Kedéra said, "I'll take you!"

"No!" said Merith sharply. "You shall help Meg in the kitchen while Juli and Innis bring the bathwater."

Kedéra caught her breath, and her fair skin went from red to white. The tension in the great hall grew thick enough to touch. Sorren said quickly, before Kedéra could speak, "In Kendra-on-the-Delta, I was a bondservant."

The girl checked whatever she had been about to say. "I thought you were a messenger," she said.

"No. Not really. I carried a message because I was asked to do it. But I was trained to shop and wash and work in a kitchen."

"I hate it," said Kedéra.

"So did I," said Sorren. "But I did it. If you will come to my chamber after I bathe, I can tell you more about my travels."

Kedéra picked up one of the silver bowls and put it on the platter. "Thank you," she said. "I'd like that." She nested the second bowl on top of the first.

As they walked from the hall, Merith murmured, "Thank you. That was very diplomatic of you." It was clear that she did not believe that Sorren had been a servant. She coughed again, a grim sound, and thrust her fingers through her hair in a gesture like her daughter's.

They walked into the courtyard. The cold struck Sorren's face and hands and throat. Her pack seemed heavier in her hand than it had on her back. Light angled steeply over the inner wall. Sorren measured it with her eyes; it was four times her height. Even in summer, she thought, it must grow dark early within the Keep. In the shadow of the wall, the air was colder. Merith went ahead of Sorren to open the door to the apartments. The corridor was narrow, dark, and smelled old.

A candle in a wall sconce sent a weak flame over the passageway. By its light, Sorren glimpsed the coarse sacking that hung from the walls of the passage. Straw crunched underfoot.

Merith said, "These used to be the servants' rooms. But with so few people here, it seemed foolish for Sark and Meg and Juli to sleep here, and for Kedi and me to sleep elsewhere." She ran her hand along the sill of a shuttered window, and held up a candle. She touched its wick to the flame of the one in the sconce.

They went up a stair. Sorren sneezed twice; the corners of the treads and the threadbare sacks that lined the walls were coated with dust. Once her bow caught in a fold of cloth.

Gently, she freed it. Something scuttled at her feet. "Mice," said Merith apologetically.

It was warmer in the upstairs. Merith pushed open the door to a room. Light from several thick candles brightened it. "The sleeping room is there," Merith said, pointing to another door in the far wall of the chamber. Sorren let her pack fall. The room smelled of wax and of something softer, a perfume. It held a great dark wooden wardrobe, two chests, a wooden chair, a firescreen, a footstool, a table. . . . Sorren watched Merith straighten the pillows on the chair, and realized that this was not a guest room.

"This is your room, isn't it?" she said.

Merith said, "The guest chamber is so dusty. . . ."

Sorren wondered if there was a guest chamber. "I won't take your room," she said. "Where would you sleep?"

"With Kedéra."

"Then I shall do that." Sorren lifted the pack again. "Where does she sleep? Show me."

Kedéra's chamber was across the hall from Merith's. It held similar furnishings: a wardrobe, a chair, a table. Through the open door of the sleeping room Sorren saw the shadowy hangings of a great curtained bed. A tall silver candlestick stood on the table, and Merith fitted her candle into it. Light glinted off an object on the tabletop. Sorren picked it up; it was a silver brooch, shaped like a daisy. The touch of hands—over how many years, Sorren thought—had worn the curving petals smooth as silk.

"Juli! Innis!" called Merith. Sorren heard the sound of feet on the stairway. Two women appeared in the hall, carrying between them a brass kettle. It swung ponderously, suspended from a wooden yoke. They turned sideways, bringing the kettle to the hearth. One of them—she was stocky and silent and looked like Meg—knelt beside the hearth and lit a fire. The flames caught with a gasp. The other woman brought in towels, a soapball, a wooden dipper, and a flat porcelain basin and put them beside the kettle.

Sorren realized that, in order to get clean, she had to strip, stand in the basin, and pour the heated water from the kettle over herself with the dipper.

"Juli will stay and help you," said Merith. Juli grinned. She had fair hair and pale coloring—northern coloring, Sorren thought, and she put her pack down once more. Merith hesitated, and then left with Innis. Sorren took her furs off, slowly, waiting for the room to get warm. A chewed bone lay beside the fire. There was a piece of braided-harness on the wardrobe knob, and a thin riding whip draped over the chair.

She could not help thinking, with longing, of the baths in Kendra-on-the-Delta. With a sigh, she swept the whip off the chair and sat down to work her boots off. Then she peeled her layers of clothing off and stepped into the basin. Juli took the lid from the kettle; steam filled the room. Lifting the dipper, Juli poured water down her back. It trickled down her belly and breasts. She lathered herself all over with the coarse, un-perfumed soap, and then knelt on the hard porcelain and closed her eyes. Juli rinsed the soap from her head. "Chea, that's good," Sorren said, sighing with pleasure as the heat flushed her clean skin.

Juli touched her upper left arm. "What's that?" she said.

It took Sorren a moment to understand the question. "It's the mark of a bonding bracelet. I was a bondservant until a little while ago."

Juli pursed her lips. "We don't do that in the north," she said. She sounded disapproving. She put a towel in Sorren's arms. "Better move to the fire, or you'll chill." Sorren moved closer to the fire, rubbing herself briskly with the towel. The warmth was making her sleepy. She reached for her pack; there were clean clothes in it, beneath everything else, saved for this moment. She put them on. Juli wiped the floor where water had splashed on the stone.

"I never heard they wore such in Nuath," she remarked.

She was talking about the bonding bracelet. "I don't know if they do," Sorren said. The silver bracelet Arré had given her had fallen to the bottom of the pack. She plucked it out and worked it over her knuckles. "I only passed through Nuath."

"Did you meet the lord?"

"You mean Tarn Ryth? Yes. I delivered a message from him to your lady."

Juli nodded; her blond braids swung. "That would be about the betrothal."

"What betrothal?"

"The one of our girl to the lord's son," Juli said. Dumping the soiled cloths in the basin, she rose to her feet.

"Wait." Sorren stretched out a hand. "Tell me of this be-trothal."

Juli settled the basin against her hip. "The lord wants his

son to wed our Kedi. She is to go and live in Nuath, in that big stone house they say he has. In exchange, the Ryth lord will send masons and smiths and horsemen and guards to Tornor, and it will be rich again." She jerked a thumb at the kettle. "I'll get Innis and we'll take that away." She left. Sorren picked up the towel. So that was what Tarn Ryth's message said, she thought. A shutter banged in the wind. Sorren rubbed the dampness from her hair. She wondered what Arré would say to Tarn Ryth's scheme. If Kedéra married Dennis Ryth, Ryke would inherit Tornor. Prosperity would return to the Keep. And Kedéra—Sorren scowled. Kedéra was a child.

What, she wondered, did Tarn Ryth want with Tornor?

Arré would know. Vigorously, she massaged her hair. She wondered if Arré had knowledge of Tarn Ryth's plan. Perhaps she could contrive to send a message south. She rose from the chair, took too long a step, and banged her hip against the table. "Damn!"

Juli's voice called from the corridor. "Can we come in?"

"Come," called Sorren. The two women entered. They went to the hearth and put their shoulders beneath the yoke that held the kettle. When they straightened, it swung ponderously between them. Matching strides, they walked to the door.

Sorren said, "What do you think of these betrothal plans?"

Juli said, "The chea should be praised. All those new folk coming north will bring work to the village."

"Does Kedéra want to be wed?"

Juli snorted. "She's a babe. She wants to ride and play with her dog. Who would not want to be wed to a lord, and living in a fine house?"

Innis said, "I would not."

"You!" Juli was contemptuous. "What do you know of life? You've never been past the peat bogs. I've been to Nuath, and it's a fine place. Go on, move your big feet out that door."

Innis moved. Juli nudged the door closed with her hip. The open door had chilled the room. Sorren hunkered down beside the fire, bending her head toward the blaze. A thump at the door made her turn. "Come in," she said.

The door opened. Kedéra stood there. The black hound leaned against her leg. "I didn't want to disturb you," she said.

"This is your room," Sorren said, and realized that her voice was not entirely steady. "You must come and go as you like."

Kedéra did not seem to notice the quaver. "You said you'd tell me about your travels," she explained.

Sorren felt a moment of panic. What could she say to this girl? She was a picker's daughter, a bondservant, no more. She felt cloddish, stupid, a huge clumsy intruder. "There's not much to tell," she said. Her words had deserted her.

Kedéra picked the whip from the floor, and curled it round her fingers. "Would you like to see my horse?" she said.

"Certainly," said Sorren. She reached for her boots.

"I'll help you," Kedéra said. She reached down, fitting her hands between Sorren's on the boot's rim. Sorren almost let go. The light contact made her heart leap in her chest as if she had touched a fire-eel.

Guardian, she thought, what's happening to me?

Kedéra seemed not to have noticed. "I'll do it!" Sorren said. Kedéra let go. Stupid, Sorren thought, now she thinks you're angry at her! She jammed her foot into the second boot, and stood.

Kedéra had picked up her bow. Gently she limned the outer edge with her fingertips. "This is beautiful," she said. "Did you make it?"

"No," Sorren said. "A—a friend had it made for me. Can you shoot?"

Kedéra frowned. "No. My mother does not wish me to learn; she says women do not need such skills." Her smoke-gray eyes gleamed suddenly. "Can *you* ride?"

Sorren reached for her cloak. "No."

CHAPTER TWENTY-FIVE

The stable was warm and aromatic; it smelled of hay and horses. There was one horse standing in the boxlike stall, and one brown mule. Kedéra brought Sorren to the horsebox. "This is Lightfoot," she said. "She's mine." She caressed the horse's glossy jaw. "Touch her. She won't hurt you."

Sorren put out a tentative hand and let the mare smell her. The breath was warm on her palm. Kedéra grinned. Slipping into the box, she hugged the mare around the neck. "Isn't she beautiful?"

To Sorren's eyes she simply looked big, though even Sorren could see the ways she differed from southern horses. She was smaller, and rounder, and her gray coat was shaggy. "What kind of horse is she?" she asked.

Kedéra slid fearlessly beneath the mare's belly. "She's a mix. She's part Asech and part northern breed, out of the old Anhard stock." She lifted her palm to the mare's muzzle; it had a carrot on it. The mare lipped it and began to chew noisily, blowing carrot chips over Kedéra's hair. The girl swung casually back under the mare's belly and leaned on the door. She looked at home, happy, and not fragile at all.

A sharp-faced youth with red hair came down the passage, arms full of harness. He nodded to Kedéra. "That's Embri," Kedéra said. She tilted her head. "You don't like horses, do you?"

Sorren said, "I've never had a chance to get to know them." She thought of the ride in Nuath. The soldier who had taken her to the Ryth mansion—what was his name? Pitor, that was it. "Have you been riding long?"

"Since I was six," said Kedéra. "My father taught me."

"Is he dead?" Sorren asked gently.

"He died six years ago," Kedéra said. Her voice was even. "I was ten."

"I never knew my father," said Sorren. "My mother died when I was thirteen."

Kedéra said, with sympathy, "Have you been alone since then?"

Sorren thought of Arré, and of Paxe. "No," she answered. "I was not alone."

They walked from the stable into the courtyard. The sky was blue; in the west, a few stars glimmered. Eastward clouds moved steadily forward. In the north, mountains made a shadow on the sky. The moon was down beyond the curve of the world. Ryke came galloping out of the twilight, bright hair flying, clutching Sorren's staff to his chest. It was longer than he was. "Do you want this?" he said hopefully.

Sorren smiled at him. "You can keep it for me, until I need it."

"When will you need it?"

"When I decide to travel."

"When will that be?"

Sorren tucked her hands inside her cloak. "I don't know," she said.

Satisfied, Ryke whirled the staff above his head and careened out of sight. Kedéra said, "Why did you come here?"

Sorren drew a deep breath. Her chest felt tight. "I had dreams," she said. "Dreams about the mountains and about Tornor Keep. But now I'm not sure why I was led here, if I *was* led. My dreams have gone."

Kedéra hunched her shoulders into the russet fur of her vest. "I have dreams, too," she said. "I dream of mountains—not these mountains, but taller, redder ones. I dream of a valley, and people living there. I dream I see them dancing, and that I am with them."

Sorren said, "I know that dream."

Kedéra swung in a circle, arms open to the sky. "I thought you did," she said. She stopped, and looked toward the windows of the apartments, where a dim light sifted through the shutters. "My mother wants me to marry Dennis Ryth, and leave my dreams behind. But I won't."

She sounded clear and determined. Sorren was glad for the darkness that hid her face. Her emotions battered her like contrary winds. She wanted to protect Kedéra—from Tarn Ryth, from Dennis Ryth, from Merith—and she wanted to run away, run from this turmoil that was seething in her bones.

"What will happen to Tornor," she said, "if you do not marry Dennis Ryth?"

Kedéra crossed her arms on her chest. "My mother will never forgive me," she answered.

That was not what I meant, Sorren started to say, and then she realized that Kedéra had answered in the only way she could. She did not care about Tornor, the Keep. She cared for her family.

Slowly, they walked to the apartments. Lauf was waiting for them inside the chamber door. His tail thumped when he saw Kedéra. But it ceased thumping at Sorren's entrance; his ears went back, and he rose, growling. Kedéra roughed his ears, and the growl died. "He hates it when I share my bed," she explained.

The fire in the hearth had burned to embers, and the room was cold. Sorren took her cloak off. Juli came to the door, carrying a cloth in which two bricks nestled. Kedéra took the candle and they went into the sleeping chamber. Sorren started to follow them. The wolfhound growled, deep in his throat.

Sorren knelt, extending a hand. "Lauf," she said, "I mean her no harm. Be friends." But the dog stiffened, and his lips pulled back from his teeth. Kedéra came from the inner chamber, with Juli at her heels.

"Juli says she knows where there are clothes that will fit you," she said. "You'll need them." She hesitated. "I can lend you a sleeping gown."

A gown for sleeping in? "I don't need it," Sorren said.

Juli went out, and returned with a bucket. There was a tall, three-legged brazier at the foot of the curtained bed; she poured coals from the bucket to the well of the brazier. Kedéra pointed her finger at the dog. "Lauf, stay," she said gently. Putting his head on his paws, Lauf watched his mistress with wide eyes. "Come," she said to Sorren. They went into the sleeping chamber. Juli had gotten the coals lit in the brazier, and heat seeped through its iron grate. A candle burned in a wall sconce. It was a small room. A washstand with a basin and chamberpot stood in one corner; in another stood a tall pole with wooden hooks radiating from it. Kedéra hung her vest from one of the hooks.

Juli tugged back the curtains at the foot of the vast bed. It was piled with quilts, and was so high off the floor that there were, Sorren saw, little steps on one side of it. Juli walked around it shaking the curtains. There was a shutter set high in the wall; through it Sorren could see a sliver of sky. In Kendra-on-the-Delta, the lamplighters would be finishing their rounds. Arré would be finishing her dinner. Paxe would be—she shut off the images abruptly, angry at herself. She realized that she was alone in the sleeping chamber. Juli was gone; Kedéra was in the outer chamber, whispering to Lauf.

She sat on the bed. It dipped beneath her weight. She took off her cloak and boots and let them fall to the floor. The room suddenly felt icy. Methodically, Sorren removed tunic, pants, undertunic, socks, undergarments, and hung them on the pole. Then she climbed into the bed. It took her a moment to find where the quilts parted. She slid downward, wrapping the coverlets around her, feeling with her toes for the warmth at the foot. . . .

"You're quick," said Kedéra. Sorren looked out from the nest she had made in the quilts. Kedéra stood naked by the clothes' pole. Her skin was white where the sun had not marked it. Gold hair powdered her breasts, grew thicker on her belly, and fleecy between her thighs. She lifted a brass snuffer from a hook on the wall and snuffed the candle. Now the only light in the room was the light from the brazier. She climbed into bed. Sorren's palms were sweaty. The linens whispered as Kedéra curled between them.

"Am I crowding you?" she said.

"No," said Sorren. Her mind was filled with the image of Kedéra naked. She lay very still in bed.

"Good night." Kedéra tugged the curtains closed, shutting out even the glow from the brazier.

The air grew heavy, motionless, and very dark.

In the morning, it was snowing.

Lauf woke them, whining outside the curtains. Kedéra leaped out of bed to reassure him and use the chamberpot. Sorren listened with half an ear to the sounds. She was stiff, as if she had not rested but she knew she had slept. If she had dreamed, she could not remember it. It was very dark in the curtained bed. She stretched, easing her muscles. The curtains opened, and Kedéra's grinning face appeared in the gap. "Are you awake?" she said.

"I'm awake."

"Juli's bringing tea." She vanished, and Sorren heard the noise of the shutter being opened. Light brightened the sleeping room. Cold air washed in, and Sorren hugged the quilts to her shoulders. The light was gray, unwelcoming, and flat.

Steps sounded in the outer chamber, and Sorren heard Juli's voice. Kedéra exclaimed. The odor of fresh-baked bread wafted through the curtains. Sorren's mouth watered. Heedless of the cold, she lifted on an elbow and pulled back the curtain near her. Through the arched doorway, she saw Juli with a tray on which stood a teapot, mugs, and a dish of biscuits. Kedéra was standing with Juli, wearing a red robe trimmed with white fur. Her arms were heaped with what seemed to be clothes.

She turned and saw Sorren. "Look!" She came to the bed and dumped the clothes at the foot. "These are for you." She laughed. "Some of them are men's, but not all of them." She stroked the topmost garment, a tunic made of blue velvet. "Such fine work." She lifted the tunic up. It was trimmed at collar and cuffs with heavy lace, and smelled of cedar. "She got it out of the chests in the apartments." Letting the tunic fall, she pulled the curtains back the rest of the way. "Come and have tea." She thrust an arm into the heaped clothing and pulled out something long and purple. "This is a robe, I think. Yes." She held it against her. It fell around her feet in soft folds.

She laughed. "It'll fit you." She laid it on top of the pile and went into the outer chamber. Sorren climbed from the bed. Cold bumps sprang forth on her arms and breasts. She wriggled into the robe, breathing cedar. . . . It was wool, and very warm.

She wondered who had worn it last as she walked into the outer chamber. Juli had gone, leaving the tray. A fire bloomed in the hearth; Kedéra knelt beside it, poking it with tongs. Lauf lay next to her. He lifted his head as Sorren entered, but did not growl.

"I poured tea for you," said Kedéra.

"Thank you," said Sorren. She picked up the steamy mug. It was brown, earth-colored, and so was the tea. Its strong bitter taste made her eyes water, but it was warming. She glanced toward the shutter of the window, which was ajar, and saw the flakes of snow drifting toward the ground.

She went to the window. The snow made a smooth blanket over the world. It covered the outer ward, lined the top of the outer wall. . . . "Look," said Kedéra. She laid one hand on Sorren's shoulder, and pointed with the other. "See that road? That leads west."

"To Cloud Keep," said Sorren, remembering her map.

The pressure of Kedéra's fingers lifted. "Yes. And Pel Keep, beyond that. And the western mountains."

Sorren turned to look at her. She was smiling; her eyes were wide, and luminous.

She went to the tray and took a biscuit. "Did you dream?" she said.

"No," said Sorren.

"I did," said Kedéra. But she did not go on. Instead—"Tell me about the south," she said.

Sorren took a biscuit. "What do you want to know?"

"What do people do?"

"They farm," Sorren said, "and fish, and build. They spin silk."

"We weave wool," said Kedéra.

"They work metals and clay."

"Do they dance?" said Kedéra.

"Some. The Asech dance with snakes. And the city-born become acrobats and tumblers and a few of them, the highborn, learn the true dance. I was a drummer for a dancer."

"Who was she?" asked Kedéra.

"He. Isak Med. He is gone from the city now. Banished." Even now, even here, it was hard for her to speak of Isak. She could not use the ugly word, *outlawed*.

Kedéra said, "You were a bondservant, now you are a messenger; you have been a drummer, you are a witch—is there anything you can't do?"

Sorren grinned. "Sing," she said. "And ride a horse. And read and write," she added.

They finished the biscuits. Kedéra flung back the quilts to air the bed. Lauf paced from Kedéra's knee to the door. "He's restless," she said. "He wants to run." She dressed, and they went into the inner ward. Lauf writhed like a puppy in the powdery snow. Sorren tilted her head to the sky. The snow-flakes rained down like icy feathers. She reached out a hand to try to catch one, but they evaded her. She opened her mouth, wondering what they would taste like.... Her breath clouded the air, melting them. One flake brushed her lip; she licked the place. The snow had no taste. Obscurely disappointed, she turned to find Kedéra.

Sark, Ryke, Kedéra, and Merith stood by the inner gate. The brown mule stood stolidly beside them, hitched to what seemed to be a cart. As Sorren neared them, she saw that the cart had no wheels; instead, it had smooth flat pieces of wood that curved upward at the tips. She said softly into Kedéra's ear, "What's that?"

Kedéra said, "A sled."

Merith smiled at Sorren. "Did you sleep well?" she said. "Were you warm enough?"

"Yes, thank you," said Sorren.

"It must be difficult for you to stand the cold, coming from the south," Merith said graciously.

But I am not a southerner, Sorren thought, and I have winter in my blood. "Not really," she said to Merith. "I feel right at home."

Merith's smile soured a little. She turned to Sark and her son. "Give my regards to Varin when you reach the village. Ask if they can spare us some fish."

"Fish?" said Sorren.

Kedéra said, "In winter, we fish through the ice."

Sorren thought, I'd like to see that. Sark slapped the mule's rump. "Ya!" he said. The mule snorted and moved. The sled ran smoothly over the fallen snow. How sensible, Sorren thought. Lauf followed it beneath the outer gate. Kedéra called to him; he barked once and then trotted back into the courtyard, holding something between his jaws.

She coaxed the object from him. "It's a quail." She turned the small brown body in her hands. It was stiff, its feathers covered with a net of ice crystal. "There's no blood on it," she said, "It must have died from the cold."

"Or from sickness," said Merith.

Kedéra's fingers probed. "It has a broken wing. I can feel where the bone is split. It couldn't fly to find food; that's what killed it, Mother. I'll take it to Meg; she'll put it in the soup pot." She snapped her fingers. "Come, Lauf." She loped off with the dog frisking at her heels.

Sorren said, "What are Sark and Ryke bringing back on the sled?"

"Wood," said Merith. "And fish, I hope."

Sorren said. "I can hunt. That will bring in some fresh meat."

Merith coughed. "Thank you," she said. "It's kind of you to offer. But if you delay your return to Nuath, you will be forced to spend the winter here."

"But—" Sorren began. She hesitated, thinking back to all she had told Merith the day before. She had not said outright that she planned to stay in Tornor. Did Merith want her to leave? "I had not intended to go back to Nuath."

Merith crossed her arms over her chest. "But you must return," she said. "There is barely enough food here to feed the household now. Besides, you are a messenger. You cannot stay locked in Tornor all the winter."

"I am not a messenger," Sorren said.

"You brought me a message," Merith said. "If you wish to do Tornor a service, you may carry a message to Tarn Ryth from me. Tell him I would look more kindly upon his greetings if they were accompanied by substance—like grain, and cloth." She turned to walk to the apartments.

Do your daughter's wishes mean nothing, then? Sorren thought. "My lady," she said, "what do you want?"

Merith said, her voice brittle as the snow, "I want Tornor Keep to survive. I want the villagers to prosper. I want Tarn Ryth to send goods and gold and soldiers north, and for this to happen, Kedéra must wed Dennis Ryth."

"Can you not make a treaty with Tarn Ryth for these things?"

"No," Merith said. "The Council of Houses in Tezera would object to any treaty I made with Tarn Ryth. But if Dennis Ryth and Kedéra wed, they cannot object if Tarn Ryth sends guards and supplies to Tornor Keep."

"Will they not help you?"

"The nobles of Tezera?" Merith laughed. "Shall I go to them and beg? I would rather starve. Tarn Ryth came to *me*." The snow covered her brown hair with a web of white. Sorren saw her as she would be in twenty years, small and pale and white-haired and bitter. She suddenly saw why Tarn Ryth wanted Tornor. His power came from the river, but his control of the river halted at the borders of Septh. His patrols stopped there. If he could possess Tornor, he would control the river above *and* below Tezera, which would give him great power. If he tried to take Tornor by force, the Tezeran Council would object, and there might be war. But the Council could not object to that most traditional of alliances, a wedding.

It made a pattern. Sorren swallowed. It was so easy to see, once you knew where to look. Living with Arré Med for seven years, she had learned some of Arré's skills. But Arré was far away, and could not help her now. "Can the other Keeps assist you in your need?" she asked.

Merith had reached the door of the apartments. "They are in like case," she said. "It is said that Lord Meth of Zilia Keep has made a separate treaty with Anhard. But I will not believe it." She glanced into the courtyard. Kedéra was coming toward them. "We will speak no further of this," she said.

Kedéra said, "Meg was pleased. She gave Lauf a bone."

Merith said, "I have weaving to do. Will you come and help me, Kedi?"

Kedéra thrust her hands through her hair. "I wanted to show

Sorren the castle," she said. "Can you spare me for an hour?"

Merith shrugged. "I suppose I can." She went into the apartments. Sorren and Kedéra stood alone. Kedéra's eyes were bright as a child's.

"What do you want to show me?" Sorren said.

Kedéra pulled the fur vest closer around her neck. "I thought you might want to take a walk on the wall."

Sorren said, "I'd prefer to be indoors."

Kedéra looked disappointed. "We could look at the apartments," she said. She pointed to the larger building. "I know the way in."

"Let's do that," Sorren agreed.

They went inside through the door Merith had used. But instead of turning right and going up a stairway, Kedéra turned left. Almost at once, Sorren was aware of the cold. She crossed her arms across her chest, holding in warmth. Kedéra said, "We never come here." She pointed to the walls, bare of tapestries. "Mother had us move the hangings into the servants' chambers, all that could be moved."

A stairway appeared in the shadowy passage, rising into darkness. Sorren sniffed. A scent hung about the walls. She wondered if age had a smell. Kedéra crouched, hands busy. Sorren heard the clash of flints on each other. Kedéra rose with the stump of a candle in one hand. "Come on," she said.

"Wait," Sorren said. "What's down here?" As she gazed along the passageway, she could see the indentation in the smooth stone of the hall that meant there were doors.

"Storerooms," said Kedéra. "They're empty now." She touched Sorren's arm. "Come."

"Were they always storerooms?" Sorren persisted. She followed Kedéra up the stairway. The wooden treads creaked beneath her boots with a noise like laughter. The candle bobbed ahead of her, a small pool of light in a vast darkness. Sorren felt the hairs on her neck stir, and told herself not to be a fool. Nothing could hurt her in these empty rooms.

"No," Kedéra said. "I think not. People lived there once. But when there was no more fighting, Tornor began to empty, and the people who were left looked for the warmest places to live. It's always warmer upstairs." She held the candle high suddenly. An iron shape leaped out at them. It was a wall sconce in the shape of a fish. As Sorren gazed at it, she remembered what Marti Hok had told her, about the rebel from

Kendra-on-the-Delta who had been banished by his city and
sent north, to thrive or die in the wilderness. He had built
Tornor. She wondered if he had told his smiths to make him
sconces in the shape of fishes, and what they thought of that.
For a moment, a picture slid into her mind, so vivid that she
thought at first she was aftseeing, of a man drawing fish over
and over again on a piece of parchment, trying to make them
look like the fish he knew, the dwellers of the ocean. She
blinked. The mouth of the fish gaped upward; the tail curved
into the wall. She went to her toes, reaching, and touched it.
Her fingers came away slippery with dust. She sniffed them.
That was what she smelled: the dust.

There were ghosts here, she thought. No wonder her own
ghosts had not followed her here. She trailed her hand along
the ancient wall.

"Come on," Kedéra said impatiently.

The upstairs corridor was lighter than the one downstairs.
The doors hung slightly ajar. Light came through them. Kedéra
put her shoulder to one massive slab of wood, and pushed.
"Look," she said. Sorren went a few steps into the room. A
great bed took up most of the spare in it. It was made of some
heavy dark wood. Velvet hangings, pulled from their support,
lay draped across it. A washstand and basin stood near it. At
its foot was a chest with the lid up. A brass ewer stood on a
small table. Wax coated the floor near the bed. "Whoever lived
here was careless with candles," Kedéra said.

A shutter banged. Sorren jumped at the noise. She gazed
at the bed, wondering who had slept there, and if, in her
visions, she had ever seen her. The brass ewer caught her eye;
its maker had hammered out a tree on its side. She stepped to
the table and picked the pitcher up. It was cold. She tipped it,
half expected water to trickle out, but all that emerged was a
sprinkling of soft gray dust.

She put the ewer down. "Let's go elsewhere," she said.

"All right," said Kedéra. They went into the next room.
Here the bed was missing. "My bed came from here," Kedéra
explained. The next room was larger, and it had a separate
sleeping chamber. A tapestry on the wall over the washstand
showed a picture of a girl reaching across a wall. The picture
was inexpert; the stitching sloppy, and Kedéra said, "Some
child made that."

"Maybe," Sorren said. Or a woman, she thought, bored and
inexpert with her needle, expressing her longing for the south

in the only way she could. . . . Why the south? Sorren thought. The faded color disturbed her. Suddenly, she wanted to see no more. "I'm cold," she said. She rubbed her arms with her hands. "I want to be warm."

Kedéra grinned. "We'll go bother Meg."

They ran down the stairs, across the courtyard, and into the kitchen. It was steamy and huge and it smelled wonderful. Meg stood in front of the huge open hearth, peering into a pot, brandishing a spice jar. As Kedéra and Sorren entered, she whirled, frowning. "I told you—" She stopped. "Oh. I thought you were Embri." Kedéra went to her and kissed her cheek. "I know you, you want something from me. Those cakes on the shelf are for the big meal."

"We don't want cakes," Kedéra said loftily. She collapsed onto a stool. "Sorren wants to get warm, and this is the warmest place in the castle."

"And the busiest. How am I to work with you underfoot?" Meg gave the stew in the pot an officious stir. "Here, you stir this." She put the spice jar on its shelf. Sorren wondered what the Med cook would think of this kitchen. It was much bigger than his. Great hooks hung from the wooden beams; she wondered what they usually held—spices, meat, pots, and pans? Kedéra stirred the pot. She dipped up a taste.

"Needs more salt," she murmured.

Meg said, "Do I need you to tell me how to cook?" She scowled. "Wait until you live in Nuath; you can order your kitchen to your heart's content."

Kedéra stopped stirring. "I am not going to live in Nuath," she said quietly.

"Humph," said Meg.

The change in temperature had brought cold bumps springing up on Sorren's arms. She moved closer to the fire. Kedéra's face was set and still. Suddenly, she let the dipper fall. "I'm going to the wall," she said. She looked at Sorren. "Coming?"

Sorren nodded, with some reluctance; she had just gotten warm. Kedéra pointed to a stair leading up along the bulk of the chimney. "Watch your step," she said.

The stair was narrow but it did not creak. At the top was a door. "It used to be barred," Kedéra said, touching the iron brace where the bar would have been. "I made Sark take it off." She pushed at the door. It opened; cold air and soft powdery snow scudded in. She thrust at it and it fell back. "Come on." She climbed three more steps. Sorren followed.

Snow whipped at her face. She wondered what to do about the
door. . . . "Leave it," said Kedéra.

Snow swirled in their faces. Sorren put her hands beneath
her cloak. Head down, blind, she followed Kedéra. Suddenly,
the wind dropped. She looked up. They were in the shadow
of a block of stone. Before them stretched the inner wall.

It was taller than the outer wall: massive, dark, imposing.
Sorren tried to imagine climbing it, and failed. Kedéra stepped
from the shelter into another blast of wind. They were on the
east side of the Keep, the cold side where the wind swept in
across the steppe. . . . Kedéra halted again, breathing heavily.
Sorren took a deep breath; the chill cut her chest like a knife
thrust. "Why do you come here?" she said, trying not to shiver.

Kedéra said, "So I can see." She leaned against the wall,
ice crystals glittering on her cheeks—no. She was crying. Sorren put both hands on her shoulders and discovered that she
was shivering, too.

"It's too cold to be up here," she said.

Kedéra nodded. "Let's go to the gatehouse stair." Without
waiting for Sorren's answer, she started off. Their boots echoed
on the stone walkway. They turned the corner; the wind now
blew at their backs, tugging at their clothing.

Kedéra stopped at one of the openings in the wall. They
gazed south, at the field below the castle. It was white, un-
stained, its purity broken only by the wooden bridge and the
dark irregular track of the river. As they watched, a mule
pulling a loaded sled broke from beneath the trees and rattled
across the field. Sark was riding the back of the load; Ryke
was sitting on the mule, leaning forward, face against its neck.
Sark was shouting. "They're coming awfully fast," said
Kedéra, puzzled. As she spoke, Ryke slapped the mule's rump
with a switch. The laboring animal stretched its neck and
moved even faster.

They were nearing the bridge. Suddenly, a rider galloped
from the trees—and another, and another. "What—" said Sorren, but she said it to Kedéra's back. Kedéra was running. The
gatehouse loomed in front of them. Kedéra dived inside it.
Sorren followed as swiftly as she could. She glimpsed a great
wheel with a rope around it. Kedéra was sliding down a ladder,
her feet barely touching the rungs. Sorren climbed after her
and caught her in the dark of the gatehouse. "What is it?" she
said.

Kedéra flung open the door and sprinted into the ward. Panting, she said, "Outlaws!"

Sorren grabbed her. "Where are you going?" she demanded. Kedéra shook free of the grip.

"To the stable. Get your bow!" She bolted toward the stable. Lauf bounded out of nowhere and raced at her heels. Sorren ran toward the apartments. The snowflakes spiraled past her in their inexorable flight to earth. . . . She heard distant shouts, and a shriek of terror that seemed to burst from the earth—the mule, she thought. She pounded up the stair, passing Merith. Merith's eyes were wide, and her broad face was chalky.

She took the narrow steps two at a time. In the courtyard, Lauf was barking, deep, furious barks. She burst into Kedéra's chamber. There was the bow, bowstring wrapped about it, leaning against the wall; she snatched it. She whirled in a circle, heart surging in her chest, seeking the quiver. There it was. She seized it. There were two arrows left. She thought of Paxe, who had given her the arrows—the thought was like a prayer. Guardian, I don't want to kill, she thought, but as she thought it she was running down to the courtyard. The snow had thickened. She saw Embri running toward the gate, clutching a pitchfork. The gray horse shot from the stable with Kedéra on her back. The girl beckoned, leaning, one arm extended, legs wrapped tightly around the cavorting, bridleless mare. I can't, Sorren thought in panic, but she slung the quiver onto her shoulder and put out an arm. Kedéra grabbed it.

"Hold my waist!" she shouted. The mare stamped as Sorren scrambled to a seat on her back. This is crazy, she thought; what can we do against armed men? But the mare plunged forward, with a jar that almost unseated her. She gripped Kedéra's waist with one arm and her bow with the other. The hood of her cloak fell back in the wind, and her hair streamed out, blowing like a banner.

The riders had made a ring around the laden mule. Sark was flailing at them with a piece of wood. Ryke, still seated on the mule, swung Sorren's staff like a cudgel. Sorren counted, three, four, six men, on skinny horses. She wondered why they lingered, why they did not take the mule and run, and realized that they were not armed. Lauf streaked at Lightfoot's side, belling his rage. Even the mule was striking out with teeth and forefeet.

She had not strung the bow, and that took two hands.

Chea. . . . ! The word was prayer. She leaned against Kedéra, feeling their pulses rock in unison, and fumbled with the waxed string, feeling for the tip of the bow. She bent it against the inside of her thigh, stretched, and slid the loop of the string into the notch—it held. She felt Kedéra draw an immense lungful of air. Then she screamed; a high shout that seemed to rise from her core. The mare leaped forward. Kedéra leaned until her cheek touched the mare's crest. She was whsipering to the mare, guiding her with hands and knees and thighs, keeping her steady. . . . Sorren gripped the bow and reached for an arrow. She looked up and saw the faces of outlaws; beneath their shaggy fur hats their eyes were wide and fearful. Run, she thought at them. Run!

They ran. She saw them scatter—all but one, who had his hand on the bridle of the mule. He had turned her half toward the trees. Ryke sprang at him from a snowdrift, and the outlaw's booted foot struck him in the ribs. He crumpled. Sorren drew the bow. Her hands were numb; she could barely feel the arrow.

She shot. The arrow wobbled in the gusting wind, and fell with a clatter to the bridge planks. But the outlaw dropped the rein and kicked his horse toward the trees. His hat flew off. Lauf sprang at it, barking. Kedéra shouted in triumph and brought the mare to a skidding halt. Sorren grabbed for a hold but her fingers would not grip. I knew this was stupid, she thought, as the ground came to meet her. She curled her arms around her head, letting the bow drop. Powdery snow geysered as she struck the ground. "Unh." Her ribs and side felt hammered. She lifted her head. Kedéra wheeled the mare around and leaped to the earth.

"Are you hurt?" she said. Her hands felt Sorren's back and neck, patting, poking. Her breath clouded the air. "Sorren, talk!"

"I'm not hurt," Sorren said. Gritting her teeth, she sat. A fall from the back of a horse was not so bad. "How's your brother?"

Ryke said, above her, "I'm fine!" He waved the cudgel. "He kicked me; did you see that, Kedi?"

"I saw," said Kedéra. She scooped Sorren's bow from the snow, and laid it across her knees.

"You looked like—like—" Words failed the boy. "Like soldiers!" he said. He looked worshipfully at Sorren. "I didn't know you could shoot an arrow from horseback."

"Neither did I," Sorren said. She wondered what the outlaws had thought when two women, one waving a bow, one shouting at the top of her lungs, bore down upon them. Her side ached horribly. I didn't have to kill anyone, she thought. Thank the chea, I didn't have to kill.... She wondered what she would have done if the outlaws had been armed. Died, probably, she thought.

Kedéra said, "They've never done that before. Attacked us, I mean. They steal sheep from the village sometimes." At her back, Sark was soothing the mule. Some of the wood had fallen into the snow. Kedéra lifted one end of a log. "Help me," she said.

Sorren bent—it hurt—and lifted the other end. They tossed the log onto the sled. Embri arrived, pitchfork in hand. He bent to help. Quickly, they loaded it and urged the mule forward. Sorren glanced back at the trees, but there was no sign of the marauders; resistance had cowed them. Lauf trotted by the sled with the fur hat between his jaws. Kedéra walked beside the mare, patting and praising her. They trudged through the drifting snow while the wind bit their cheeks, making its own music. Under the gate, Merith waited. Ryke ran ahead of them into her arms.

They gathered in the hall. Ryke, swinging his cudgel, was inclined to be boastful, until Sark spoke sharply to him and made him sit down. Sorren went to the fire and warmed her hands. Kedéra came to stand next to her.

"Who were they?" Sorren said.

"Who?"

"The outlaws."

Kedéra frowned. "Outlaws—are outlaws. Their villages make them leave. Some are thieves. They live on the steppe, in the little round stone huts the peat spaders build. They raid the villages for sheep. They've never attacked the Keep before."

Sorren remembered their pallid faces. "They must be hungry," she said. It hurt her to think of people living like that. "They should go to the city and find work."

Merith said, "Life in Tezera is not easy, when you're used to the steppe." She stroked Ryke's hair until he jerked away, irritated.

"Now what will they do?" Sorren said, not expecting an answer.

Sark said, "Steal a sheep." He leaned heavily on the table. Sorren wondered if he was feeling ill.

Merith said sharply, "Sark, are you tired?"

"Na." But his head drooped.

Kedéra went to him. "Of course you're tired," she said. "Why don't you go and sit on a stool in the kitchen, and rest?" She coaxed the old man from the bench and walked him to the kitchen. She came back with a tray bearing goblets and a wine carafe. "Meg will make him rest," she said.

Juli served the meal. "You should have shot them all," she said belligerently. "Thieves and villains, they are."

Kedéra said, "They're just cold, and hungry."

"Then they should find some honest work to do."

Merith said, "There is no work." She looked at her daughter. "Nor will there be, unless things change."

Kedéra stiffened. "I don't want to talk about it now," she said.

Merith said, "We must." Two red spots, like fever, lit her cheeks. "Kedi—" her voice grew pleading—"these folk are our charge. Even the outlaws. We must find a way to help them, to ease the poverty that makes them steal."

Kedéra shook her head. To break the tension, Sorren reached for the wine carafe and filled the goblets all around. This was the northern wine that Arré served to the Council. She wondered if Arré knew it came from Tornor. She wished Arré were here. She would know what to do for Tornor. She did not believe in insurmountabilities. If there was no evident solution, she would invent one.

She sipped the wine, thinking of Arré. Smooth as music, an idea came to her—no, she thought. That would—she would—She wondered if the wine was making her drunk.

"My lady," she said, "can you see no other course to save the folk of Tornor, but for Kedéra to wed Dennis Ryth?"

Merith said, "I cannot." She put her spoon down beside her plate. "Kedi—"

"I will not marry Dennis Ryth," said Kedéra. "I am of age, and it is my choice."

"Do you care nothing, then," her mother said, voice lifting, "for me, for your brother, for your heritage? What will you do? Run away to the west, like a child chasing sparrows with a handful of rock salt, while Tornor decays into rubble?"

At Kedéra's feet, Lauf raised his head and growled. Kedéra bit her lip. "Hush, Lauf," she said. She turned the wine goblet in her hand. "I do care," she said. "But I do not wish to marry Dennis Ryth, and I am not a child."

Sorren stared at the hall's patterned walls. The tapestries seemed to wink at her, as if she and they were in complicity. "Others share Tornor's heritage," she said.

Merith said, "I told you, the other Keeps are in like case."

"I didn't mean the other Keeps," Sorren said. She leaned her elbows on the table. "I mean the Med house in the south. That house built Tornor Keep. I know the ties have long been lost. But if Arré Med knew your plight, she would want to help you."

Merith said angrily, "I will not ask charity of the south!"

"It would not be charity," Sorren said. "I know Arré Med. She cares deeply for her house, and she has just lost a brother. The Council outlawed him. Only ignorance parts her from you. In Kendra-on-the-Delta they think the Keeps are empty."

Her words echoed off the remorseless stone. She watched Merith's face. "And so they will be," said Merith, "if we receive no help." The rage had left her voice, and only the pain remained. She stretched her hand to her daughter. "I don't want you to marry Dennis Ryth against your will."

Kedéra slipped from the bench and went round the table to her mother's side. She put her arms around Merith. "I am glad," she whispered, "because I cannot. Mother, listen to Sorren. She knows more of the world than you or I."

Sorren wanted to laugh. She knew the world—*she*, the picker's daughter, the northern girl? "Arré Med has strong ties with Tarn Ryth," she said. "If she were to assist you, Tarn Ryth would not be offended. He might find a way to send his soldiers to Tornor anyway, with Arré Med's consent. After all, she cannot do it. It's too far."

She pictured Paxe in the snow. Paxe would hate it here, she thought.

"And how do I establish contact with the Lady Arré?" said Merith.

Sorren's heart began to race. "Write to her," she said. "Recall the ancient tie. Tell her of your need."

"She will refuse," Merith insisted. "Why should she help us, who cannot repay the debt?"

Sorren said, "We all have debts." She thought of Paxe, of Kadra, of Isak. "I think she will not refuse." Merith frowned. She does not believe me, Sorren thought. Chea. . . . She hunted for other words. Perhaps she should tell Merith about the L'hel. But Merith was not Arré; it would only make her uncertain to hear of the L'hel's ambitions. She laid her palms flat on the table, as if she could draw Merith's trust out of the wood, or the stone, or the silent earth.

The feel of the table made her memory wheel back to another table, in a silent room. She rose. "I'll be back." She went into the courtyard. What had Tukath told her? *Give up the Cards for your own purposes*. She walked through the swirling snow to the door of the apartments, and up the stairs to Kedéra's chamber. She took the box of Cards from her pack. She closed her eyes, waiting for the world to blur, for the tapestried walls to vanish. . . . But nothing happened. The Cards stayed dumb. This was home to them, these walls, this silence. Here they did not need to speak.

She brought them to the hall. Merith and Kedéra were sitting side by side, hands clasped. She held out the box. "Here."

Merith said, "What do you want me to do with those?"

"What you like," said Sorren. "They are no use to me here. Sell them, if you wish. Marti Hok of the Hok house in Kendra-on-the-Delta would buy them from you. Sell them to Tarn Ryth." She laid the box on the table. Merith freed her hand and picked it up. Kedéra glanced at Sorren, question in her eyes, and Sorren shook her head, hoping that Kedéra would stay still, ask nothing, make no demand.

Merith frowned. Then her face smoothed. Gently, she held the box out to Sorren. "No. I will not take them. I appreciate your giving them to me. But they are part of Tornor's heritage, and they did not travel across the world with you to be sold. You said they gave you visions."

"Not any more," said Sorren.

"But they did. They may again. Vision is too uncommon to be sold. I would rather—" she turned her head from side to side, looking at the walls—"strip the gold thread from the tapestries, and sell it. We may have to do that, when winter passes and the traders return."

Kedéra said, "Mother, write to Arré Med."

Merith sighed. She touched her daughter's cheek with a knuckle. "Stubborn. The folk of our line are always stubborn." She looked at Sorren. "As you are, messenger. Meg said you were a northerner, and she was right. If I write it, will *you* take my letter to Arré Med?"

Kedéra gasped. "But—" Her eyes sought Sorren's. I thought you would go west with me, they said.

Sorren's heart clenched in her chest. She did not want to. What if she met Paxe; what could they say? The smell of the ocean rose like a ghost in her mind. Moist and salt, it called to her. "I will take it if you write it," she said. "And if you can find no other messenger."

"That seems fair," said Merith. She pushed her plate away, and stood. "I have weaving to do this afternoon. Kedéra, will you help?"

Kedéra said, "Yes. In a moment."

Merith said, "I shall be in the storeroom, winding wool." She walked out. Juli came from the kitchen and began to clear the plates. She was whistling. Sorren knew the tune; it was the song that Arré could not bear. *I am a stranger in an outland country.* . . . It made her think of Isak, and of Kadra. Perhaps Kadra's bequeathing her the cloak had been an omen. Perhaps she was doomed to wander, making other people's journeys, carrying other people's messages.

Kedéra touched her arm. "Sorren?"

She roused herself. "I'm here." Her head felt heavy. "Walk with me," she said. Kedéra nodded. They strolled toward the entrance to the hall. Lauf woke, whined, and bounded to Kedéra's side. She stroked his ears.

"Good dog," she said lovingly, "Outlaw-chasing dog."

The snow was still falling, but lightly now through the gray afternoon light. Sorren clutched the box in one hand. "I don't want to go south," she whispered to the castle.

It did not answer. Perhaps it had never really felt her presence, or noticed her visitations. She was less to it than the river. When the thaws came, the river went south. She remembered the faces of the outlaws. Desperation, not evil, had driven them. The order they knew had failed them. She could not hate them. She wondered if they would be back, and if so, when. Perhaps the gate could be mended.

She felt pulled in two, torn as she had never been in Kendra-on-the-Delta. She wanted to stay in Tornor, and—she smiled to herself—she wanted to go with Kedéra, wherever Kedéra went.

Kedéra said, "Sorren?"

"I'm here."

"I'll teach you to ride if you'll teach me to shoot."

Sorren looked at her. The snow glittered in her hair. I was wrong, Sorren thought. She looks like no one. She is herself, unique. "And if I must go south?" she said.

Kedéra said, "Then I'll go with you."

She might have been talking about a ride to the village. "You don't know what you're talking about!" Sorren said, and blinked. She sounded like Kadra. How childish she must have seemed to Kadra, with her schemes and plans and certainties. There were no certainties, she thought. Only the past is certain, and the past is dead.

Kedéra was watching her with that fervent look. It made her tingle. She reached with her free hand and brushed the melting snow from Kedéra's hair. It was flyaway, feathery, soft as sunlight, delicate as cobweb or milkweed.

Kedéra turned her head swiftly, and her lips brushed Sorren's hand. "You look unhappy," she said. "I don't want you to be unhappy."

A growl interrupted them. They looked down. Lauf was glaring upward, legs stiff.

Kedéra laughed. "He's jealous!"

He has cause, Sorren thought. She wondered how far the western mountains really were, and if, in some forgotten valley, chearis danced. Or was that, too, in the past? "Better teach him not to growl at me," she said.

Kedéra seized Lauf's collar. "Lauf, listen. This is Sorren. She is my friend, you stupid dog, and I will not have you growling at her. She is not going to go away. She belongs here, and you'd better get used to that." Her voice lifted, ringing off the stones. "Her name is Sorren. Can you learn that? Sorren. Sorren."

APPENDIXES

I: PRONUNCIATION

Most proper nouns and words of two syllables are pronounced with the primary stress on the first syllable: Árun, Sórren, *níji*. Exceptions, like Arré and Koré, are marked. Nouns of three syllables—*sharíza, chelíto*—are pronounced with the accent on the middle syllable, as shown above. Proper nouns of three syllables—Tázia, Méredith, Ísmenin—should be stressed on the first syllable, with some exceptions, e.g., Tezéra, Arúna, which have primary stress on the middle syllable. Longer names, such as Berénzia and Terézia, are accented.

The plural is usually formed by adding *s* to the word, as in *seji, sejis; cheari, chearis*; and occasionally by adding *as*, as in Jalar, Jalaras. When the word ends in *se* or in *as*, as in *doisse, chearas*, the same word is both singular and plural.

The sounds of the language are much like those of English. *A* is pronounced like the *a* in *father*, except when it appears as the first syllable of a word, e.g. Arun, Alis, where it is pronounced like the *a* in *act*. *E* is pronounced like the *e* in *set*, except when it is the first syllable of a word, e.g. Elath, where it is pronounced like the *e* in *equal*. *I* is pronounced somewhere between the *i* of *big* and a long English *e*; *o* is pronounced like the *o* in *over*. *U* is pronounced like the *u* in *run*. *Y* is pronounced like the *i* in *if*, as in Lyrith, except in those cases where there is an unvoiced terminal *e*, e.g. Ryke: it is then pronounced to rhyme with *tyke*. The *th* sound, as in Sereth, Thule, is pronounced like the *th* in the English *path*.

A major exception to the above rules is the word *chearas*, which is stressed on the first, not the middle syllable, e.g. *chéaras. Cheari* and *chearis*, however, follow common usage.

0   *The Dancer:* is the Card with no number. *Description:* A young man wearing only a loincloth. His left foot is off the ground. His hair is gold and very long. His eyes are gray. He is beardless. Behind his head the sky is dark blue. A crescent moon ascends. His expression is jcyous and transcendent.

1   *The Weaver:* is a woman in a green dress, seated at a loom. Her hair is dark and long and hangs unbraided down her back. She is framed in a window. She holds the shuttle in one hand. The picture on her tapestry is of a blossoming tree.

2   *The Dreamer:* is a woman sleeping. A window overlooks her couch: through it we see two bright red stars. She lies on her back with her hands folded on the coverlet. Her hair is bright gold and long.

3   *The Lady:* is a golden-haired woman standing outdoors. It is day. In the distance we see fields, a barn, an orchard. She carries a sheaf of flowers. A sleek white greyhound stands beside her. She is smiling.

4   *The Lord:* is a stern-faced man seated on a high-backed wooden chair. He wears red and silver. His eyes are blue; his hair is gold. He wears a ruby ring on his right hand. A black wolfhound lies beside his booted feet.

5   *The Scholar:* is a man in a black-cowled robe edged with silver. He stands beside a table; one hand rests on a stack of parchment. Most of his face is hidden in the shadow of his hood.

6   *The Lovers:* are a man and a woman holding hands over a wall. The wall is covered with ivy and blue flowers.

7   *The Archer:* is a woman wearing only a loincloth. The crescent moon is at her back. She stands in profile, drawing a bow. Her hair streams out behind her; it is gold.

8   *The Messenger:* is a cloaked and hooded figure, in green, riding a sorrel horse across snow. It cannot be seen if the figure is a man or a woman. The sky is clear and dark blue.

9   *The Horseman:* is a man riding across the steppe on a black horse. The man's hair is gold and streams behind him, as does the mane of the horse. The steppe grass is pale green. The horse is without saddle or bridle.

10 *The Stargazer:* is a woman standing on a balcony. She is looking up at the stars. Her hair is dark. Her eyes are gray. She wears a blue gown. In the foreground stands a table with the suggestion of the two curling ends of a scroll. Her face is stern and unsmiling.

11 *The Illusionist:* is a young man dressed in red and orange, standing on one foot. He is smiling. He is juggling a number of brightly colored balls. He wears a blue ruff around his neck.

12 *The Wolf:* shows the head and shoulders of a gray wolf. Its lips are pulled back: it is snarling. Its fangs are long and yellow. Its eyes are red.

13 *The Eagle:* shows an eagle soaring over a precipice. Its talons are extended as if to strike. The tips of its feathers are gleaming white. Behind it the sky is dark blue. The rocks are red with the sunset.

14 *The Phoenix:* shows the phoenix perched unharmed in the midst of a fire. We see it in profile. Its wings and plumage are of myriad colors.

15 *The Mirror:* shows a landscape of a house, trees, and a lake in which the landscape is perfectly reflected so that one cannot tell which is the real and which the mirrored scene. There are no human figures in this Card.

16 *The Tower:* shows a tall stone tower in the act of splitting apart. It has been struck by lightning. Very far beneath it, there are running people and horses.

17 *The Wheel:* shows a great circle with eight spokes. Within each space between the spokes are people, all different, some men, some women, all ages from infant to crone, pressing against the spokes as if they want to get out of the space.

18 *The Demon:* is a monstrous semihuman form. He has scales and horns. He is naked: his body is green. He has a barbed tail. He has fangs and is grinning.

19 *Death:* is a human skeleton standing in a cornfield. The skeleton has red eyes. The sky is gray, as at twilight.

20 *The Moon:* shows a full moon rising over water. A woman stands at the water's edge, both hands uplifted to the rising moon. Her back is toward us. Her hair is pale and long. A black cat sits at her feet.

21 *The Sun:* shows a circle of people with their hands linked. The number varies: sometimes there are six, sometimes more, but there are always at least three men and three women, counting male and female children. Behind them we see a barn, a mill, a herd of goats. A bright sun illumines the landscape. The hair of the women is bound with flowers.

III: CHRONOLOGY OF ARUN

Year 1: Founding of Kendra-on-the-Delta
Year 32: Founding of Shanan
Year 56: Founding of Tezera
Year 60: First major raid into Arun by Anhard forces
Year 77: Building of Cloud Keep
Year 82: Terenth Med attempts to overthrow the rule of his sister Berénzia in Kendra-on-the-Delta. He is exiled to the north.
Year 84: Tornor Keep begun
Year 85: Tornor Keep completed; Terenth Med is named 1st Lord of Tornor Keep.
Year 121–123 Pel Keep built
Year 140–42: Zilia Keep built
Year 166: Erection of the watchtower at Tornor Keep
Year 245: Col of Iste born
Year 247: Raven Batto born in Kendra-on-the-Delta
Kerwin, 11th Lord of Tornor, dies.
Morven is named 12th Lord of Tornor.
Year 263: Ryke of Tornor born
Year 266: Norres of Tornor village is born.
Morven dies. Athor is named 13th Lord of Tornor.
Year 267: Errel, Athor's son, is born.
Sorren, Athor's daughter is born.
Year 280: Raven Batto kills Ewain Med in Kendra-on-the-Delta. He is banished.
Year 281: Founding of Vanima
Truce signed between Anhard and Arun
Year 290: Col Istor invades the north.
Athor dies.
WATCHTOWER
Year 322: Death of Sorren, Lady of Tornor
Year 376: Establishment of the Council of Houses in Kendra-on-the-Delta (Council Year One)
Year 380: Marriage of Kerwin of Tornor and Alis of Elath
Year 383: Kel of Elath is born.
Year 390: Morven is named 19th Lord of Tornor.
Year 393: Kerris of Elath is born.

413

Year 396:   Alis of Elath dies. Kerris is maimed by Asech raiders.

Year 398:   Kel goes to Vanima.

Year 400:   First Asech raid on Elath

Year 404:   Second Asech raid on Elath

Year 405:   Kel is named cheari by Zayin.

Year 406:   Kerris links with Kel for the first time

Year 410:   *THE DANCERS OF ARUN*

Year 425:   Establishment of the White Clan

Year 435:   Building of the Tanjo in Kendra-on-the-Delta

Year 437:   Truce with Asech tribes is arranged by the witches.

Year 442:   Founding of Shirasai

Year 459   Marti Hok is born.

Year 464:   Edged weapons are banned from Kendra-on-the-Delta.

Year 465:   The Ban is upheld by the witches.

Year 468:   The Ban extends to Shanan and Tezera.

Year 472:   Sul and Minto Houses are admitted to the Council.

Year 478:   Arré Med is born.

Year 485:   Paxe-no-Tamaris born

Year 489:   Isak Med is born.

Year 501:   Paxe gives birth to a daughter.

Year 503:   Paxe gives birth to a second daughter.

Year 504:   Plague in Kendra-on-the-Delta
               Paxe's daughters die. Paxe goes to Tor's Rest.

Year 505:   Plague continues. Shana Med dies. Arré Med becomes head of the Med house and a member of the Council.

Year 506:   Paxe returns.

Year 508:   Ricard is born.

Year   Arré and Paxe are lovers.
509–11:

Year 512:   Isak Med receives the shariza.
               Paxe is named Yardmaster.

Year 513:   Isak Med marries Myra-no-Ivrénia.

Year 514:   Kadra-no-Ilézia is maimed by a fall.

Year 515:   Arré brings Sorren to Kendra-on-the-Delta.

Year 520:   Paxe and Sorren become lovers.

Year 522:   *THE NORTHERN GIRL*

The choice of a Year 1 is arbitrary; no such dating system occurred in Arun. In the north, events were dated by the year of the local ruler's reign; in the south, the dating system varied from town to town and city to city. The scholars of the Black Clan maintained a separate dating system for their records, but this was of no use in day-to-day affairs, since the Black Clan considered such things secret, and guarded its records jealously.

In Kendra-on-the-Delta, a common system of dating began when the Council was formed. Shanan, Tezera, and Shirasai adopted the system established in Kendra-on-the-Delta. In the Galbareth and in the mountain villages, weather, local events, and the richness or poverty of the harvest distinguished one year from another.

The folk who came from Anhard to trade or settle adopted Arun's customs while they were within her borders. The Asech tribes did not, but since they kept no written records (preferring oral history which they could embellish), their methods of dating are irrelevant to this story.

THE FANTASTIC
WORLD OF FANTASY